Dedication

For all the divers in the world

Diving Into Her

Diving Into Her

Alyson Root

ISBN-13: 9798376372913
Imprint: Independently published

Cover design by: Cath Grace

Table of Contents

Chapter 1

Kim pinched the bridge of her nose. The headache she'd been battling since yesterday was wearing her down. Even with copious amounts of pain relief tablets, the pounding continued. It wasn't much of a surprise though because Kim always developed headaches when she was overly stressed, and these past 48 hours had been one of the most stressful times of her life.

"Greg, if you just shut up for five minutes, maybe I could explain why I'm so upset," Kim barked. The day before last, Kim's long-term boyfriend had yet again cancelled their plans to have a weekend outside of Paris. So far, he had cancelled five times and Kim was done with his excuses.

"Five times, Greg. That's how many times I have had to cancel this reservation. The woman of the Airbnb must think I'm a right mug," she sighed. Kim could feel the fight in her wane. What was the point? She knew he wouldn't change his plans for her.

"Kim, I told you this meeting was more important than a bloody weekend in some shitty backwater town. I can't let the boss down," he argued.

In a flash, Kim's anger erupted. "No, but you have zero problem letting me down. You don't even consider my feelings at all anymore." She was breathing hard. She couldn't believe she had let Greg treat her like this for so long.

Where the hell was the little firecracker she once prided herself on being? Why the hell had she let this man disregard her thoughts and feelings all for the sake of a bloody job title? She was worth more than that. "We need to take a break, Greg."

"I agree. Let's chat tonight. I'll probably be home a little late, but I'll try to get away before eight," Greg chirped.

"No, you misunderstand. I want a break from us. I need some time to figure out what I want because I can't keep living like this. I won't be cast aside for a job. Not by anyone. I'll stay with Anna for a while." She rang off before Greg could even take a breath to reply.

Well, that was that then. Now she just had to hope that Anna didn't mind her crashing at her apartment. Kim couldn't see a reason her best friend would mind. She wasn't even in the country at the minute, so her very nice and very big apartment in the sixteenth arrondissement was standing empty. It would be just the right place for her to take a breather and do some reassessing.

She took a couple of deep breaths. The pounding in her temples had lessened since she had verbalised her wish to get some distance from her boyfriend, proving just how much stress he had been putting her through.

Kim
Hello my lovely, hope you and Sam are good. Any chance I could crash at yours for a while?

2

Kim didn't know if Anna would be awake yet. It was just after two in the afternoon in Paris, which would make it around seven in the morning in Texas. Kim tapped her finger on her desk in anticipation. She really hoped Anna wouldn't take too long to reply. As if she'd willed it, her phone buzzed. Anna was calling.

"Did I wake you?" Kim asked.

"No, no, it's fine. Sam was up early anyway and she's like an elephant stomping round, so she woke me," Anna said sleepily. Kim smiled. Sam was going to be in trouble later. Anna was not a morning person, and she hated being woken earlier than her alarm.

"I'm sure she'll make it up to you," Kim giggled, knowing full well that Anna and Sam were insatiable and found any excuse to ravish each other. Kim was envious of their relationship. She couldn't remember a time that she had ever been ravished by Greg.

Their sex life had been a lot more active in their earlier years, but as of late, it had stalled to nothing. Kim spent plenty of time self servicing, which was fine, but sometimes she just wanted someone to take her and worship her, just like Sam did with Anna.

"Oh, she'll make it up to me alright," Anna replied. Kim could hear the smile through the phone. "Anyway, enough of that. Why do you need to use the apartment? I mean, of course you can use it for as long as you like, but why do you need to? Are you okay?"

"I told Greg I need a break," Kim said plainly. She'd told Anna before that she was sick of coming second in his life.

"What happened?"

"He cancelled again, something to do with a meeting that was more important than a weekend in some shitty backwater

3

town. His words, exactly," Kim growled. She could feel herself getting angry again.

"He really said that?" Anna gasped.

"Oh yes, he really said that. I've had enough Anna, I need to do a little soul searching."

"In that case, stay in my apartment as long as you like, and I think you should take our reservation in Saint Tropez next week."

"I can't do that. Anyway, why won't you be going? I thought it was going to round off your travelling before you come back to work?"

"Sam got an offer to go to California to work with a big shot photographer. I could see how excited she was, so I told her we would go there instead of Saint Tropez. I haven't got round to cancelling everything yet. If you go, I won't have to. Please say you'll save me from having to spend my day on the phone," Anna whined. It would be a wonderful way to de-stress. August was always slow in the office and Kim was due to take a few weeks off after Anna returned.

"Who is going to take over for me in the office? We've never both been away at the same time?"

"Please, we have plenty of people to take over. I'm working on my laptop, so it's not a major issue. Rachel and Emmanuelle are more than capable of running the place for a while. Say yes, Kim, you deserve it."

Well, how could she say no to that? A few weeks away in the South of France sounded delightful, and she knew all too well that the place Anna had booked would be far nicer than anything she could afford.

"Okay, yeah why the hell not, thanks Anna, you're a doll." A smile blossomed for the first time in two days across her face. She was feeling better already.

"*Bien*, I'll call the hotel and let them know there is a change of name. Call me anytime you want, Kim. You were *the* best friend I could have asked for when I was working through my stuff. I want you to know I'm here for you."

Anna had leaned on Kim when she'd finally left her boyfriend and came out. Kim was so proud of her friend, especially when she met Sam. They were made for each other even if it had taken them both a little time to accept it. Kim and Anna had become close friends during that time and she knew without a shadow of a doubt that Anna would be there for her in a flash if she needed it.

"Thanks love, don't worry though, I'm okay, a little time away will clear my head and help me decide what I want."

"Still, I'm only a phone call away."

"I know. Now try to get back to sleep. I'm sure Sam has plans to exhaust you later." Kim laughed.

"You know us too well. I probably need to stop telling you so much about our sex life," Anna giggled.

"Don't you dare. I live vicariously through you."

"Take care, Kim, I'll talk to you soon."

"Bye, doll, give Sam a kiss from me."

Kim rolled her shoulders. She felt the tension radiate in her neck. It was no wonder her head had been giving her trouble. Looking at the clock on her computer, she realised she'd worked through her lunch hour again. Something she'd done all week.

Instead of continuing with her work, Kim took the afternoon off. Her apartment was only twenty minutes away, leaving enough time to pack a few items and head over to Anna's. There was no point waiting around for Greg to get home.

The August heat in Paris was stifling. There was no way in hell Kim was going to subject herself to the heat and smell of the metro. Walking meant that her twenty minute commute time would double, but it was necessary.

There wasn't a cloud in the sky as Kim walked the streets to her apartment. The café terraces were full. People of all ages crammed under little umbrellas sheltering from the sun's relentless heat. Kim felt beads of sweat roll down her back. How anyone could wear suit trousers in this weather was beyond her.

Kim was a dress gal. She owned a lot of them. Her love of vintage dresses was well known. Her friends and family were all taken aback at the sheer number of pin-up style dresses she owned. Today was one of many days that she was thankful she had plenty of dress options at her disposal. She might sweat, but at least the bit of breeze that was blowing cooled her legs and her arse. There was nothing worse than having an overheated crotch!

Finally, her street came into view. The walk had taken longer than expected and she was positive that she'd caught the sun on her face and neck. The last obstacle she faced was the three flights of stairs in her black patent heels. For most women, it would have proven to be too much, but not for Kim. She was like a ninja in high heels. She'd learnt to walk in them from an early age.

Kim was small, and she'd been teased relentlessly as a child. As she got older, she'd silenced the bullies by strutting around masterfully in heels that were not for the fainthearted. Kim drew confidence through wearing high-heeled shoes. They made her feel invincible, and they made her legs look fabulous. No one could bring her down when she had her trusty heels on.

Kim cracked open the door to the apartment. A bit of her hoped Greg would prove her wrong and she would find him waiting for her. Her heart sank a little when she realised she was alone in the apartment. She let herself have a moment before straightening her shoulders. She was here for a reason, and she needed to get on with it.

Pulling her suitcase from under the bed, she began picking out her clothes. Swimwear was a definite for her trip to Saint Tropez. She picked out a range of dresses that made her feel confident and carefully packed them away. Kim was naturally organised, so packing took her less than half an hour.

The thought of lugging her suitcase to Anna's in the heat filled her with dread. A taxi was the sensible option, so she ordered one from her phone. Slowly, she descended the stairs. As good as she was at navigating stairs in heels, doing that with a suitcase in tow was a different matter entirely. The last thing she wanted was to fall or worse, break a heel.

After what seemed a lifetime, she finally reached the ground floor. Parts of her hair had come out of her signature high ponytail and were sticking to the side of her face. God, she couldn't wait to get to Anna's and freshen up.

The taxi was idling outside her apartment building. Kim had never been so happy to see a Parisian taxi driver in all her life. She noticed him look her up and down, clearly appreciating what he saw.

Being noticed wasn't something new. Kim seemed to draw attention from both men and women, which suited her just fine. It was nice to be seen, nice to have someone look at her and make her feel good about the way she looked. Greg used to do that, but not anymore. She was lucky if he even noticed her at all lately.

Forcing a smile on her face, she greeted the driver. He'd raced out of the car to take her suitcase. The car was wonderfully cool, the A/C soothed her overheated skin deliciously. The driver hadn't said very much apart from a quick "Bonjour". He was, however, throwing her glances in the rear-view mirror, his eyes travelling to her cleavage. She wondered if he would drum up the courage to ask her for her number before the journey was over.

Kim paid the driver using the contactless card machine. It was so much easier than carrying cash. As soon as the payment cleared, the driver scrambled out to open her door. He looked as if he was going to ask her something, but was interrupted by the doorman, who offered to take Kim's luggage. Anna had probably called ahead to let him know she would be arriving.

The taxi driver left looking a little crestfallen, but he wasn't to know that even if he'd found the courage to ask for her number, he would've been shot down. As much as she enjoyed a bit of attention now and then, she certainly wasn't the type of person to lead someone on. Even if things with Greg were rocky, she wasn't in the right headspace for anyone right now.

Kim loved Anna's apartment. It was luxurious, yet homely. Anna had originally rented the apartment temporarily when she was taking some time for herself a couple of years ago. It was in this apartment that she met Sam, who turned out to be renting the apartment across the street. Sam and Anna's story was complex, but utterly adorable. They'd been thrown together only to find out they knew each other at university.

Kim's story with Greg was far from adorable. She'd met him in school, they'd dated and that was that. No big romance, no fairytale. Maybe that's what was wrong. Maybe their relationship should have been a high school romance and nothing more. Kim sighed. *It can't have all been a mistake, surely?*

After throwing her suitcase in the bedroom, Kim ordered a pizza from her favourite restaurant. Nothing made her feel better than a tomato and pesto pizza. There was no need for her to unpack. She knew which dresses she would wear for the rest of the week and all her other clothes could stay packed, ready for her holiday.

The thought of Saint Tropez filled her with excitement. It had been years since she'd been able to go on a proper holiday, one where she could completely relax. Holidays with Greg usually ended in bickering. They wanted to do different things. Greg wanted to find a sports bar, sit there all day drinking, watching football. It was Kim's worst nightmare.

For her, a holiday should be filled with culture and adventure. A few days of sitting by a pool to relax was also necessary, along with cocktails with little umbrellas, of course. Yes, this was just what she needed, no stress, time for herself to unwind and figure some stuff out.

The stress of the day was weighing heavily. Her body ached and after inhaling an entire pizza, she was suffering from a case of "food coma fatigue". Her eyes felt like lead weights. Anna's enormous bed was calling her. Her head barely touched the pillow before she was unconscious.

* * *

Saint Tropez was an undiscovered land and Kim was more than excited to spend her vacation exploring every nook and cranny.

The week in Anna's apartment had been fabulous. She'd worked a couple of days remotely, taking full advantage of the little table that sat by the full-length French windows. Her days had been spent tapping away on her laptop, stopping now and then to peer down to the street below, people watching as the sun shone down, kissing her face.

Greg had called twice and left a few messages on her phone. From what Kim heard, he wasn't taking their separation seriously. He'd asked her to pick up his dry cleaning next week and told her that his friends were visiting in ten days, therefore he expected her to plan a dinner party. Kim had simply shaken her head after listening to his voicemails.

The flight to Nice had been easy. Thankfully, the flight had only lasted an hour and a half and there had been no turbulence to deal with. If flying was that easy all the time, she'd travel more. Kim loved the idea of jetting around the world, if only her bank balance allowed her to do more than dream about it.

The car Anna had rented for her was sat waiting outside the airport. It was a beautiful and expensive convertible, perfect for the drive along the coast to Saint Tropez. So far, her vacation was off to a wonderful start.

Kim pulled into the assigned parking space that was listed on the confirmation email that Anna had forwarded to her. A young bellboy in a very smart uniform opened her door, gesturing for her to exit the vehicle.

"Welcome to The Sapphire Hotel and Spa," he said in perfect English.

"Oh, thank you," Kim replied, feeling a little out of her depth.

"Please head inside and register at the front desk. Thomas is currently on duty and will take care of all the paperwork. I'll have your luggage waiting for you."

"Right, thank you again." Her voice shook slightly out of nerves.

The lobby boasted clean, sleek lines. It was everything Kim imagined a modern luxury hotel and spa would look like. If the rooms and spa area were anything near as nice as the lobby, Kim was going to be one lucky woman.

"Hello, I'd like to check-in please," Kim said sweetly to the man behind the desk she presumed was Thomas.

"Of course. Can I take your name, please?"

"Kim Richmond."

Thomas set about clacking on the keyboard in front of him, his brow furrowed in confusion. "I'm sorry, but I don't have a reservation in that name," he said after a few more seconds of clicking his mouse.

"Really, that's strange. My friends booked the master suite. They couldn't make it, so she called to change the reservation to my name." Shifting from foot to foot, Kim was getting the feeling that her vacation was about to become less than perfect.

"Can I have the original name?" Thomas asked.

"Anna and Sam Chambers." Thomas clicked and clacked for a little while longer, his face still a picture of confusion.

"I'm very sorry, but that reservation was cancelled. The suite has since been booked. We don't have any vacancies until the beginning of September."

"That can't be right, look I have the confirmation here," she said, showing Thomas the email that Anna had sent her.

"That's the original reservation, but since then, Ms Chambers has cancelled the room. We received the call last week," he said calmly.

Kim was feeling anything but calm. "No, she called to amend the booking, not cancel," Kim shot.

"One minute, please." Thomas picked up the phone that sat next to his computer. Kim listened as he conversed quickly in French. She saw his face drop and a blush form around his neck.

"I can only apologise, Ms Richmond. The call to amend the booking was taken by a summer intern and instead of changing the name, she cancelled it by mistake."

Kim stood stock still, glaring at Thomas. She was willing herself to keep her temper in check. "So what now?" She demanded.

"There isn't anything I can do. All the rooms are booked. I'm so sorry. Ms Chambers will receive a full refund."

"What good is a refund when I'm on holiday without a room?" Kim barked.

"I'm so sorry." Thomas twiddled his thumbs together nervously.

Kim needed to calm down. It wasn't his fault that a mistake had been made. "Sorry, Thomas, forgive me for getting upset. It's not your fault. I just don't know what to do now."

"Let me make some calls. Maybe another hotel will have some availability." His face was sincere with regret.

"No, it's okay, this was a treat from my friend. I couldn't afford a hotel like this. Do you mind if I sit for a few minutes to organise myself?" she asked, pointing to one of the large white sofas that lined the lobby.

"Of course. Take as long as you want."

Kim felt the sting of tears in her eyes. Her perfect holiday was over before it even started. What was she going to do? She couldn't face the idea of returning to Paris. She desperately needed space from Greg and her life.

In reality, though, what choice did she have but to jump on the next flight home? She couldn't afford anything in Saint Tropez, not even a cheap room. Her budget only covered a bit of spending money for the duration of her trip.

She felt the tears spill from her eyes. Her shoulders shook as she fought to keep control of her emotions. Just as she was about to lose all hope and control, she felt a hand on her shoulder. Kim looked up and saw a familiar face laced with concern.

"Kim?"

Chapter 2

Hélène smoothed down the front of her dress. She was nervous. Today would be her fourth date with Jenny, an Australian reporter who had moved from Sydney to work in Paris for eighteen months. The time limit wasn't ideal, but Hélène tried to remain hopeful. No reason to sabotage a new relationship, all because the other person might leave for the other side of the world in a year's time. Right?

They'd hit it off from the moment they'd met. Hélène had literally bumped into Jenny as she was exiting her local café. After a few apologies on both sides, they'd grabbed a coffee together, which led to their first date that night.

Jenny was fun and adventurous, she had a zest for life and travel. It surprised Hélène to learn how many countries Jenny had lived in. In normal circumstances, that would have been a red flag. Clearly, Jenny wasn't someone who stuck around. Hélène had buried that little red flag all the way in the back of her mind though, because beggars couldn't be choosers.

Okay, so Jenny wasn't the ideal candidate at first glance, but Hélène chose to remain positive, test the waters by going on a second date, which had been a success. On the third date they'd slept together, and it had been great, not just because it ended a rather long dry spell on Hélène's part, but because they seemed compatible between the sheets.

Fourth date territory was promising. Surely Jenny wouldn't be investing her time if she was just going to up sticks and leave. No, tonight's date was going to be a step in the right direction. Hélène could feel it in her bones.

She gave herself another look over in the mirror. She looked good. The dress looked like it had been tailored to her body, which it had been. She ran her hand through her long ash blonde hair, giving it a little ruffle. Yes, now she was ready.

Henry opened the car door. *"Bonsoir,* Hélène," he said with a brief nod. Hélène was very fond of Henry. He had been her driver for years.

"Bonsoir, Henry," she replied before slipping into the back seat.

The ride to the restaurant would have been achievable by foot if Hélène wasn't wearing ridiculous heels. Hélène was much happier in trainers or flip-flops, however because of her job, she was used to wearing uncomfortable footwear. She was the office manager for one of Paris's top photography houses, therefore not a place for comfortable shoes, more's the pity.

The car pulled up, and Henry was out of his seat in a flash. Another reason Hélène loved Henry as her driver, he was efficient. "Thank you Henry," Hélène said sweetly.

"Have a good evening, Hélène," he replied before closing her door and getting back in the driver's seat. She knew he would only drive around the corner and wait for her to call him when she was ready to leave.

Hélène squared her shoulders and headed into the restaurant. She was getting excited at the prospect of sex again. It really had been too long. Her excitement crashed and burned as she spotted Jenny, who was sitting at the bar. Jenny was not dressed for a date. In fact, it didn't appear to Hélène that Jenny planned to stick around for any length of time if her packed bag was anything to go by.

"Hey, you," Jenny chirped.

"Um, hi." She couldn't match Jenny's enthusiasm.

"So… this sucks, but I have to leave. Work stuff." Jenny didn't elaborate.

"Oh, okay, when will you be back?"

"Probably won't be, in all honesty. Listen, it was awesome meeting you, maybe in another life, eh?" Jenny chuckled. What could she possibly find amusing?

"Right, in another life," Hélène parroted. What else could she say? Jenny swooped down and hauled her bag over her shoulder. She leant in and gave Hélène a chaste kiss on the lips.

"See ya." Jenny winked before leaving Hélène standing by herself at the bar, feeling like a fool. She was in shock. How had a promising night of drinks and sex turned into such utter garbage?

Feeling the sting of tears in her eyes, she knew she had to get out of that goddamn restaurant. It was one thing having people witness her being broken up with. It would be another thing entirely for them to see her break down.

Turning on the spot, she marched out with her head held high. Thankfully, she had been right about Henry sticking close because within a minute he'd pulled up and opened her door. He said nothing, and Hélène was grateful. She wasn't sure she could hold herself together if he asked if she was okay.

The brutal truth was she was far from okay. Hélène's luck in love was nonexistent. In fact, she often thought she was

15

cursed. Every woman she connected with left. As her mood grew more morose, Hélène knew she couldn't be alone right now. The thought of going back to her empty apartment was too much. *I don't need a relationship, I just need a good fuck.*

Hélène was so sick and tired of feeling like this, feeling unlovable. It was time for her to make a change. If she couldn't get a woman to stick around for the long haul, she'd change her way of thinking. If a quick fling or one-night stand was all she could manage, then fine, fuck settling down, fuck a quiet domesticated life, she'd play the field.

Honestly, Hélène had always found it easy to get a woman into bed. Maybe that's what she should stick to. She asked Henry to drop her off at her old haunt, a pub for queer women. It was years since she'd last visited. Maybe it had changed, but she doubted it.

The pub hadn't changed in the slightest. The decor was exactly the same. It was supposed to mirror a traditional English pub, but Hélène wasn't convinced English country pubs had statues and posters of naked women all over the place.

"Martini please," she half shouted at the bar woman. The music was a little loud. *God, I'm getting old.*

Sitting there nursing her drink, her resolve to become a carefree womaniser was quickly disappearing as she looked around the pub full of baby dykes. This wasn't what she'd envisioned for herself at 34. She'd left her party days behind at the end of her twenties.

Where was she going wrong?

All her dates started off well. Some even made it to the relationship stage, but then they all crashed and burned. Every single woman left her. The hard part was that none of them left because of *her*. Each one had a personal reason to go. Hélène started mentally checking off her list of exes.

16

Amelie: Left to care for her dad after he suffered a stroke.
Lucie: Won a grant to work in Antarctica.
Clara: Went into business with her brother in Italy.
Lauren: Took a job in the UK.
Sam: Only wanted to be friends once she realised Hélène had ties to her ex.
Ella: Moved to the US to complete her PhD after taking a year sabbatical from studies (something Hélène wished she'd mentioned before they'd started dating) and finally…
Jenny: Work stuff!

Hélène rolled her eyes at the last name on the list. Jesus, surely she was worth more than a two word explanation.

The music was getting louder and Hélène's mood was not improving, especially since she'd been hit on several times by women who were at least ten years younger than her and drunk.

Swallowing the rest of her drink in one, she stood up to leave. She had no desire to take anyone to bed tonight. Maybe she needed a break from dating and women. Maybe she should use up her many holiday days to get away and regroup.

Yes, that's what she needed, sun, sea and absolutely no lesbians!

* * *

Hélène's bathroom came into focus as she woke. Her cheek was stuck to the toilet seat. Never in all her 34 years had she regretted drinking wine like she did at that very moment. Two bottles, that's the amount of wine she'd consumed after arriving back home from the pub. *Oh dear god I'm dying.*

Hélène wasn't usually the type of person to drink her feelings away, but last night had really taken the biscuit. Gingerly, she lifted her head, testing her capability of movement. Unsurprisingly, she felt as if she was being fucked in the skull by a sledgehammer.

Staying propped against the loo wasn't an option. Deciding to brave the pain, she crawled over to her walk-in luxury shower. Her bathroom wasn't huge, but she was lucky enough to have both a shower and a separate bath. Uncommon for small Parisian apartments.

God knows what kind of tragic mess she looked right now. That was something to worry about later though, because now she needed to shower, brush her teeth and consume her body's weight in water and grease.

Showered and smelling less like a pub carpet, Hélène walked slowly into her kitchen. Although the last thing her stomach wanted was food, she knew she needed her miracle hangover cure. Eggs, bacon, and cheese in a toasted roll. A combination which had never failed her.

A little slower than usual, Hélène cooked her saviour sandwich. It took her around half an hour to eat it. Her stomach protested with every bite, but she finally ate it all. Now she had to wait. The longest it had ever taken her to feel better after said sandwich was two hours.

Three hours and forty minutes later, Hélène could finally feel her hangover subside. Now she was just left with the memories of her less than stellar night. Jenny. Being alone. The pub and last but not least, sadness.

Wow, she really was a ray of sunshine. Although she also remembered the idea of getting away for a while. That thought was what she needed to cling to. In fact, she needed to get organised. Hélène knew herself too well. The longer she thought about it, the less likely she would do it. Spontaneity was key.

"No time like the present," she said to absolutely no one because that was her life, alone and talking to herself. Pulling herself out of her momentary dark cloud, she grabbed her phone and hit speed dial. The phone rang for what seemed a lifetime. It was a long shot trying to get JJ on the phone, but she had to try. He was the one that could grant her the wish of a luxury vacation. Just as she was about to hang up, the call connected.

"Hélène, how are you, squirt?" JJ chuckled. Hélène knew full well he loved winding her up using a nickname he had given her as a child.

"Oh, I'm peachy," she said dryly.

"Uh oh, what's up?" JJ or John Spencer Junior was Hélène's step brother. The world, however, knew him as one of the most successful entrepreneurs to have ever walked the earth. Hélène just saw him as her irritating older brother.

They shared a father — if you could really class him as a father; he was more like a sperm donor to both her and JJ. Phillipe DuBois was a wealthy businessman, known for his cutthroat business practices and his womanising. Hélène never really understood what her mother had seen in him. She realised he was a waste of space early on. God knows why her mother kept his surname after the divorce.

The one positive relationship she'd got out of her father was JJ. They'd always been close. She'd never seen JJ as a stepbrother. He was her brother in every way. Hélène was a little ashamed that she'd asked JJ to keep her name separate from his own. If the public knew she was related to him — well, let's just say trusting new relationships and friendships would be impossible. She couldn't stand the thought of people trying to build friendships with her just to get close to the wonder that was John Spencer.

It was a jaded way to look at it, but she'd seen it happen enough times with her mum and JJ's late wife Claire to know

19

that people rarely had the best intentions when they knew you were related to John Spencer. So as far as the world was concerned, Hélène DuBois was just another employee in one of his many businesses.

Obviously, as she got to know someone, whether that be someone she was dating or just making new friends, she eventually introduced them to JJ, but nine times out of ten that never worked out either.

"Oh, you know, another woman bites the dust. This time, though, I thought drowning my liver was a good idea." Hélène grimaced when her stomach rolled at the thought of alcohol.

"Ah, right, how did that work out for you?" he chuckled. At least someone found her situation funny.

"Wonderful, I feel like a million euros. The highlight of it all was waking up glued to the toilet seat," she huffed.

"Oh Christ, squirt," he laughed. "What can I do to help?"

"Actually, I was hoping I could borrow *Connie?*"

"Sure, I'm not using her. She's free all summer." To anyone listening in, their conversation could be taken the wrong way. Hélène was definitely *not* asking to borrow a woman. *Connie* was JJ's super yacht that was moored in Saint Tropez.

"I'll call Bobby and get him to set her up. How does next weekend sound?"

"That's fantastic, thanks JJ, I owe you one."

"No, you don't. Just go and chill. Maybe I can fly down for a weekend, spend some quality time with my sister?" For the first time in twenty-four hours, Hélène smiled. She might not be able to get a woman to love her, but at least she had her brother. JJ was the type of guy who had no problems showing his feelings.

"That would be the best thing ever!" She bellowed. "You know I might spend the week at The Sapphire. It's been ages since I've had a good spa treatment."

20

"Brilliant idea. The penthouse will be reserved already. I like to have it booked just in case I need to have a weekend of calm."

"You sure you don't mind me using it?"

"Not a bit. I can't get down there for a few weeks, lots to do here in London, but I promise to find time when you're aboard *Connie*. Probably in three of four weeks."

"I wasn't planning to be away that long, JJ. I've got a business to oversee."

"Oh bollocks. Listen, squirt, this is the first time in years you've asked for a holiday. I am insisting you take the next five weeks off. The office will be fine. No arguments." His tone was final.

"Well, if you insist." She couldn't help but chuckle. JJ, getting all bossy on her, was hilarious. Most people quaked in their boots when John Spencer got stern. Hélène was not most people. She knew the teddy bear behind the "big boss" persona.

Once they'd rounded up the conversation with a quick catch up, Hélène called and arranged for JJ's jet to take her to Saint Tropez. She'd need a day to organise and pack, and then she was free to start her holiday. Letting out a long breath, she could already feel the tight knots in her back ease. Sun, sea, and NO lesbians, just what she needed.

* * *

There were some definite perks to being related to JJ. The company's private jet was just one of them. Normally Hélène had no problem taking a commercial flight, but this time she wanted to indulge a little. The flight to Nice had been smooth flying all the way. The Champagne and cheese had been a bonus mid flight.

21

Organising cover for the office had been a cinch. JJ was right, as usual. The Paris office had always run like a well-oiled machine. Hélène had plenty of support. Sébastien had agreed to fill her position whilst she was away. There was no one more suited than Seb. She trusted him completely, often wondering if he should really hold her position full-time.

Managing the office was okay. It filled her days, but it wasn't her passion. The formidable Veronique DuBois — Hélène's overbearing and critical mother — would have preferred that her daughter had followed her into the fashion business, but to her immense disappointment, Hélène had never wanted that life.

The drive to Saint Tropez was just as easy as the flight. Henry had agreed to fly down with her and drive her around as needed. Hélène sometimes worried that she was asking too much of her loyal driver. When she'd voiced her concerns to him one evening, he'd told her in no uncertain terms that his job meant the world to him and that it gave him a sense of purpose.

Henry was a widower with no children. Driving Hélène around was what kept him sane. How could she argue with that? Anyway, the perks of being her driver were pretty damn good. Henry had travelled the world with Hélène, benefitting from fancy hotels and upscale restaurants.

Hélène rolled her neck as the car swung into the hotel's parking area. As usual, Henry was out of the car like a shot, holding the door open for her. The bell boy had already begun unloading her luggage.

Hélène had stayed at The Sapphire Hotel and Spa several times. Once with Claire, JJ's late wife, twice with her mother — those had not been the most relaxing days — and once more on her own. It was the ultimate experience in indulgence and Hélène couldn't wait to bask in it once again.

Hélène strode into the lobby. Thomas was at the desk as usual, but this time he looked a little ashen-faced. It was only then that she heard someone sniffing behind her she understood something was wrong. It was the kind of sniffing someone did when they were trying to keep themselves from crying.

Following Thomas's gaze over to the white couches, Hélène saw a familiar face. It was a face that was pretty unforgettable. Hélène's brow creased as she looked at Kim, attempting to keep herself together.

Something was seriously wrong. There was no way she could walk away and start her holiday when someone she knew was in distress. Hélène gave Thomas a little smile and walked over to Kim. She didn't want to frighten her, so she gently lay her hand on Kim's shoulder. "Kim?"

Hélène's breath hitched when Kim looked up into her eyes. Kim was a blonde bombshell. Her eyes were the colour of the Mediterranean sea, crystal clear and shining, but they were shining with unshed tears. Whatever was happening, Hélène knew her holiday was about to change drastically. "Hélène, what are you doing here?" Kim spluttered.

"I'm staying here for a week on holiday. I presume you're doing the same?"

"I was," Kim cried, tears falling down her face.

"Hey, no crying. Tell me what's wrong."

"I was supposed to be staying in Anna's room. She and Sam are still in the US, so they gave me the reservation. I got here and the intern who was supposed to amend the booking cancelled it instead of changing it." Kim hiccupped. Hélène began rubbing soothing circles on Kim's back, desperately trying to get her to calm down. "All the other rooms are booked and I can't afford any other hotel in the area," Kim stuttered. "I've got nowhere to go and I can't go home yet. I needed this holiday so much."

Hélène could certainly understand that. What could she do, though? It seemed her mouth had the answer because before she registered what was happening, she'd invited Kim to stay in the suite with her.

"I can't do that," Kim protested.

"Why not? I've got a penthouse suite with three bedrooms and it's only me in it. You need a room, so stay in one of the spares, no big deal." Clearly, it was a big deal because Kim started crying even harder. Hélène didn't know what to do. She was usually excellent in a crisis and at comforting people, but she was really struggling with Kim.

"Thank you, Hélène, thank you so much. You don't know what this means." Hélène was almost knocked off the sofa when Kim launched herself into her body, hugging her hard. Hélène relaxed a little and hugged Kim back. It seemed she was finally calming down.

"I'll just let Thomas know you will stay with me." Kim sat back and gave a brief nod. Hélène could see she was trying to compose herself. Thomas appreciated Hélène's offer and was very apologetic. He gave Kim free treatments for the entire week as an apology, something that went a long way to cheering Kim up.

Warning bells sounded loudly in Hélène's head as she felt a warm sensation spread over her body at the sight of Kim smiling. Until she reminded herself that Kim had a longtime boyfriend, that was. Her rules of sun, sea, and no lesbians were still intact. She had no reason to panic. In fact, having a little eye candy to look at was a bonus to her trip, not that she objectified women, but who was she kidding? Kim was beautiful. *I wonder what she looks like in a bathing suit?*

Chapter 3

A three-headed Martian could have turned up and Kim still wouldn't have been as shocked and surprised as she was when she looked up to see Hélène standing in front of her as she'd had a complete and utter fucking meltdown.

Hélène offering Kim a room in the penthouse suite was such a kind offer it left Kim feeling all kinds of things. Kim and Hélène had only met a handful of times outside of their friendship group. Hélène had slept with Sam once, but for a reason Kim wasn't completely clear on, they'd decided to be friends and nothing more, which was the right call. Sam and Anna belonged together.

Aside from those meetings, Kim, and Hélène had exchanged a few emails and messages when organising things between their friends, Sam's leaving party, for example. That was before Sam and Anna had got their shit together. Kim still rolled her eyes at the stupidity of them both to this day.

After Hélène had arranged everything with Thomas at the front desk, she motioned for Kim to follow her over to the lifts. Kim was still in a bit of a weird headspace, considering the day she was having. To her relief, Hélène didn't fill the silence with chatter. She was quite happy to let the quiet surround them as they entered the lift and ascended to the penthouse suite.

If Kim thought the lobby was special, she was gobsmacked when Hélène keyed them into the penthouse. Kim had never seen anything so luxurious in her life. The suite was bigger than any apartment Kim had ever lived in.

Everything was a crisp white, with hints of colour woven throughout the room in the canvases and ornaments that were expertly placed on the walls and furniture. The large corner sofa was sunk into the floor facing a wall of glass windows. The view itself was breathtaking. Kim was struggling to take it all in. She was sure that the suite Anna had booked would've been nice, but not this kind of nice.

"Pick a room. I usually take the one on the left," Hélène said, pointing down the corridor. Kim had almost forgotten she was there.

"Oh, sure, I'll take the one on the right then." Why was she nervous? Kim was an upbeat, confident woman. This was ridiculous.

"You look like you've had one hell of a day. Care to talk about it over a cocktail?" Hélène was already dialling the phone on the table by the door for room service.

"Oh god, I'd kill for a drink." Kim was feeling infinitely better already.

"Great, what's your poison?"

"Will you judge me if I say a piña colada?" Kim grinned. Hélène laughed. Kim's stomach clenched. She'd never noticed Hélène's low and velvety laugh before.

"I promise not to judge. In fact, I'll join you," she said before putting in their order along with some appetisers. "They'll be up in a few minutes. Why don't we drop our cases in the rooms and get comfortable? After all, we have to get ready for some serious rest and relaxation," she added with a wink.

Kim grinned again like an idiot. She couldn't wait to shed her dress, put on a ridiculously comfy bathrobe and pig out on food and cocktails. The fact that Hélène was here with her was icing on the cake. *Why is having her here icing on the cake?*

Kim's bedroom—or should she say the massive fucking room that was once again bigger than her own apartment combined—was stunning! Just like the rest of the suite, the colours were bright, crisp and clean. The bed was enormous and Kim could not wait to starfish the hell out of it.

The door had barely clicked shut before she stripped off her dress, followed by her underwear. She hated feeling claggy after a day of travelling, so she needed to freshen up pronto! Heaving her case onto the bed, she unzipped it, looking for her thinnest pyjamas. The heat wasn't suffocating because of the air conditioning, but it was still warm.

Kim laughed out loud and shook her head as she entered her private bathroom. The room was covered from floor-to-ceiling in marble. The shower was a large walk-in that could easily accommodate five people. Or two very horny and adventurous people.

Kim shook her head again. Jesus, she needed a shag or at least give herself some self love. The thought of sex excited and confused her though, because when she looked at the shower and envisioned all the naughty things she could get up to in it, it wasn't Greg she saw in there with her.

27

Even though she had made it clear to Greg they were taking time apart, she wasn't ready to think about jumping into the sack — or shower — with anyone else yet, not until they'd had time to really talk and explore where they were in their relationship. That would be if Greg could get his head out of his arse and take Kim seriously.

Feeling her mood sour at the thought of Greg and their questionable relationship status, Kim snapped on the shower and dived under the rainfall of water. Instantly her worries washed away along with the grime of the day.

With no idea how long she'd been under the water because she'd been in a trancelike state, she jumped when she heard Hélène call her from the living room. The food and alcohol had arrived.

Quickly drying herself off, she removed her contact lenses. How did she always forget to take them out before showering? Slipping on her silk camisole and matching shorts, she wrapped herself up in the plush robe that hung on the back of the bathroom door.

Another thing she frequently forgot to do was put her glasses in reaching distance for when she'd removed the aforementioned contacts. She let out a huff of irritation at her mistake and slowly felt her way to the bed and suitcase. Thankfully, she'd put her glasses in an easy access part of her luggage. It was as if her brain knew she would need to find them through the sense of touch alone.

After a couple of seconds of rummaging and opening her glasses case, she could see clearly again. Suddenly, a knot tightened in her stomach. No one ever saw Kim in her glasses. Greg obviously had, but even Anna had only seen her in them once, and that was by mistake.

Kim felt uncomfortable with people seeing her in her specs. She'd been the same from a young child. Her mum had always told her she looked "super cute", which didn't make her feel any better. Kim didn't want to be cute, she wanted to be fierce and commanding.

That feeling came from the fact that her height had always been a subject of ridicule. She'd mainly dealt with that through impressive heel skills, but the glasses were a different matter. Kids were cruel, and their words had left a lasting impression on her. Nothing made her more self-conscious than her glasses.

It had taken years for her mum to agree to contact lenses. After Joy finally relented, Kim swore she'd never let anyone see her in her glasses, which made her feel less than her confident self. But now, in this gorgeous suite, she was going to have to let one more person see.

Breaking open a new set of lenses had floated through her mind, but her eyes were sore and dry from all the crying she had done in the lobby. No, she just had to suck it up and let Hélène see. First, she needed her trusty high heel slippers. Glasses were one thing. No heels as well? Out of the question.

Hélène had her back to Kim as she entered the open plan living room. She was clearly enjoying the view of the sea. Kim gave a nervous cough to signal her arrival. Hélène turned slowly. Kim held her breath, hoping that Hélène wouldn't make a comment. She watched Hélène's eyes grow a little wider, but she said nothing. After a beat, Hélène gestured to the food and cocktails that had been laid out on the coffee table.

"Feel better now?" Hélène's voice sounded a little husky.

"Oh Jesus, much better. I could spend the week standing in that shower." Kim smiled, remembering how wonderful the cascading water had felt on her skin.

"Tell me about it. The first time I came here, my friend had to drag me out of mine," she laughed. Kim saw a shadow of a memory pass over Hélène's face. *What is she remembering?*

They both sat down on the sofa, clearly a little uncomfortable with each other. Kim made the first move and grabbed her drink. "Bottoms up," she cheered before gulping down two-thirds in one go. Hélène laughed, reached for her own drink and followed Kim's lead. At this rate, they were going to be half-cut within an hour. "I'll call down and order a steady stream of these bad boys." Kim's confidence was back with a vengeance. Hélène simply giggled as she watched Kim strut over to the phone, to call in their order.

"I'm not sure The Sapphire is ready for the likes of me," Kim laughed, half joking. Kim liked a good time, although it had been a while since she'd felt so carefree.

"Should I be worried?" Hélène replied with an affable grin. Kim's stomach did a little flip. She'd always found Hélène stunning, but let's face it, in Paris there were stunning women around every corner.

"Depends."

"On?" Hélène asked, a little quieter. Her voice was even huskier than before.

"Do you intend to let your hair down and have some fun?"

"Oh, that is a given. I desperately need some fun."

"Stick with me, doll, I'll get you there," Kim winked, amused at the red tinge that had appeared on Hélène's cheeks. Hélène cleared her throat before finishing her drink and nibbling on some appetisers.

"So, do you want to talk about today?" Hélène asked through mouthfuls of mini quiche. Kim weighed her options. Yes, today had been a rollercoaster of emotions and it would probably do her good to vent a little, but she was more interested in having fun with Hélène. Maybe they could become proper friends outside of the group dynamic?

"Maybe later. Right now, I want to devour some pastries and cocktails. It's been far too long since I've had a proper holiday and I can honestly say I've never had one this luxurious."

"Yes, it's definitely a good way to spend your time." Hélène was looking directly at her and although Kim's gaze had been surveying the suite in more detail, she didn't miss the fact that Hélène was staring intensely. Interesting.

* * *

Kim was several piña coladas in and she was thoroughly enjoying the buzz. From the looks of Hélène, who was now sprawled on the other end of the sofa, she was enjoying herself, too. More time must have passed than Kim was aware of. She felt like they had only been chatting for an hour or so, but when she glanced at her phone, she saw that they'd been eating and drinking for nearly four hours.

The sun had started to set, and they were in for one hell of a view from where they sat. "Have you seen the time?" Kim slurred, clearly she was a little more than buzzed.

Hélène giggled. "What does time matter when you're having fun?"

"You speak wisely." Kim tried to keep her features serious. She lost the battle and laughed. God, they were having a blast. "I'm so glad you rescued me today, H."

"Well, I couldn't exactly leave you in the lobby, could I? I'm a gentlewoman."

"Gentlewoman?" Kim giggled.

"What, too butch?" Hélène smirked.

"Not at all. I think more women should be called 'Gentlewomen'. I was just thinking how right you are to call yourself one. There aren't many people who would offer a room

31

on their vacation to an acquaintance," Kim stated as a matter-of-fact.

"Can I let you in on a little secret?" Hélène whispered, raising her index finger to her mouth, making a little "*shh*" sound. Kim leaned forward, which was harder than it sounded, considering the room felt as if it was spinning.

"I'm a vault. Lay it on me, H baby."

Hélène laughed harder, which made Kim smile. She couldn't get enough of that low, sexy laugh. "It was a little selfish on my part. I came on holiday because I was feeling super sorry for myself and a little lonely, if I'm honest. Meeting you here and offering you a room was just what I needed. You're fun." Hélène smiled widely.

Kim knew she meant every word, which was very kind of her, but she was also concerned that Hélène had come here feeling lonely. "Why were you feeling sorry for yourself? Do you want to talk about it?"

"How about we take a raincheck on it for tonight? We're having too much fun to get mopey again." Hélène shuffled herself off the couch to her knees. "Wow, I'm getting old. Who knew getting off a couch at thirty-four would be a problem," she chuckled.

"Getting off a couch with a litre of rum inside you would be an issue for anyone," Kim added before gracefully standing up. The look on Hélène's face was highly amusing. She looked at Kim's face, then down at Kim's high-heeled slippers and back again several times.

"How can you say that when you have just risen off the couch like a Norse goddess in heels?" Hélène shot, her tone laced with surprise and admiration. "I'd have rolled both my ankles by now."

"I can do anything wearing heels." Fact.

"Anything?" Hélène said, raising her eyebrows.

"Yes, anything," Kim shot back with a knowing smirk. Kim knew Hélène was gay, but she was sure that Hélène didn't know she was bi. Everyone assumed she was straight for a couple of reasons—first Greg. They'd been together for years. Second, how she presented herself, the heels and dresses, and thirdly because Kim didn't discuss her sexual orientation. Not because she found it difficult, or she was hiding, it was more because she didn't feel the need to explain herself to anyone. She was bisexual, she knew it and she was the only person it concerned.

Kim was thoroughly enjoying this playfulness between them. She assumed Hélène was usually the confident go get 'em kind of woman. Kim wanted to see how she fared when she was up against someone just as confident and playful. Judging by the look on Hélène's face, she was confusing the fuck out of her. Kim smiled internally. This was going to be a lot of fun.

"Want to see something amazing?" Hélène asked. She hadn't broken eye contact with Kim since their last exchange.

"Always," Kim replied, not missing a beat.

Hélène rose from the floor and turned towards the large sliding doors that gave them that incredible view. "Follow me."

Kim had no idea what Hélène was going to show her. A small part of her, well, okay, a large part of her was hoping their playfulness was going to take a turn towards something more. That thought was unsettling. She was still technically in a relationship. But for how long she couldn't say.

Kim stepped through the double doors and onto the terrace that wrapped around two-thirds of the penthouse suite. There was an area for grilling, two sun loungers, and a beautiful dining table. The view was outstanding. Scanning her surroundings, she noticed Hélène had walked out of sight. Kim followed the sound of Hélène's flip-flops around to the left of the suit. To her surprise, Hélène was ascending a set of terracotta stairs.

"Keep up, you're going to love this," Hélène called over her shoulder.

When Kim reached the top step, she froze in place as she took in what lay before her. The stairs led up to the roof, which had been transformed into a tropical getaway consisting of a fully stocked bar, a large jacuzzi, and a large swimming pool. Oh, and if that wasn't enough, the space was filled with beautiful plants and trees, making it into a true secret garden.

"Oh my days," Kim gasped. "This is just beyond stunning," she added, shaking her head as if the image in front of her would disappear like a dream.

"I knew you'd like it," Hélène beamed.

"Like it? I want to marry it and have its babies. Jesus, I thought the suite and view were decadent. This takes the biscuit and the barrel."

"Drink?" Hélène called. Kim hadn't noticed her slip behind the bar. "I make a fabulous spiced rum and coke," she said jovially.

"Hell, yes!" Kim shouted. "I'm not leaving this roof, ever."

"Get comfy." Hélène pointed to one of the wooden sun loungers. Kim wasn't one to argue with a beautiful woman who was mixing her a drink in paradise. She lay down, crossing her legs. The air on the roof was significantly warmer than in the suite and she was feeling sweaty, with her fluffy robe still wrapped around her.

Tugging on the loose knot, she let the robe fall away. It took her a millisecond to shrug it from her shoulders. Although the sun was setting, she still saw a shadow cross her closed eyes. When she opened them, she saw Hélène standing over her, clearly checking out her best assets.

Kim grinned. "Is that for me?" she said, pulling Hélène out of her ogling. Hélène at least had the decency to look mortified that she'd been caught staring, which made Kim want to laugh out loud.

"Yep for you, one rum and coke," Hélène choked, her voice raspy.

"It's okay to look, you know. I flaunt what I've got, I'm body positive." Kim said playfully.

"Well, I'd be body positive too if I looked like you."

"Doll, you've got plenty to flaunt," Kim replied honestly.

"If that were the case, maybe I'd be able to keep hold of a woman." Hélène blushed. She'd clearly said more than she'd meant to. Kim had a decision to make. She could try to push Hélène into talking or keep things light. Considering the amount of alcohol they'd both consumed, maybe it wasn't the best time to be delving into deep feelings.

"Is there music up here?" Kim asked, hoping Hélène would go with the flow. She didn't want the night to end with Hélène feeling low. Her plan worked. Hélène threw her a heart-stopping grin before heading back to the bar. A few moments later, soft music played through two small speakers attached to the roof of the bar. God, Kim was in heaven.

"Challenge time," Hélène said as she walked back over to Kim.

"What do you mean by that?"

"I want you to prove that you really can do anything in those heels." Hélène was grinning widely.

"I wouldn't even class these as heels, to be honest," Kim smirked.

"Fancy putting your money where your mouth is?" Hélène shot back quickly.

"What are the terms of the challenge?" Kim replied just as quickly.

"You have to get through a song of my choice in the highest heels you have here. You dance without stumbling and I will be your personal bartender on this very roof terrace for twenty-fours hours straight. I win and you have to be my personal chef for twenty-four hours straight. How does that sound?"

"Honestly, not worth the challenge. If you want to make it so, I can't say no, then you need to up the reward, H." Kim was teasing. Hélène didn't know that Kim never shied away from a challenge or dare, and she certainly didn't turn down a way to prove how much of a boss bitch she was in heels.

"Alright, I'll bite. What are you proposing?" Hélène was clearly intrigued.

"You win, and I'll answer every room service request in my underwear. I win, you streak through the lobby."

"Naked?" Hélène squeaked with alarm.

"Not naked, in your underwear," Kim replied calmly. She could see Hélène regretting the whole challenge idea.

"We can't do that!"

"I thought you wanted a bit of fun and adventure?"

"Yes, but I know these people. What will they think?" Hélène replied, panicked.

"Hey, this was your challenge, not mine. I'm just trying to make it worth my while. I could slip and break something," Kim said seriously, even though the chance of that happening was infinitesimal. She watched Hélène mulling it over.

"Okay, you're on!"

"Wow, you're confident," Kim chuckled.

"I am. I can see you're well skilled in heels, but I don't believe for one second you can 'do anything' in them, especially dance to the song I have in mind."

"Bring it on. I'll go get my winning pair."

Chapter 4

Hélène repeatedly chastised herself as she watched Kim scurry back to her bedroom to collect her heels. What the hell had come over her? Challenging Kim to prove her heel skills was the adult equivalent of pulling her pigtails in the playground, because she secretly liked her. Hélène was way beyond that type of infantile behaviour. Well, so she thought.

Everything was going swimmingly when they'd arrived in the suite. The place was just as wonderful as Hélène remembered, and she really was happy to have Kim there as company. In fact, she was really looking forward to becoming Kim's friend.

That notion had come crashing down with a bang when Kim had come out of her room wearing the sexiest fucking glasses Hélène had ever seen. Well, maybe it wasn't the glasses themselves but the person wearing them. Kim was Hélène's complete fantasy, rolled up in a fluffy robe. A sexy blonde bombshell in heeled slippers and wingtip glasses.

Hélène had wanted to make a comment, but she got the distinct impression that it would have been a fatal error. So instead she'd tried to swallow down her lust—because let's be honest, that's exactly what it was—and hoped they could have a lovely evening in each other's company.

Mostly, they'd had a really enjoyable night together. It had been a while since Hélène had felt so comfortable around a woman. The problem was that Hélène could've sworn their interactions so far had been laced with flirtation, which was confusing as fuck.

Kim has a boyfriend, so even if she *did* slide over to Hélène's side of the rainbow scale, it was a no-go. So why was Kim flirting? Or was she? Was Hélène seeing things that weren't there? Possibly, actually, it was more than likely.

Hélène couldn't spend any more time over analysing because the sound of Kim's heels tapping on the floor was getting closer by the second. It didn't matter now. She'd offered up the challenge and Kim had accepted it. It was going to happen no matter what. But why oh why had she agreed to Kim's terms? Hélène's confidence that she would win had taken a severe nose dive.

"Right, I'm ready," Kim chimed, pulling Hélène out of her head. Hélène swallowed hard. Kim had replaced her slippers with the tallest heels she had ever seen. There was no way in hell Kim was going to dance along to Hélène's chosen song in them.

"Jesus, they're not shoes, they're stilts," Hélène blurted. She was getting a little worried that Kim could legitimately hurt herself. "Listen, it was a stupid challenge. I don't want you getting hurt and ruining your holiday, seriously let's just forget it and have another drink."

"Ah, I see, you're scared," Kim grinned.

"Not scared, just wanting to stay out of the emergency department."

"I don't buy it, you're chicken. Scared, you might have to give Thomas a glimpse of the goods, eh?"

Hélène's concern was ebbing. She did not like to be called a chicken. Fine, Kim wanted to dance in her death shoes, then that's exactly what would happen. Hélène was looking forward to Kim's smug smile being wiped off her face.

"Okay, let's do it, but the song I picked will not be an easy one to dance to," Hélène warned.

"I'd be disappointed in you if it was." Kim walked to the centre of the terrace and stood with her hands on her hips, waiting. Hélène pulled out her phone, ready to play the song.

"Ready?" Helen's thumb hovered over the play button.

"Always," Kim replied confidently. Hélène pressed play. The opening bars to a Disturbed song rang out through the speakers. She studied Kim's face, gauging her reaction. To Hélène's horror, she saw a smile cross Kim's face in recognition.

"I love this song," she shouted. Hélène could not believe what she was witnessing. Kim was full out moshing. She was holding nothing back and to Hélène's disbelief it looked as if Kim wasn't wearing shoes at all with the way she was jumping around, clearly having the best goddamn time of her life.

Hélène couldn't move, she couldn't speak. The sight of Kim in her silk camisole and shorts paired with the red patent heels was doing things to her in a very sensitive area. She could have come on the spot when Kim reached up and released her platinum blond hair, which was now swishing around her face as she gyrated. Holy mother of God.

The song finally ended. Kim did one last jump before taking a bow. "I believe I won," she said triumphantly.

"I don't believe it," Hélène blurted. "That was the best thing I think I have ever seen." Hélène wasn't lying. That had been a stunning display of grace and style, even if Kim had been rocking out.

"Why thanks, doll!" Kim was beaming. "So about the terms of our deal." Hélène's stomach dropped. Oh shit, she'd completely forgotten about that. Oh god, did Kim really expect her to streak through the lobby in her underwear?

"How about I take you out for a super delightful meal instead?" Hélène asked hopefully.

"Oh no, no way, you agreed," Kim said seriously.

"Kim, I wouldn't be able to show my face here again." Hélène was almost pleading.

"You knew the risks. Now it's time to pay up. Come on, H, live a little."

Live a little, really? Hélène was no stranger to fun. She'd done a few questionable things in her youth, but she was an adult now. She needed to act like one.

"We're too old to be doing silly things like that."

"It was your bloody idea and I'll tell you something. If you'd have won, I would have taken my punishment without question."

"Really? you're telling me you would have honestly answered the door in your knickers and bra without questioning it?" Hélène replied, her tone a little on the mocking side.

"Absolutely, no problem," Kim said firmly. "Tell you what, follow me." Kim turned on her heel and walked off towards the suite downstairs.

For the second time tonight, Hélène was watching Kim walk away, leaving her feeling out of her depth. She shook herself out of her stupor and followed Kim into the suite.

Hélène entered the suite. Kim stood by the small table by the door. Putting the room service phone back in its cradle, Kim

40

stood and stared at Hélène, which felt a little uncomfortable. She wasn't sure what the hell was happening. Just as she was about to break the silence, there was a knock on the door. Kim stared directly at Hélène. She didn't once break eye contact as she shimmied the camisole over her head to reveal a matching bra underneath. Hélène couldn't breathe. Kim dropped the camisole, turned around in her silk shorts and bra, and opened the door wide.

"Oh, thank you so much. I just really fancied a hot chocolate." Kim spoke sweetly to the poor young man who was beetroot red, trying desperately not to look at Kim's boobs. Hélène felt for the guy. She was having difficulty herself.

"Hélène will tip you." Kim took the hot chocolate, turned back around and strolled straight past Hélène, looking very smug. Hélène rushed forward, shoving a fifty euro note in the boy's hand before shutting the door.

"Are you insane?" she cried, turning to face Kim, who was now perched on the sofa, sipping her hot chocolate.

"Nope, just not a chicken." What was Hélène supposed to say to that?

* * *

"This is insanity," Hélène grumbled as she checked herself over in the mirror. How had she got herself in this mess? After Kim called her out as a coward, Hélène didn't have much of a choice but to go through with her dare.

So here she stood, a thirty-four-year-old woman looking up and down at herself in a mirror, deciding if the underwear she was currently wearing was suitable for a quick streak across the posh hotel lobby.

"You ready?" Kim called through her bathroom door.

"No," she said emphatically.

41

"Fine, don't do it then," Kim said calmly.

"Oh, and have you lord it over me for all eternity, I don't think so."

"Stop stalling then, and let's go." Kim sounded far too smug for Hélène's liking.

A myriad of curse words streamed through her mind. She couldn't exactly stay mad at Kim for asking her to go through with something that had been entirely her idea in the first place. Hélène looked herself dead in the eye, summoning all the courage she could find. "You are Hélène DuBois. You can do this," she said to her reflection. Reaching for her robe, she opened the bathroom door.

"Hey, no robe remember," Kim shot.

"No robe in the lobby. You didn't specify that I couldn't wear it until I get down there."

"Fair enough. So ground rules, first no robe, second you have to do a full circuit of the entire lobby and third no running."

"No running? How's that fair?"

"Fine speed walking only," Kim smirked. She was enjoying this far too much.

"Fine," Hélène grumbled.

Hélène's heartbeat picked up several notches as she followed Kim out of the suite. It wouldn't be out of the ordinary for them to be seen walking around the hotel in plush robes. After all, it was also a world class spa. What would be and what was going to be out of the ordinary was a mid-thirties French woman power walking around the lobby in nothing but her delicates.

Hélène wasn't a complete stranger to dares and challenges. She'd taken part in many skirmishes as a teenager. Few people in her adult life knew that she was the daughter of the very impressive Veronique DuBois, a name that commanded respect in the world of fashion.

The downside to Hélène's parentage was that she'd grown up with a mother who demanded perfection from everyone around her, including her daughter. Hélène had responded to those demands in a typical teenage way and rebelled.

From the age of sixteen through to her late twenties, Hélène had enjoyed pushing her mother's buttons by partying and generally misbehaving. She'd never pushed it so far that she truly embarrassed her. She wasn't cruel, but she wanted her mum to understand that she wasn't one of her sheep. Hélène was her own woman.

For the most part, Veronique had let Hélène get away with her roguish behaviour. That was until she turned twenty-eight. Hélène recalled her mother swooping into Paris after being in the US for a year. Hélène had been spending a large amount of time in the company of lovely ladies, enjoying everything that the DuBois name afforded her. It was after a heavy weekend that Hélène had been subjected to her mother ripping off her bed covers, demanding an audience.

Veronique spent hours dressing Hélène down, pointing out that Hélène was no longer a child. She was a grown woman wasting herself on childish pursuits and loose women.

Over the years, Hélène's rebellion had become less and less about proving she was her own woman and more about feeling lost. Hélène's career was nonexistent. She only had a job because of her brother. The women she bedded only wanted a taste of her privileged life. They wanted nothing substantial from her.

That weekend was when Hélène let go of her inner rebel and child. Deciding she wanted more out of her life. A partner, a home, and a career.

The idea of embracing that side of herself again was unnerving. She'd worked hard to change. Her managerial job

43

wasn't her dream career, but she was happy enough. As for a partner and a home, she hadn't been able to check those off her list just yet. God knows she'd tried, though. Could she let herself go a little without coming undone? Would word of her behaviour get back to her mother?

The elevator started its descent before Hélène even registered she was in it. She'd been in a world of her own. The bell signalled their arrival. "Okay, it's all on you now, H." Kim's eyes twinkled with excitement.

"I don't think I can do this," Hélène whispered. She felt the blood drain from her face as she pictured her mother being informed that her irresponsible daughter had been caught half naked running around the family's favourite hotel.

Kim must have seen Hélène's colour fade. Wrapping a hand around Hélène's bicep, Kim gently squeezed. "Hey, it's okay. You really *don't* have to do it Hélène, I'm truly sorry if I've made you feel bad."

"It's not you," Hélène whispered again. Her voice had lost all its strength.

"What is it then?"

Hélène pulled Kim to a sofa that sat next to the elevators.

"Have you heard of Veronique DuBois?" Hélène asked, averting her eyes to the floor.

"Of course, who hasn't?" Kim replied, looking confused.

Hélène took a deep breath. "She's my mother."

"Okay."

"Okay?"

"Yes, okay, what about her?"

Hélène sat silent for a minute, looking at Kim. She couldn't recall the last time a person had been so unaffected by her mother's name. Clearing her throat, she told Kim all about their relationship and how Hélène had behaved. She explained about her mother's harsh words and how she had been trying to change herself to become more responsible, more of an adult. When she finished, she looked into Kim's eyes, waiting for her reaction.

"I can understand your reticence to let yourself go," Kim eventually said. "The thing is, Hélène, you haven't come here to cause trouble. You're not partying and womanising. You came to relax and enjoy yourself. Having some silly fun is all a part of that. It doesn't mean that you're irresponsible, it means that you can find a balance. Being an adult is hard. The preconception that you have to lose your childish side is bullshit." Kim squeezed Hélène's hand, which was pulling at a thread on her robe. "We spend our days stressed and anxious, juggling everything that life throws at us. It's not possible to take all that on and not let off a little steam. I would think you speed walking around here in your pants is the tamest of ways to let it all go."

Hélène felt her anxiety drain away. With just a few words, Kim had calmed her. She had a way of making everything feel manageable and lighter. Hélène loved Kim embraced her silly, fun side, even if it meant she could be a little pushy when excited about something.

"Thanks," she said after a moment of silence. "You're right, I know that. It's just a difficult thing to let go of."

"I know, doll, really I get it. Look, you're under no pressure. It really was just a silly bet." Kim ducked her head to look into Hélène's eyes.

Hélène was momentarily transfixed. Kim's eyes were mesmerising. In that moment, with Kim's words echoing in her head, Hélène felt a jolt of something she couldn't name. It was a feeling that made her want to let it all go, consequences be damned.

"Fuck it. You're buying shots after this." In a flash, Hélène was on her feet, disrobing. Without looking back, she dropped the robe to her feet, squared her shoulders and strode off.

The moment she stepped away from Kim, it was as if time slowed down. She saw Thomas casually look up from his computer. She saw his features turn to surprise and maybe embarrassment as he scanned her scantily clad body up and down as she walked past his desk.

With a straight face as if it was any other day, Hélène slightly turned her head and greeted him. "Good evening, Thomas." She continued to walk to the plush sofas at the other end of the lobby. She heard Thomas stutter, a reply which made her grin.

Now that she'd committed, she might as well do it right. She arrived at the sofa, bent down to the coffee table, picked up a magazine, flipping a few pages, feigning interest before replacing it in its original place. All she had to do now was make her way back over to the elevators and she'd completed her dare.

On her return journey, she heard the distinct sound of the double doors swish open. Other guests had arrived. Hélène looked over and gave the couple that had just entered a swift nod. "Lovely evening, isn't it?" The couple faltered in their steps. The man who was probably in his late fifties blushed. His wife or companion did a double-take before planting an elbow in the man's ribs.

Hélène continued on her journey, stopping only once more at a floor-length mirror that was halfway between the entrance and the elevators. She looked herself up and down once more before running her hands through her hair and adjusting her bust. She'd definitely chosen the right underwear. It was sexy as hell and in that moment she felt confident, beautiful and free.

When she was satisfied that she'd given enough of a show, she sauntered over to the elevators to press the call button.

As the doors opened, she looked over at a stunned Kim, gave a teasing smile and said, "You coming?" before walking into the car and leaning casually against the back wall.

"Sweet Jesus, that was incredible," Kim blurted when she crashed into the elevator after Hélène. "You boss bitched the hell out of that."

"I did, didn't I?" Hélène burst into laughter. "Did you see the look on Thomas' face? I'm going to have to tip big after that."

"I think what you just did was the biggest tip he will receive all year." Kim laughed just as hard as Hélène.

"Oh, I hope I haven't scarred the poor man."

"Scarred him? You've got the body of a goddess. He'll feel like the luckiest fella alive right now. He'll probably need to take his break soon just to relieve himself."

"That is a hideous thought." Hélène shivered. Gross.

"Well, I certainly have a lady boner for you, so I fully understand his predicament," Kim said seriously.

"Oh my god, who says that?"

"I only tell the truth," Kim said, leaving Hélène to roll her eyes. "Here, put this back on before I combust." Kim drooped Hélène's robe over her arm. Hélène felt herself blush. She knew Kim was just being playful and was not being serious, but the thought that she could make someone as gorgeous as Kim hot under the collar turned her on massively.

As soon as they entered the suite, Hélène headed for the bar. She wasn't joking when she said she'd need shots.

"Tequila?" she asked Kim, who was draped over the sofa looking all kinds of sexy.

"Tequila goes straight to my knickers," Kim said seriously.

"I beg your pardon?"

"You've never heard that expression before?"

"Nope, I presume it's an English thing?"

"Probably, but it basically means that Tequila leaves me horny."

Hélène nearly choked on the shot she had just knocked back. Kim flung her head back, laughing. "Everyone has a drink that leaves them like that. What's yours?"

"I don't know." Hélène was still choking and her shot.

"Rubbish, of course you do."

"Okay fine, rum." Hélène poured out another shot for herself.

"We were drinking rum earlier. Does that mean you've had a fire raging in those delicious panties all evening?"

"Oh my god Kim, do you not have any boundaries at all?" Hélène laughed.

"Not with my friends," she giggled. "Sorry, am I being too much? Greg says I'm too much sometimes."

Hélène saw Kim shrink back. She saw her bubbly, outgoing friend become smaller, her eyes dimming. Hélène's heart clenched. Who the hell felt that they could tell this vibrant woman she was "*too much*"? Hélène put the shot glass down and went over to Kim. She didn't know what she was going to do, but she desperately wanted to comfort her somehow.

"You are not too much. Never think that, Kim." Her tone was firm.

Kim gave her a half-hearted smile. "Thanks."

"No, you listen to me." Hélène pulled Kim, so she sat flush against Hélène's side. Hélène turned her body so she could look Kim straight in the eye. "Kim, you are a rare woman. You are smart, funny and confident. You have the ability to make people feel included and seen. Never let anyone tell you that you're too much. It's them that aren't enough. Do you understand?"

Kim nodded, her smile a little brighter. "Thanks, H," she breathed. "Do you mind me calling you that?"

"What, H?"

"Yeah."

"Not at all. You'll be the only one who does though, everyone calls me Hélène or Hels."

"I like I get to call you by a nickname only I will use."

"Me, too. Now you're ready for a shot? I think we both earned one tonight," Hélène chuckled.

"Oh yes, make mine a double. I'm just going to grab my phone. I haven't looked at it since we arrived."

"That's how it's supposed to be on holiday, isn't it?"

"Yeah, but…" Kim started before drifting off. Hélène then understood she was probably thinking about her boyfriend.

"Of course you probably need to check in with your partner." She moved, creating a bit of room between them. As much as Kim made Hélène feel all kinds of things, she couldn't forget that Kim was with someone else. Although it struck her as odd that Kim had come away on her own. If Hélène was Kim's partner, there would be no way in hell she would miss out on a week of private time with her.

Kim gave her a tight smile. "Yeah right, need to check in."

Hélène watched Kim walk away for the third time.

Chapter 5

Needing a few minutes to herself, Kim closed the door quietly behind her. The evening had not turned out how she thought it would. Sharing laughs and drinks had been wonderful, but at some point it had turned into something else. She'd found the challenge funny at first. She was guaranteed to win. There had been no doubt. Why had she insisted that the consequence for the loser required them to be in underwear? What was that about?

Walking over to the bed, she had no intention of looking at her phone. She'd just said that to give herself a plausible reason to take some space. Dancing in front of Hélène had felt sensual. The music might have been a heavy rock song, but it didn't change the fact that she'd felt Hélène's gaze on her the whole time and she'd liked it a lot.

Dropping her head in her hands, she blew out a frustrated breath. The purpose of this vacation was not supposed to be getting all hot and bothered over a friend. She was supposed to be taking the time to decide if she wanted to stay with Greg.

Maybe her behaviour around Hélène was telling her a lot about her state of mind regarding her relationship with her boyfriend. Surely if she was still committed to Greg, she wouldn't be entertaining the idea of jumping Hélène, because in truth that's exactly what she wanted to do.

Surely the alcohol she'd consumed played a big part in her feeling this way, plus Hélène saving her from a ruined holiday was also a factor. Nevertheless; it didn't change the fact she wanted to see more of Hélène with even less clothing than she already had.

The ping of her phone drew her attention. Her screen showed multiple notifications. *God, can't I just have some fucking peace?* Ten messages and fifteen calls all from Greg made her anger sizzle. He was unbelievable. How many goddamn times did she need to tell him she needed space? The phone rang twice before Greg answered.

"Kim, where the hell are you?" he demanded. Kim's anger almost erupted, but she quashed it before she said something she'd regret.

"I'm on holiday," she replied calmly.

"What the fuck does that mean?" He barked.

"It's not rocket science, Greg, I'm. On. Holiday."

"Where?"

"Saint Tropez?" No reason to lie to him.

"Saint Tropez? How the hell have you afforded that?"

"If you must know, Anna couldn't go on her holiday, so she gave it to me."

"Oh, right, fine." His voice came down a few notches.

"What do you want, Greg?" Kim sighed.

"I want you to come home. I understand I upset you and I understand it's hard for you when I can't be around, but I think this is a bit drastic."

Kim shook her head in defeat. He just wasn't getting it at all. "Greg, listen and listen carefully. I'm not some bored little housewife who sits around pining for my man. I have my own life away from you, as you do from me, and that's great. It's healthy. What's not healthy is that you've checked out on being an equal partner in this relationship."

"No, I haven't."

"Yes, Greg, you have. You treat me like your little woman."

"Hey, that's not fair," he shot.

"Isn't it? You've started questioning why I haven't got your dinner on the table for when you get home, for Christ's sake."

"I'd do it for you!"

"That's bullshit. As soon as you know I'll be home late, you schedule drinks with your bloody boss."

"I don't see why I should wait around. Not when I have meetings, I can attend. I'm a busy man."

"Even on my birthday?" she snapped. The line went silent. He couldn't talk his way out of that. "You've also started volunteering me to organise dinner parties for work. Since when have I ever wanted to do that? Never, Greg. You've been trying to anchor me to the goddamn kitchen for months and I don't get it?"

"Forgive me for thinking that you might enjoy being a lady of leisure. Plenty of other wives do that. All my colleagues' wives are stay-at-home mothers."

Kim shook her head furiously. "First, I am not your wife, second who the hell do you think you are making that kind of decision for me? You know me much better than that. You're trying to railroad me into something you know I fucking detest. Don't let my dresses and heels fool you, Greg, I am one hundred percent my own woman and will never be anyone's property. Regardless of what I look like, I'm not a '50s housewife. I never will be." She seethed.

"Alright, so I went a little overboard. I just wanted to provide for you."

"NO! you wanted to match up to your slimy colleagues and bosses. I never thought you'd become that guy, Greg, never."

"I'm sorry, Kim, please come home, let's work it out," he pleaded.

"No, I'm on a well-deserved holiday, one which I intend to enjoy."

"Maybe I could come down to you then for a weekend? That would be nice, right?"

"Oh, now you want to join me?" she shouted.

"Yes I do, really. I was wrong to cancel on you. I want to make time for you and us. Come on, Kim, we've been together for ages. Surely, that deserves a second chance?"

"Let me think about it," she sighed. Yes, she was furious with him, but he had a point. They'd been a couple for years and it had been a good relationship on the whole. Maybe they could work on it.

"Great, just let me know and I'll be there," he said enthusiastically.

"Fine, I'm going now. Good night."

"Night, Kim, I love you,"

"Yeah, me too." Her voice lacked conviction.

The phone line went dead and Kim felt numb. All the pleasant feelings she'd felt mere minutes ago evaporated. She felt stuck. If she were being honest, in that very moment she did *not* want Greg in Saint Tropez, but that could change after a few more days, once she'd calmed down.

Feeling the weight of the day, Kim dropped her phone on the bedside table and crawled onto the bed. The only thing she needed now was sleep. Maybe tomorrow would come with some much needed answers.

* * *

The sound of the ceiling fan brought Kim out of a fitful night's sleep. Her eyes fluttered open slowly. She was momentarily confused by her surroundings. Sitting up, she propped herself against the headboard, her head pounding. She couldn't be sure if it was the alcohol, conversation with Greg or her overwhelming feelings of attraction towards Hélène that made her feel as if she was having a hole bored into her skull.

Hélène. Jesus, she'd just left her sitting in the living room last night, probably expecting Kim to return for another drink. "I'm the worst."

The first thing she had to do was drink a pint or two of water along with some painkillers. The second and the most important was to apologise to Hélène. Kim had to get a grip on herself. It wasn't fair to mistreat Hélène because she was going through some personal crap.

After a quick shower to freshen up, she dressed in one of her bathing suits that paired with a sheer wraparound. Oh, and not forgetting her trusty heeled sandals. No need to look bad whilst grovelling.

Heading into the living room, she saw no sign of Hélène. However, the smell of coffee permeated the air. Maybe she was in the kitchen? Nope, not there. Kim wondered if Hélène had already gone out. After all, they hadn't said they would spend

54

any time together, just that Kim could stay in a spare room. The thought made Kim's stomach tighten and not in a good way. Had she ruined a chance at friendship with Hélène already?

After pouring herself a large cup of coffee, she headed to the balcony, the doors already open. The bright blue of the Mediterranean engulfed Kim's vision. Wow, it was breathtaking.

"Gorgeous isn't it?"

Kim almost launched her coffee mug over the balcony railings. "Jesus Christ," she blurted. She'd not seen Hélène lounging on one of the many chairs on the terrace. "You almost gave me a heart attack." She gasped, clutching her chest.

"Sorry," Hélène chuckled, not looking in the least bit sorry at all.

"No, it's fine." After a few moments of deep breathing, she looked down at Hélène. Her breath hitched. Hélène was in the smallest bikini Kim had ever seen. Her toned body was already turning a delicious tanned brown. Her skin looked so soft Kim had to mentally slap herself to stop from reaching out and caressing the beautiful body laid so tantalisingly close.

"Listen, I owe you a huge apology," Kim said after clearing her throat, which had suddenly dried up like the Sahara.

"Apology, what for?" Hélène looked genuinely confused.

"Well, for a start, buggering off and leaving you sitting in the living room last night."

"I figured you just crashed out. It was a long day, and we drank a lot," she grinned.

"True, but no, I mean yes, I crashed out, but it wasn't that. I had a phone call with Greg and it drained me." Kim wasn't able to look at Hélène.

"Oh, is everything okay?"

"Honestly no," Kim sighed. "The reason I came on holiday is that I needed a break from him, from us."

"I'm sorry Kim, do you want to talk about it?" Hélène sat up, sliding her sunglasses into her beautiful, shiny, soft hair. *Get a grip.*

"You didn't come on holiday to listen to my personal issues."

"How about you let me decide what I came on holiday for? I wouldn't have offered to listen if I didn't want to," Hélène said gently. "Tell you what, I'll make you a deal."

"Ha, you sure that's a good idea?" Kim smiled.

"Yes indeed," Hélène laughed. "The deal is, you use me as a sounding board and in return, I'll use you. I came here after some messy personal stuff, too."

Kim mulled it over. "Yeah, okay, that sounds fair."

Hélène nodded and patted the seat next to her. Kim sat down, nursing her coffee. She wasn't sure where to start. Well, from the beginning would be the best place, but when was that? When had she first noticed a change in Greg?

After a breath Kim launched into her personal misery, Hélène sat listening closely.

"So now he wants to come down here for the weekend and sort it all out," Kim finished.

"How do you feel about that?"

"Right now, it's the last thing I want. I was really serious about needing some time and space. I think I've lost a part of myself and I want to get it back."

"So tell him."

"I have, several times, but he just isn't hearing me."

"So tell him again until it sinks in."

Kim sighed, "You're right. Surely he should understand that it's better for me to take my time now. It's better in the long run, right?"

56

"I can't answer that for you, Kim, but if that's how you're feeling, then you should run with it."

"Thanks, H." Kim's head and heart felt better for unloading her thoughts and feelings that had been percolating inside for far too long. "Now your turn." Adding a little levity, she shoulder bumped Hélène.

"Right, I don't think it's as much as you're going through. It's just me feeling sorry for myself, really."

"Don't dismiss your problems, doll."

"I just got sick and tired of failing with women," Hélène said shyly.

"What do you mean?" There was no way that someone as great as Hélène couldn't get a woman, no way.

"I mean I'm cursed," Hélène said plainly. Kim didn't know what to say to that, so instead she stayed silent, waiting for her to continue. "Everyone I meet leaves me. Not because of me, but for one reason or another, they leave. I'd just been left again before I decided I needed to get away."

"Were any of them serious?"

"No, not really. We never seem to get far enough into a relationship before they leave." Hélène sighed. Kim scooched a little closer until she was shoulder to shoulder with Hélène.

"You know what that tells me?" Kim gently bumped Hélène, who shook her head. "That tells me you just haven't met the one. Because you, Hélène, —" Kim said pointing at her, " — are one hell of a catch and I'm positive the universe will send you that one woman who sees how fantastic you are and will not leave, she'll be your happy ever after."

"Maybe, but for now, I just want to focus on this wonderful holiday," Hélène replied truthfully. She'd had enough of overthinking and moping. "How about we spend today on the terrace by the pool sipping cocktails and tomorrow we take advantage of those free spa treatments you were given?

Perhaps tomorrow evening we could go for a nice meal in Saint Tropez. There are some wonderful places I know you'll love."

How could anyone say no to an offer like that? The past 24hrs had been pretty manic and even though they had indulged in a few drinks last night, neither of them had had the time to really relax and enjoy their time at The Sapphire.

"That is exactly what we should do." After all, they were in no hurry. They could get to their personal baggage later on.

* * *

Kim couldn't remember having a more relaxing day. True to Hélène's word, they'd spent the day lazing by the pool, sipping delicious cocktails that Hélène cooked up. Kim was certain that Hélène must have had training as a mixologist. So far, her favourite had been Hélène's piña colada. But that was probably because she would always be biased towards the coconut-y goodness.

"Shit," Kim mumbled. She could feel a patch on her shoulder burn. Kim wasn't someone who could indulge in the sun for too long, her naturally pale skin burnt quickly. Anyone would think that she would have learnt how to properly cover herself in sunscreen, but alas once again she'd missed a spot and was going to pay for it if she didn't get under some shade.

"You okay?" Hélène replied lazily, she had obviously been dozing.

"Yeah, just missed my bloody shoulder and now I can feel it burning," Kim said, pissed at herself.

"Let me see." Hélène sat up, beckoning Kim to show her. Kim turned her shoulder. She could see by Hélène's reaction that she had burned.

"*Oui*, you got caught. Hang on, I have some magic cream that will sort you out." Hélène skipped off towards the stairs,

58

leaving Kim to watch her very firm arse in those tiny bikini bottoms. *Christ, I think she just gave me sunstroke, too.*

Moments later Hélène came bounding up the stairs, taking them two at a time, something Kim appreciated, especially when the momentum made Hélène's breast bounce. *My god, I'm such a creep!*

"Here, let me put this on you. I promise you'll feel better in no time." Hélène was completely unaware of Kim's less than friendly thoughts running through her mind.

"Thanks." Kim cleared her throat. Hélène must have been a miracle worker because the moment the cream soaked into her skin, Kim felt the sore tightness disappear.

"What the hell is that stuff? And where has it been all my life?" Kim chuckled.

"It's wonderful, isn't it? I often burn myself in the kitchen, so I carry some around with me everywhere. Just let me know if you need it again."

"It sounds like you spend a lot of time cooking?" Kim wanted to know everything about her new friend.

"Oh yes, I adore cooking. It's soothing." Hélène's passion was visibly shining through her eyes as she spoke. "I love trying to put my spin on traditional recipes."

"I'd love to try something sometime. I'm okay at cooking but it's not something that comes naturally." Kim hoped she wasn't coming across as pushy again.

"I will cook for you anytime." They sat looking into each other's eyes, something stirring in the air between them.

"Awesome. I can be your guinea pig."

"Deal." Hélène held out her hand to shake on it. Kim looked from Hélène's face to her extended hand. She couldn't help but laugh.

"We seem to make a lot of deals," she said, grinning.

"You're fun to deal with." Hélène wore an equally brilliant grin. Kim sucked in a quiet breath. Was Hélène flirting again?

"Right back at ya, doll." Kim winked, hoping to inject some levity into the conversation. It worked. Hélène threw her head back and laughed before sliding back down on the sun lounger.

* * *

Dusk fell. The colours from the disappearing sun were phenomenal. Kim had never seen anything like it. After they were both showered, they sat at the large table overlooking the sea. The food they ordered from room service was delicious, and the wine that Hélène picked paired perfectly.

"You've had some training, I think," Kim said after she'd taken a sip of her red wine.

"What do you mean?" Hélène replied between bites of the lamb tagine they'd ordered.

"I mean, you can mix a cocktail like a pro, you have excellent taste in food, and you know how to pair it with the perfect wine. That makes me think you've had some training or experience in the culinary world."

"Ah, you caught me." Hélène laughed. She put her cutlery down and gently dabbed her mouth with her napkin. "I spent a lot of my childhood touring with my mother. It wasn't something I enjoyed and most of the time I got in the way. After a while, my mother would send me away to entertain myself and I would always end up in the kitchens of any hotel or resort we were staying at. I got to know a lot of chefs, some famous, some not. I spent my time shadowing them and learning."

"She sent you away?" Kim couldn't imagine ever wanting to offload her child to a stranger. Hélène shrugged her shoulders in response.

"How old were you?" She didn't know why, but she felt anger bubbling up.

"Too young, but it's the way it was. Can't change it now and besides, I really enjoyed my time learning how to cook."

"Well, now I really can't wait to try your food," Kim quipped.

"What about you? Where did you learn to cook?" Hélène asked, tucking back into her food.

"Not sure, really. My mum is an excellent cook, but I didn't spend any time in the kitchen with her. I think I just picked things up as I went."

"Are you close to your parents?"

"Absolutely! They still live in the UK. My mum, Joy, is a Doctor of Applied Physics. She works at the University of London. Although she's pretty much retired now, she only takes a few classes. My dad Peter is a Doctor of Engineering. He stopped working about five years ago after he had a minor heart attack. They both seem happy now they've got more time together."

"Putain, Kim, they sound impressive."

"Oh, they are, but you'd never guess if you looked at them. Picture me but twenty years older and that's my mum. You can imagine her students' faces when they meet her for the first time," Kim laughed.

"I bet her classroom is full to burst. If I'd had a teacher that looked like you, I would've turned up every damn time for class," Hélène laughed. Kim felt her cheeks colour. Did Hélène just imply she was hot?

"Well thanks, I'll let my mum know you think she's a hotty."

"Please do," Hélène winked. "So I take it you didn't want to go down the academic route?"

"What makes you think I didn't?" Kim was used to people thinking she wasn't academically minded, unfortunately people still judged on looks and hers didn't scream academia.

"Sorry, I didn't mean to presume, it's just that with you working with Anna…"

"I get it. I have a MSc in Biology. I considered going for my PhD, but life just took a different turn."

"In what way?"

"Greg, to be blunt. He'd waited around whilst I finished my degree working for a bank in central London. He got offered an excellent position in Paris, which was too good to turn down and to be honest, I was excited at the idea of living abroad. I always thought I could go back to uni at some point."

"Do you still want to?"

"Honestly, I haven't thought about it for a long time. We came to Paris, and I started working for Anna. I love my job and I love living in Paris."

"It is a wonderful city," Hélène nodded.

"What about you? Do you always want to work at JHS photography?"

"God, no, but right now it will do."

"What do you want to do, then?"

"Do you really want to know?" Hélène almost looked shy, which Kim found intriguing.

"Of course I do."

"I want to open up my own diving centre somewhere tropical."

"Diving, as in scuba diving, as in underwater?" Kim spluttered.

"*Oui absolument.*"

"Wow, that's, that's amazing, Hélène, what an adventure that would be."

"You really think so?"

"Oh god yes, I'd love to learn. I always wanted to, but as I said, life took me in a different direction."

"I could teach you," Hélène shot. Kim studied her face for a second. Was she being serious? Kim had always wanted to scuba dive, especially after she'd taken some extra classes in Marine Biology at university.

"Really?"

"Yes really, I'm actually diving after I leave here." Hélène shuffled in her seat. "You could join me if you wanted. I know you were supposed to be here for a couple of weeks, which got ruined. You could come with me and continue your holiday. I have a boat for a few weeks."

"Oh, wow, that's really generous Hélène, can I think about it?"

"Of course, no pressure."

The idea of spending extra time with Hélène was enticing, especially if it was on a boat far away from everyone. They could really get to know each other that way, just as friends, obviously.

Chapter 6

"Was I ever dropped on my head as a child?" Hélène barked down the phone.

"Erm…. what?" A groggy voice on the other end of the line spluttered.

"You know, dropped, leading to some sort of brain damage," Hélène shot back.

"It's four in the morning, Hélène, are you having a genuine emergency, like have you actually hurt your head?"

"No, I'm not hurt. I think I'm just suffering the aftereffects of a childhood trauma because that's the only logical reason to explain my behaviour right now."

"Okay, back up, try to catch me up because I have no idea what the hell you're talking about and you have never called me this early to have a meltdown."

"JJ, I think I'm in trouble as in 'woman' trouble." She exhaled harshly. There was zero point in Hélène denying that she was smitten with Kim, a woman she'd known only "casually" as of three days ago. Three days was all it had taken, though. Hélène had come away to find herself and regroup, but instead she'd smacked straight into a woman that was now invading her thoughts and dreams entirely.

"I didn't know you went away with someone?" JJ replied, still sounding utterly confused and half asleep.

"I didn't. I turned up at the hotel to find a woman I know through a friend sat crying on the sofa. Long story short, her booking got screwed up, so I offered her a bedroom and now I have invited her to spend time on *Connie* with me."

"You invited a woman to sail around the Mediterranean on *Connie* and you barely know her. Am I getting this right?"

"In a nutshell, yes. We have been spending a lot of time together and she is wonderful, fun, adventurous, oh and straight with a long-term boyfriend," Hélène quipped. She was staggered by her own stupidity.

"I thought you'd already gone through the 'fall in love with a straight woman' phase. Isn't that like the first thing lesbians do, sort of like an initiation," JJ chuckled at his own joke.

"Yes, I have already done that. Thanks for reminding me, but I just get this feeling with her. I think she's been flirting, but I also think I could be so desperate that my brain is making it up."

"Just ask her." JJ said it as if it were the simplest thing on the planet.

"Have you lost your mind?" Hélène barked, jumping at the level of her own voice had reached. She quickly shot a look at her bedroom door, listening to see if she'd disturbed Kim, who was sleeping across the hall.

"You're the one who thinks you've lost your mind, Hélène. It's only difficult if you make it. Just be honest with her and see where she's at. If you've got it wrong, apologise and move on. You're both adults, it's not high school. Talk to her and then you can stop freaking out and enjoy your holiday."

Hélène didn't know quite what to say. She wasn't by any means lacking in experience with women but lately her confidence had taken a bit of a battering. This was probably the first time in a decade she'd rung her big brother for advice. Normally, she was more than capable of sorting out her own love life. Well, maybe not if recent events were anything to go by.

"I don't know, JJ, I think we could become really good friends and I do *not* want to ruin that by saying something. I think my last break up has affected me more than I realised, the final straw almost. I just want to settle down with a woman who loves me and who I love in return. Is that so much to ask?"

"You will, Hélène, but maybe you need to stop looking so hard. The right one will come along and be everything you want and more, I'm sure of it." Hélène felt a pang of guilt course through her. Here she was moaning about a lack of love life when John had lost the love of his life forever.

"*Merde, désolée* JJ, I'm an insensitive ass."

"No, you're not, and Claire would be furious to hear you speaking of yourself like that. I had a wonderful marriage to the love of my life. It's painful that she's gone, but my god I wouldn't change a second of it. You have every right to want that too, so don't apologise. I'm your big brother. I want you to come to me when you need a shoulder, compris?"

"*Oui, merci grand frère.*"

"So what you gonna do?"

"Nothing. Take some time to sort my head out and enjoy my time away with my friend."

66

"And that's all you want to do?"

"Yeah, it's not right for me to say anything. Kim's going through a rough patch with her boyfriend and I would be out of line to add any more drama to her life." She would do the right thing and support her friend, talk, and comfort, nothing more. They both had a lot going on in their lives, and Hélène knew she'd rather have Kim as a friend than not at all. "Sorry for waking you."

"No worries, I was going to have an early start, anyway. I'll let you know when I can join you on *Connie*. I could do with a break, too," JJ sighed.

"You work too hard JJ. Claire wouldn't want you to burn out. You never stop." John Spencer was a hard worker. She knew that and she knew that he loved what he did, but it didn't stop her worrying about her brother, the man who had lost so much and had never really stopped to grieve.

"You're right. I've been thinking lately that I need to slow down a little. There will always be more work, but I feel like I'm missing out on life."

"Are you okay?" Hélène wasn't used to hearing JJ talk like this. He was always so focused on work, always ready to move on to bigger and better opportunities.

"Yeah, I'm okay. The anniversary is coming up in a couple of weeks and I guess it's got me thinking."

"Thinking what?" She wanted to be there for him as much as she could. He was her rock, and she knew she could be that for him, too.

"Thinking that Claire would be angry with me for throwing everything I have into work. She constantly told me she wanted me to move on, find someone else, start a family. I promised I would, but after she'd died, the thought made me sick. How could I let anyone in after her? She was perfect."

"And now?"

"Now, I think I'm letting her down," he croaked.

"You could never let her down, John, but I think that if you're ready for something new, then you should go for it. You have more money than God. There is no reason you can't step back and evaluate your life, find out what comes next." She hoped she was saying the right things.

"You're a wise woman, sis," JJ chuckled.

"Hmmm, try telling that to the ladies," she laughed. There was a moment of silence.

"Did you know Claire froze her eggs?"

"You British are so odd. Why would you put eggs in the freezer?" she quipped.

"You're hilarious," he deadpanned. "Seriously, she froze them, they're still in cold storage."

"Okay?" Hélène was unsure of where this was going.

"Would you think I'm insane if I told you I wanted to have a baby?" His voice was laced with nerves. Hélène had to take a moment to process what he'd just said.

"You want to use Claire's eggs and make a baby?"

"Erm… yeah. We always wanted kids, and it was me that put it off, too fucking busy building The Spencer Empire. By the time we were in a position, I thought we could try, Claire got sick."

"Do you want to be a dad? I mean really want it? Having Claire's baby won't bring her back." She didn't want to piss on his cornflakes, but she wanted to make sure her brother wasn't just reacting out of sadness, especially with the anniversary of Claire's passing just round the corner.

"Yeah, I do. For the longest time, I couldn't imagine living in a world without her. It took me a long time and a lot of therapy to deal with everything. I'm finally in a position where I want to move on. Claire will be with me forever and I want nothing more than to fulfil our dream of having a baby together.

That doesn't mean that I'm stuck in the past. I know she's gone, but I also know the world would be so much better with some of Claire still in it. I can do that, I can offer the world that gift, and I think I could be a wonderful dad."

Hélène had to suck in a breath to stop her emotions from spilling out. "You would be the best dad and I would be a fucking fantastic aunt," she laughed.

"No doubt about that," JJ chuckled.

"Will you tell dad?" John's relationship with their father was as tense and distant as her own.

"No need. It has nothing to do with him." John's tone was sharp; Hélène knew that was the end of that conversation.

"So, when will you do it?"

"I've already set up an appointment with my lawyers and a fertility agency just to get the ball rolling."

"Wow."

"Yeah," he sighed.

"This has been a really intense discussion," Hélène laughed.

"What do you mean, it's completely normal to delve into super personal and painful shit at four a.m.," he laughed.

"I'm proud of you, J, so very proud."

"Right back at you, Hélène. Keep your chin up okay? You will find your person, I'm positive of it."

"Funny, that's what Kim said."

"Sounds like a wise woman, too."

"Yeah, I think she is," Hélène sighed.

* * *

By the time Kim ventured into the suite's living room at half nine, Hélène had already swum fifty lengths, showered and eaten a healthy breakfast. The phone call with JJ had helped her clarify some things.

First, she was so proud of her brother after everything he had gone through. She was so proud of the man he'd become despite his poor parental role model. She knew he was going to be the best dad any child could have. Second, she was going to cool her jets with Kim.

After hours of thinking and dissecting her feelings, she was sure that the only thing that would come of it would be pain and heartache. Hélène's inability to keep a woman was depressing, and she certainly didn't feel like adding another name to her growing list of rejection.

Kim was a wonderful person. Anyone with eyes and a brain could garner that from just a few minutes with the firecracker. So to that end, Hélène was going to be happy with the fact that they would be friends.

Hélène still hoped that Kim would take her up on her offer to teach her how to scuba dive. No need for Kim to miss out on the chance to fulfil one of her dreams. Maybe after their day in Saint Tropez, Hélène would broach the subject again.

They only had another three days until their holiday together would end and she wanted to get an answer sooner rather than later because arrangements would need to be made.

Pulling out a pad, she started jotting down a list of people she would need to talk to, mainly the boat crew, who would need to prepare another suite. The chef too, just in case Kim had any food allergies or requirements.

"Are you working?" Kim asked as she waltzed into the living room. Today's outfit was in the form of short dungarees made of light linen fabric. She sported a tight ribbed tank top underneath and high wedge sandals. As usual, her hair was in a tight ponytail, but today, she had a bandana wrapped around it. She reminded Kim of the "We Can Do It" poster.

"Not working, just noting some things down, so I don't forget." No point telling Kim what she was actually writing until she knew Kim would come along for the ride.

"Okay," Kim chirped. "I'm going to have a coffee, is that okay? Do we have time? You haven't actually given me any details of our day."

Hélène's heart momentarily betrayed her as she looked into Kim's delicious eyes. "Take all the time you need. I thought we could skip the spa and just head into town. I think you will enjoy it far more than a mud mask," Hélène chuckled.

"You would be right about that." Kim nodded in agreement. "Is it sad that I'm really quite excited?" She looked a little embarrassed at her confession, which Hélène found curious.

"Not at all, that's what exploring is all about!" Hélène said quickly. "I want you to enjoy everything."

"You're too good to me." Kim winked, and Hélène's heart skipped a beat. "Do you want a cup?" Kim held up the coffeepot questioningly.

"No, I'm already on my fourth." She was certain if she had any more caffeine, she would start vibrating.

"Fourth?" Kim barked. "What the hell time did you get up?"

"Oh, er, around four," Hélène mumbled.

"Four, really?"

"Yes, I couldn't sleep, so I called my brother."

"I bet he really appreciated that."

"Not at first," Hélène grinned, "But actually we ended up having a great chat."

"Ooooh, do tell." Kim slid onto the sofa next to Hélène. "Shit, sorry, that was really rude. You don't have to tell me at all!" Kim quickly interjected before Hélène could speak.

"No, it's fine. He's going to be a dad." Hearing it out loud sent a rush of affection through her body.

"Congratulations." Kim squealed in delight before putting her mug down carelessly on the coffee table and then pulling Hélène into a tight hug. "I bet he and his partner are so happy," she said into Hélène's hair. Hélène now had the arduous task of explaining JJ's loss.

"Actually, he is a widower." Kim slowly retracted herself from the hug and looked at Hélène quizzically.

"Erm, okay, so...." Kim said, trailing off waiting for Hélène to fill in the blanks.

"JJ, that's my brother, lost his wife a few years ago. They'd had Claire's eggs frozen. It seems he is now at a point where he wants to make their dream a reality."

"Wow, that's beautiful and heartbreaking all at the same time," Kim breathed.

"It is, but I'm just so happy that he is ready to move forward. Claire's death shocked us all, but for JJ, it was like having half of his own heart carved out. They were soulmates."

"Oh, Hélène." Kim shuffled forward to take Hélène in her arms again. Hélène relished the embrace. The feel of Kim holding her was like nothing she'd ever felt before.

"You must be excited to be an aunt?" Kim sat back, picking up her coffee cup again. Hélène missed the contact immediately.

"Oh god, I'm going to spoil that kid rotten," she laughed. Kim followed.

"I can well imagine it. Do you want kids?" Kim's eyes widened. "Oh, shit, I did it again, didn't I? I don't know what's wrong with me asking you all these personal questions."

"Relax, it's fine. If I didn't want to answer, I wouldn't. And yes, I would like a child. I wouldn't want to do it alone, though. But as I told you before, I have serious problems in the

72

romance department, so I can't see children happening anytime soon."

"Oh, stop." Kim playfully swatted Hélène's arm. "You will be with the woman of your dreams and have beautiful babies."

"What about you?" Two can play this game.

"Oh yes, I would love children, two max I think. I would love to travel with my kids, show them the world." Kim looks off into the distance, a dreamy look in her eye.

"Does Greg want Kids?" Hélène knew that was a risky question but she just couldn't help herself.

"He was always on the fence. He never committed one way or the other, which I saw as a bad sign. I mean, to bring a life into this world needs to be a decision that you're one thousand percent sure on, there can't be any half measures, right?"

"I'm in complete agreement." Hélène couldn't help but relate the conversation to her own parents. Phillipe and Veronique were *not* good paternal and maternal role models. They *definitely* should have had a conversation about kids before jumping in the sack.

"You okay?" Kim's voice was low and soft.

"Better than okay," Hélène chirped. She wouldn't let her time with Kim be spoilt, not after the rocky start they'd already had. "Are you ready to do some exploring?"

Kim's face erupted in childish joy at the mention of their outing. "Yes totally, am I dressed okay?"

"You look wonderful."

"Great." Kim was beaming.

"I'll call Henry and have him pull the car round." Hélène got up and walked to the phone by the door. She stopped when she heard Kim giggling to herself. "What are you laughing at?" Kim had an adorable giggle.

"I just remembered it's going to be the first time since you took a stroll around the lobby in your undies that we will see Thomas." Hélène felt the heat climbing up her neck. God, she'd completely forgotten about that. How the hell was she supposed to face him now?

"Stop panicking, I can see your brain melting from here," Kim laughed.

"Easy for you to say. Thomas didn't see you in sexy lingerie, did he?" she shot back playfully.

"True, but let's be honest, you looked so hot you have zero things to be embarrassed about. If anything, Thomas will be the embarrassed one. I think he had to remain seated for a while after he saw you, if you catch my drift." Hélène didn't understand what Kim was saying. Her face must have given her away, because Kim sauntered over and whispered in her ear.

"I think he was standing at attention for a long time." Hélène suddenly registered what Kim was saying, and the heat she had felt before came rushing over her like molten lava.

"Oh *Merde*, that's a horrible image you've just put in my head." Hélène shivered, which made Kim throw her head back in laughter.

"You're too easy to wind up. Stop fretting, doll, he won't make a big deal out of it, so just go on as normal." Kim patted Hélène's arm.

"Fine," Hélène grumbled.

"Let's go." Kim laughed, grabbing Hélène by the wrist and out of the door, giving Hélène only a split second to grab her purse and shades.

* * *

After a day crammed with exploring, Hélène and Kim finally sat down to have dinner. The restaurant Hélène picked was one of

74

her favourites. She often came here with JJ when they had the chance.

"This is wonderful." Kim gazed around the space, her eyes alight with wonder. Hélène looked at their surroundings and tried to see it from Kim's point of view.

They were seated in the patio area. A beautiful wooden gazebo covered the entire space with vines creeping up the posts. There was a wonderful stone water fountain that bubbled quietly in the corner. The tables were donned with white cloth and bright silver cutlery. There was no mistaking it was a high end eatery.

The best part—in Hélène's opinion—was the lighting. Along the gazebo hidden beneath the vines were soft, glowing lights. Candles shone delicately from every table. Even the perfectly pruned trees had soft lights hanging from their bows.

"It's my favourite place to eat in all of Saint Tropez." Hélène cast her eyes back to Kim.

"I feel underdressed," Kim muttered. Hélène could understand Kim's worry. The restaurant wasn't exactly casual.

"You look wonderful, don't worry." Just as Kim was about to respond, a man stopped at the table.

"Hélène, my darling, how the hell are you?" He barked, making Kim jump. Hélène gave a little laugh at the jolly man she loved and knew so well.

"Christophe," she said, rising to give him a hug and kiss. "I'm very well."

"And who is this?" He'd turned his attention to Kim. Hélène saw the sparkle in his eye. Not surprising, considering how beautiful Kim was.

"This is Kim."

"*Enchanté.*" He pulled Kim's hand close to his lips.

"Nice to meet you, too." Kim smiled, but it wasn't one of her genuine smiles. Christophe was laying it on a bit thick, in

Hélène's opinion. Hopefully Kim wasn't feeling too uncomfortable.

"You are a rare beauty, my dear." Hélène could feel her eyes roll. Christophe was the owner of the restaurant.

"Thank you, that's very kind," Kim said graciously. Christophe dropped her hand and turned back to Hélène.

"Everything is on the house, darling."

"That's unnecessary, Christophe," Hélène objected.

"Hush, it's done." He turned back to Kim. "After your dinner I would love to buy you a drink, Kim." Hélène watched in anticipation. It wasn't the first time Christophe had asked out one of Hélène's companions. She saw Kim's perfectly sculpted eyebrow rise and a smirk form on her beautiful red lips.

"Sorry, Chris, old chap, you're barking up the wrong tree," Kim said sweetly. Hélène couldn't stop herself from sniggering. Christophe's face was a picture worth savouring. He wasn't used to being rejected in such an obvious way. After a beat, she saw him square his shoulders.

"Are you sure, my dear? I have a wonderful bottle of Champagne chilling behind the bar." Hélène had to give him kudos for trying after that spectacular brush off. She looked over at Kim, who rose from her seat. Oh god was she going to throw water in his face?

"I'm sure it's a delightful bottle. Maybe we could buy it off you?" Kim rounded the little table and stood next to Hélène. Before Hélène could register what was happening, she felt Kim's arm snake around her waist.

"What do you think, lover? A bottle of Champagne in the hot tub tonight?" she cooed in Hélène's ear, pinching her arse for the full effect. Hélène felt Kim's touch in every fibre of her being. Her voice had left her and all she could do was stare at Christophe, who looked just as equally stunned. He was the first one to pull himself together.

"I apologise, Kim, and of course, you may have the Champagne. I can't think of anyone better to have it than Hélène and yourself."

"Appreciated," Kim replied, landing a kiss on Hélène's cheek, which jolted her out of her shock.

"Erm, yes, thank you, Christophe," Hélène stuttered.

"I shall bid you farewell, Hélène. I hope to see you again soon. You too, Kim. You are an adorable couple." He bowed his head and left. Hélène felt Kim's arm leave her body.

"Sorry about the groping. I just couldn't think of a way to get him to back off. He seems like the type of man that doesn't give up."

"Yes... Indeed" Hélène's mind was still scrambled.

"Sorry, I made you uncomfortable, didn't I?" Kim said with a frown. Truthfully, Hélène was far from uncomfortable. Her body was still revelling in Kim's touch. She was on fire and it was taking all her strength not to admit everything to Kim, her feelings, her thoughts, all of it. Friends be damned at this point.

"No, don't be silly. Christophe is a nice man, but he really shouldn't be hitting on you or anyone in his restaurant. You did the right thing."

"Are you sure?" Kim looked unsure whether she should believe Hélène.

"Of course, you can grab my ass anytime you need saving," Hélène grinned, hoping Kim would laugh it all away. Hélène internally gave herself a high five when Kim gave her a killer smile.

"Good to know." They fell silent as they looked at each other. The air felt charged again. Kim's phone chimed. Hélène saw Kim's disappointment as she looked away and to the screen.

"Sorry one minute." Kim read the text. Her brow creased in anger. "You've got to be fucking kidding me." The other patrons in the restaurant all stopped and looked over at her outburst.

"What's wrong?" Hélène asked urgently.

"Greg is here!"

Chapter 7

"What the hell are you doing here, Greg?" Kim raged as she stomped towards the door of the suite. "I specifically told you not to come. I specifically told you I needed time."

Kim had called Greg after her chat with Hélène. She realised that Greg coming to Saint Tropez for the weekend would be a bandaid on a gaping wound. She knew he would arrive and say all the right things, as usual, but she also knew that once the weekend was done, he would go back to work and nothing would change. Kim wanted — no, needed — time to be on her own, to figure out if their relationship was worth the work.

"You can't expect me to just do nothing, not after I've made the effort to take time away and come here to be with you," he shouted.

"I expect you to fucking listen to me, GOD!" she screamed. She could feel the blood pumping in her ears. She watched Greg shuffle from side to side, peering over her shoulder.

"Do you think we could discuss this in private? We don't need a fucking audience," he spat. It was only then that Kim remembered Hélène had followed her back to the suite, looking very concerned. She spun around to look at her friend. Hélène had hung back. She was looking more than concerned now.

"I'll let you in so you can talk," Hélène said quietly. Kim closed her eyes and took in a large breath. She needed to calm down. It mortified her that Hélène was witnessing this.

"Thank you," she whispered as Hélène passed her to open the door. They walked in silently. Hélène dropped her purse on the table and headed to the balcony.

"I'll be by the pool. Call if you need anything." Kim simply nodded and waited for her to disappear. Once Hélène was out of sight she whirled round and glared at Greg.

"What the hell are you doing? Why can't you respect my wishes?" she asked as calmly as she could. Shouting wouldn't help.

"I'm trying to fucking understand, Kim. One minute you're happy I'm coming for the weekend and the next you're telling me to leave you alone. I'm a part of this relationship, too." He was obviously trying to keep calm, too.

"You took me by surprise when you offered to come down and I didn't actually agree to it. I said I would think about it and I did. I thought about it and decided that I need time on my own. That's what I told you when I called you back and instead of listening to me, you once again ignored me and turned up, anyway." She was seething.

"So what? You get to swan off to Saint Tropez, living it up whilst I sit at home?"

"I deserve a fucking holiday, Greg. I've been begging you for years to spend time away with me. I am sick of waiting around for you. I'm sick of taking a back seat to you."

"God, you're ungrateful," he spat. "I've worked my fingers to the bone to provide for you. I waited around like a fucking idiot in London whilst you went to school and now I need the same support you're getting bitchy about it."

"I can't believe you just said that." Kim felt as if he'd just slapped her across the face. "I asked you repeatedly if you were okay with waiting for me to finish school. You promised me I never had to worry about it and now you're throwing it in my face, like I forced you to wait around against your will."

"I'm not throwing it in your face, just stating facts."

"Stating facts? I'll give you fucking facts," she bellowed, unable to hold her anger in. "You have turned into a horribly misogynist. I don't recognise the man standing in front of me. You are so far from the sweet man I loved all those years ago," she cried. "I'm not doing this anymore, Greg. I want you to leave. I'm not in this. I'm not fighting for us anymore."

"You can't leave me," he roared. Kim looked on, shocked, as she saw his face turn red in anger. He lunged towards her, grabbing her arm painfully. "You are coming home now," he screamed. He looked almost unhinged. The veins in his head were bulging.

Kim froze. Greg's hand clamped down on her hard. For the first time in their lives together, she feared him. She had never seen Greg act like this. He had never scared her, never laid a finger on her that wasn't gentle. Her mind went blank. She couldn't move, she was paralysed.

Without warning, she felt his arm being ripped off of her. The tug jolted her back to reality. She watched as Hélène manoeuvred Greg's wrist in such a way that he crumpled to the floor as she pulled his arm behind his back.

"You will never lay a hand on her again," Hélène hissed. Her eyes shone with utter rage. Greg whimpered as Hélène forced his arm higher.

"Fuck… stop okay… stop, you're going to break my arm," he cried.

"Say it. Say you will never touch her again." Hélène's voice was almost at a whisper. It dripped with disdain for the man.

"I won't, I swear. I'm sorry Kim, please."

Kim shook her head, clearing the fog that had descended on her mind. She looked at the man she used to love, his face writhing in pain. What happened to him?

"Hélène, can you let him go?" she asked quietly, laying her hand on Hélène's arm. Hélène looked into her eyes, looking for assurance that she was okay. "Please." She nodded and dropped Greg's arm. He rubbed it, trying to ease the pain. "Greg, I want you to leave. I will have my things collected when I return. If you ever touch me like that again, I will have you arrested," she said calmly.

Her previous fear had melted away in Hélène's presence. She knew she was safe. Greg looked up at her from the floor, tears stung his eyes.

"Kim, I'm so sorry. I don't know what came over me. Please forgive me. I love you," he pleaded.

"No, leave now."

Greg slumped, his shoulders shaking as his tears fell. Kim stood tall and waited until he'd collected himself. She walked confidently to the door and held it open. Greg looked at her and then at Hélène, his face resigned in his dismissal. Trying to reclaim some of his dignity and pride, he brushed down his trousers and shirt and walked out the door. Just as he was about to turn around to say something more, Kim gently closed the door on him and their relationship.

* * *

Kim let her hand rest on the door handle. She needed to steady her breathing before she could face Hélène. She didn't know what felt worse, Greg's sudden and frightening behaviour, or the fact that she had subjected Hélène to her drama.

"I'm sorry," she whispered, her forehead almost resting against the door. "I'm so sorry, Hélène." She felt Hélène's body gently press into her back.

"What on earth are you apologising for?" Hélène's disbelief was clear in every word. Kim dropped the handle and turned around. Hélène was well within her personal space with a look of sympathy and worry etched on her face.

"You did *not* sign up for this. You didn't even sign up to take me in. You should be enjoying your break. All I have done is bring you trouble." Kim's voice cracked, the weight of the situation finally catching up.

Just as she felt as if she was going to crumble to the ground, she felt Hélène's arms hold her up. The dam broke, all Kim's emotions that she'd been trying so desperately to hold in came flooding out.

"Shhh, it's okay, I've got you," Hélène whispered in her ear. Minutes later, Kim finally pulled herself together enough to take a step back from Hélène's embrace.

"I'm sorry," she repeated.

"No more apologising. You have nothing to say sorry for. You are not responsible for that man's actions." Hélène's face betrayed how angry she was towards Greg. "What he did was inexcusable and he must face the consequences now. My only concern here is you, Kim. Do you understand?" Kim watched Hélène's hand gently caress Kim's arm where Greg had grabbed her. Kim was sure that Hélène wasn't aware of what she was doing.

"Thank you." Kim looked into Hélène's eyes, hoping that she could convey how grateful she was in one look.

"What do you want to do now? Are you tired? It's been a long day." Kim didn't know what she wanted, but she was sure that sleep would elude her. Hélène must have seen her indecision. "Why don't we go up to the roof and do some stargazing?"

"Yes, I think I'd like that." Kim needed some quiet time to reflect, but she didn't want to be alone. Hélène made her feel safe. They slowly made their way to the roof. Kim followed Hélène's lead and lowered herself onto one of the loungers. Hélène picked up a little remote control that lay on the table next to her and hit a button. All the lights went out and Kim almost gasped at the sea of stars covering the night sky.

"Oh, wow."

"Beautiful," Hélène whispered, but Kim saw Hélène wasn't looking up at the sky but at her. A flutter of something swam through Kim's body. Even though the events of the past half hour had been shocking, Kim's body couldn't help but to react to Hélène's attention.

"I'll come with you," Kim said, turning her face towards Hélène.

"Hmm?" Hélène's mind was obviously elsewhere.

"I'll come away with you. That's if the offer still stands?" Her heart jolted as she watched Hélène's face transform into something so wonderful she couldn't possibly put it into words.

"You'll stay on the boat with me?"

"Yes, if you still want me to?"

"Absolutely!" Hélène beamed. They looked at each other for a few minutes, their smiles matched in size before turning their attention skywards. Kim felt Hélène's hand slide into hers, their fingers entwining. No words were spoken, something was changing between them, but no explanations were necessary, not yet.

Some time needed to pass. Wounds needed to heal before either of them was ready for that conversation, but Kim already knew that what was transpiring between them was something worth waiting for.

Kim had no idea how much time had passed. They'd laid down, watching the night sky for what seemed like hours, their hands remaining intertwined. "Do you want a drink?" Hélène asked.

"No alcohol, please. I don't think that would be a good idea tonight." The last thing she needed was an anxiety attack. Hélène gracefully lifted off the sun bed and headed to the little bar. Kim continued to look up. Millions upon millions of stars twinkled. She even saw several shooting stars, which made the experience even better. A calm settled over her. Hélène had given her exactly what she needed.

"Here." Hélène passed Kim what looked like a piña colada. "It's virgin," she supplied.

"Thanks."

"Well, we are still on holiday, after all." Hélène grinned. Kim appreciated the gesture. She was sure it couldn't be easy for Hélène to navigate such turbulent waters. Kim took a long sip of her cocktail. It was just as good as its alcohol-infused twin.

"Mmmm," she moaned. "Delicious." Hélène gave her a smile and settled back down into her seat.

"He wasn't always like that." Kim sighed. She was completely perplexed by Greg's behaviour. In all their years together, Greg had never shown a hint of aggression the way he had tonight. "I just don't understand," Kim spluttered, her lower lip trembling. What had happened to the sweet man she fell for all those years ago?

"Tell me about him." Hélène reached for Kim's hand once again. Kim took a big breath in, wondering where to begin.

"We went to school together. In fact, we only lived a street away from each other. He's my oldest friend." Kim shifted herself into a sitting position, pulling her legs into her chest with her arms wrapped around them. "We did everything together. His parents were quite old when they had him, so he would always hang with me and my parents, who could do a lot more than his own. We got together at the end of high school. Shortly after his parents died, he was seventeen. But even after that happened, he never lashed out. He had a moment where he hung around the wrong crowd, but that didn't last long.

"We ended up at the same university together. I wanted to complete my Master's, and he said he was happy to wait around until I was finished. We had all these plans to travel together after uni but my decision to stay on changed that. Toward the end of my Master's, Greg was offered a really great opportunity in Paris. I was more than happy to move to France with him. It was the beginning of our adventure, well, that's how I saw it.

"As the years went on, I think he got frustrated. I don't think he was moving up the ladder as easily as he thought he would. I think that's when I really saw a change in him. He got close to his boss, Hervé, who is a complete and utter arsehole. No other way to describe him. The man hit on me so many times in front of Greg it was embarrassing. Greg said nothing."

"Do you think he was worried about upsetting his boss?" Hélène asked.

"It must have been. It hurt, though, because in the past, he would never have stood by whilst someone disrespected me or him that way. He started working all the time and instead of talking things through with me, he started freezing me out, letting me down. This last year has been miserable. The only thing I had was Anna and my work."

"Does Anna know about all this?"

"Not all of it. I didn't want to burden her with it," Kim sighed.

"I think you need to stop believing your problems and experiences will be a burden to those who care for you, Kim."

"Maybe… oh god," she whined. "What am I going to tell my parents? Greg is like a son to them."

"You tell them the truth."

Kim stared silently up, contemplating what Hélène had said. The last thing she wanted was to lump her parents with her mess, especially the part about Greg getting aggressive. What choice did she have, though? She was close to her parents and they would sniff out a lie all the way from England. She'd tell them when she was back in Paris. The thought sent a wave of nausea through her. Paris was her home now, but where would she go? The apartment that she shared with Greg was in his name only.

"Hey, what are you thinking?" Hélène said, interrupting her melancholic thoughts.

"I just realised that I'm probably homeless now, too." Her emotions were overwhelming her again.

"Hey, don't even worry about things like that. You have people around you who won't let anything happen to you, okay?" Hélène said with a confidence that lifted Kim out of her misery.

"Thank you, Hélène, really. You've been such a good friend, even though you don't really know me that well."

"You're a good person, Kim. I'm honoured that I get to be your friend and get to learn about you. I know it sucks right now, but you will get through it and I will be here for as long as you need me." Kim swallowed hard. She was overcome with a feeling that she couldn't quite name, but it was akin to adoration, maybe something more. "Let's enjoy our cocktail and then get some sleep. Things will be clearer in the morning, I promise."

* * *

The sound of music woke Kim with a start. She'd been in a deep and dreamless sleep. She'd slept well, considering everything that had transpired the night before. Her mind still buzzed with unanswered questions, unsurprisingly. Pushing her thoughts aside, she headed for the shower.

Kim relaxed as the water massaged her aching muscles. She looked down and saw the bruises forming where Greg had grabbed her. A shudder took over her body. The fear she felt yesterday crept back into her mind. "No," she said forcefully out loud. "No, you don't get to have that power," she said louder. She closed her eyes and willed herself to think of happier things. Yesterday's excursion swam into her memory. Hélène had been just as excited as Kim to explore Saint Tropez.

First, they'd gone to the Citadel Saint Tropez, which overlooked the bay. They'd both wandered around the structure in awe. They'd read every word in the brochure, learned everything they could, and then discussed it in depth.

Kim had thoroughly enjoyed talking to Hélène. She was sharp and witty. She knew her own mind, but was more than happy to open herself up to something that challenged her preconceived ideas.

After they'd spent a couple of hours walking around the Citadel, they'd visited the Annonciade Museum, which Kim had enjoyed but not as much as Hélène. By the time they got to the market, it was very busy, but they persisted and battled through the crowds.

Hélène introduced Kim to all kinds of different food, which was the highlight of the day for her. Kim couldn't remember the last time she'd been challenged and educated as much as she had been yesterday.

Feeling refreshed, Kim followed the sound of the music to the kitchen. Her step faltered when she took in the sight in front of her. Hélène was dancing along to the music, swaying her hips as she cooked, her body moving effortlessly to the rhythm.

Hélène was wearing a white and gold bikini with a sheer robe wrapped around her body. Her hair swayed back and forth over her back as she moved. Kim was frozen to the spot. She knew she should let Hélène know she was there, but she didn't want the dancing to stop. She was mesmerised.

"Oh, hey," Hélène called, finally noticing Kim standing by the breakfast bar. "Hungry? I went a little crazy with the pancake batter," she chuckled. Sure enough, Hélène had made enough pancakes to feed a small army.

"Starving," Kim replied truthfully. The smell was making her mouth water.

"Sit down and let's tuck in. We have a long day ahead."

"Really?" They hadn't discussed doing anything today.

"Of course, but that's only if you want to. You can do whatever you want. I thought it would be a good idea to do some shopping for the next leg of our travels." Kim smiled broadly. She was happy beyond measure that she'd bit the bullet and taken Hélène up on her offer to join her on *Connie*.

In truth, it hadn't been a tough decision. From the moment Hélène had comforted Kim in the lobby on the first day, she felt safe and welcome. She still harboured some residual guilty feelings about airing her dirty laundry in front of Hélène, but she was trying to take on board what her friend had said last night and not feel like a burden. Surely Hélène was upfront enough to say something if she felt uncomfortable helping Kim out.

"What do we need to buy?" She asked enthusiastically.

"Oh, wow, where to start?" Hélène laughed. "I'm going to take you to my favourite dive shop." Kim balked at the idea of spending money. Scuba gear wasn't cheap, everyone knew that.

"And before you panic, we're going to rent most of it. I've already called Ivan and put the charges on my account."

"But…"

"No buts. Let me do this for you, Kim. It really would be my pleasure. After all, you're doing me the favour of spending your time with me. I can't wait to teach you how to dive, so it's purely selfish." Hélène nodded resolutely.

"That's very kind, thank you. I will find a way to pay you back though, even if that means serving you drinks for the rest of our holiday."

"I'm sure we can come up with a much better way than that," Hélène winked. Kim felt that wink through to her core. Holy shit, she was in trouble.

Chapter 8

The last two days at The Sapphire had flown by, and Hélène had enjoyed them immensely. It had been a bit touch and go to begin with. Kim had suffered quite a shock with Greg, a thought that made Hélène's blood boil with rage, just as it had on the night it all happened.

Watching Kim's reaction when she'd received the text informing her that Greg was waiting outside their suite had been difficult. She wanted Kim to figure out her relationship with Greg, but she was also feeling something akin to jealousy at the connection Kim had with this man. She was also pretty pissed he had interrupted their plans.

The day spent in Saint Tropez had been wonderful. Hélène didn't think it was possible to connect with someone so quickly and on so many levels, but with Kim it was effortless. The restaurant had been the perfect choice, even if Christophe had tried to hijack her date, okay, not a *date* date, but still he was out of order. The memory made Hélène chuckle. Kim putting him in his place was highly entertaining and satisfying. Then came the downfall of the evening. The text.

They hadn't really spoken on the way back to the hotel. Hélène knew Kim was struggling and trying to make idle chit chat wouldn't have helped. They'd ridden the elevator in silence. Hélène's own heart rate had kicked up a notch at the thought of the showdown she knew was going to happen.

The man standing at the door to their suite had been exactly the type of man Hélène would have expected to work in a bank. His suit probably cost a few thousand euros, along with his designer Italian shoes and silk tie. He looked around six feet, his belly was overhanging his trousers slightly. His hair was slicked back, and he wore a huge dose of some repugnant aftershave.

Then the show began, Kim and Greg began to converse, well, more like seethe at each other. Hélène had felt more than awkward, which is why she'd jumped at the chance to let them into the suite as soon as she was given the chance.

Kim seemed to have had everything under control and they'd needed privacy, which is why Hélène had made herself scarce and ducked out of the room to the balcony. A decision she now regretted. She should have stayed by Kim's side, protected her more.

She'd heard their voices raise, but something else had her hackles up. It was something in Greg's voice, a warning of something worse to come. That's when she returned to the room. She felt as if Kim needed her there.

When she'd stepped through the door and seen Greg lunge for Kim, grabbing her arm forcefully, Hélène had seen red, it was as if she'd got tunnel vision and the only thing she could think of was getting that asshole's hands off of Kim.

Before she'd known what she was doing, she'd marched over to Greg in three large strides—putting to use her many years of martial arts training—and rendered the man incapacitated. Truthfully, If Kim hadn't stopped her, she would probably have snapped his arm.

It had taken Hélène several deep breaths to calm herself down enough to comfort Kim. She'd been glad that after the initial shock, Kim had wanted to talk it through with her.

That night had turned out to be one of the best in Hélène's life. Yes, she'd had to watch Kim get hurt, which hurt her just as much, but in the end Kim had taken Hélène up on her offer to board *Connie*.

The feeling that Hélène had felt when Kim uttered those words was indescribable. She'd wanted to jump off of the sun lounger and take Kim into her arms. She'd refrained, though. It certainly hadn't been the right time to be doing a happy dance, not when the trauma Greg had inflicted was so raw.

Hélène understood Kim would need space and time. She wanted to do whatever she could to make Kim feel better. That's when the idea of shopping had occurred to her. She thought that maybe a distraction would do Kim good, and she'd been right.

The morning after "The Event"—that's what Hélène had decided to call it—Kim had looked a little flushed when she'd first walked into the kitchen. Hélène thought she must have still felt embarrassed about Hélène witnessing the altercation with Greg. Hélène had been a little embarrassed herself. She hadn't realised Kim was standing there when she was dancing about the kitchen, making them breakfast.

The trip to the diving shop had been a lot of fun. Kim seemed to be a little overwhelmed at first, but soon got into the spirit of it. Hélène smirked at the memory.

"Jesus, how much bloody gear do you need to buy?" Kim chuckled as she perused the shelves in the shop, which were stuffed with everything a person could ever need for diving.

"It's great, isn't it?" Hélène beamed. Hélène had already purchased most of the things in the place, but she always found one more thing she "needed" to buy when visiting. The second bedroom in her apartment had been transformed into her very own diving boutique.

"You're telling me I need all this?" Kim's eyes went wide at the very thought.

"Of course not," Hélène laughed. "You'll need the basics. A lot of this stuff is for serious divers and those who like gadgets, like me," she grinned.

"Okay Jacques," Kim smirked. "Lead the way."

"Did you just refer to a diving legend, Ms. Richmond?"

"Why yes I did. I'm more than a pretty face, you know."

"Oh, I know that," Hélène said, unable to help herself. "So first things first, let's get you a mask."

"Mask, yep great idea." Kim nodded, following behind Hélène as she wound through the shop to the section that displayed every type of diving mask you could think of.

"Right, so where do we start?" Kim bounced on her heels.

"Well, is there one that grabs your attention?" Hélène watched Kim as she inspected the shelves.

"That one." Kim pointed to a bright yellow one.

"Good choice, Ms Richmond. That's a great mask to start with. It's a *Beuchat*, made in France." She took the mask down to give Kim a closer look. "It's seamless, the glass is moulded directly into the silicone. The other good thing is that it's a nice bright colour. No way I can miss you in this."

"Are you telling me there's a chance you could lose me underwater?!" Kim almost shouted, making Hélène laugh.

"Calm down, I will not lose you," Hélène replied. "We will be in shallow, clear water. I'll have you in my sight at all times, okay?"

"Okay." Kim was a little subdued. Hélène was going to have to work on her confidence and make sure Kim trusted her completely.

"Next item." She tossed the mask in the basket she'd pick up at the front of the shop. "Flippers!" she said excitedly, unable to contain her enthusiasm. Hélène saw Kim smirk at her as they headed to the wall covered in paired flippers.

"Now, you need to choose a pair that aren't too rigid, otherwise, you will expel a lot of energy unnecessarily." She perused the options, wondering which one's Kim would choose.

"What about these?" Kim motioned to a pair just above them.

"Great choice. I have those, just in a different colour." Hélène was impressed that Kim seemed to have a good eye for quality equipment. "Plus, they match your mask."

"Really?" Kim said, feigning ignorance, making Hélène chuckle. "You chose them so your outfit would match, didn't you?" Hélène laughed.

"No idea what you're talking about. What's next?" Kim smiled.

"Hmmm, I'm sure." Hélène muttered, still smiling like an idiot. "I have a tank and breathing equipment for you already on the boat, so we just need a wetsuit and vest."

"Vest? What kind of vest?"

"In French it's called *Gilet Stabilisateur*. It's what holds your tank and what helps you to stabilise underwater. Don't worry, I'll explain it all properly when we get on *Connie*."

"Alright, lead the way." Kim's earlier anxiety seemed to be gone.

95

"There are several *Gilet Stabilisateur* or *Stab* for short. A dorsal style *Stab* is a good idea. I think you will feel more comfortable and it will help you stay horizontal easier."

"I have no idea what those words mean, but I trust you. Maybe you should pick the *Stab*." Hélène nodded and took one off of the rack.

"Try this on." She beckoned Kim forwards. The *Stab* fit Kim well. Hélène always did have a knack for sizing up a woman.

"What do ya think?" Kim gave a little twirl.

"Perfect," Hélène spoke more about the woman in front of her than the *Stab*. "Okay last but not least, a wetsuit. This isn't going to be very fun. Putting on a dry wetsuit is easier than when it's wet, but it's still going to be a pain to do, so prepare yourself."

"Oh, blimey," Kim mumbled.

"There are different thicknesses of wetsuit. Depending on where you will dive depends on the thickness you need. So, for example, if you were to dive in the North of France you would opt for a 7mm suit, something thick to combat the cold. Thankfully, we will dive in water that will feel like a warm bath, so no need to get a super thick one. I usually dive in a 5mm wetsuit around Corsica."

"5mm it is then."

"All these suits are of good quality. Just pick a few you like and you can try them on." Hélène rifled through the suits hanging up. Kim took her time. Hélène enjoyed watching her as she weighed up the options. That seemed to be Kim all over.

When they had first met, Hélène thought Kim was a little rash and pushy, but over the week she realised Kim thought over everything before acting. She considered her actions using the information she was given. Hélène understood now why Kim was so good at science. Her brain was wired that way.

"Here, I've picked three. What do you think?" Kim looked a little nervous, which Hélène found adorable.

"Great choices. Now try them on." Whilst Kim changed, Hélène continued to shop. There was a new diving computer she'd seen when they'd first entered. It was expensive, and she didn't need it at all, but it was also full of cool new features, so that trumped everything.

"Erm, H," Kim shouted.

"Yeah, you okay?" Hélène called back

"Erm no, not really, I'm stuck," Kim groaned. "Can you help me?"

"Okay, I'm coming." Hélène laughed. She'd had her fair share of situations with wetsuits herself, so she knew how Kim was feeling.

"Can I come in?" she asked through the changing room doors.

"Well, unless you're able to get me out of this thing through a solid piece of wood, I would say that it's essential you *do* come in."

"Alright, snarky." Hélène chuckled as she pushed open the door. "Oh, dear." She laughed as she caught sight of Kim, who was red-faced and flustered.

"I got the thing to my thighs and then it became like glue. It won't budge."

"You just have to put a little effort behind it, do you mind?" Hélène pointed to the suit, hoping Kim understood she wanted to help pull the thing up.

"Go for it." Kim straightened up. Hélène approached carefully. She needed to keep her wits about her because being this close to Kim was dangerous.

"Okay, I'm going to pull it up. I'm sorry in advance if I pinch your skin. It's sometimes unavoidable." Kim nodded and braced herself. With years of practice, Hélène quickly got the wetsuit in place. "There, all done. How do you feel?"

"Like a piece of shrink-wrapped meat," Kim groaned playfully.

"You get used to it. The good thing is that because of your heel obsession you have excellent posture, which always makes wearing the suit easier and more comfortable,"

"I do not have a high heel obsession."

Hélène raised her eyebrow in mock objection. "Really?"

"Fine, but it's only because I can rock the shit out of any heel," Kim shot back with a smirk. Hélène was instantly transported back to the night Kim danced in her heels. The memory sent all of Hélène's blood rushing south.

"Do you like it?" *Yes, stick to the wetsuit.*

"I do." Kim nodded, satisfied.

"Excellent, I think we're done," Hélène smiled. "I'll get it all packed and sent to the boat."

That had been the end of their shopping trip. They spent the rest of their time exploring and stopping for food. Hélène spent the last day in the hotel packing and coordinating their schedule with the captain of the boat. Hélène left Kim to soak up the sun whilst she was busy. Now and then she noticed Kim look at her mobile. A shadow would cross her face for a second, but it never seemed to last long.

* * *

Finally, the day had come for them to board *Connie*. Hélène was ridiculously excited. She could only imagine how Kim was feeling. Hélène hadn't said much about the boat. She knew Kim was going to be blown away when she saw her moored a kilometre outside of Saint Tropez.

"Ready to go?" she called to Kim, who was still in the suite.

"Aye Aye, captain," Kim called back, making Hélène roll her eyes.

"Are you going to be making these kinds of jokes for the entire time?"

"Probably," Kim laughed as she wheeled her bag out of the suite.

"The car's waiting. Let's go. We have an adventure to begin."

The car was idling outside the main entrance as they approached the doors. Hélène quickly looked over at the reception area and gave a polite nod to Thomas. She had to stop herself from blushing and laughing at the same time. She'd made sure that the staff got a hefty tip.

The drive to the port was short. It was a perfect day to be heading out to sea. The sun was blazing down, but the heat was offset by a wonderful breeze. Hélène made her way to a small boat that was docked at the closest gangway. She heard Kim's heels clicking close behind.

"Erm, H?" Kim sounded nervous. "Please tell me that's not *Connie*?" She was pointing to the little boat Hélène had stopped at.

"Don't you like her?" Hélène enjoyed teasing Kim.

"Oh, er… no, she's lovely," Kim spluttered. Hélène tried her hardest to keep her face as serious as possible, but she failed miserably. Her laughter echoed across the marina.

"Kim, of course this isn't *Connie*. It's our boat to get to *Connie*."

"Phew, Jesus, I was having palpitations," Kim chuckled. "So which one is she?" Kim scanned the marina, looking at all the boats.

"None of these," Hélène chirped. "*Connie* is too big to moor here. We need to travel about a kilometre to meet her."

"Too big? Really? There are some beast-y boats here. How bloody big is *Connie?*"

"You'll see, come on." Hélène hefted her bag on board and then Kim's. She jumped on deck, turning to offer her hand to Kim, who rolled her eyes before skillfully hopping on board. Hélène still couldn't believe such things were possible in the shoes Kim was wearing.

The boat rumbled into life. The smell of the sea permeated Hélène's senses. It was like coming home for her. She was never as happy as she was when she was on or in the water.

The little boat zipped out of the harbour, breaking through the water with ease. Hélène and Kim sat back and relaxed, taking in the sights. There wasn't a cloud in the sky and the sun reflected off of the water, making it look like there were thousands of diamonds on the surface. It was peaceful and exhilarating at the same time.

Hélène spotted *Connie's* gargantuan body. She looked over to Kim, who in turn followed Hélène's gaze back to the horizon. Hélène remained silent. She wanted to watch Kim as they approached the boat. Kim's eyes got wide. She looked back and forth between Hélène and the boat.

"Are you kidding me?" Kim gasped, standing to get a better look at Connie. "That's not a boat, Hélène. That's a sodding cruise liner."

Hélène let out a laugh. "She's not a cruise liner, she's a 300-foot yacht to be precise."

"Oh well, only 300-foot, my mistake," Kim replied sarcastically.

"*Elle est belle,*" Hélène whispered. Kim nodded in agreement.

Connie was one of the biggest super yachts in the world. Hélène had been lost for words when JJ had first flown her out to board *Connie*. She boasted a helipad, swimming pool and jacuzzi. She could hold over a hundred guests and the suites were nicer than most five-star hotels.

Hélène thought JJ had gone a tad overboard with his purchase at first, but she'd quickly changed her mind when she'd spent two weeks cruising around the Mediterranean, diving with her brother and hosting parties.

That summer had been one of the best in her life. Unfortunately, over the years, they'd only been able to stay on Connie a handful of times together. Hopefully, JJ could fly out in a week or so. She really wanted him to meet Kim.

"I'm lost for words," Kim gasped as she surveyed the yacht. The little boat slowed to dock with *Connie*. "I mean, I figured that your family was well off, but this is another level, Hélène."

"It's solely owned by my brother." Hélène wondered whether she should come clean about her relationship to one of the world's richest men.

"What the hell does he do?" Kim was still gawping at *Connie*.

"Erm, well, you sort of already know, actually." Hélène's old anxieties were surfacing. What if Kim acted differently? What if this perfect woman turned out to be not so perfect when the subject of money came up?

"How is that even possible?" Kim enquired, her brow arched.

"Well, he owns your publishing house, well, half, actually." Kim looked at her in a way that made her nerves tremble.

"Are you talking about John Spencer?" Hélène remained silent. Instead of answering, she gave Kim a quick nod of her head.

"Well, that would explain *Connie* then," she laughed. Hélène waited for the other questions that usually followed when she revealed she was related to the great John Spencer, but Kim never asked them. Unsure of what to do, Hélène collected their bags and passed them to the waiting crew members.

"Hi, everyone," she chirped as she stepped aboard. "I hope you're ready for some fun."

The crew on *Connie* were some of the nicest people in the world. They were passionate about their careers and put one hundred percent into their jobs. Hélène had quickly formed friendships with them all. She loved that they were laid back but always professional; they were guaranteed to have a wonderful time.

"Come on, I'll show you to your suite," she said over her shoulder to Kim, who was still ascending the steps.

"I have a suite?" Kim almost shouted.

"Yes, Kim, you have a suite," Hélène replied, smiling.

"Jesus."

Hélène had asked the crew to set up the suite that was next to hers. There had been several other options, but Hélène wanted Kim to be close. Her resolve to remain friends had been slowly ebbing away as the days had gone by.

Her heart and brain were at constant odds, which was proving to be utterly exhausting. Hélène was sure she'd received some signals from Kim. At least, she thought she had. Surely she wasn't making them up? They had flirted several times in the past forty-eight hours, but Hélène had to be mindful. It was possible that Kim was simply reacting to everything that had happened recently.

This is so confusing!

Chapter 9

Kim was a bright woman. No, actually she was more than bright. She was very intelligent; she was gifted with her understanding of biology and yet here she sat, confused beyond measure with her own body and mind. She simply didn't understand her body's reaction to Hélène.

After the hideous incident with Greg, surely she should feel sad, upset at the end of their long relationship. However, even after all that, the only thing she felt was warmth and comfort because the only thing or only person who was on Kim's mind was Hélène.

Talking to Hélène calmed her. She felt supported when she'd told Hélène about her past with Greg. Hélène had taken it all in her stride, offering words of comfort where needed, just being there to help Kim get through it all.

Sleep hadn't come easy the night of the incident, especially after receiving a barrage of messages from Greg begging for forgiveness. She'd replied calmly, asking him to give her space. Kim knew in her heart that their romantic relationship was done, however, they shared so much more than that. They'd been best friends for decades, and that wasn't something she was willing to let go of just yet.

She meant what she'd said, though. If they were to ever move past what had happened, he needed to back off. The back-and-forth of text messages had drained her, but she finally felt as if Greg had understood and accepted what she was asking of him.

The next morning Kim had had every intention of telling Hélène about the messages until she'd walked in on Hélène dancing in the kitchen. From that point on, it seemed as if all the drama was irrelevant. The only thing that mattered was right then and there. They'd been flirting all holiday even if neither of them admitted it. Kim knew what was happening.

It had been a long time since Kim had felt a fire like this inside her. She felt alive and wanted. Hélène had no idea that Kim was bisexual, so she knew it was unlikely that Hélène would make any kind of move. Kim had to decide if she was ready to make it for them both.

Would all the drama in Kim's life be too much for Hélène? Who in their right mind would get caught up in all that? But something kept niggling in the back of Kim's mind. It was a feeling that something special was between them, something that could change their lives if they were brave enough to explore it.

The shopping trip to the diving store had been fun. Kim was in awe of Hélène, who radiated passion when explaining all the different equipment and their uses. Kim longed to see that passion again.

104

After the shopping trip, Hélène had busied herself organising and packing. Kim had chuckled several times as she'd watched Hélène buzz around the suite with a look of pure excitement spread across her face.

Kim had given herself the last day to take stock of how she was feeling. More than hurt, she was feeling confusion towards Greg. His behaviour was so out of character. Eventually, she decided she would call her parents when she was settled on *Connie*. They knew Greg just as well as she did, and maybe they could offer her some insights as to what to do next.

Once she'd squared that decision away, her mind focused solely on Hélène and their upcoming trip. Weeks alone with her on a boat, sunbathing and diving. Kim was excited that she would have quality time with Hélène to help strengthen their bond. She wanted Hélène to know everything about her, and vice versa. Kim also wanted that time to be sure that she wasn't just having some sort of reaction to the past week, which had been chaotic, to say the least.

So here she sat, in the most luxurious suite she had ever seen, on the biggest boat she had ever seen, trying to decide what to do next. Hélène had shown her to her suite and told her to get comfortable.

Kim had been quiet since boarding *Connie*. Her shock and awe had proven too much for her to hold a full conversation. She shook her head, trying to engage her brain. Fumbling in her pocket, she retrieved her phone. Hopefully, Anna would be free to talk. It was so much easier now that she and Sam were back in Paris.

"Anna, you will never guess where I am right now?" She said louder than she meant to. The pent up excitement had become too much.

"Whoa, Jesus, Kim, why are you shouting?" Anna grumbled. Kim thought she sounded as if she'd been asleep. She looked at the time. It was 11 a.m., far too late for Anna to be still in bed.

"Did I wake you?" she replied, much quieter than before.

"Oh, er… yes… I was just taking a nap."

Kim giggled, *taking a nap my arse*. Kim rolled her eyes, laughing. "You just had morning sex, didn't you?"

The line went silent before Anna pushed out a breath of air, laughing along with her friend. "Yes, okay, I've just had morning sex and was drifting off into a sated sleep."

"Good for you, doll, say hi to Sam for me."

"Will do, but she's out for the count right now." Anna sighed happily. Kim could see the loving look that Anna was giving Sam even over the phone.

"You pair are like rabbits," Kim laughed.

"Did you call for any other reason than to chat about my amazing sex life?"

"Actually, yes. As I said, you will never guess where I am?"

"Aren't you at The Sapphire?"

"No, I'm not at the hotel. Some shit has gone down, Anna, like some major life altering things." Kim heard Anna shuffling about. She presumed she was taking herself into another room.

"Okay, go." Anna had an edge of concern in her voice. Kim took a deep breath before spilling everything that had happened with Greg and Hélène over the past week. Just the act of talking to Anna had a therapeutic effect. It made her feel as if she could see things a little clearer now. Kim also wanted Anna's opinion on it all.

"That is a lot," Anna breathed. "Okay, first, I'm so sorry that the hotel screwed up like that. I will have words," she said

106

sternly, making Kim smile. "Second, Greg has a lot to answer for. No matter what the circumstances, laying a hand on you is inexcusable, and you did the right thing asking him to leave. As far as the breakup, only you know if that's what you want. The big thing in this is the Hélène situation. I didn't know you're bi. You never said a word when I came out to you."

"I didn't purposely hide it from you, doll. It's just something I don't feel the need to bring up."

"Okay, fair enough. So what do you want to happen with Hélène?"

"Something more than friendship. I know that much. Anna she's the most caring person I've ever met. She's beautiful on the inside and out."

"Well, it seems clear to me you know what you want."

"That's the thing, though. It's what I want. I don't know if that's what she wants."

"But you said there has been definite flirting."

"Yes, pretty much from the moment she rescued me in the hotel lobby."

"So I think it's safe to say she's interested. You just have to talk to her. Don't do what I did and keep your feelings to yourself. The worst outcome is that she just wants to be friends, the best outcome is, well…"

"You're wiggling your eyebrows right now, aren't you? Do you just think of sex all the time now?" Kim laughed.

"I said nothing about sex," Anna protested playfully.

"You implied it," Kim shot back.

"No, I didn't. You're just horny."

"Doll, you have no idea," Kim chuckled.

"Joking aside, you guys could have something wonderful, but you'll never know until you talk."

"You're right, I know you are. I suppose I'm just nervous. I've only been with Greg, so this is new to me."

"Relax, you're in no rush. I think you'll know when it feels right. In the meantime, enjoy this break, laugh, swim and drink. It's the first holiday you've had in a long time. Take advantage of it and relax," Anna said warmly.

"You're the best, do you know that?" Kim chirped back. She was very fortunate to have a friend like Anna.

"I am, it's true," Anna laughed. "Now, if you don't mind, I think I just heard Sam, so I need to get back to bed."

"Enjoy yourself," Kim chimed.

"No doubt about that. Speak soon."

"Speak soon."

The line cut off, leaving Kim to mull over her conversation with Anna and all its implications.

* * *

Kim allowed herself a few minutes to think, to decide how she was going to proceed with Hélène. First and most importantly, she needed to be sure that Hélène felt the same. There wasn't an easy way to do that. Well, there was, but that meant that Kim had to put her big girl pants on and have a frank discussion with the French beauty.

Could she be that bold? She'd let that idea percolate for a while. In the meantime, she had to process her surroundings because, frankly, *Connie* was stunning. The name of the boat made her laugh. Who the hell called a luxury yacht *Connie*?

Kim slowly walked around the suite. It was on the left side of the boat. Was that Port side? Kim needed to brush up on her nautical terminology. The large queen bed faced a wall of windows that allowed her to gaze out into the blue paradise that surrounded them. Kim couldn't wait to see the sun rise in the morning.

Everything in the suite screamed money and wealth. The carpet was so thick that Kim considered just taking a nap on it. The furniture matched the boat's trim, which was a rich mahogany. It was a wonderful contrast of clean white against dark wood. The spotlights made the suite sparkle. Kim could easily spend the rest of the trip in her room without getting sick of it.

When they'd first come aboard, she'd followed Hélène through the boat in a daze. Now she couldn't for the life of her remember anything she had seen. Maybe it was time to explore? Hélène had said that she was going to change and then catch up with the crew.

After throwing on her bikini and a wrap around robe, Kim set off to find Hélène. She noted the door a little further down the corridor. It was the door to Hélène's room. Should she knock, see if she was still in there? No, Kim was sure that Hélène was already on one of the four decks.

Kim looked at a floor plan that was attached to the wall. The deck she was on now was where the suites were located. There was a deck with a dining area, another with the lounge and pool out back, or at *the stern*. Kim praised herself for remembering the correct term. The top deck seemed to be where the captain would be, also an observation area with sun loungers by the look of the map.

Kim walked towards the stairs that lead to the other decks. Of course, they weren't any old stairs, no, they were spiralling solid mahogany. Kim was almost certain the staircase alone cost more than the entire building she lived in.

Throughout the boat the light was a mix of natural sunlight which was let in by the tinted windows that spanned the entire length of each side of the boat and brighter, more crisp light from spot lights which had been strategically placed to enhance the high cost features in each room.

Eager to find Hélène, Kim rushed through each room, trying to get her bearings. After a few minutes, she could hear Hélène's distinct laughter filtering through from the outside where the pool was located.

"Hey, there you are," Hélène said, smiling as Kim joined her and a woman who she didn't know sitting with their feet dangling in the water.

"Sorry, took me a while to navigate my way here," Kim replied sweetly. She didn't like how close the unknown woman was sitting next to Hélène.

"Navigate? Are you really going to be throwing in as many nautical terms as you can on this trip?" Hélène chuckled.

"Well, when in Rome and all that?" Kim replied nonchalantly.

"Here, here," the unknown woman chimed. Hélène chuckled, then squeezed the woman's arm, making Kim's insides squirm uncomfortably.

"Sorry, this is Holly. She's part of the kitchen crew and one of my best friends. We've been diving together on *Connie* for years." Hélène was smiling fondly at Holly.

"It's a pleasure," Holly chirped, holding out her hand to Kim.

"Right back at you," Kim smiled, shaking her hand. So one of Hélène's best friends was a gorgeous Ozzy. Kim didn't like it one bit. Jealousy really was an ugly bitch.

"So," Hélène began, "I think we will have a couple of chilled days relaxing by the pool before we arrive in Corsica. How does that sound?" She directed the question to Kim.

"Fantastic, I'll do whatever you want," Kim replied, her voice a little lower—almost sultry—than she meant it to be, causing Hélène to raise an eyebrow.

"Really, anything I want, hmm?" She replied playfully.

110

"Anything." Kim was done playing games. She wanted Hélène to understand she was interested, especially now Holly had turned up. Her flirting was obviously having an effect as Hélène swallowed deeply before clearing her throat, suddenly unable to look Kim in the eye.

"Wow, it just got real hot out here," Holly announced, her eyes darting between Kim and Hélène.

Not wanting to make Hélène too uncomfortable, Kim extricated herself from the situation. "I'm going for a swim if that's okay, Holly's right, it is a touch warm out here." Kim headed to the pool's steps before anyone had time to reply.

The water was refreshing. It was a wonderful contrast to the heat that was beating down from the cloudless sky. Kim swam the length of the pool slowly, watching Hélène and Holly from the corner of her eye. They seemed to whisper, which made Kim's green-eyed monster rear its ugly head again.

Had she been fooling herself this whole time? Had she imagined Hélène flirting? One thing was for sure, Holly and Hélène looked comfortable together. It was definitely possible they were more than just friends.

Kim continued to swim even when she saw Holly get up and leave. She wondered what Hélène would do. Would she follow Holly? Her question was quickly answered when Hélène stood and stripped off her T-shirt and shorts, revealing a very sexy black bikini. It took all of Kim's concentration to carry on swimming and not drown.

Hélène slid her golden body into the water and made her way over to Kim. "How are you finding everything so far?" she asked Kim as they swam next to each other.

"H, this is paradise. I don't know how you stay away for months on end?" It was the absolute truth. She'd live on *Connie* if she had the opportunity.

Hélène laughed. "I know what you mean. If I were the type of person to live off of family money, I would probably spend all my time here, but, alas, I'm not, I enjoy making my own money which means, like you, I have to work a lot and take vacations when I can."

Kim didn't really have a response to that. She felt as if anything she said would take them into a conversation that was a little too deep. That was always the case where money and family were concerned.

"So Holly seems nice." It wasn't the most subtle of conversation changes, but Kim just couldn't shake the feeling that was growing in her stomach. She needed to know if Hélène and Holly were more than just best friends.

"Holly is great. We've had some amazing times on this boat." Hélène smiled, clearly reliving some of those memories. Well, that kind of said it all, didn't it? Kim's heart felt as if it had just been punched. From the look in Hélène's eyes when she spoke of Holly, Kim was convinced they were more than friends.

"Right," Kim said curtly, her jealousy seeping out. "Well, if you both need some time together, just let me know and I'll busy myself elsewhere."

"That's unnecessary, but thanks?" Hélène looked a little confused. "She'll be joining us for dinner later, along with a couple of other crew members, if that's okay with you?"

"More than okay," Kim lied. "I think I'll go freshen up before dinner. What time should I be ready?" She wanted nothing more than to escape to her suite.

"Oh, okay," Hélène's eyes dropped from Kim's in disappointment. "Dinner will be at seven, so you have plenty of time. How about a cocktail?"

"Thanks, but I think I'll take a nap. Long day." Kim swam to the steps. She was struggling to keep her emotions in check. Typical! Just as she'd decided to go after what she wanted, it was too late. Hélène was clearly taken with Holly, and Kim was not about to be a third wheel.

Thankfully, Kim had an easy time finding her way back to her room. Throwing her wraparound on the bed, she hit the shower. Maybe a nap *was* what she needed. They'd had a long day and Kim had dealt with a lot of emotional baggage recently. Perhaps that's why she was feeling so eaten up at the idea of Hélène and Holly.

* * *

A light knocking drew Kim out of her sleep. After taking a couple of seconds to adjust to her surroundings, she padded over to her door. Hélène stood outside looking like a fucking model. She wore a dress that looked as if it should be worn on a red carpet. Her hair was swept over one shoulder, revealing her long and slender neck. Kim had to check that she wasn't dribbling.

"Sorry to wake you," Hélène said, her voice as soft as velvet. Kim almost wondered if she was dreaming.

"No, it's fine. What time is it?" she replied sleepily. The nap had turned into a full slumber. Kim had clearly needed to rest.

"It's seven fifteen. I was beginning to think you'd jumped ship when you didn't come to the dining area."

"Shit," Kim barked. She'd overslept and kept everyone waiting. "Give me like twenty minutes and I'll be there," she shouted over her shoulder as she ran back to the bedroom to dress.

"Take your time. I'll meet you there."

"Okay," Kim shouted through the dress she was pulling over her head. She heard her door close and sank onto the bed. *Fuck.* Now she had to pull herself together enough to spend the evening with Hélène, who looked like a fucking goddess and her probable girlfriend.

Shaking her head, Kim grew frustrated with herself. Why the hell was she giving up so easily? She'd made a snap decision about Hélène and Holly and she'd all but walked away without knowing any facts. Which was not like her at all.

Hélène may or may not be involved with Holly, but until Hélène told Kim specifically, either way, she wasn't going to back down. It had only been a few hours since she'd decided to see if there was something more between them, and she was damned if she was going to turn and run now.

Drawing herself up, she flattened down her dress, which looked as if she'd been sewn into it and picked out her favourite heels, the ones that Hélène had salivated over when she'd danced in them. It took her a few minutes to do her hair and makeup before she surveyed herself in the mirror. God damn, her mum would be proud. Kim looked like a fucking bombshell, and it was all for Hélène.

I'm coming for you, doll!

Chapter 10

Something was off with Kim. Hélène knew that much. As to the reason, that was a complete mystery. Everything had been fine when they'd left the hotel and headed to *Connie*. They'd both been in high spirits, excited for the next leg of the trip.

It was clear that Kim had found the boat a little overwhelming, but Hélène didn't think that was the reason Kim had acted strangely by the pool. Maybe it was because Hélène had left her alone in her room? At the time, she'd thought it a good idea to give Kim a bit of space to acclimatise herself to her new surroundings, but maybe that had been a mistake.

Hélène had been riding a high since she boarded *Connie*. Seeing her friends, especially Holly, was just what she needed. Hélène had met Holly the first time she'd boarded *Connie*. Holly was new to the kitchen crew, and they'd hit it off immediately.

To begin with, they'd seen each other as a potential love interest but they soon realised they were better suited as friends.

"So where is your *friend*?" Holly smirked as they sat at the dining table, waiting for Kim to appear. The fact that Kim hadn't turned up for dinner was another reason Hélène was convinced there was something wrong.

"I'm not sure why you said friend like that?" Hélène was used to Holly baiting her, especially when there was a beautiful woman around.

"I said it like that because I don't believe for one second you just want to be friends," Holly answered smugly.

"We *are* just friends." Hélène was not having this discussion with Holly. It was already a complicated mess. She didn't need her friend's input, which she knew would likely suggest she bed Kim and move on.

"Just friends, really?"

"Yes," Hélène said emphatically.

"Excellent, you won't mind if I have a crack at her, then?" Holly gave Hélène a smirk, causing heat to rise in her chest. Sometimes Holly really tested her patience.

"She's just broken up with her long-term boyfriend, Hols. She needs support and relaxation, not a horny lesbian coming on to her." Hélène's tone was a little harder than necessary.

"You never know, Hélène, a roll in the sack with a gifted lesbian may be just what the doctor ordered." Holly wiggled her eyebrows. Hélène looked at her friend stunned, had she always been this egotistical?

"Did you miss the 'boyfriend' part of my sentence?"

"No, but I'm not gonna assume she's straight. I'd like to hear that from her," Hélène said matter-of-factly.

"Holly, seriously, she's vulnerable right now. Please leave her be."

116

"Fine, but just for now, Hélène. The moment I think she's into me, I'm taking my shot," Holly said confidently. "Anyway, are you gonna have the same chat with that pair?" Holly directed her eyes to Leo and David, the two other members of the crew that often went diving with Hélène and Holly.

They always got together for meals on their trips, and Hélène had thought it a good idea to introduce Kim to them. Thinking about it now, though, maybe it wasn't such a good idea. They were two good looking fellas, both single and very good with women. How had Hélène surrounded herself with people that were definitely going to hit on Kim? People who probably had more chance of succeeding than she did.

"Yes, I will be," Hélène said as she moved toward the men talking at the other end of the room. Her progress was halted though as she watched Leo and David both stare wide-eyed at the door to their left. Hélène followed their line of sight and walked straight into the corner of the table. Kim had just entered the dining room and turned every single head. Hélène thought she was going to hyperventilate.

Kim was wearing one of her signature dresses that moulded itself to every inch of her sumptuous body, and dear god those heels. The same heels that had set Hélène on fire when watching Kim dance in them.

Hélène was dumbstruck, her voice had abandoned ship completely, her mind could only process Kim's movements, which were confident and seductive. Kim strode into the room as if she fucking owned it, her hips swaying and head held high.

"Evening all, I'm so sorry I'm late," she purred. No one moved. Every eye was fixed on Kim, who clearly knew the effect she was having, considering the small grin that was etched on her face. Holly was the first to move. She shot out of her chair to greet Kim.

"No apologies necessary," she said smoothly. *So much for waiting, Holly!*

"I'm David," David said, hurrying over to take Kim's hand. Seconds later, Leo was by her side.

"Leonardo, *enchanté*," he said, grasping Kim's other hand and kissing her knuckles.

"You look stunning," Hélène said, almost in a whisper. She'd meant to say it in her head, but her voice had returned at that very moment and embarrassed the shit out of her. Kim's eyes snapped to Hélène's.

"So do you," Kim replied.

They all stood in silence for a few seconds. Holly, David, and Leo looking between the two women who had yet to break eye contact. Hélène felt the tension rising. She had to break it for her own sanity. "Shall we eat?" Prying her gaze away from Kim, she moved to stand behind her seat.

Without a word, everyone headed to the table. It was a large solid wood table that could easily seat twenty. It wasn't often that Hélène used the room. She much preferred less formal meals by the pool, but she was determined to give Kim the full luxury yacht experience.

"This is breathtaking," Kim said, her gaze scanning the room as she sat in the chair next to Hélène. Unsurprisingly, the other guests fought to get to the chair that was on the other side of Kim. Leo won out through sheer force.

"It is beautiful," Hélène replied, sinking into her seat, Holly taking the one to her left, followed by a pissed off David.

"Is this your first time on a luxury yacht?" Leo asked. His Italian accent had suddenly become 100% stronger. Hélène internally rolled her eyes at him.

"It is," Kim replied sweetly.

"And what do you think so far?" Leo pressed, his body getting ever closer to Kim.

"No complaints from me?" Kim chuckled, causing everyone to smile because even Kim's chuckle was fucking gorgeous.

The door hidden at the back of the room swung open. Sal the chef came bustling over to Hélène, kissing her on each cheek. "*Salut*, ma cherie."

"*Salut* Sal," Hélène beamed. "Sal, this is Kim. She's my guest."

"Welcome, Madame," he said with a little bow towards Kim, which made her blush. "I hope you will enjoy the meal I have prepared."

"Oh, I have no doubt," she said and then paused, her face paled a little. "Erm, that is unless you have done a lot of seafood… I… I don't eat fish."

"No fish, Madame, Hélène already filled me in on your aversion to '*Fruit de Mer*'," he smiled. Kim's face filled with colour again.

"I can't believe you remembered. I only mentioned that once, and it was an off-the-cuff comment, if I recall." Kim looked at Hélène, who blushed. Hélène remembered everything Kim had told her over the course of their time together. She'd tried to soak in every bit of information that Kim had been willing to give during their talks.

"I have an excellent memory," Hélène smiled back

"So, are you all ready?" Sal interjected. Everyone nodded in agreement.

* * *

The food was excellent as usual. The conversation flowed between the group, however Hélène wanted to reach over and pour some cold water over Leo's head. He had spent the entire meal fixated on Kim, his body inching closer every time he spoke.

"Cocktails by the pool?" Hélène asked the group.

"Crackin' idea, darl," Holly said excitedly. Hélène had seen her friend drink twice the amount of alcohol than everyone else during dinner, which meant that she was in the party zone. If they weren't careful, Holly would turn their little soirée into a full blowout.

"May I escort you out?" Leo asked Kim, holding out his arm for her to take. With a polite smile Kim took Leo up on his offer.

"He's going to get in her knickers," David grumbled.

"No, he is not. Kim has standards," Hélène laughed. Her true feelings about David's statement were far from funny. Her gut was twisting at the thought of Kim going to bed with Leo. What could she do, though? If Kim wanted to blow off some steam with a hunky Italian, there was nothing Hélène could do about it.

All the levity of the evening drained from her body. She was suddenly tired and regretted the cocktail suggestion. She had to be a suitable host, though, so she squared her shoulders and followed David down the stairs to the pool.

Leo had already taken care of the cocktails. He stood close to Kim by the railing, chatting away. Hélène watched them momentarily. By the fake smile that was on Kim's face, Hélène knew she didn't have to worry about Leo's advances.

"Hey, do you want to take a walk around the boat?" Hélène asked Kim as she drew up next to her. She tried to ignore Leo, shooting daggers her way.

"We were just in the middle of a conversation," Leo interjected, his voice strained.

"A walk would be lovely," Kim replied, giving Leo a sweet smile before wrapping her hand around Hélène's offered arm.

"We can walk all the way around if you like. It's a beautiful evening and the sun will set soon."

"Perfect." Kim tightened her grip ever so slightly on Hélène's arm.

They walked slowly in comfortable silence for a while. The view from the ship was astonishing, especially since the setting sun was casting radiant colours across the sky. Hélène heard Kim let out a sigh. "Are you okay?"

"I'm…" Kim began, but trailed off. Hélène could see she was struggling with something.

"Hey, you can tell me," she whispered, bringing them to a stop so they could lean against the railings. A splash caught Hélène's attention. She whipped her head towards the sound and smiled brightly. "Look."

Kim looked out and gasped. Hélène's heart soared at Kim's sheer delight as they watched a small pod of dolphins play. "Oh my god," Kim cried, her whole body coming alive. Hélène sent a little thank you into the universe. This couldn't have happened at a better time.

"Beautiful," Hélène remarked. She was in awe herself as she watched the playful creatures twist and turn underwater before leaping into the air. Seeing such things reminded her how fortunate she was to be able to have these types of experiences.

She cast her eyes towards Kim, who was no longer looking out to sea. She was regarding Hélène with a look that could only be described as determined. The tension between them was charged. Hélène wasn't sure what had happened in those few seconds to have changed the atmosphere so much, but she was scared that if she didn't diffuse it soon she would do something stupid.

"We're really lucky to see dolphins. I've only ever seen them twice in this area so it's…" Her voice was muted when she felt Kim's lips on her own. Those soft, warm lips sought permission to delve deeper. It took Hélène's brain a millisecond to decide that she absolutely wanted the kiss to evolve.

Hélène's hands automatically went to Kim's waist, pulling her in closer. She felt Kim's hands travel to the back of her neck, massaging and pulling her in. She felt Kim's tongue brush against her lips, causing her to groan.

Hélène was having an out-of-body experience, but there was something nagging in her mind, something telling her to pull back. She gripped Kim's hips once more before withdrawing her hands and her lips. Her breath was coming fast, the blood in her body seemed to pool between her thighs, leaving her head dizzy.

"Kim…" she panted. She watched Kim's eyes open slowly.

"That was…"

"Remarkable."

"Yes."

They stood silently, looking at each other. Hélène's mind was running a million miles an hour. She was struggling to understand what the hell had just happened. She needed answers, however Kim had other ideas. Before Hélène could open her mouth, Kim leaned in, kissed her cheek and bid her good night.

Hélène stood rooted to the spot, unable to move. Had that really just happened? Had Kim, the woman she'd been dreaming of, just kissed her? Hélène sucked in a big breath. She had to figure out what it meant. They were going to be living in the same space for a couple of weeks with no means of escape.

It wouldn't be a problem for her, but it was more than possible that Kim would instantly regret her actions and want off of the boat.

* * *

After several hours of staring at the bedroom ceiling, Hélène eventually made her way to the pool. The stars were shining in their infinite glory. The Milky Way stretched out above her as she lay on a lounger. Nothing Hélène did stopped her mind from buzzing. Kim's actions had really thrown her.

Throughout the entire trip, Hélène had concentrated on making sure that Kim was okay, that she felt comfortable and safe. Now, lying under the starry sky, Hélène had to make sure all those things were true for herself.

The strength of her feelings made no sense. She'd known Kim for just over a week—discounting the handful of times they'd interacted with each other through Anna and Sam. How could she be so far gone already? What happened when Kim left? Hélène's breakups in the past had been difficult. It was always hard to watch someone she liked walk away for whatever reason. With Kim though? She wasn't sure she could come back from that kind of heartache.

As a young girl, Hélène had always believed that she could fall in love at first sight but that had just been the fantasy and hopes of a girl, she was now a woman, a woman that had learned that true love and love at first sight was rare and unlikely to happen to her.

JJ and Claire had had that kind of love, which made Hélène's heart sing and cry at the same time. She was so happy that her brother, whom she loved more than anyone, had been given that gift, and so angry that he'd had it so cruelly ripped away.

"Are you going to make a habit of waking me up in the middle of the night?" JJ grumbled sleepily. Hélène smiled. She felt bad for calling him, but she needed some guidance.

"Sorry J, I just needed to hear your voice." She was aware of how silent the boat was. Her voice echoed as she spoke.

"What's up, kid?"

That was the question wasn't it? What was wrong? Nothing and everything. The woman she craved had kissed her. She should be on cloud nine right now, but she felt hollow.

"Kim kissed me." Just hearing the words out loud made her stomach flip excitedly.

"Wow," he replied with a chuckle. "I take it you weren't expecting it?"

"Not at all. She kissed me and then said good night."

"Maybe it was just as much of a shock to her as it was to you?"

"Yeah, maybe," she muttered.

"What's wrong?"

"It was the best kiss I have ever had, JJ. She literally took my breath away, but then she left, just walked away. She's had so much going on lately I can't help but wonder if it really meant something or just that she's struggling with her life right now and needed an outlet."

"You could be right. The only way you'll know is by talking to her, or letting her come to you. You're the one that knows her. Judge your reaction on the way she acts with you when you see her. Let her know that you're willing to let her set the pace."

"What if it was just a mistake to her, though? I'm not sure how I would handle it."

"Are you falling for her?"

"I think I am, which is stupid. I'm setting myself up for heartache. There's no way she's in the right headspace. I'm not even sure she really likes women for Christ's sake."

"You're making a lot of assumptions right now, without knowing all the facts. Like I said, let her come to you and then talk to her. Honestly."

"I don't know, JJ," she huffed.

"Yes, you do, otherwise you wouldn't have called me. I'm only telling you what you already know."

"Hmm." *Real mature Hélène.*

"Go get some sleep. Tomorrow, or I should say this morning, continue as you were. Let her know that you're not freaking out. Get on with your day and be patient. Okay?"

"Okay, thanks, JJ, sorry for waking you. Again."

"No worries, kid."

"Okay night." She could do that, right? Just get up and carry on like nothing had happened without making Kim think she was dismissing the kiss. Yeah, simple. It was decided then. She'd carry on with the trip and wait to see if Kim wanted to talk.

Even though the talk with her brother had helped, her mind was still whirring. It seemed sleep was not on the cards. Picking herself up from the lounger, she trudged back to her suite.

Chapter 11

Kim stretched out her legs until they rested on the balcony rail. The low morning sun warmed her as she settled back into her chair, hot cup of coffee in hand. After kissing Hélène the night before, Kim hadn't expected to sleep, but she had. In fact, she'd slept so soundly that when she woke at seven a.m., she felt wonderfully rested.

Her spur-of-the-moment decision to kiss Hélène hadn't caused the expected reaction she thought would follow. Instead of anxiety or panic, Kim felt oddly calm. It was as if Hélène's lips had given her all the answers to the questions she'd been asking herself over the past week.

Hélène was something special. That kiss had been something special. The timing had been perfect with the sun setting across the sea. The dolphins had added magic to the air, and in that moment Kim couldn't think of a more perfect time to let Hélène know how she felt.

The melodious sound of a Skype call filtered through from Kim's suite. The picture identified the caller as Kim's mum. *Strange, it's only about six a.m. in England.*

"Hi," Kim chirped as her mum came into focus on her screen.

"Darling, how are you, love?" Kim's mum Joy bellowed down the phone.

"Mother, you do not need to shout." Sometimes Joy Richmond forgot she wasn't addressing a large lecture hall full of adoring students.

"Sorry, doll," she chuckled. "You okay? It's been a while since we heard from you."

"Is that why you're calling so early?"

"Well, yes, and the fact that we've both been up since five prepping for next week's trip."

Kim had forgotten that her parents were due to travel to the States to be guest speakers at two ivy league schools. They seemed to work more now, when they were supposed to be retired, than they did when they were in full-time employment. Kim couldn't fault them, though. They were doing something they loved together. "I completely forgot. Are you both ready?"

"Ready as we'll ever be," a faceless voice chimed in from somewhere behind Joy.

"Peter, would you come and sit down? We are not having a three-way conversation with you in another room," Joy huffed, rolling her eyes, causing Kim to laugh.

"What is he doing?" Kim chuckled, her dad finally making an appearance, his arms full of files.

"He's over preparing as usual."

"I am not," Peter scowled.

127

"Yes, you are. Don't argue," Joy said without looking at her husband.

"Dad, do you really need all those?"

"No, he does not. Now, will you come and sit your cute bum down?"

"Mum, don't call his bum cute when I'm on the phone."

"Why, it's true. You should thank him for it, considering you inherited it," Joy laughed.

"Don't worry, honey, you inherited all of your mum's delicious curves, too." Peter smiled lovingly at his wife as he scooted to sit next to her.

"Geez, give it a rest, you two," Kim laughed. Her parents had always been openly loving with each other. It had set a high standard for Kim as far as her love life was concerned. Then it dawned on her. That's what had been missing between her and Greg. Kim wanted the kind of love that her parents had and she hadn't had it with him.

"Is that a new dress?" Kim asked, pulling herself away from her straying thoughts.

"Do you like?" Joy asked, running her hands down it. Kim had the exact same taste as her mother. Even though Joy had never tried to influence her style one way or the other, Kim had followed in her footsteps.

"I love it," Kim beamed. It really was a sublime dress. Forest green with thin white embroidery around the seams of the arms and collar. Kim could see that the bodice was tapered to fit snugly around her mum's waist. The skirt section flared out. It was gorgeous.

"She doesn't need any more dresses," Peter interjected.

"A woman can have as many dresses as she damn well pleases! Cardigans, on the other hand, should be limited to two, not two wardrobes full, so you're not one to speak." Her mum huffed playfully.

128

Where her mum had fabulous fashion sense, her dad did not. He really was the stereotypical professor, cardigans and all.

"Dad, you *do* need to cut down on the wool," Kim giggled.

"Never!" he declared loudly, making them all laugh.

"Anyway, love, are you having fun?" Joy asked once they'd all calmed down.

Was she having fun? The events of the past week flashed in front of her eyes. Kim had had every intention of calling her parents and filling them in on everything, but she'd wanted a few days out at sea to fully relax before tackling what she knew was going to be a tough conversation.

"Yes, I'm having fun. I'm currently on a super yacht in the Mediterranean."

"I thought you were in a hotel?" Her dad piped up.

"I was, but... well, the holiday didn't start off great. There was a mix-up with the room and I ended up staying with a friend that happened to be there."

"Which friend?" Joy asked casually.

"Hélène DuBois. She's actually more of a friend to Sam, but we've seen each other around. She was so kind and let me crash in her suite.

"That was very kind of her," Peter said. Joy nodded in agreement.

"It was." Kim's voice trailed off.

"What's going on, Kim?" her mum asked, leaning towards the screen. She had to talk to them. It was no good putting it off, especially if she wanted to enjoy the rest of her time on *Connie*.

"So look, the reason I went on holiday was because I needed a break from Greg. He'd cancelled our plans again, and I'd had enough. Things between us have changed, so I thought getting away would be beneficial to us both."

129

"Okay," her parents said simultaneously.

"During the week, Greg showed up, unannounced." The hard part was coming up. "We got into a fight and he…"

"He what?" Peter asked, his brow creasing, as if he knew what she was about to say.

"He got a little physical."

"HE WHAT?" Peter bellowed.

"Calm down, Dad, Hélène handled it and then I threw him out. Needless to say, our relationship is over."

"Are you okay, love?" her mum asked softly. Joy was always the one to calm a fraught situation.

"I'm okay, I was shocked at the time, but Hélène has been a wonderful friend and helped me."

"Well, I'm really starting to like Hélène," her dad quipped.

"You will love her," Kim shot. Her mum arched an eyebrow at her enthusiastic outburst. "I decided to tag along with her on the next part of her holiday, hence why I'm now on a yacht."

"Good, you deserve it, love, but I need to just go back to the whole Greg thing for a minute, if you don't mind." Joy's tone was insistent.

"Okay."

"We've known that boy for a long time. It's worrying that we never saw that he could get physical."

"*I* never saw it, Mum, and that's because he never would have. Whatever is going on with him is really out of character. Now, because you're both super pissed at him right now, my next request is going to be difficult."

"And what request is that?" Peter barked.

"I need you to get hold of him and help him. I can't right now. We need space. I need space, but that doesn't mean that I'm not worried about my best friend. He *is* my best friend and even though we'll need time to heal before we can get back to that, I still need to know he is okay. He doesn't have anyone apart from us, Dad."

"I'll call him," Joy nodded.

"He put his hands on our little girl, Joy," Peter said irately.

"He did, and I will address that with him. However, Kim is right. We've been like parents to him since he was a young lad and to hear that he acted in such a way is very worrying," Joy shot back.

"Please Dad," Kim pleaded. "Call him and talk to him. Something isn't right."

"Fine, but he will answer for his actions," Peter barked.

"Yes, he will," Joy placated.

"Thank you." Kim sighed. Knowing that Greg had someone on his side made her feel better. The three of them sat silent for a minute.

"There is something else," Kim mumbled. She hadn't planned on telling her parents about Hélène yet, but it just felt great getting it all off her chest.

"Bloody hell, what else? You're not pregnant, are you?" Peter moaned.

"No, not preggers, Dad," Kim laughed. "Erm… well, something might have happened between me and Hélène," she said shyly. Her parents knew she liked both men and women.

"Something like what?" her mum asked.

"Er, well, I kind of kissed her last night." She couldn't look at them.

"Christ almighty, Kim, you've only just dumped Greg," her dad snapped.

"Hey, watch your tone, mister," Joy shot at her husband. "Kim has every right to kiss whomever she likes whenever she likes. She's the one who knows her own feelings. Who are you to judge?" God, Kim loved her feisty as fuck mum.

"Well... I mean."

"Well nothing, hush your mouth until you're ready to support your daughter." Kim had to bite her lip to stop herself from laughing. Her dad looked like a scolded child.

"Sorry, love," He mumbled.

"It's okay, Dad, I get your worry. The thing is, she's just a wonderful person, and she makes me feel really good. We hit it off last week and whether or not you think it's too soon, I know I'm attracted to her. Things between me and Greg have been broken for a long time, something I probably should have told you before, so for that I'm sorry. Things with Hélène are new and I'm not even sure how she feels yet. It could be just a flash in the pan."

"But you don't want it to be just a flash in the pan, right?" Joy asked, even though it wasn't really a question.

"Yes, I can feel it's something more than that and I want to explore it."

"Then go for it, honey. If it's going to make you happy, dive right in. All this stuff with Greg will work out. I don't think you should wait around if you've found something worth pursuing, something your father should know all about."

"Alright, love, I get it. Sorry I shouldn't have reacted that way. I think it was just a lot to process in one sitting."

"I'm just glad I got to tell you. I've been a little confused by it all."

"That's what we're here for, doll," Joy winked. "When do we get to meet her?"

"When I know what the bloody hell is going on between us," Kim chuckled.

"Well, keep us updated, alright?"

"I will and you guys call me and let me know when you've arrived in the States, okay?"

"We will," Peter nodded.

"Alright guys, I love you both. I'm going to go grab some breakfast."

"Bye, love," they said together.

Kim dropped her phone on the bed and sighed. She'd done it. It was out in the open and now she could focus on how she was going to face Hélène. She wanted Hélène to know that she didn't regret what she did, and that she was hoping they could do it again.

Kim had to be careful though, their week had been full of ups and downs, a lot of emotions had been shared, Hélène might need convincing that Kim wasn't just going through some sort of post breakup breakdown.

* * *

Kim stopped just inside the door that led to the pool. She rolled her shoulders and moved her head back and forth. Anyone would think she was a prize fighter waiting to enter the ring.

Hélène was sitting at a small table near the back of the deck furthest away from the door and the pool. Kim stood silently watching as she lifted her coffee cup to her lips, those same lips that had sent fireworks through Kim's body. She continued to watch as Hélène looked out to sea now and then before dropping her gaze back to the book she was holding with her free hand.

The day was already shaping up to be hot. Hélène had a vest top on over her bikini and a sarong wrapped around her bottom half. One of her legs was perched on the seat opposite her. Kim had an overwhelming urge to walk over, drop to her knees and lick every inch of that golden leg, all the way up to…

"Morning," a voice boomed, thoroughly ejecting her from the fantasy she was arse deep in. Kim turned her head to see Holly leaning against the stair bannister.

"Morning," Kim parroted back.

"Sleep well?" Holly asked as she pushed herself off the bannister towards Kim.

"Like a baby," Kim answered sweetly. She wasn't sure why, but there was something about Holly that made her feel uncomfortable. Maybe it was just some residual jealousy from seeing how close she was to Hélène. "You?" she countered.

"Always sleep well when I'm at sea." Jesus, how long was she going to have to keep up the small talk? "You want some brekky?"

Kim nodded and followed Holly outside. She held her breath slightly, waiting for Hélène to see her. Hélène shifted her head when she heard them walk out. Her eyes flicked to Kim.

"Morning, H," Kim called.

"Morning, Kim." Kim studied her for a second before taking the seat next to her. The table had a plate of croissants and pain au chocolates, plus freshly cut fruit and orange juice.

"God, this looks delish," Kim chirped, her stomach rumbled loudly, making her giggle. She glanced at Hélène, who was smiling affectionately at her. *Okay that's a good sign.*

"What's on the agenda today, boss?" Holly mumbled through a mouth full of croissant.

"Don't talk with your mouth full Holly, *putain, c'est pas possible*," Hélène grumbled, her face contorted in disgust. "We have today and tomorrow to relax and then we will moor up to dive. I've got this for you," Hélène looked at Kim, pointing to a book that rested on the table. Kim picked it up. It was a guide to diving.

"It's full of all the information you will need. It explains the equipment, the terminology, hand signs..." Kim looked from the book to Hélène. Her excitement was endearing. "I mean, you don't have to read it. I will guide you through your baptême. That is your first dive. In English you call is a baptism. Just a little dunk in the water. I will tell you everything you will need to know. I just thought maybe you would enjoy a bit of extra reading," she finished eagerly.

"Who the hell likes extra reading?" Holly scoffed, sending a flare of irritation through Kim.

"I do," she snapped. "Thank you, H, that's very thoughtful. I'll demolish this bad boy today so I'll be ready for you come dive time," Kim replied with a wink.

"I can help explain anything you don't understand if you like. There are some maths and physics involved," Holly blurted, clearly unfazed by Kim's earlier snap.

Holly looked at Hélène, who had laughed. "Thanks, Holly, but I think I'll be okay," Kim said, gently slapping Hélène's shoulder to get her to stop laughing.

"Am I missing something?" Holly asked, looking between the two women.

"No, sorry, it's just the idea of Kim needing any help."

"Why's that funny?"

"Because she is ridiculously smart. There is nothing in that book that will remotely test her wonderful brain."

"You think my brain is wonderful?"

"Yes."

"I wouldn't have pegged you for a bookworm," Holly grinned, looking Kim up and down, her eyes lingering uncomfortably on Kim's chest.

"And why's that?" Kim fumed.

"Well, it's not like you look like one."

"And what does a 'bookworm' look like?"

"You know, geeky glasses, no friends, fugly. Oh god, was that you?" Holly chortled.

Kim stilled. A flashback to her childhood loomed in the front of her mind. People like Holly were the reason she often felt uncomfortable with herself. She was about to open her mouth when she saw Hélène lean forward. "Holly, I'm not sure what has got into you recently, but your attitude sucks right now. In the space of five minutes, you've insulted Kim's intelligence whilst making yourself look like an ignorant fool. You yourself were a 'bookworm' when you were younger, glasses included."

"I was just joking around," Holly retorted.

"No, you weren't. You were being purposefully combatant, which is unlike you."

"Whatever, darl, I'm going to see if Sal needs a hand."

Kim watched Holly retreat inside. Their interaction had been odd and Kim was certain there was more behind it than Holly just being playful.

"Sorry about Holly, I really don't know what has got into her."

"It's fine." For the first time since their kiss, they found themselves alone. Kim studied Hélène's face, trying to work out how to approach the conversation they most definitely needed to have.

"H, last night I kissed you."

"Yes, you did." Hélène shifted in her seat, looking just as surprised as Kim was at herself for being so blunt.

"I want you to know that I don't regret doing it and I'm not having some sort of breakdown. I'm attracted to you, because, well, for one you look like that—" Kim wagged her finger at Hélène's body "—and, well, I hoped maybe you had similar feelings. There, I've said what I needed to, so you just take your time, mull it over and get back to me."

136

Take your time, mull it over and get back to me? What the hell was she blabbing on about? She was trying to woo the woman, not sell her fucking car insurance.

"Right," Hélène muttered. Jesus Kim needed to extract herself from this blatant cluster fuck.

"Oh darn, I… er, forgot my sunglasses," she both blurted and stuttered as she desperately hauled herself away from the table, knocking her half glass of orange juice all over the fruit. "Bollocks."

"It's fine," Hélène said, scrambling to move things out of the puddle of juice now seeping over the edges of the table. "Kim, really, it's fine."

"Sorry," Kim mumbled, fleeing the scene.

Alright then, that could have gone a tad better.

Kim reached her suite in record time. Her face was the colour of a tomato and her nerves were fried. Everything had been going great apart from Holly's odd behaviour. She'd been up front about her desires and had got straight to the heart of the matter. That was, until she panicked midway through her confession, which for some bizarre reason had turned into more of a sales pitch than a confession of the heart.

Oh, let's not forget the ridiculous attempt to leave, citing "forgotten sunglasses". Those were the same sunglasses that were on her face the entire time. Last but not least, drowning the table in orange juice. *Smooth Kim, real smooth.*

Well, there was nothing for it. She was just going to hide away in her suite until either she could live down her embarrassment or—the more likely scenario—the world ended.

A knock on her door interrupted her pacing. She could ignore it, right? Apparently not because whoever was doing the knocking was getting louder by the second. Huffing out a breath, she stomped over to the door. Better to get it over with, she supposed.

She cracked open the door slowly. Hélène stood there with her hands clasped in front of her. She was clearly trying to stop herself from laughing. "Can I come in?"

"Fine," Kim huffed again, opening the door wider to let Hélène pass. Kim took a deep breath and closed the door. There was no time for embarrassment because as soon as she turned to face Hélène she was pushed up against the door, Hélène's face an inch from her own.

"I'm not sorry either," Hélène whispered, her mouth crashing into Kim's.

Chapter 12

There were probably a hundred reasons this wasn't a good idea, but Hélène was willing to listen to zero of them, not when her mouth was attached to the most sensual person she had ever met.

Kim was sexy, intelligent, and charismatic. She exuded warmth and joy, everything that Hélène wanted in a partner. Granted, they were no way near partner status, in fact they were no way near any kind of status, but that didn't matter. Kissing Kim with her body pinned up against her suite door mattered.

Hélène had taken Kim by surprise. She just couldn't hold back any longer. The moment she'd seen Kim looking sheepish and adorable as she opened the door, Hélène knew she was going to make a move. How could she not?

Kim had been beyond cute at the breakfast table. Hélène had had to stifle a laugh as she'd watched Kim try to convey her feelings, getting flustered and then making a real cockup of her exit. Even though it had been an amusing sight to see, the only thing Hélène could focus on was that Kim had said she was attracted to her and that she had feelings.

That was more than Hélène could ever have hoped for. Considering how brave Kim had been to open herself up like that, Hélène felt it was only fair to talk to Kim and let her know she did indeed feel the same.

When Hélène had arrived at Kim's door, she'd had every intention of doing just that, having a conversation that would hopefully lead to something else at a later date. She did not think she would be pressed up against Kim and her magnificent cleavage.

"Kim?" Hélène panted into her mouth.

"Hmm?" Kim mumbled as she captured Hélène's mouth again. Kim's tongue slipped over Hélène's top lip, extracting a low moan.

"God, you feel good." Hélène pulled herself back, their lips popping as they parted. "Do you want to talk?" she asked, because as great as their make-out session was, Hélène needed to know that Kim was in the right headspace for what they were doing.

Kim brought her hands, which had been pressed against the door to steady herself as they kissed up to Hélène's shoulders. She pushed Hélène back a little further, creating a foot of space between them. Hélène held her breath. She was certain that she'd just broken the spell and Kim was about to throw her out of the room. Hélène could *not* have been more wrong, or more taken aback by Kim's next move.

Without a word, Kim reached up to take out her hair tie. Her platinum locks cascaded down around her shoulders. She mussed her hair with both of her hands, leaving Hélène speechless. The vision of Kim running her hands through her hair whilst holding eye contact with her was almost too much.

Hélène continued to observe Kim without uttering a word or sound. She was completely captivated by this woman. She saw Kim steady herself, parting her legs slightly, resting her back against the door. Hélène ran her gaze down the length of Kim's scantily clad body. *Thank Christ for bikinis.*

Hélène's attention was brought back to Kim's face as she felt a hand cup under her chin, forcing her head up. Still, Kim remained silent. Her eyes were almost entirely black, her pupils were blown open with want. Hélène took some quick breaths, wondering what the hell was going to happen next.

What happened next was beyond her imagination or any fantasy she could concoct. Kim trailed her hand down herself, starting from her clavicle, brushing her fingers lightly against her skin, lingering momentarily over her left breast, never breaking eye contact. Kim's hand continued its downward trajectory until she reached the hem of her bikini bottoms, her fingers skimming just underneath, causing Hélène's breath to hitch.

Hélène couldn't keep her eyes from following those fingers all the way to her left hip, where Kim plucked at the string that was knotted to keep the garment on her body. She watched as Kim repeated the same action on her right side. Then she watched as they fell from her body, leaving Hélène with a view that could only be described as heaven on earth.

Sun-kissed and smooth, Kim stood tall and proud as she confidently exhibited her toned and curved body. Hélène hadn't taken her eyes from the almost white hair that nestled between Kim's legs. She felt her mouth water and was only partially aware of Kim reaching up to discard her bikini top.

Hélène felt the familiar touch of Kim's hand under her chin, pulling her gaze back to those mesmerising blue eyes. She opened her mouth to speak, but was silenced by a single finger pressed to her lips. Hélène snapped her mouth shut and waited.

141

Kim brushed her finger across Hélène's lip, down to her neck and across to her shoulder. That's when Hélène understood what was about to happen and she was almost positive that Kim was the woman of her dreams.

Hélène felt pressure on her shoulder, pushing her down. Hélène complied, dropping to her knees in front of Kim. She looked up, waiting for her next instructions. Kim snaked her hand around Hélène's neck, gently squeezing, divulging exactly what she wanted.

Hélène looked up into those captivating eyes one last time before she dropped her gaze to the object of her want. Kim shifted, draping her left leg over Hélène's shoulder. Hélène leaned forward and gently rested her face against Kim's mound. Her breath skimmed over Kim's clit, her nose buried in Kim's curls. She saw Kim clench as her breath sent shock waves of pleasure through her pussy.

"I'm going to worship you," she whispered before taking Kim fully into her mouth.

Hélène wrapped her hands around Kim's thighs to bring her closer so she could drive her tongue deeper. She felt possessed, every lick and suck delicious, but not enough to satisfy her greed. Hélène felt every pulse of Kim's pleasure, every twinge of desire as she ran her tongue from Kim's entrance to her swollen clit.

"Yes," Kim gasped as Hélène sucked her clit again and again. "Right there." Hélène needed more. She needed to be inside her. She needed to feel Kim envelop her fingers as her walls clamped down with pure pleasure.

Hélène released one of Kim's thighs, bringing her fingers to Kim's pussy, drenching them in the liquid that covered her mouth and chin. She slid two fingers in with ease. Kim bucked her hips as she adjusted to the fresh sensation.

After several moments, Hélène thrust harder and deeper. The pressure from Kim's hand on the back of her head intensified, telling her she was doing exactly what Kim needed her to do.

Kim's hips had taken on a life of their own as her orgasm built rapidly. Hélène was no longer in charge of the pace. She let Kim fuck her face and ride her fingers until she heard Kim's breath falter as a scream of sheer elation consumed the room.

"Jesus Christ." Kim steadied herself against the door, letting her leg drop from Hélène's shoulder. Hélène remained kneeled. Her mouth rested on Kim's mound again. She needed a few seconds to soak in everything that had just happened. She wanted to etch every moment of that experience into her memory.

Time passed in silence, neither of them wanting to break the moment. Hélène could feel her own need pulse between her legs. She couldn't recall ever being so turned on. It would have to wait, though. She needed to have Kim again. Hélène grasped Kim's hips and looked up. Kim leaned her head back against the door.

Hélène watched, fixated on Kim's chest, which was still rising rapidly. The beauty of Kim's breasts almost made her groan out loud. She rose swiftly from her knees up Kim's torso, her mouth capturing one of Kim's nipples whilst her hand caressed the other. Hélène felt Kim's stance change. She felt hands clutch her hips, pulling her closer.

"Bed," Hélène growled. Kim pushed herself off the door and walked Hélène backwards toward the bed. Her legs hit the edge, forcing her to sit down.

"My turn," Kim whispered into her ear, causing her to clench her thighs. After the last few minutes, Hélène was sure that she wouldn't take long to reach orgasm. "Tell me what you want." Kim leaned into Hélène, ushering her back so she was lying down.

"I want you between my legs," Hélène replied as she pulled herself further up the bed until her head rested on the pillows at the top. Kim crawled her way up the bed, her eyes fixed on Hélène's.

"You have too many clothes on." Kim reached for Hélène's bikini bottoms and tugged them down, throwing them unceremoniously to the floor. Hélène watched as Kim surveyed her pussy, instinctively licking her lips. Kim obviously wanted to taste her, but Hélène wanted something else.

"Take my top off," she ordered. Kim's gaze flicked up to Hélène. She looked as if she was deciding whether she wanted to protest Hélène's command.

Hélène was far from dominant in bed. For most of her dalliances she would go along with whatever her partner wanted, but with Kim she had the overwhelming need to have Kim's clit pressed against her own.

She briefly worried that Kim wouldn't enjoy Hélène's demanding tone. The last thing she wanted was for Kim to feel uncomfortable. Hélène could have kicked herself as it occurred to her that Kim had just broken up with someone because they'd tried to control her. *Fuck.* Hélène desperately tried to read Kim's facial expressions. She almost cried out in happiness when she saw a wide smile radiate from Kim's face.

Kim leaned in, whipping off Hélène's tank top before reaching round her neck to untie her bikini top. The garment was quickly discarded. Kim then leaned back on her knees between Hélène's legs, her eyes roaming over Hélène's naked body.

"You're beautiful." Hélène blushed. She wasn't someone who handled compliments well under normal circumstances. A compliment coming from someone as breathtaking as Kim felt unbelievable. Her face must have conveyed her feelings, because

144

a slight frown graced Kim's perfect face. "Hey —" she squeezed Hélène's thighs to get her full attention, " —you *are* beautiful."

"Come here." Hélène reached for Kim, spreading her legs wide, allowing Kim to slip between them so she was lying over her completely. A low groan escaped Kim.

"Fuck, you feel good." Kim licked down Hélène's throat.

"Spread me." For the first time since they had started, Kim looked unsure of herself. Hélène reached down between them, spreading open her lips. Kim followed her every move.

"Now you," Hélène whispered. Kim's nimble fingers moved gently. She lifted herself a little to allow her hand to stroke down her slit, spreading herself open as she went. Hélène's free hand gently grasped Kim's arse, wasting no time pulling her back down so their clits were touching. Kim let out an audible gasp. Hélène drew in a sharp breath.

"I've never done this before." Kim spoke so softly, Hélène had almost missed what she had said.

"Are you uncomfortable?"

"No, not at all, it just feels... I just feel —"

Hélène cut her off by drawing Kim's head down into a scorching kiss. Kim's hips immediately started rocking into Hélène's. The feeling was deliciously intense. Hélène already knew that she would come quickly. She'd been so turned on it was unlikely she would last even a couple of minutes.

"Oh, my —" Kim gasped. Hélène took Kim's head into her hands.

"Look at me," she said with ragged breaths. "Look at me while we come together." Kim didn't reply. She simply nodded as she struggled to keep her eyes open.

"Hélène."

"Yes... yes, Kim, keep going."

"I can't hold on," Kim cried. Her hips were rocking furiously, her arms shaking as her body relented to her orgasm.

Hélène's own pleasure was building so strongly she thought she would pass out.

In a moment of pure ecstasy, Hélène felt a clarity of mind like never before. She felt as if she was floating above herself. Her brain and body felt nothing but absolute rapture as she came loudly and with abandon. Blood pulsed through her ears as she regained her senses. She looked at Kim, who had collapsed to her chest, her breathing heavy and deep.

"Are you okay?" she asked, lifting Kim's head with her hands that were still clutching the side of Kim's face.

"That…" Kim panted.

"Was divine," Hélène finished. Kim nodded her head in agreement.

"I've never come so hard before or so fast," Kim said, letting out a breathy laugh. Hélène smiled at her. She should tell Kim that she too had never come so hard, but she wouldn't, in fear of everything else she was feeling tumbling out.

Hélène had felt something break open inside her as she'd climaxed, something that was terrifying because she was guaranteed to get hurt if she dared speak it out loud.

* * *

A warm breeze licked Hélène's skin, stirring her from a most delightful sleep. She stretched her body, which ached, reminding her of what had transpired earlier. Her eyes whipped open at the memory of her and Kim together. Her head instinctively turned to look for Kim, but she was gone. Hélène's heart rate picked up. A sense of dread seeped through her veins.

Willing herself to remain calm, she propped her body up against the headboard. She just needed a few moments to compose herself before she went looking for Kim. If Kim had

146

decided that what they'd done was a mistake, Hélène would be devastated, but she would also have to respect Kim's wishes.

The sound of the balcony door interrupted her dark thoughts. Kim stepped through, wrapped in the sheer robe she had been wearing earlier. Hélène's heartbeat was dangerously high as she waited to see what Kim would say.

"You sleep like the dead," Kim chuckled. The levity in her voice washed over Hélène like a cleansing bath.

"You wore me out," Hélène replied, allowing herself to breathe normally for the first time since she had woken to an empty bed.

"Clearly. Who knew you were such a lightweight?" Kim smirked. Hélène saw Kim's eyes slip down to her chest. Under Kim's gaze, Hélène suddenly felt self-conscious. It was different when they were in the throes of passion, but now in the cold light of day, Hélène worried Kim wouldn't look at her with the same adoration.

Reflexively, she drew the sheet up to cover herself. After a few silent moments, Hélène cleared her throat. "Maybe we should talk about what happened?"

"Probably." Kim walked over to the bed, where she sat looking at the floor. Hélène understood she needed a little time to arrange her thoughts. What they had done couldn't be taken lightly. Hélène never took sex lightly. Yes, it could be fun, a great way to blow off steam, but it still involved two people with emotions.

"Can I start?" she asked. Kim turned her head slightly.

"Yes, of course."

"I need you to know that for me, it wasn't a mistake. I am very attracted to you, Kim, and what we did was beyond anything I could dream."

147

Kim puffed out a breath. "Wow, okay," she stated, "I don't regret it either Hélène, I told you this morning that I am attracted to you."

"Okay, so why do I feel there is more going on? You wear your emotions on your face, Kim, it's adorable, really."

"I wasn't honest with you, well I was, but I don't think you quite understood at the time," Kim began. Her eyes were wide, and she was looking uncomfortable.

Hélène stilled in the bed. What had she lied about? Oh fuck, was she still with Greg? Hélène was no cheat, she would never get involved with someone that was attached. "You need to tell me, Kim, because my mind is coming up with things that are frankly terrifying."

"Oh no, no don't panic, it's not that bad, well I hope not."

"Okay, can you just tell me?"

Kim straightened her shoulders, gearing herself up. "Okay, so when we were... you know..." Kim gestured her head, her finger pointing between them.

"When we were having sex," Hélène supplied.

"Yes... well, I told you I'd never done that before."

"Didn't you like it? Oh god."

"No, I loved it, Hélène, it was like nothing I have ever experienced before. Can you stop interrupting and let me finish?"

"Sorry," Hélène mumbled.

"What I meant was that I'd done none of that before, with a woman, I mean."

"Okay," Hélène breathed. If that was the only thing that Kim wanted to confess, she would be over the moon.

"You're not bothered?" Kim was clearly surprised by Hélène's lack of reaction.

"Of course I'm bothered, but not in the way you probably think. I'm honoured to have been your first experience with a

148

woman. I pray it lived up to your expectations. Kim, you're a grown woman. I don't believe you would have slept with me if you didn't want to. I was more worried that you have only just split from Greg and now we are doing this."

"I have a lot of feelings at the minute. A lot has happened recently. I can't argue with that, but I don't want you to think that you're some kind of experiment or rebound. You're so much more than that."

"I must admit, it's nice to hear you say that. Where do we go from here?"

"I honestly don't know. I have things to work through, but I really, really enjoyed what we did earlier."

"Me, too."

"Could we just carry on as we have been? Enjoy spending time together, getting to know one another on this beautiful boat?"

"You didn't answer the part about the sex living up to your expectations," Hélène said earnestly.

Kim reached out and took her hand. "You do not know how far beyond my expectations that was, Hélène."

Relief washed over her. She wanted Kim to revel in the experience. The first time with a woman was precious and Kim deserved to be treated like the goddess she was. Plus, Hélène was only human. Her ego needed to be placated, too.

"Okay, good. I would like to enjoy our time together, but what happens when I want to kiss you again? Because I'm going to want to kiss you again, Kim."

"Then you kiss me. I would just like us to take our time."

"Of course, you set the pace."

"Thank you." Kim shifted a little further up the bed toward Hélène. "I don't think you really need this." She tugged the sheet down from Hélène's body. Hélène smiled widely. She liked this pace, she liked it a lot.

149

"Come here." Gesturing for Kim to lie over her. "I have a lot of things to show you," she grinned. Oh yes, she had plenty of things she was going to show this wonderful woman.

Chapter 13

This was the second time that Kim had woken before Hélène. The first was after Hélène had blown Kim's mind with breathtaking sex. Her initial reaction when she'd woken the first time had been to panic as she'd looked down at Hélène sleeping soundly.

Panic because it was the first time Kim had slept with a woman, panic because she'd jumped into bed with someone just after leaving her long-term boyfriend and panic because she had no idea how the woman sleeping next to her would react when she woke.

After watching Hélène for a few minutes longer, Kim had had to get some space so she could get some perspective. The last thing she wanted was for Hélène to think she'd done a runner, so the only safe place to go was the balcony. Far enough from Hélène to think clearly, but not too far that she looked as if she was trying to escape.

The sun had been high in the sky when she'd sat down in one of the chairs just outside her suite. Hélène was obviously a deep sleeper because Kim had made more than enough noise to wake her as she'd made coffee and grabbed a leftover pastry to nibble on. She'd work up an appetite. The thought made her grin like the Cheshire cat.

Kim needed to organise her thoughts. Number one on her list was to examine how she felt about sleeping with a woman for the first time. Kim had dated one other person apart from Greg in her life, a girl called Heather, but that had been when she was in high school; so apart from a few pecks on the lips, her only experience had been with Greg.

Sex had never been an issue with Greg. They were compatible. It wasn't earth-shattering, but it was good. Kim hadn't spent any time fantasising about sleeping with a woman because she'd been happy with her boyfriend. When things between her and Greg had soured, she could admit she'd thought about women more often.

Sleeping with Hélène had been a complete surprise. Admitting her feelings had been a big step. She'd hoped that Hélène would reciprocate how she felt, but having her turn up at her suite and take her so goddamn thoroughly had been astounding.

Also, to Kim's complete shock, she'd been the one to take the lead. Guiding Hélène down to her knees, demanding she ate her out, was very much out of character for Kim.

Greg had always initiated sex. They'd always followed the same pattern; that being Greg feeling up her boobs before entering her. Foreplay hadn't been very important to them, but now Kim realised she'd been missing out.

After several minutes of correlating all that information, Kim concluded that she was very much okay with her first experience being with Hélène. The pleasure she'd experienced was indescribable; plus, she'd felt safe and in control.

The next area of her discomfort was that she'd slept with Hélène without considering Greg. They'd been together for a long time. They'd shared all their achievements and life goals with each other. Yes, Greg had crossed a line and Kim knew she couldn't go back to being his life partner, but that didn't stop her from feeling that she'd effectively dumped him and moved on.

How could she reconcile the fact that she was so attracted to Hélène that she'd been unable to stop herself from touching her and being touched with the fact that she still cared about Greg? She wasn't in love with him, but she also didn't want him to be hurt by her actions.

As she'd sat thinking about it on the balcony, she'd realised *that issue* needed time. She just hoped that Hélène would be okay with it. Speaking of, would Hélène be okay with everything that they'd done?

As she'd swallowed the last dregs of her coffee, she'd noticed the time. Kim had sat on the balcony for almost an hour, thinking. The rustling of bed sheets had alerted her to Hélène waking.

Steeling herself, she'd gone back into the suite to find Hélène sat upright with the sheet barely covering her body. Kim had had to stop herself from flinging herself at the French beauty once again. Thankfully, she'd controlled herself and they'd talked.

Hélène regretted nothing and was happy to go at a pace that Kim set. She hadn't even reacted strongly to her being Kim's first sexual experience with a woman. Once they'd finished talking, Kim's resolve had shattered. The sight of Hélène laying there, naked and wonderfully tussled, had been too much. So, Kim had started another round of life-altering sex.

So, here she was again, staring down at Hélène's perfect body. This time, however, she felt no panic, only the remnants of pleasure that she'd experienced an hour earlier. Kim looked at the time. They'd been locked in her suite for going on six hours. They'd missed lunch completely, and it made Kim wonder if Holly and the others had noticed their absence, or worse, heard them going at it?

Slipping out of the bed, Kim headed for the bathroom to clean up. It wasn't the best idea to wake Hélène before she had the chance to shower and dress because she knew they would end up fucking in the shower and then probably again after. As much as Kim wanted to — and boy, did her body want that — she really *did* want them to take it slow.

Yes, they were explosive between the sheets. Their chemistry was incomparable, but they needed time to get to know each other. They'd had plenty of discussions over the past week, but Kim recognised there was still a lot more to learn.

Kim also needed to know that Hélène was going to be okay with Greg. Whatever happened between them, he was always going to be in her life in some way or another, and Hélène had to be on board with that.

The warm water of the shower caressed her skin. Her body ached, but she was sated and happy. She took her time washing and drying her hair, applying a little light makeup before donning the bikini she had stripped off hours earlier. Hélène was still out for the count, which made Kim laugh out loud. It made her wonder how much noise she could actually get away with making before Hélène would finally be disturbed.

As she pondered the idea of putting on some music to test her theory, there was a knock on her door. Kim positioned herself so that Hélène would be out of sight when she opened it up to whoever was on the other side.

"Hi, Kim." Of course it was Holly on the other side of the door. Who else? If Kim were a petty person, she would have shut the door in her face, but alas, she was a mature adult. Holly's behaviour toward her had been out of line this morning, especially considering they didn't even know each other and, to Kim's knowledge, had done nothing to warrant it.

"Hi, Holly, what's up?"

"Have you seen Hélène?"

"She's asleep," Kim said curtly. Why should she pander to a bully? She also wouldn't hide the fact that she and Hélène were more than just friends now, either.

"Oh, okay, could you get her to go to the bridge when she's awake? We're going to be docking off Corsica soon and she wanted to talk to the captain before they dropped anchor."

"I'll tell her, thanks." Kim gave a tight smile as she softly closed the door.

Putting her ill feeling towards Holly aside, Kim made her way over to the bed. Hélène was lying on her front with her head buried between the pillows. Kim found it miraculous the woman could still breathe.

"H," she cooed gently as she rubbed Hélène's back. She repeated her ministrations with no success. Kim laughed again. Hélène was too fucking adorable. "Hélène," she called louder. "Doll, you've got to wake up." Kim shook Hélène's shoulder repeatedly until she finally got a response.

"Mmmmm," Hélène groaned sleepily, causing another chuckle to escape Kim.

"Come on, sleepyhead, you have to see the captain. We've arrived in Corsica."

"Two more minutes," Hélène grumbled, pushing her head farther into the pillows. Kim took an exasperated breath.

155

She had to do something drastic because at this rate, she would still be trying to get Hélène out of bed at nightfall.

"H, you have ten seconds to roll over and open your eyes or there will be consequences." Hélène grunted, leaving Kim no choice. "Okay, you asked for it," she sang as she made her way over to the fridge to retrieve a bottle of water. It was going to soak the sheets, but Hélène was stubbornly refusing to wake up.

In point five seconds, Hélène flew out of bed as the water Kim poured out of the bottle hit her square in the head. "*Putain bordel*," she cried, staggering to get her balance.

"I'm sorry, H, but you left me no choice." Hélène stood naked as the day she was born with water dripping down her neck. If Kim wasn't slightly terrified at the look in Hélène's eyes, she would have laughed.

"You're going to pay for that."

Kim did not like the gleam in Hélène's eye. "Now hold on a minute—" Kim held her palms raised up in a surrender, " — you forced me to do it." She backed away from Hélène, who had a maniacal grin etched on her face.

Kim rounded the bed as Hélène stalked her with the grace of a lioness stalking its prey. "H, I've just done my makeup," Kim pleaded because she knew exactly what kind of punishment Hélène was going to deliver, and she was very turned on by it.

Her pleas fell on deaf ears as Hélène launched herself at Kim, causing them to tumble on the bed, both of them laughing wildly. It was safe to say that Hélène was late visiting the captain and Kim had to shower and reapply her makeup.

* * *

After Hélène departed to speak to the captain, Kim took the diving book Hélène gave her at breakfast to read by the pool. It didn't take her long to be completely lost in the text. The book

156

explained all the different aspects of diving, including the pieces of equipment that Hélène had brushed over when they had shopped in Saint Tropez.

Kim was especially taken with the theory side of it. She thoroughly enjoyed learning about dive times at different depths. Hélène had been right this morning. The physics and math involved were ridiculously easy for Kim, and, in no time, she could calculate how long they could dive on a tank of air at different depths.

She was testing her memory retention when Hélène stepped out of the sliding doors. "Hey." Hélène had a bright smile, lighting up her face.

"Hey you, did you get everything sorted with the ol' cap-i-tain?"

Hélène chuckled. "Yes, we are anchoring just off of Corsica, a place called Calvi. Have you heard of it?"

"Sorry, no, I'm a bit shit with French geography outside of Paris," Kim confessed.

"That's fine. I'll enjoy teaching you," Hélène winked.

Kim was pleased that they could carry on as normal. She'd worried that sex would change their dynamic and make things awkward, but so far, it was business as usual. Well, not quite. They were now free to ogle each other openly and steal kisses. "Oh yes, I am an outstanding student."

"Lesson number one then—" Hélène grabbed Kim's hand, dragging her out of the chair and through the doors Hélène had just exited, "—you need to know where we are, so let's take a peek at a map."

They made their way up the stairs to the top deck. A table sat in the centre of the room with several maps strewn across. The captain sat in his chair at the front, scanning the horizon. Kim was impressed with all the equipment laid out in front of him. It made her wonder how long it would take someone to learn to captain a vessel of this size.

"Here, look." Hélène gestured to a map she had rolled out covering the others. Kim bent over the table to look. Sure enough, it was a map of Corsica with a red cross jotted just off of the North coast. "We are here." Hélène pointed to the cross. "We will eventually traverse the entire west coast of the island, stopping to dive several times." Kim nodded in silent understanding. "I've started us off in Calvi because it's a great place for you to learn to dive. Look." She pointed, drawing Kim's eyes to the place Hélène's delicious finger rested. *Stop it*, she chastised herself. Hélène was trying to teach her something and all she could do was lust after the woman's talented fingers.

"This is Calvi, and this is the Citadel. It's beautiful at night. The entire Citadel and the surrounding cliffs are lit up with coloured lights. If you want to see it, we can have dinner tonight on the observation deck?"

"Yes, please, that sounds wonderful." Hélène beamed at Kim's response, eliciting a wide smile in return. Hélène cleared her throat and tore her eyes away from Kim, which left her feeling disappointed.

"So, my plan is for us to complete your baptême at the base of the Citadel. It's a perfect place for you to learn. Once I'm confident and you're confident, we can dive deeper. There is a sunken bomber plane that lies around twenty-seven metres down. I think that after a few dives, you could handle it."

"You haven't seen me dive yet. I could be terrible." Kim's nerves were bubbling up to the surface. Learning to scuba dive was wonderful, and she was more than excited, but she was also worried about letting Hélène down if she wasn't a natural. Hélène was clearly passionate about the sport and Kim wanted more than anything to share in that passion.

158

"Stop worrying. I have a gut feeling that you're going to be great," Hélène replied reassuringly.

"Okay, well I'll do anything you ask." Kim spoke before realising how that sounded. She could see that Hélène's mind had gone to the same place because she smirked and raised one of her perfect eyebrows. "You know what I mean," Kim whispered playfully, shoving Hélène's shoulder.

"I know what you mean," Hélène laughed. "I saw you were reading the book I gave you. How did you find it?"

"Oh, it was fascinating, thank you. I finished it just before you came to get me."

"You finished the whole thing?"

"Yes, I'm a fast reader," Kim smiled. Little did Hélène know how fast she was. Kim devoured books. Her parents had encouraged her to read as much as possible when she was small and when it became clear that Kim was gifted, they did everything in their power to encourage Kim's learning.

"Great, do you want to go grab a cocktail and let me test you?"

"Bring it on." Kim wiggled her eyebrows, making Hélène laugh, rolling her eyes playfully. They headed back down to the pool and sat at the table that had been set up for breakfast earlier in the day.

"Okay, let's run through some hand signals." Hélène began. Her posture said she was all business.

"Hit me."

"Okay, what does this mean?" Hélène clenched her hand into a fist, leaving her thumb sticking out, pointing it down.

"That means that we are going to submerge."

"Correct, next." Hélène spread her hand out, palm facing down, moving her wrist back and forth, causing her hand to look like it was a seesaw.

"That means that there is a problem. You would make that sign and then point to the thing that is causing an issue. So, for example, I would make the sign and then point to my head if I had a headache, or to my leg if I had a cramp."

"Perfect. You really are a fast learner," Hélène chimed.

"It's fun to learn," Kim supplied.

"Okay, let's go over some other important things you need to learn." Kim nodded. She was having a lot of fun.

Over the space of several hours, Hélène took Kim through the book, making sure she understood everything. Kim was more than impressed with Hélène's knowledge.

They briefly separated so that they could dress for dinner, which Hélène informed her would be a casual affair. Kim still attempted to look good, though. She couldn't help but want Hélène's attention focused solely on her.

The view of Calvi and the Citadel was breathtaking. Multicoloured lights lit up the Citadel and the cliff it stood on. Kim was in heaven as she sat on a comfy sofa with Hélène gazing out over the city with a piña colada in hand.

They'd continued to talk about diving, Kim throwing questions at Hélène now and then. Kim learned that Hélène had been scuba diving since she was sixteen and she was licenced to teach diving commercially, which made sense considering her dream was to open her own dive centre.

Over the course of the evening, David, and Leo joined them. Kim sat back and listened to them discuss the first dive, which was scheduled for first thing in the morning. Holly waltzed over several minutes after Leo and David, looking as if she'd already had a few to drink.

"What we talking about?" Holly said, slurring slightly.

"Just planning Kim's baptême tomorrow. Will you be joining us?" Hélène was a little colder than usual.

"I'm surprised," Holly began.

160

"Surprised with what?" Kim interrupted. Her gut feeling was telling her that Holly was about to ruin their wonderful evening.

"Surprised Hélène can keep her head out of your pussy long enough to do some fucking diving."

The silence that encompassed the observation deck was potent. Holly's remark had left Kim breathless in the most horrible of ways. She chanced a look at Hélène, whose face was so severe it scared Kim a little.

"What did you just say?" Hélène seethed.

"I'm fucking about, calm down," Holly said, backtracking, she knew she'd just fucked up royally.

"Repeat what you just said," Hélène barked.

"I was joking. C'mon, Hélène, you used to laugh at the stupid shit I say." Holly squirmed in her seat.

"*Répète maintenant.*"

Holly's eyes darted from one person to the next. "I said that I was surprised you could keep your head out of Kim's pussy long enough to dive." Her delivery was flat.

"And you think that is an appropriate way to talk to me and my guest?" Hélène was almost shouting. "Get out of my sight, Holly, go to your cabin and sober up, I will deal with you tomorrow. *Comprendre*?"

"I'm sorry, Hélène, please. I was thoughtless, my stupid sense of humour, that's all."

"No, Holly, you don't get to use that excuse this time. I will find you tomorrow. Now leave." Holly cast one more gaze around the people staring at her before leaving. Kim sat silently, not knowing how to handle the situation.

"Kim," Hélène said cautiously. "I'm so very sorry for that. I have no excuse to give for such poor behaviour."

"It's not your fault, H." She hated the pained look Hélène now sported.

161

"You are my guest on this boat and should not have to deal with such an unsavoury character as the one Holly has displayed this evening." Kim looked at David and Leo, who were both looking at their feet. She needed to turn the night around. She was damned if she was going to let Holly spoil it for them all.

"Thank you for saying that. Now I, for one, could do with a top up. David, would you do the honours, kind sir?"

"Of course, my dear lady." David stood and gave Kim a little bow and a wink.

"Leo, could you put a bit of music on? I feel the need to dance."

"Sí," Leo shouted enthusiastically. Kim turned to Hélène, who was watching her curiously.

"Hélène, can you let go of what just happened? For me? Tomorrow I'm putting myself in your capable hands, but I'm still a little nervous. I need to unwind tonight and have fun so that I don't take any kind of negativity with me underwater. Can you do that for me? Relax and enjoy the evening?" Kim watched as Hélène studied her silently. Kim waited patiently for Hélène to decide. After several silent moments, Hélène let her chest deflate. She reached for her drink and downed it entirely.

"Care to boogie?"

Kim's head rocked backwards as she laughed loudly in relief. "Who the hell says boogie nowadays?"

"I do," Hélène replied, sticking out her tongue.

"Yes, Hélène, I would love to dance." They made their way over to the centre of the observation deck, where Leo was already gyrating alone. They applauded his effort and danced right alongside him.

The music pumped, vibrating through Kim's body. She watched as Hélène let herself dance without care. This woman utterly dazzled her. She had to keep her wits about her because

162

she knew it would be far too easy to lose herself in Hélène DuBois.

Chapter 14

The sun was just making an appearance over the horizon as Hélène made her way through the boat to the wheelhouse. It was a habit she had formed over the years.

"Hélène, good morning."

"Good morning, Bobby, how's it looking out there today?"

"Like paradise, as usual, Hélène."

"A good day to dive, then?" Hélène already knew the answer. She'd been awake an hour already to do her pre-dive checks, and she'd studied the weather fastidiously to make sure conditions would be perfect for Kim's baptême. She certainly wasn't above cancelling the dive if the weather would be anything but perfect. Thankfully, this morning report informed her it was going to be a calm day with little wind.

"You know it, kiddo, you champing at the bit to get in the water?" He chuckled, knowing her far too well.

"God, yes," she laughed. "It feels like an eternity since I've been down there."

"How do you think Kim will do?" Hélène loved that Bobby paid attention to the guests she brought on board. He always made sure they felt welcome. Hopefully, Hélène could spend some time with him and Kim before they departed for home.

Bobby was in his late fifties and had joined *Connie* as her captain when JJ had purchased her. Bobby and her father were friends from school, although Bobby was a few years younger than her dad. The great thing about the captain was that he was nothing like Philippe DuBois, in that he was affectionate and kind. Philippe could barely pass as cordial most days.

"We'll see when we're out there, but I'm confident." Hélène knew that Kim would succeed. It was just how she was. She excelled at everything she did, in Hélène's opinion.

"Is it the same crew diving?" Hélène hesitated before speaking. On a normal day, Hélène would dive with Leo, David, and Holly, but after last night's performance, Hélène didn't think she could be within a few metres of Holly because she wanted to rip her fucking head off.

Hélène had been mortified when Holly belligerently spewed her venomous words out in front of Kim last night. She had absolutely no idea what the hell had gotten into her friend. No doubt they would have words, but Hélène couldn't focus on that right now. The most important thing for her to do was make sure Kim's baptême went off without a hitch and, for that to happen, Hélène had to have her head firmly in the game.

The dive wasn't due to happen for a couple of hours, but there was plenty to do before then. Leo and David had stowed the gear onto the Zodiac that was mounted to the back of *Connie*.

Hélène had already checked and rechecked their breathing apparatus, vests, and tanks. It was likely she would check them several more times before they hit the water.

Her primary goal was to make Kim feel comfortable and safe. Scuba diving was a sensational experience, and Hélène hoped Kim would get as much out of it as she had when she'd first started.

Hélène scanned the water one more time from the giant window before saying her goodbyes to Bobby and heading down to the dining room. David had already asked the kitchen staff to provide a healthy and light breakfast for them all.

Hélène had told Kim the time she needed her to be ready, which was quickly approaching. Pushing through the doors to the dining room, Hélène was surprised to see Holly sitting at the table eating breakfast, her wetsuit hanging around her waist.

"Are you kidding me?" Hélène spat, her anger from last night returning in force.

"No, it's no joke. I know we need to talk about my behaviour last night and we will. You can scream and shout all you want. I know I deserve it, but for now, we need to put it on the back burner. We always dive together on *Connie*. It's been that way for years and I will not tank our tradition just because I was an arsehole."

"There is no need for you to come along."

"No, you're right. There isn't a practical need, but that doesn't matter. Our issues will be dealt with later. Please don't freeze me out. It's the first dive of the trip. You know how special that is."

"*Our* issues?"

"My issues," Holly stated.

"I'm not sure Kim will want you around either, to be frank. I think she's had quite enough of your unwarranted

166

outbursts against her. Today is supposed to be fun and relaxing. How the hell is she supposed to do that with you there?"

"I have already been to her cabin, Hélène. I have apologised profusely and assured her I will never again speak out of turn like that."

Hélène stood for a second, deliberating her next words. "Fine, if Kim is okay with it you can come, but you will stay on the boat. Whether or not you have apologised, Kim will still be on edge with you, and I can't afford that when she is trying to learn."

"Fine, no problem and then after the dive, we'll talk," Holly stated, more than asked. Hélène could agree to those terms. They had been friends for a long time, and Hélène desperately wanted some answers.

With a curt nod, Hélène took the seat opposite Holly and ate her breakfast. A few minutes later, David and Leo sat down, their wetsuits also hanging around their waists. Under normal circumstances, Hélène would be happy to see her friends sitting around the table excited about the first dive, but this morning was proving to be difficult.

Holly had really upset Hélène with her outbursts and she was struggling to find her equilibrium. That was until Kim swayed into the room like a goddamn angel. Hélène couldn't stop her face from lighting up even if she tried.

Holly had put a downer on everything, but one look at Kim's beautiful face made everything alright again. Hélène was momentarily lost in her memories of their early hour activities together. Back to the hours of touching, licking, and kissing.

"Morning, all," Kim chirped, shifting her gaze from one person to the next to make sure they knew she was talking to them all, even Holly.

"*Buongiorno*," Leo returned, raising his glass of water up to Kim.

167

"Morning," David mumbled — he was worse than Hélène at waking up in the morning. His grumble didn't seem to faze Kim though as she lowered herself into the chair next to Hélène, laughing.

"Not a morning person, David?" she teased.

"Mmm," was the only response she got, which made her laugh more.

"Morning you," Kim said a little quieter to Hélène when she'd stop laughing.

"Morning. How did you sleep?"

"Wonderfully, for some reason I was tuckered out," she winked. Hélène grinned and blushed. She shot a quick look at her tablemates to see if they were listening. The only person looking at her was Holly, but she quickly diverted her eyes when she caught Hélène's gaze.

"Well, I hope you're good and rested. You'll be tuckered out again by the end of the day. It can be quite taxing when you first dive."

"I'm ready and raring to go." Kim grabbed for a banana. Her body looked as if it was twitching with excitement.

The group sat for another half an hour before Leo and David excused themselves to prepare the diving boat.

"Okay, let's go, I sat all your gear on the deck. We will get you ready and then go over some ground rules, okay?" Hélène had to put herself into work mode, she couldn't afford to be distracted by Kim and her orgasm-inducing body that was covered by a black one-piece suit but still showed off all of her best assets.

Hélène helped Kim with her wetsuit. It was just as funny as the day she'd tried to put it on in the shop. Kim, looking all flustered, was sexy as hell. *Keep it in your pants, DuBois.*

"Okay, so the wetsuit is on, finally," Hélène teased. "How are you feeling?"

"Good, now that bit's over with," Kim huffed.

"Okay, next I'm going to take you over your equipment. I have already attached your vest to your tank and fitted the breathing equipment, but I would still like you to get into the habit of checking it yourself."

"Gotcha!"

"Okay, first, check that the tank is secured to your vest." Kim leaned down and tugged on the tank.

"Seems okay?" she said unconvincingly.

"The best way to check is to grab the top of your vest and lift. If the tank is properly attached, there will be no movement. If the tank slips at all, it means the strap needs tightening."

Kim gave a nod and lifted the vest. "Holy cow, how heavy is this thing?"

Hélène laughed. "You know how heavy it is, but I understand that knowing the weight and feeling it for yourself is quite different. Remember, it's easier in the water."

"It better be," Kim grumbled playfully.

"Okay, so the tank is secure. Now we want to make sure all the tubes to the breathing apparatus are secured. The best way to do that is to open up the tank, allowing air through. Once that's done, we are going to inflate the vest a little, making sure the system is working whilst also checking the amount of air in your tank."

Hélène pointed Kim to the areas she needed to check when the tank was open. She explained as much as she could and in as much detail as possible, knowing that Kim would appreciate it. Once she was sure that Kim was comfortable with their equipment, she signalled Leo to haul it on board the Zodiac.

"I can't believe you have another boat," Kim said, disbelievingly.

"I chose it actually, after JJ bought *Connie*. We knew we would want to dive a lot when we were together and it seemed silly to rent something. So, JJ gave me the all clear, and we bought this. Now we can dive whenever we want," Hélène smiled.

"Sounds heavenly," Kim sighed.

"It is, and now you get to enjoy it, too." With one last smile and one last ogle, Hélène ushered Kim onto the Zodiac. David and Leo were occupying themselves with the boat whilst Hélène and Kim stood up front next to Holly, who was driving.

"All ready?" she called to no one in particular.

"Yup, let's go," David answered. Holly nodded and threw down the throttle. Hélène was used to the sudden thrust, but Kim wasn't. She stumbled backwards, straight into Hélène's waiting arms. If Hélène had the choice, they would stay like that for the rest of the trip, but she didn't want to distract either of them from the task at hand.

"You okay?" she shouted over the roar of the engine.

"Perfect." Kim's face beamed back. Hélène sighed in contentment. Being here with Kim gave her the exquisite feeling of unbridled happiness.

* * *

The journey to the dive spot took them five minutes. The sea was completely flat, which allowed the Zodiac to glide over the surface with ease. Hélène turned her face to the sun for the entire ride. This was her happy place, where she was completely at ease. She cast her attention to Kim as the boat slowed. "Stop worrying, I can see it on your face."

"Sorry, I'm just nervous."

"To be expected, but I promise, as soon as you go under, your worries will evaporate. Trust me."

170

"I trust you."

Hélène nodded. Their eyes were still locked onto each other. Hélène could feel her heart race. She wanted to lean in and kiss Kim, but she wasn't sure if that would be okay. Kim captured her lips in a sweet and all too brief kiss, silencing any worries. Hélène smiled shyly, touching her fingers to her lips. God, all Hélène wanted to do with this woman was dive into her. No holding back. Give her everything, all in, all the way. *Stop it, focus.*

"Are we all set?" she called to her crew.

"Set, Hélène," Leo shouted. He and David had already put on their gear.

"Okay, Kim, let's get your wetsuit zipped up."

"Let's do it," Kim said with a confidence that had been missing before the kiss. Hélène hoped it was the contact they shared that had bolstered her.

"Alright Kim, I'm going to enter the water first. Once I signal, you can drop in. Myself and Leo will help you put your vest on, in the water, okay?

"Okay."

"David, can you be our designated photographer?"

"Aye, aye, captain."

Hélène turned back to Kim. "Your first dive is all about fun. You just have to come along for the ride. Me and Leo will do the hard work," she winked.

Satisfied that Kim was doing well, Hélène put her kit on, double-checking that everything was as it should be. Hélène took a calming breath before she tumbled backwards into the water. As usual, her world spun out of control for a second as she rolled underwater. Once she was the right way up, she inflated her vest, broke the surface and gave the obligatory "okay" sign.

171

Her body hummed with delight as she adjusted herself to her watery surroundings. Hélène gave the nod to Holly, signalling she was ready for Kim to enter the water. Hélène watched and laughed out loud as Kim joyfully jumped off the side of the boat as carefree as a child.

"Okay?" she called to Kim once she had resurfaced. Kim nodded with a big smile on her face. Slowly Hélène made her way over to Kim. They bobbed up and down, waiting for Leo to join them.

"Let's get you dressed." Leo inflated Kim's vest and gestured for her to slip her arms through. The process only took a couple of minutes. Leo and Hélène were like a well-oiled machine, although trying to get Kim's flippers on was a fun experience. They had to stop several times because Kim couldn't control her laughter as she rolled about in the water.

"We're going to descend now. I will regulate the air in your vest so you don't have to worry about anything. Just enjoy yourself."

"Okay," Kim sang.

"Leo and David, can you go first? I'll stick with Kim and we'll come down together. We are stopping at five metres."

"Roger that," Leo supplied, emptying his vest of air, allowing him to slip beneath the surface with ease, David following close behind.

"I know there is a lot to remember, so you must tell me if you're feeling overwhelmed. Remember the most important thing I told you about when we go down? If your ears hurt, signal and we will stop immediately. Take your time to clear the pressure in your ears. There is no rush," Hélène said seriously, holding onto Kim's vest.

"I'm good. I remember what you said about pinching my nose and swallowing to clear my ears." Kim was showing no signs of stress or anxiety, which helped Hélène relax.

"I'll be with you every step of the way. You will never be out of my sight and I will have a hold on you all the time."

"Okay then, I'm ready to scuba dive." Kim slipped her mouthpiece in and nodded, signalling her readiness. Hélène followed suit and lifted their inflating hoses. She gave the sign for them to dive, using the signal they had practised yesterday.

Hélène kept a watchful eye on Kim as they went down. Reaching five metres wouldn't take long, but she wanted them to take as much time as necessary. Kim was dealing with the alien notion of breathing underwater, plus the building pressure in her ears. Hélène didn't want her to rush. Safety first was paramount.

There were no signs of distress at all from Kim. Hélène signed to her asking if she was okay, which Kim signalled she was. They hit five metres and Hélène slowed them by pumping a little air into their vests. They levelled out and waited for Leo to join them. David swam around the trio, taking pictures.

Satisfied that everyone was okay, Hélène finally took the time to scan her surroundings. The cliffs of the Citadel were just off to their right. The visibility was excellent. Hélène had been on several dives where the visibility had been so low she could barely see her hand in front of her face.

She motioned to Kim, Leo, and David that she was ready to move. Hélène had explained the principles of swimming with flippers, but she was a firm believer that you could only learn by doing. Kim seemed to get the hang of it quickly, which didn't surprise her at all.

The four divers made their way slowly over to the rocks. Hélène stopped now and then pointing at the different corals and fish that were swimming around, she watched as Kim took it all in, she could see each time Kim saw something new that excited her because her eyes went wide and then creased as she smiled.

Hélène kept track of their depth, and the time they had been under. As much as she was enjoying herself, she understood Kim would tire out soon. She didn't want to exhaust her on the first dive because they could go again later in the afternoon.

Hélène turned herself gracefully in the water to face Leo, David, and Kim. She crossed her arms in an X shape to tell them the dive was over. Ascending could be tricky for beginners, but she had no intention of letting Kim attempt it on her own. Making sure that her grip on Kim's vest was tight, she moved them closer to the surface.

They broke the surface with no issues. Finally, Hélène felt as if she could breathe properly. It had been a textbook dive. Holly leaned over the side of the boat as they approached. Hélène was the first to get her gear off and hauled onto the boat. Leo and David followed next, allowing Hélène to help Kim.

Taking the vest and flippers off whilst bobbing about in the water was harder than it looked, but Kim managed it without too much trouble. Hélène grabbed hold of the handles that were placed on either side of the Zodiac, and with one pump of her feet, catapulted herself out of the water and onto the deck of the boat.

Holly had already dropped the steps for Kim, who was slowly making her way up and out of the water. Hélène recognised the signs of Kim's tired limbs, but her face registered nothing but elation.

"What do you think, then?" Hélène asked Kim when she had stepped onto the deck fully. Hélène was taken by surprise when Kim tackled her in a hug.

"Oh, Hélène, I can't even tell you," she panted. Hélène laughed. Kim's joy was infectious. "It was the best thing I've ever experienced. I mean, did you see all the little fish and the coral? Did you feel how warm the water was? I mean, it was a little

174

weird at first, but after I got used to the whole breathing underwater thing, it was as if we had entered another world."

"I knew you'd like it." Hélène tried desperately not to show how excited she was at Kim's reaction.

"Liked it? I loved it, doll," Kim squealed. Even Leo and David were grinning like idiots at Kim's exuberance.

"We can go again later if you want? As long as you're not too tired."

"Really?"

"Yes, really." Hélène laughed, still in Kim's arms. It felt good. Too good.

"Let's head back, grab some food and then reassess after." Everyone aboard nodded in agreement. Kim nodded with a lot more enthusiasm than the rest. *She's the perfect woman.*

The journey back to *Connie* was quick, the time flew as the group chatted animatedly about the dive and everything they had seen. Kim was firing off questions about the different corals and fish, which seemed to please David, who was an expert in marine life.

Once they were back on board *Connie,* Hélène spent some time filling out the necessary paperwork. She also spent some time with Leo and David debriefing. The morning had been so perfect that Hélène could only hope that the rest of the trip would be the same.

Chapter 15

Kim dived a total of ten times in Calvi. Her first experience underwater had been so exhilarating she was practically bouncing with excitement at the thought of doing it again.

Kim could fully understand why Hélène was so passionate about it. As soon as she descended into the depths, a calm washed over her. All the noise of the world vanished, replaced by the sounds of the ocean.

Hélène had explained that the sound underwater was magnified, it made the experience even more magical in Kim's eyes. She loved hearing her breath and the little bubbles crackle around her ears. The little swoosh sound that came after a fish zipped off to hide was wonderful.

On their third dive, Kim had almost forgotten to breathe properly when they were ascending to the surface. The sun was sending rays of light through the water, which highlighted the clouds of fish swimming around them and the vast amount of bubbles that the group produced.

It really was a wonderland and Kim couldn't wait to come back for more. She'd made Hélène laugh on several occasions with her impatience and eagerness to get back in the water. Hélène had repeated several times that they couldn't dive continuously, which Kim understood, but it didn't make her feel any less excited for the next time.

Now that Kim had reached ten dives, Hélène suggested they move on to the next dive site. The main town was called Galéria. Hélène seemed to be excited to dive there. There was a tunnel they could go through — if Kim was feeling confident — and a shipwreck. Kim was more than happy to try something a little different.

"Do you think you would be interested in taking the test today?" Hélène asked as they sat by the pool sipping cocktails. They'd gotten into somewhat of a routine lately. They would normally dive in the morning, sometimes again in the afternoon — if Kim wasn't feeling too tired — then they would retreat to their suites for a while to wash up or take a nap. Once they were feeling refreshed, they would sit by the pool with cocktails until the evening. Leo and David joined them now and then. Holly had kept herself busy, only stopping by to say hello and ask if Kim was enjoying herself.

"Yes, I'm ready." Kim could have taken the test days ago if she were being honest. It wasn't as if the questions were difficult. If she passed the written test and Hélène signed off on her proficiency, Kim would officially get her Level 1 diving title.

"Great, I'll grab the paper and let you get to it. I don't think it's going to take you very long," she scoffed playfully.

"Let me get some water down me first. I've had three of these bad boys already." Kim grinned, hoisting up her piña colada.

"No rush." Hélène winked as she made her way inside, presumably to get the test paper.

So far, they'd been on *Connie* for a week and a half. It was the longest time that Kim had ever been away from solid ground and she was loving every minute. Maybe in another life, where she hadn't settled down with Greg, she could have had a job as a Marine Biologist living life on the sea. It was a fantasy that Kim had been envisioning a lot recently. Her phone ringing brought her back to reality.

"Hey, Mum, I thought you would be in the air by now?" Kim had tried to keep track of the days which proved difficult sometimes, especially when she had purposefully limited her phone time, instead enjoying the ocean view and conversation.

"Change of plan, love," Joy replied. Kim heard a sliver of anxiety in her mum's voice.

"Everything okay?"

"It is with me and your dad," Joy sighed. "Greg, not so much."

"Greg? you've spoken to him?"

"Yes, after our conversation, I didn't want to wait too long to check up on him."

"Thanks, Mum. So what's going on?"

"Honestly, I'm not sure, doll. He is in a real mess. I've convinced him to come here for a few days. Whatever he's going through is impacting him severely. I stopped your dad from blowing off at him because, well, frankly, I don't think he could handle it. Did you notice anything out of the ordinary before you went away?"

Kim felt an enormous amount of guilt settle on her shoulders. She'd been so upset with his lack of effort in their relationship and how it was affecting her she hadn't really taken a close look at her partner. Had she missed something? Not that she could recall. Greg's behaviour had changed gradually over months. Nothing that would indicate something terrible had happened to him.

"No, nothing I can think of. Honestly, I thought it was just us growing apart, wanting different things, but from what you're saying, it seems that I should have picked up on something else."

"I didn't say that, love. Actually, I don't think that Greg really knew he had a problem until he became aggressive with you. When I spoke to him, he just kept apologising about the way he'd treated you. He sounded so broken, Kim, it was worrying. That's why I told him to come home. I don't think it's a good idea for him to be alone right now."

"Should I come home?"

"No, don't do that. He needs time and I think I'll have a better chance of getting to the bottom of things if it's just us. Your dad will talk to him about the incident. I can't stop him, but once that's done, I think we need to concentrate on the root cause of his behaviour."

"Can you let me know what happens? He's still my best friend. I hate to think that there has been something going on right under my nose and I didn't know."

"Kim, even though he is clearly having some troubles at the minute, that doesn't diminish the fact that your relationship changed and that he acted the way he did towards you. Please don't think I'm calling to make you feel bad because I'm not."

"Okay, it's just so upsetting. I can't help but feel guilty, Mum. Here I am swanning about on a luxury yacht with a woman that I'm attracted to when my ex-boyfriend of two weeks is having a breakdown. What kind of person does that make me?"

"Human. Kim, if you have been miserable for months, you have no reason to feel bad about getting away and taking care of your own well-being. I, for one, am thrilled that you love yourself enough to do it. As for your attraction to Hélène, well, that's not something you can control. You ended it with Greg. No one gets to determine how much time must pass before you are ready to move on, but you. Did something more happen with her?"

Kim remained silent. Her feelings for Hélène had increased tenfold since they'd slept together. Hélène was an amazing woman and an incredible lover. She made Kim feel seen and, if she dared say it, loved. But surely it was far too early for Kim to be ready to move onto something more serious.

"Yes, something happened. It wasn't planned."

"It's okay, love. As a parent, the only thing I want is your happiness. If Hélène is your happiness, then you have to take the risk."

"It's a tad early to know that, don't you think?"

"No, I don't think. I believe people can meet their soulmates and know instantly, call it love at first sight if you want. It doesn't matter, only you know what you feel and how strongly. Yes, the situation at the minute is hard, but don't let that stop you from going after the thing that will bring you joy, sweetheart."

"I just need some time to figure it all out. One reason I finally ended it with Greg was because I felt I'd lost a part of myself. I need to spend some time on me before I can get involved with someone again. Hélène understands that, she's been great. I told her I needed to go slow, and she seems fine with that."

"She sounds great, Kim."

"She is."

Kim spent the next half an hour on the phone with her mum, recapping all the diving adventures they'd been on. She explained in detail about the sights they'd seen beneath the waves. The one great thing about having professors as parents was that they were equally curious and eager to learn as Kim.

Greg lingered at the back of her mind throughout their conversation. Kim was happy that her parents were going to take care of him, but she was confused about her role in it all. Kim wanted to be there for her friend. Whatever was wrong went beyond their relationship. Greg had been suffering, and she hadn't known. Kim had been by his side every day since they were kids and it didn't sit well that she wasn't there with him now.

They wound down the conversation, promising to call with updates soon. Once the call ended, Kim took a few calming breaths. There was so much to unpack in her mind that she was feeling overwhelmed by it all.

"Hey, you okay?" Hélène asked. Kim realised Hélène must have overheard some of the conversation.

"I've been better." No point in lying.

"I didn't mean to eavesdrop, but I caught some of it. Is Greg okay?"

Trust Hélène to be kind and considerate of her ex. Kim couldn't say with all certainty that she would want to sit there listening about any of Hélène's ex girlfriends.

"No, he isn't. Not because I broke up with him, although that is upsetting him. I think he is more upset with himself for acting that way with me than with us actually breaking up. There is something going on with him. My parents have arranged for him to stay with them for a few days, to get to the bottom of it all."

Hélène sat quietly as Kim rambled on. It felt good to talk to someone. The thing she couldn't express, though, was her confusion about her feelings for the woman sitting in front of her. Even after hearing about how badly Greg was doing, Kim couldn't stop herself from wanting Hélène.

181

They'd had sex three times. They hadn't done it since the day Hélène took her by surprise in her room. Kim knew Hélène was leaving it up to her to initiate all things physical, but she secretly wished that Hélène would just take her.

But Kim had cooled things down between them — bedroom wise — for a reason. Yes, they stole kisses and touched each other, but that was all. She didn't want them to become so lost in the throes of passion that she lost sight of herself again. She had to keep a sensible head on her shoulders. Assess the risks before jumping in.

"Do you want to postpone the test?" Hélène asked cautiously.

"No, I can do it. I'll only overthink everything. I might as well do something that will focus my mind."

Hélène nodded and pulled on her hand, ushering them inside to the table where the test paper sat. Just the touch of Hélène's skin helped calm Kim down. Whatever was building between them, Kim knew deep down her feelings were real, which scared the living shit out of her.

* * *

The sun was setting, a multitude of colours filled the sky. The rest of her day had passed pleasantly. Once Hélène had got the okay from everyone on board, they made their way toward Galéria. The journey was quick, but Hélène had decided they would wait until the next day to dive again.

After Kim had completed the test, she took a little space. The conversation with her mum had taken a lot out of her, and the last thing she wanted was for her mood to dampen the trip for anyone else. Hélène had been as supportive as ever when Kim explained she would spend the rest of the day in her suite.

Thankfully, Kim's phone was full of books. She could easily waste away hours reading. Since she'd begun diving, her interest in Marine Biology had soared. Thinking back to her university days, Kim scoured the internet looking for articles and books that specialised in the subject. A tinge of regret pinched her brain. She wished she'd stayed on and completed her doctorate, but no use looking back now. She could always go back to her studies if she wanted.

Kim shook her head, trying to dislodge her thoughts. She already had too much to think about. A knock on her door disrupted her errant thoughts.

"Hey, you okay?" Kim asked when she opened the door to Hélène.

"Yes, sorry to interrupt. I just wanted to ask if you fancied getting off the boat for a while? We've been at sea for over a week and I thought that a trip to the island would be a welcomed break."

"Oh, that sounds lovely, although don't get me wrong, H, it hasn't exactly been a hardship being on *Connie*," she chuckled.

"I know, but Corsica is a beautiful place and I feel kind of bad not taking you into Calvi."

"Hélène, don't be ridiculous. You've given me the best holiday of my life. I loved all the diving we did in Calvi, so I'm not sorry we didn't get to visit the town."

"Well, if you say so. Still, a night in Galéria will be fun. Leo and David want to come. I haven't asked Holly yet. I thought I should see how you felt about it first."

"Have you spoken to her?"

"Not really, it's been over a week since her outburst and she said she apologised to you."

"She did."

"I don't really know what to say. I can't imagine what came over her to act like that. She's been avoiding me. I don't know whether to bring it up or just let it go."

"My advice would be to clear the air. If she really acted out of character, you should find out why. I'm happy for her to come along. I'll leave that decision up to you. She's your friend."

"Okay, I'll ask if she wants to join us. We'll depart in an hour if that's fine by you?"

"Yeah, that's great. Do I need to get dressed up?"

"No, casual is fine. I thought we could find a local hotspot by the beach."

"Perfect, I'll get ready."

Hélène was looking delicious. Kim couldn't help but stare as she walked away toward her own suite. It took all of Kim's willpower to stay in her room. Even though her mind was buzzing with confusion and questions, Kim's desire for Hélène was clear as day.

Now looking at Hélène's retreating form, Kim couldn't remember for the life of her why she thought it was a good idea to distance herself. It had been over a week since she'd had her hands on Hélène's body, her libido was through the roof and the thought of not having Hélène's hands on her was painful.

Kim's resolve crumbled. Just having Hélène stop by her suite was enough to send her into overdrive. She needed her, and she needed her now. Without a second thought, Kim left her room and walked the short distance to Hélène's door. She took a calming breath before knocking.

It was only a few seconds before the door opened and Hélène looked at her with a quizzical stare. The arched eyebrow was just too much for Kim. She dived forward and planted her lips on Hélène's. Hélène was taken aback, but only for a second.

They kissed feverishly. Hélène's hands made their way to Kim's hair. She felt Hélène quickly remove her headscarf, which had been wrapped around her ponytail. The release of her hair was somehow very erotic. Maybe it was because Hélène was now delving her hands through her locks, her lips devouring her neck.

"Stand by the window," Hélène demanded through her kisses.

"What?" Kim breathed. She couldn't focus on Hélène's words because the sensation of those lips was outstanding. Hélène didn't repeat her demand. Instead, she broke away and led Kim to the windows that faced the bow of the ship.

Kim hadn't been in Hélène's suite before, and she wasn't about to stop what they were doing to take a tour. What she noticed, though, was that Hélène's suite faced the front of the ship. Three quarters of the bedroom had floor-to-ceiling windows, giving them a nearly 360 degree view of the Mediterranean. Kim didn't have the opportunity to comment, because Hélène gently pushed her body up against the window.

"Don't worry, they're tinted." Hélène sucked on Kim's earlobe. In that precise moment, Kim wouldn't have cared if the whole of Corsica could see them.

Kim felt Hélène's hands untie her bikini top. Kim pushed her own bottoms to the floor. Within seconds, Kim was naked and being turned so that her front pressed up against the cold glass. There was a brief pause as Hélène stripped.

"Spread," Hélène demanded. This time, Kim could focus enough to obey. There was nothing sexier than Hélène commanding her. Not once did Kim feel out of control. She knew that if she objected, Hélène would stop in a heartbeat.

"What are you going to do to me?" she gasped. Hélène's hands were roaming all over her body.

"I'm going to fuck you from behind whilst you look out over paradise," Hélène replied. Honestly, Kim wasn't sure how she was still standing. What was it about this woman that was so intoxicating? Kim braced her hands against the windowpane and spread her legs, shoving her arse out a little to give Hélène all the access she needed.

"What about you? I want you to come, too."

"I'm going to take my pleasure. Don't worry about that." Kim felt Hélène press her body into her own. She felt Hélène's wet pussy grind against the back of her arse. Hélène's hand skirted up the back of her thigh and then delved into her folds. Kim almost head butted the window with the jolt that coursed through her.

"Oh god."

"Do you like that?" Hélène asked, even though it wasn't really a question. Hélène enjoyed talking through sex and Kim fucking loved it. Hélène's words could bring her to the brink of orgasm, she was sure of it.

"Harder, fuck me harder," Kim demanded. The feel of Hélène rubbing herself against Kim was almost too much. She could feel her climax building. Hélène was thrusting hard. Their bodies were in a perfect rhythm, allowing them both to claim their pleasure.

"H, I-"

"Hold on, a little more," Hélène begged. Kim gripped the glass as hard as she could. Hélène wanted them to come together, but Kim was struggling to keep her orgasm at bay. She needed Hélène to catch up, and quickly. Deciding she would literally give Hélène a helping hand, she reached round and cupped Hélène's sex. The added friction was all that was needed.

"Yes… yes… I'm coming," Hélène cried. Kim threw her head back on to Hélène's shoulders as she finally allowed herself to come. Her entire body shook, her legs wobbled dangerously as her orgasm took control. Miraculously, they were both able to come down from their orgasms still standing.

"That—"

"Was fabulous," Kim finished. The warmth of Hélène's hands encircling Kim's waist made her heart skip. Hélène's head was resting on Kim's shoulder as they both tried to calm their breathing.

"How long have we got until we need to leave?" Kim asked.

"About half an hour."

"Not ideal, but it will have to do." Kim turned herself round. "We are not done." Kim grinned wickedly when she saw Hélène gulp in anticipation.

Chapter 16

The sand felt warm between Hélène's toes. She dug them deeper, basking in the familiar warmth. How she wished she could wake up every day in a place like this. She looked over her shoulder at her friends, who were sitting at a wooden table close to the beach.

The restaurant they had chosen was a small local place that had seen better days. The interior was faded, and the furniture mismatched, but the ambiance was perfect. Instead of being surrounded by tourists, they were amongst the village locals.

Raucous laughter filtered out of the double doors which led to the main restaurant. A private party had booked out all the tables inside, but that was fine. Hélène was more than happy to sit on a rickety bench, sipping ice cold beer with Kim, Leo, David, and Holly.

It had been a tense week. Holly's outburst had thrown Hélène through a loop. She really had no idea how to approach her friend. The answer she found was to just *not*. For over a week, she and Holly had been civil but cautious. They had spent no time together unless it was within the group of divers. Hélène looked forward to her diving holidays all year, and part of that excitement was seeing Holly. She hated that their time away was being ruined by an underlying issue.

Diving all week had taken her out of her melancholy. Nothing could lift her mood better than sinking beneath the waves. Hélène had been over the moon with how well Kim had taken to it. She loved Kim was enthusiastic and wanted to learn. Leo and David had taken Kim under their wings too, especially David, who was more than happy to teach Kim about life underwater. Leo spent more time flirting than anything, but Hélène didn't feel the pang of jealousy like she did the first time.

Once Kim had completed her first ten dives, Hélène felt comfortable moving them on to the next dive spot. Kim had enjoyed her dives so far, but Hélène knew she would lose her mind when they dove on a wreck. She was a little disappointed that they hadn't attempted to dive over the bomber plane that lay beneath the Citadel, but she didn't want Kim to feel rushed. It would be possible for them to make a return trip on the way home so they could all experience it together.

The best part of the week, though, had to be the time she'd got to spend with Kim alone. After their first encounter, Hélène was cautiously optimistic. She understood Kim needed time, even though she'd pounced on Hélène the second the conversation had ended.

After a few days, though, her optimism had dimmed. Kim was very flirty, and she often stole kisses and touched Hélène in a way that was more than friendly, but they hadn't had sex again. Hélène wasn't a complete idiot. She understood

189

Kim was going through big changes in her life and she couldn't expect her to suddenly fall into another relationship. Giving Kim the time she'd asked for was simple enough, even if her body cried out to touch her.

Their time together earlier on in the evening had come as a complete surprise. Hélène had resigned herself to no more sex on the boat. When Kim had shown up at her door though, with a look of unfiltered lust shining in her eyes, Hélène quickly tore up that resignation and jumped in feet first.

Taking Kim up against her bedroom windows had been a fantasy she'd had ever since their first time together. Hélène surprised herself again with how demanding she'd been with Kim. The push and pull seemed to spur them on, Hélène demanding first and then Kim taking her turn. It was exhilarating. It was also explosive.

Hélène's clit ached after their fourth round. Her body was warring with itself. She was tired and aching, but still needing Kim to touch her and bring her to climax. It was good that they'd planned to visit the island because Hélène was sure that they would fuck each other into oblivion if left to their own devices.

The journey to the island took just over five minutes. Kim had sat herself at the back of the zodiac, quite content holding Hélène's hand as they sped along. The impromptu trip had been a great idea and now, as Hélène sat nestled in the sand, a little further down the beach from her friends, she could appreciate how wonderful the evening had been.

She took a big lungful of sea air as she noticed Holly break away from the group and walk over. "Hey, can I sit?" Holly asked tentatively.

"Yeah, sure." They needed to get over whatever was happening. They'd been friends too long, but that didn't mean Hélène was going to let Holly walk all over her. Holly had to know that the way she'd behaved was well out of order.

"Look, Hélène, I am really sorry."

"Okay, you've said that, but that doesn't explain why you said what you did." Hélène said bluntly.

"You're right. I was jealous of Kim."

"Why, we're not together, Holly, we never have been."

"I know. It's hard to explain."

"Try."

"Do you remember me mentioning Rebecca?"

"Yeah, last year, wasn't it? You dated for a bit."

"We were together for over a year. She dumped me just before I left to come here. Anyway, I was more messed up about it than I realised and I transferred that onto you."

"Why?"

"I didn't deal with being dumped. I just pushed it all to one side. I latched on to the idea of us having one of our getaways. You know, just the four of us like the old days. We'd drink, dive, flirt a little, go to bars and find women. I focused entirely on that. I didn't actually mind when you told me Kim would join us. I thought it would be fun. Maybe, me and her could have a brief fling. That was until I saw how you looked at her and I realised you were completely smitten." Holly sighed.

"My brain just went into meltdown. All I could see was losing you to someone else. I don't mean that romantically. It was more about losing the time with you I felt belonged to me. You were supposed to be the one who got me through my shitty breakup. I got jealous of Kim having your attention, which I know is juvenile. It was just about my broken heart, nothing to do with you or Kim. I'd been stalking Rebecca's Insta feed the night I had that outburst. She's found someone new, and it sent me off the deep end. So as the mature adult I am, I drank too much and took it out on Kim."

"That's a lot to unpack, Holly." She felt bad for her friend. She'd never known Holly to date anyone longer than a

191

couple of months, so this Rebecca woman must have been something.

"It really wasn't about you or Kim. I like her. She's good for you. It was all about me and the fact that I hadn't processed any of my hurt. I just tried to run from it. I'm so sorry, Hélène, I hate fighting with you."

"I hate fighting, too. It's been horrible this past week."

"Can we go back to normal now? I promise I will never speak to you or your 'friend' like that again," she winked.

"She is my friend," Hélène blushed.

"She's more than that and it's great, really, Hélène, I'm happy for you."

"It's a delicate situation." Hélène was so pleased that she had her best friend back. She needed to talk.

"Want to elaborate?"

Hélène spent the next few minutes telling Holly about her and Kim, and then Kim and Greg.

"Yeah, that's complicated." Holly puffed out her cheeks.

"Yeah, it really is."

"My advice, Hélène, before the trip ends, and if you still feel this strongly, you have to talk to her. I understand you want to give her the space and time she needs to process everything, but that doesn't and shouldn't mean you're left waiting for her to make the call. She can't fuck you and then keep you hanging, its not right."

"She's not like that, Hol, I don't feel like she's just in it for a quick lay. When we're together, whether that be in bed or just in each other's company, it feels deeper than anything I've felt before."

"And that's awesome, mate, but you have to make sure she feels the same, otherwise you're gonna be the one getting hurt. I'm not saying you need to ask for commitment, but you should know if it's going to carry on after you go back home."

192

Holly was right, Hélène had been burying her head. She was enjoying Kim so much that she didn't want to ask the hard questions.

"I'll talk to her." Hélène nodded.

Holly bumped her shoulder. "Let's get back to those three. Leo looks like he's well into his fifth cocktail. We might need to rescue poor Kim." Hélène laughed when she spied Leo gesticulating wildly. Kim was laughing so hard Hélène could see tears running down her beautiful face. They would need to talk, but not tonight. Tonight was about coming together as a group and enjoying life.

* * *

The five days they'd spent diving around Galéria had been fantastic. The weather and conditions couldn't have been better, plus the atmosphere had changed considerably since Hélène and Holly had buried the hatchet.

When JJ called Hélène to tell her he'd rearranged some things so that he could join them, she was beyond happy. It felt like years since she'd got to spend time with her brother — even though it was only a few months in reality — and she was secretly happy that he would have the chance to meet Kim.

Kim had spent every night with Hélène in her suite. They still hadn't broached the future which Hélène was feeling uneasy about because the longer she spent with Kim, the deeper Hélène fell.

Every night ended with sex. Some nights it was slow and passionate, others it was as if they hadn't touched each other for an age. Hélène loved it no matter how they did it, and that was becoming a problem. How was she going to cope if Kim only wanted this to be a holiday fling? It had moved way past that for Hélène.

193

Yes, the sex was outstanding, but the other facets of their relationship were just as good. Kim was fascinating. Her brain and the way her mind worked were so incredibly sexy. Hélène would lay there listening to Kim talk about biology, recounting her university days and the subjects she found fascinating.

Hélène didn't know what Kim was talking about most of the time, but it didn't matter. In return, Hélène had also opened up more. She'd talked in depth about the struggles she had with her parents. How close she was with JJ and how difficult it had been when Claire had passed.

When Hélène thought back to all their conversations, she was convinced that Kim had to be on the same page as her. There was no way either of them would discuss such private things with someone who was just a fling, right?

"You're so warm," Kim purred into Hélène's neck. They had been holed up in Hélène's suite for the entire morning, neither woman showing any signs of wanting to venture out.

"I've always been warm," Hélène murmured. She was in that stage of being awake, but not entirely.

"I like it. I get cold easily, but now I have you to keep me warm."

"Do you?"

"Do I what?" Kim asked as she snuggled closer to Hélène's.

"Do you have me?" Hélène held her breath as Kim shifted her head onto her arm so she was looking into her eyes.

"Are we having *that* conversation?"

"I think we need to. I promise I'm not trying to push you. We won't be on *Connie* forever and I suppose I'd just like to know if this is going to stop as soon as we disembark?"

"I hope not." Kim brushed the tip of her nose on Hélène's shoulder.

"Okay, well, that was easy," Hélène laughed.

194

"There will be things to talk about when we get back. I will have to sort out an apartment or at least find out if Greg wants to keep ours or move out. So much has happened that will need my attention, but I hope you realise by now that you are one of those things, too." Hélène felt a ball of emotion wedge itself in her throat. *This is too good to be true, surely?*

"Is it safe to say we're dating?" Hélène asked cautiously. Kim let her gorgeous chuckle vibrate against Hélène's shoulder, sending a bolt of energy to Hélène's centre.

"Yes, Hélène, we're dating, exclusively, I hope."

Hélène felt the smile bloom on her face. "Yes, please, I mean, I'd like to be exclusive too."

"Well, that's settled then, doll." Kim winked, pecking Hélène on the cheek and sinking back down into the bed. "What time does JJ get here?"

"Later this afternoon, so at some point we will have to get out of bed," Hélène laughed.

"But not yet, right?" Kim grinned. Hélène knew that mischievous grin, and it thrilled her to be on the receiving end.

"No, not right now. Why did you have something in mind?"

"Sit on my face," Kim blurted. Hélène slammed her thighs together because the effect of Kim saying those four words was nearly enough to get her off — no touching necessary. Kim was already getting herself into position. Hélène hadn't said a word, and she wasn't going to. If this vixen wanted Hélène to ride her face, who the hell was she to question it?

"C'mon, let's go." Kim playfully slapped Hélène's arse as she manoeuvred herself so she was hovering above Kim's face. "You're going to need to hold on for this doll," Kim said, her eyes shining. Hélène gripped the headboard and lowered herself down. Kim grabbed her arse with both hands and sank her face into Hélène.

"Oh. Mon. Dieu," Hélène exclaimed loudly. She kept her focus squarely on the wall in front of her because she was sure that if she looked down and saw the ravenous look on Kim's face, she was going to come instantly and she wanted to make it last.

Kim's tongue entered her deeply, making Hélène's vision swim. "Oh, don't stop," she cried. No matter how badly she wanted to hold on, her clit couldn't take anymore. Kim's tongue was masterful as it slid out of her entrance and caressed her so skillfully. "Right there... yes... there, Kim... Oh god, I'm coming." Hélène's fingers were hurting with how hard she was gripping the headboard. To add to what was already an earth shattering orgasm, Kim brought her hands up to Hélène's breasts and pinched her nipples, causing a second orgasm to strike.

Hélène was certain that the crew had just heard her because she had just screamed her head off. Normally Hélène was relatively quiet when she came, but good god, the noises Kim could extract from her were mind-boggling.

A repetitive *thud thud thud* noise pierced through Hélène's post orgasm bliss. Snatched back to reality, Hélène adjusted her head slightly to take in the sound. Helicopter blades, the sound unmistakable. A sudden panic zipped through Hélène's body.

"*Merde*, JJ is early," she barked as she scrambled off Kim's face and out of the bed, searching for her clothes. Her mind whirred. She'd been looking forward to JJ meeting Kim ever since he'd told her he would join them for a couple of days. In the cold light of day, though, all of Hélène's old insecurities were rearing their ugly head.

"Hey, whoa, slow down," Kim pleaded, reaching her hand out to take Hélène's arm. "You need to jump in the shower before you greet him, H."

196

"I don't have time."

"Make time, because you smell of sex," Kim said bluntly. Hélène froze in place. Of course, she needed a shower. She'd been face and knuckle deep in Kim for most of the morning.

"*Merde*," she exclaimed, ripping off her clothes again and storming into the bathroom. The water was calming, but her breath was coming in fast. Why was she getting herself so worked up?

The sound of the shower door opening pulled her back to the room. Kim snuck in behind her and pulled her in close. "I'm not sure what just happened, but you kind of just abandoned me after making me come like four times. Not cool, H," Kim teased.

Hélène blew out a breath. "Sorry, I don't know why I'm freaking out." She may as well be honest.

"Neither do I, but now you know you're freaking out. You can get it under control, okay? You've been so excited to see your brother. Hélène, just enjoy that." Hélène turned around, so she was facing Kim, who without her heels just made it to Hélène's shoulders.

"Thank you," she replied, lowering her head for a kiss.

"None of that. You're supposed to be getting clean," Kim laughed. "We can get dirty again later," she winked.

Fifteen minutes later, and with one aching clit, Hélène dragged herself out of the "no sex" shower she'd just shared with Kim. Her body did *not* appreciate the lack of stimulation it was so used to getting nowadays when in the shower.

They dressed quickly, stealing a kiss before heading to the pool deck. Hélène heard JJ before she spotted him. His laugh bellowed through the boat, causing her to smile. She loved her goofy brother.

"*Coucou,*" she called as she slipped out of the sliding doors. JJ swung round in his chair. He looked like an excitable puppy.

"Hélène," he cried joyfully, launching himself at her and cocooning her in a wraparound hug. Hélène breathed in her brother's scent. She'd missed him so much.

"How are you?" she mumbled, her face pressed hard in JJ's chest.

"All the happier to see you, kid," he bellowed. They held each other for a few more seconds. She noticed JJ's eyes flit over her shoulder. Hélène turned her head and followed his gaze. Kim stood a foot or two away from them, with a smile that lit up her face.

Hélène felt the same old nerves flutter. This was usually the time she found out that the person with her was more interested in meeting the infamous John Spencer than Hélène herself. The thought of Kim being one of those people hurt more than she could say.

"Kim, I'd like to introduce you to John Spencer." Her tone was professional, almost as if they were in a boardroom meeting instead of the back of a luxury yacht. Hélène noticed Kim frown slightly. "John, this is Kimberley Richmond."

Hélène stepped to the side slightly, allowing them to greet each other and no doubt start a conversation about John and his success. Despite how it might look to some, Hélène was not jealous of John. He'd worked his ass off to achieve everything he had, and he really was the best brother anyone could ask for. Sometimes, though, Hélène just wished *she* was enough.

"Hello, Kimberley," John said cheerfully, holding out his hand. Kim stepped forward, giving Hélène a puzzled and slightly amused look before taking his hand in a brief handshake.

"Great to meet you, John. Please call me Kim, I'm not quite sure why H introduced me as if I was applying for a job," she chuckled. Hélène blushed a little. "So John, tell me…"

And here they came, the inevitable questions; what's it like to be so young and so successful? How many companies do you own now? Have you got any new businesses lined up? I would love to pitch you an idea I had if you have a few minutes?

"How many embarrassing childhood stories can you tell me about Hélène before her head explodes?" Kim said seriously. Hélène must have misheard. She snapped her eyes to Kim, who was grinning and wiggling her eyebrows mischievously at John.

John burst out laughing, his shoulders relaxing, "Oh boy, I have some great ones, let's grab a drink and I'll start with how she tried to bake cookies for a school assembly one year and they all turned out looking like penises," he howled.

Hélène quickly came to her senses. Her feet moved quickly to catch up to the duo, who had moved to the drinks station that had been set up on the far side of the deck. "I don't think anyone needs to hear that," she huffed, causing John and Kim to laugh louder. Oh, man, she was in for a long night.

Chapter 17

John Spencer was probably one of the nicest guys Kim had ever met. It was abundantly clear that he adored Hélène as he regaled the group with stories of their mishaps and adventures together as kids. Hélène had spent a lot of the evening bright red, glaring at him to stop, but he just winked and carried on.

Kim was just happy that Hélène's earlier anxieties had fallen by the wayside. She wasn't sure why Hélène had reacted so strongly when JJ had turned up early or why she'd introduced Kim the way she had. It was a little heartbreaking for Kim to see that Hélène had taken a side step after the introductions, as if trying to get out of the way. Did she feel as if she was less than when her brother was around?

The group had enjoyed a wonderful BBQ on the upper deck. Leo had anointed himself as the grill master, which, to be fair, Kim couldn't argue with because the food had been phenomenal. She remembered him saying his family owned several restaurants in his hometown which would explain his skill. The drinks flowed freely, leaving everyone relaxed and a little tipsy.

"So, Kim, tell me about you," John said over the chatter.

"What do you want to know?"

"Anything you feel happy sharing, I suppose."

"Okay, well, you know I work for *Tower Publishing* because you own it," she giggled. "I have lived in France for a few years now but still suck at the language. I have an unhealthy obsession with vintage clothes—"

"And heels," Hélène interjected.

"Erm, excuse you, that's an appreciation of fine footwear, not an obsession," she mock scowled. "I'm an Aries, and I've always wanted a pet turtle." John raised his eyebrows, looking at Hélène, who was beaming. "What about you?"

"Oh, I'm sure you've read all about me," he grinned. Kim noticed Hélène sink back into her chair, the smile she'd sported dimming. "I have, and no offence, John, but your business doesn't really get my juices flowing. I was more thinking about JJ, Hélène's older brother."

Kim felt Hélène's hand rest on her thigh. She looked over and she could have sworn that Hélène's eyes were wet. An emotion was etched over her face that Kim couldn't decipher. Gratitude? Happiness? Lust? Love? No, scratch the last one!

"Oh right, that I can talk about."

Kim sat there and listened to John, or JJ, as she now referred to him. Kim's heart broke for him when he spoke of Claire, his late wife. She could see the love and pain that he held in his eyes. She felt fortunate that he was comfortable enough to share such intimate stories. She felt honoured to be a part of Hélène's inner circle, if she were being honest.

"Bedtime for me," John said through a yawn. Holly, Leo, and David had already retired. Kim looked at Hélène, wondering if she was going to leave, too.

"I'm going to have one last drink," Hélène said. "Kim?"

"Yeah, I'll join you."

John smirked at them both before kissing them good night. He flashed a wink at Hélène, who rolled her eyes. "What was that?" Kim laughed.

"Oh, you mean Captain Obvious wasn't all that subtle with his wink?" Hélène said sarcastically. Kim sniggered. She loved the dynamic between the two siblings.

Hélène was already mixing them both a drink. Kim moved over to the two-seat sofa. All night they had sat close to each other but never close enough that they could touch, and boy did Kim miss touching Hélène. It was crazy how much she craved the closeness.

"Here." Hélène passed Kim the drink and then settled down next to her, their thighs wedged next to each other. There was no space left between them, which made Kim happy.

"Cheers."

"Cheers."

"So, will you tell me why you introduced me to JJ like that?" It had continued to bug Kim all evening. She was sure there was something more behind it. She knew she was right when she saw Hélène shift in her seat, her shoulders sagging as she let out a long sigh.

"It's going to sound pathetic," Hélène said, unable to look Kim in the eye.

"I doubt it, H, but you don't have to tell me if you're uncomfortable."

"It's just, well, you remember me telling you I've had some issues with the way people behave once they find out who I'm related to?" Kim nodded. She didn't want Hélène to stop talking. "Well, it's just that I have got used to taking a backseat, especially around JJ. Don't get me wrong, I adore that man, but sometimes it's hard when I get cast aside by people who are supposed to be interested in me. As soon as JJ enters the picture, that's all anyone can focus on. I know he doesn't enjoy having the spotlight on him all the time. He would never want me to feel like this, but I do and I can't do anything about it." Hélène took a long breath.

"Well, that sucks. I hope I never made you feel like that when—"

"No, you didn't. In fact, you're the first person who has ever asked about me, asked JJ to talk about our childhood. It meant more than you can imagine." Kim studied Hélène's face. The raw emotion playing across her beautiful features was heartbreaking and wonderful all at the same time.

Who wouldn't want to talk about Hélène? It baffled Kim that any woman could even contemplate casting her aside just to talk to John. Yes, he was a big deal, but not compared to her.

The thought smacked Kim square in the chest. No matter how hard she tried to keep things casual with Hélène, it wasn't possible. The connection they had was too strong. "Do you want to take a swim with me?" Kim's mind was spinning, and she needed to break the tension before she said something she feared, something that was becoming painfully obvious the more time she spent with Hélène.

"You want to swim now?" Hélène asked incredulously, "It's nearly midnight." Kim stayed silent. She placed her drink on the table and made her way to the stairs. Her heart was racing. She hoped Hélène would take the bait.

The pool was lit by small lights on every side. The rest of the boat—minus the observation deck—was in complete darkness. Without having to look up, she sensed Hélène's eyes on her as she approached the pool. Dropping her dress that she'd unzipped on the stairs, Kim stood in only a black lace thong. A smile crept on her face when she heard Hélène gasp.

Keeping her back to Hélène, she slowly bent at the hips, sliding her underwear down as she went. The night air felt amazing on Kim's fevered body. Just the thought of Hélène watching her, wanting her, was enough to have her sweating.

Walking to the edge of the pool, she gracefully slipped out of her heels and looked up toward the top deck where Hélène was leaning, watching, a look of pure need radiating off of her.

"Are you coming?" Kim asked softly.

"You astound me," Hélène whispered. Kim gave her a playful wink before diving into the pool. She twisted her head toward the door after resurfacing and waited. Hélène exited the door already half naked, making Kim laugh. God knows where she'd dropped her clothes.

In a flash, Hélène dived in and emerged in front of Kim, with only an inch separating them. "You take my breath away, Kim." Hélène was so serious that Kim's heart fluttered and her stomach tensed. Hélène's low timbre made Kim clench. Hélène delicately took Kim by the waist and pulled them together.

Kim's legs instinctively wrapped around Hélène's body. "You scare me," Kim whispered. She hadn't meant to say it out loud, but it was the truth.

"You never have to be scared of me or with me." Hélène brushed her nose against Kim's. Her eyes were so sincere that Kim couldn't wait any longer. Bridging the tiny gap between them, Kim took Hélène's lips into her own, sucking gently and then nipping.

A moan from Hélène spurred her on further. Her hips surged forward, seeking friction, but the water only served to titillate her sensitive clit. Hélène slowly turned them and guided Kim so she was backed against the pool wall. Their lips never parted, they breathed each other in, consuming everything the other had to give.

"Please touch me," Kim gasped. She couldn't take anymore. It was the sweetest torture she'd ever experienced. Her body craved release, but her heart wanted the feeling to last a lifetime. "Hélène, please." Kim released her legs slightly, allowing Hélène to bring her hand between them.

Even in the water, Kim knew Hélène would feel her arousal. She almost cried when she finally felt Hélène's fingers caress her folds. Kim was all for rough and ready, but the feelings that surrounded them when they took their time were unparalleled.

Hélène's moan brought her back to their current reality. Hélène was grinding against her own hand, the hand that was deep inside Kim. "Come with me," Kim whimpered, her own gratification growing into a wave that was almost ready to crest.

Hélène doubled her efforts, her hand plunged deeper and faster, her hips rocked as hard as they could in the water. Kim's eyes clouded over. She couldn't focus on anything. Her mind was incapable of dealing with the feelings that were crashing through her nervous system.

She held Hélène tightly. Her head slammed into Hélène's neck, biting hard on her flesh as her orgasm rocketed through her. The scream that emanated from her throat pierced the stillness of the night, her pleasure echoed in the winds.

* * *

"Are you sure you don't want to come?"

"No, really, I could do with some down time," Kim said honestly. The past two days had really taken it out of her. JJ was a live wire, always on the go. They'd arrived in the Golfe de Valinco early yesterday morning.

JJ had insisted that they dive early, which had been a lot of fun. Hélène, as usual, stuck to Kim like glue, which she secretly loved, even though she had clarified that Hélène should feel free to go off with JJ. Leo and Holly were more than qualified to handle Kim underwater, but Hélène wouldn't budge.

They'd managed two dives, followed by another late night of drinking and other fun activities that only included Kim and Hélène. The lack of sleep and high energy output had caught up to Kim, and the thought of diving again was far too much. Her body required a sun lounger and nothing more.

"Hey, Hélène, I'll stick around too," JJ called. Hélène stopped in her tracks at that unexpected announcement and eyed her brother suspiciously, causing him to laugh. "Hey, I'm not as young as I was and I haven't scuba dived in over a year. My old bones need a break!"

"Hmmm," Hélène huffed. "Fine, we won't be too long anyway." Just as she turned to leave, Kim cleared her throat. Did Hélène actually think she was leaving this vessel without kissing her goodbye?

Hélène turned at the noise and smiled when Kim raised a questioning eyebrow. Crooking her finger, she beckoned Hélène to come back. The kiss they shared was slow and held a definite promise for more when Hélène returned. Kim's legs almost buckled in anticipation.

JJ and Kim spent a delightful few hours drinking and chatting. The conversation spanned a myriad of topics which Kim thoroughly enjoyed. JJ was an intelligent man. No wonder he was so successful. When the conversation hit a natural lull, Kim felt the atmosphere change.

"So…" John said, turning his head to Kim. Kim smiled internally. She now understood his reason for staying behind. He was going to do the whole big brother thing.

"So?" she replied confidently. He wouldn't rattle her.

"You and Hélène."

"Me and Hélène," she repeated.

"Blimey, you're not making this easy," he laughed.

"Why would I? This is highly entertaining," she grinned.

"I see why she likes you. You're fiery, that's for sure."

"Is that a compliment?"

"Sure it is. Hélène needs someone with a bit of fire. She also needs someone who will use that fire to have her back," he said pointedly. Kim wondered how much of Hélène's insecurities JJ was aware of.

"She does and I will have her back, no matter what. Even if we don't work out romantically, we're friends."

"Do you not think it will work out?" John asked with a frown.

"I can't predict the future, JJ. You know I have baggage. I would be surprised if Hélène hasn't told you about Greg."

"She did, but I can't see how that would be a problem. It's over, right?"

"Yes, but I had a life with him, a life that I have to go home and deal with. It won't be easy and I don't want Hélène to feel trapped. That's a lot for a new relationship."

"So it's a relationship, not just a fling?"

"Oh no, it's a relationship. As much as I tried to keep us casual, it's definitely more than that."

"Okay, that's good to hear. Hélène deserves the best. I know she struggles with her association to me and believe me when I say I hate it when she puts herself second. I see her do it every time she introduces someone to me. It doesn't help that her mum is who she is. Veronique was never good at boosting Hélène, so she learned to just stay quiet and out of the way."

"That makes my blood boil," Kim growled.

"Good, I'm glad. Like I said, Hélène needs that protection from someone and from the way you two have been behaving, I think she's found it, just like you have found what you were looking for. Can I give you some advice?"

"Sure." Kim didn't know where this was going and it was certainly a heavy subject, but she was happy to hear what he had to say. JJ was the closest person to Hélène, the one who knew her the best.

"You might have baggage and things might be shitty, but what you have found with Hélène is rare. Take it from someone who had it and lost it. Life is wonderful all on its own, but living it with the person who was made just for you is priceless. No amount of uncertainty or fear is worth missing out on it. When you get home, talk to each other properly, work out how to be together because Kim, from the way Hélène looks at you, you are her person."

Kim was floored. That was one hell of a speech, and she had no idea what to do with it. The universe gave her no time to dwell, though, because the incoming call from Greg wouldn't allow it. Kim looked from the phone to JJ, who gave her a kind smile before leaving her alone by the pool.

Taking a deep breath, she answered the phone. They hadn't spoken since the incident at The Sapphire, and she wasn't sure how she was supposed to feel. Relieved was one emotion because at least Greg was getting help from her parents. Anger was the other emotion, especially as she replayed the events of their last conversation.

"Hi," she said cautiously.

"Kim, thank you for answering. I was afraid you wouldn't." Kim noted he sounded much more like his old self.

"Ignoring you won't get us anywhere. How are you?"

"Desperately sorry. The way I treated you is unforgivable and I understand completely if you never want to talk to me again."

"I considered it. I'll be honest, Greg, you scared me. The thing is, you're my best friend and I want to help you, but I can't do that as your girlfriend. I hope you can understand that." It was important that she clarified their positions immediately.

"Honestly, I think it's the right thing," he sighed. "I was just hoping that I hadn't lost you completely. There are things we need to talk about, things I'd prefer to do in person. Would it be possible for you to come to your parents' for a weekend? It's not a good idea for me to be in Paris right now."

Kim tilted her head to the sky. It seemed her perfect getaway was ending. Realistically, she knew she couldn't stay away from home and everything else for much longer. The idea of leaving *Connie* made her heart sink. Leaving her perfect paradise with Hélène sounded like hell, but what choice did she have?

Travelling to England to hash things out with Greg sounded about as fun as contracting an STI, but she had to put that part of her life to bed. It would probably be better if she dealt with it in England. That way, Hélène wouldn't be drawn into anything. Kim could return to Paris with a fresh start.

"Okay, I can come over, but it will have to be in a couple of weeks."

"That's great, really Kim, thank you." An uncomfortable silence filtered through the phone receiver. What was there to say? They still had a cloud of shit hanging over them.

"I'll talk to you soon, okay," she said lightly, not wanting Greg to feel dismissed.

"Alright, and Kim?"

"Yeah?"

"I really am sorry, and I love you."

"I love you, too." She pressed the end call button with a sigh and then stilled when she saw the look on Hélène's face.

Shit, she must have heard her tell Greg she loved him and by the look of it, without knowing the context in the way it was said.

"Hélène—"

"Just wanted you to know I was back, but I obviously disturbed you, sorry. I'm going to shower for dinner." And with that, Hélène turned and swiftly left. Kim let her head drop to her chest in defeat. So much for her having a relaxing day.

After downing the remains of her cocktail, Kim heaved her tired body up and headed for Hélène's suite. In the space of a few hours, she'd faced her past, present and most scarily the possibility of her future, that's if she took what JJ said to heart.

Deep down though, she saw how Hélène looked at her and she probably mirrored that look, too. But her past with Greg was what worried her the most at that moment. Hélène's face had been gut wrenching when Kim had looked up from the phone. Hélène looked stricken and Kim had been the one to cause that, which was unquestionably the worst feeling in the world.

The best thing to do though was to hash it out with Hélène now, not leave it to fester. Nothing good would come of that. She knocked on Hélène's door. No reply. With the force of a rhino, Kim pounded on the door.

"Hélène, let me in," she said forcefully.

The door opened, with Hélène looking chagrined. "Kim, I was just getting in the shower," she said curtly. Right, so this was how she was going to play it!

"The shower isn't even running yet and you haven't taken your clothes off. So my guess is you were ignoring me because you are upset that you overheard me tell Greg I love him. About right?" Hélène grumbled something inaudible. "So I'm right," Kim continued, surging forward into the room.

"I'm not upset," Hélène said weakly.

"Sure, you look simply chipper." Kim rolled her eyes. "If you had heard the *entire* conversation, you would have heard me telling Greg that we would not be getting back together." Kim took a breath and waited for Hélène to respond. Hélène remained silent, looking at the floor. "Hélène, look at me." Hélène pulled her focus to Kim's eyes. "A few days ago, we decided we were giving this a try." She pointed from Hélène to herself. "That hasn't changed for me. Yes, I will see Greg. He is my oldest friend and we have history. I want to be there for him because he is going through something, but that does not mean that you come second, do you hear me?" Kim desperately wanted Hélène to absorb her words and take them to heart because she meant every goddamn one of them.

"Okay," Hélène mumbled, looking away from Kim. Jesus, Kim couldn't take that look anymore. It was as if someone had stomped on her dog or something. In a flash, Kim was standing in front of Hélène, holding her face in her palms. "Kiss me, please." Hélène's face softened as she leaned forward and placed a delicate kiss on Kim's lips.

"Sorry," she whispered against Kim's mouth.

"Don't say sorry, but next time, please don't run away. Talk to me."

"Okay."

They kissed softly for a long time. Kim didn't want to let Hélène go. Her emotions were feeling raw, and even though what she had just said to Hélène was true, the reality of having to juggle her feelings for Hélène, her past with Greg and everything else in between weighed heavy.

Chapter 18

The last dive of their holiday was one of great excitement and sorrow. Hélène hated having to say goodbye to her friends and the crew of *Connie*, especially when she didn't know when she would get to see them again.

JJ had extended his trip so that Hélène and Kim could take the chopper back to Paris with him. He'd rearranged some meetings so that he could spend a little more time with his sister in the city.

Hélène had a constant stream of anxiety running through her veins ever since she'd overheard Kim on the phone with Greg. Even though Kim had tried to put her mind at ease, her feelings were conflicted. She so desperately wanted to believe Kim, believe that whatever was going on between her and Greg wouldn't come between them.

Hélène knew they had a lot of history and it would take time for them to really work through their issues so they could get back to being best friends. That wasn't her problem, her problem was the goddamn universe, which always seemed to screw with her.

Kim was perfect in Hélène's eyes, everything she could ask for, so it stood to reason that Hélène would lose her, eventually. Maybe it wasn't rational thinking, but if she took her past into account, it stood to reason that she was going to get hurt.

Instead of talking to Kim — which would have been the sensible and mature thing to do — Hélène buried her feelings deep down, deciding to put all her efforts into making the last days of their holiday the best they could be. Drinking, dancing, and laughing had been at the top of the bill every evening. It had been immensely gratifying to listen to Kim boast about her diving achievements and recount all her favourite parts.

JJ and Kim got on like a house on fire which warmed Hélène through to her bones, and the cherry on top had been Holly's turnaround. Having her best friend back was wonderful. The back-and-forth banter between Holly and Kim was more than pleasing to witness. All in all, the choice to get away from the city and therefore her lacklustre life for a while had been a roaring success.

Connie set sail north. Hélène wanted them to stop at Calvi again, to dive over the sunken bomber. The team had been more than happy to do it, especially Kim, who had kissed Hélène with such ferocity that she had to stop herself from throwing Kim over her shoulder and dragging her back to her suite. Kim was an expert at riling Hélène up within seconds.

"Everyone ready?" Hélène called as they finished loading the Zodiac for the last time. The trip back up the coast had only taken a few hours and Hélène didn't want to lose any

213

more time considering they would start their journey home early the next morning.

"All good, boss," David shouted. Hélène cast an eye over the boat and the group one last time to make sure everything and everyone was where it should be. She let her eyes linger on Kim for a few seconds. What a difference a few days made.

On their first dive, Kim had looked overly nervous and a little shy around the others, a stark contrast to Kim now who lounged on the side of the boat, her wetsuit hanging by her waist, laughing at something Leo was saying.

There was no doubt Kim looked as if she had always belonged to the little diving family. As usual, Hélène's heart gave a little flutter. It was the first time she'd ever been with someone who fit in so well, with her and her friends. Shaking herself out of her thoughts, Hélène gunned the throttle, laughing when she saw JJ tumble from his perch.

"Drop anchor," she shouted to David as they circled above the wreck. It had been years since she'd dived on the site. David threw the anchor over and began prepping for their dive. Today, they would go in two groups, which allowed everyone to dive.

"Kim, get suited, JJ too. David, Leo, and Holly, you good to go second?"

"Yeah, no probs," Holly chimed. They worked quickly to get organised. Holly helped Kim with her vest and tank, whilst Leo helped JJ and David helped Hélène. They were ready in less than ten minutes.

"I'll hit the water first, JJ you second, and then Kim. We'll meet at the front of the boat. Everyone okay with that?" Two "okay" signs were given in response. Pulling her mask down and inserting her mouthpiece Hélène rolled backwards and into the warm sea. There was no current and no wind. The surface was so still it looked like glass. Hélène made her way to the anchor point, keeping her eye on JJ and Kim as they entered the water.

"Everyone okay?" she asked as they convened.

"Good."

"Ready." Kim smiled. Hélène gave the sign to descend. Today would be one of Kim's deepest dives. The wreck sat at twenty-seven metres, which was well within her capabilities. They made their way down slowly, stopping every few metres to allow their ears to adjust to the pressure.

The water was crystal clear. It was easy to see the shadow of the wreck approach as they sank further down. Hélène checked over her shoulder to make sure that Kim and JJ were close by. She didn't have to worry, though. Kim was right on her tail. JJ gently swam a little further back, taking his time to look at the wreck.

The bomber was in great shape, but it was an eerie sight to see. The history of a wreck was never lost on Hélène. It was a very sobering experience. The structure of the plane was almost intact. The propellers were still attached to the four engines.

The nose of the plane had been torn away, leaving the two pilot seats visible, which caused a chill to run through her body. Even though she'd dived on this site many times, the thought of the people who had been trapped in the plane as it went down left her horrified and solemn every time.

They circled the bomber several times, each circuit noting different things. Nature had well and truly taken over. The fish and coral flourished over nearly every inch of the metal carcass.

Noting that her air was getting low, Hélène signalled to JJ and Kim to end the dive. As usual, they ascended at a slow pace. There was no way she was letting their holiday end with one of them getting "the bends". The sun's heat hit Hélène's face immediately as she broke the surface. None of them were overly chatty as they boarded the Zodiac, which wasn't unusual after experiencing a dive like that.

"You okay?" Hélène asked Kim once they'd shed their wetsuits, flippers, and masks.

"That was… wow," Kim replied forlornly.

"Yeah, it's something."

"I can't imagine how scared those men must have been."

"It's unimaginable. It gets me every time I dive on it."

"Thank you… for making sure we came back to see it."

"You're welcome. You know, Kim, I really hope you carry on diving after this. Not because I like it, but because you do. You're a natural."

"Oh, I'm definitely carrying on. I already googled diving clubs in Paris. Did you know they have them?"

"Yes, I did," Hélène chuckled. She loved seeing Kim light up like an excitable child at Christmas. "C'mon, let's get dry and have some rum whilst the others take their turn."

* * *

Car horns and engines assaulted Hélène's senses as she stepped out of the car JJ had hired to take her back to her apartment. Gone were the lazy days of Saint Tropez and Corsica, gone were the cocktail hours looking out over the sea and gone was her alone time with Kim. Strictly speaking, those weren't completely gone. She hoped Kim would come over to her apartment for dinner, where they would most definitely have some quality alone time.

Holly had sent her off with the promise of a visit. Leo and David had given her and Kim a bear hug before waving them off. It was unlikely Hélène would see the boys until she was ready to set sail on *Connie* again. They would be off to their respective countries to work now that the summer was done.

216

A message had come through halfway through their return journey from Sam wanting Hélène to set up a drinks night. JJ had spent most of the time on the way back talking shop, which really pissed Hélène off. They hadn't even got back to Paris and already she was feeling her stress levels rise. Thank god for Kim, who had held her hand the entire journey, shooting sympathetic looks as JJ yapped on about business.

Feeling weary from the day, Hélène climbed the stairs to her first-floor apartment slowly. She missed the sun; she missed the sea, and above all, she already missed Kim. They'd had a quick kiss goodbye after dropping her off, and that was it.

For nearly three and a half weeks they'd been inseparable, just the way Hélène liked it. Tomorrow, though, they would both be back at work.

Hopefully Kim would take her up on the offer to come over this evening, but she wasn't hopeful. Kim had looked just as tired, and Hélène also knew that Kim going back to her apartment was throwing up some hard feelings for her.

Heaving her luggage up one flight of stairs had been more than enough to sap the last bit of Hélène's energy. Normally, she would sort out her clothes as soon as she got home, but that would have to wait. The only thing Hélène wanted was a hot bath and a nice glass of wine.

Dumping her bags in her spare room, she set about checking her messages and post. One voice message snagged her attention. "Where are you? I thought you would be back from your little escapade by now. We need to talk about your behaviour at The Sapphire. I cannot begin to fathom the reason you were parading yourself around the foyer in your underwear, Hélène. I really thought we'd moved past this childishness. Why you need constant attention is beyond me. Call me back immediately."

Hélène's stomach clenched. Oh shit, she'd completely forgotten about the hotel stunt. It had taken a whopping thirty seconds for her mother's message to drain away all her holiday cheer and relaxation. She could already feel her shoulders bunching as she thought of having to deal with Veronique.

There was nothing for it. She would have to call back and get it over with. If she waited any longer, she feared Veronique would turn up at her door and that was the last thing she wanted.

"Mother," Hélène chimed as the call connected.

"About time. Explain yourself," Veronique spat. Hélène scrunched her eyes closed. The sound of her mother's anger sent shivers down her spine.

"There is nothing to explain. It was a bit of fun at the beginning of my holiday. I tipped the staff well when I left. There was no damage."

"No damage. What about the damage to my name and image? What will people think? Hélène, do you ever think of anyone else but yourself? Hmm?"

Hélène shook her head. Of course, her mother was only thinking about how it looked for her. "There was nobody of note in the foyer, only Thomas at the front desk. I was not streaking naked. It was a silly dare between friends. That's it, you're taking this way out of proportion."

"When are you going to grow up?" Her mother shot.

"I have. I've changed a lot since you last lectured me, because you were right then, I needed to grow up. What happened at the hotel wasn't like before. It was a silly way to de-stress."

"I don't know what to do with you."

Hélène gritted her teeth. No matter what she did or said, it would never be good enough, not for Veronique fucking DuBois. Hélène was just a constant letdown to her mother. Jesus, she was so tired of feeling like she wasn't enough. Not enough as a daughter, not enough as a partner, just not enough.

Hélène wasn't sure what made it happen, but right then, as she listened to her mother breathing disapprovingly down the phone at her, Hélène snapped. "Stop," she bellowed. "Stop talking right now. How dare you ask me what *you're* going to do with me? You haven't been interested in being my mother since the day I was born. I'm well aware of my failings, thanks to you. You're the first person to let me know how much of a disappointment I am," she raged.

"I am sick of feeling less than. I have done my very best to make you notice me, and yes, that included acting out. Forgive me for wanting my mother to *want* to take an interest. Everything was in vain, though, wasn't it? Unless it was to do with your fucking 'brand', you weren't interested. I am worth more respect than you give. I am worth so much more than what you give me. Mother, I'm done. Until *you* are ready to make some changes, I don't want to hear from you. Oh, and on one last note. There is absolutely no way my behaviour at The Sapphire will damage your precious image because not one person knows who I am to you. That's how insignificant I am in your life." Finished with her rant, Hélène ended the call.

Oh shit.

She'd well and truly done it now. Hélène had never spoken to her mother that way before. But on reflection, it felt damn good. Yes, her initial reaction was to vomit, but after a few deep breaths that feeling subsided and another emotion took over. Maybe for the first time ever, she'd shown herself some self-respect.

Her body wasn't quite on the same page because the hand that held her mobile was trembling violently. What the hell should she do now? This was foreign territory. Hélène was used to her mum being the one to lose her shit and hang up, not the other way round.

A melodic rap on the door snapped her out of her anxiety riddled brain. Hélène whipped open the door, hoping that Kim had turned up out of the blue to surprise her. It wasn't, but it *was* one of Hélène's favourite people.

"Sam, oh, it's so good to see you."

"Give me a squeeze. It feels like forever since we saw each other." Hélène wasted no time pulling Sam into a hug. "You okay?" Sam must have sensed Hélène's tense muscles. Her body felt as stiff as a plank.

"I think I just did something really stupid."

"Haven't you just got back? I wasn't sure you'd be in. Sorry for just turning up. If I'm being honest, Anna sent me to get the gossip. She's headed over to Kim's as we speak."

"Gossip?"

"Don't play dumb. Did you really think Kim wouldn't tell her best friend about you and her?"

"Er…"

"Ha, you should see your face right now. I cannot believe you didn't call me!"

Balls! What was she supposed to do now? Sam was staring her down, her eyebrow raised. "I didn't think interrupting your holiday was a good idea, that's all."

Sam scoffed. "Nice try. What's the real reason?"

"Okay fine. I thought it might be weird."

"Why?"

"Anna is Kim's best friend. It feels odd telling you about me and Kim, knowing that she'd doing the same with Anna."

"Ah, you're worried we're going to be comparing notes."

"Yes, a little."

"Look, you're my friend. Whatever you tell me is between us and it stays that way unless you tell me differently.

Yes, Anna told me you and Kim were becoming something more than friends, but she didn't tell me anything else. I promise you have nothing to worry about. I just want to be there for you."

It was a relief to have someone other than JJ to talk to. He was great, but he wasn't a gay woman. He could only relate so much, and she certainly couldn't share any sexy details with him. "Oh, Sam, it's been one hell of a holiday."

"I gathered," Sam laughed.

Hélène directed them to her living room. Thankfully, she'd done a deep clean a few days before going away and the place looked great. It wasn't a large apartment. Honestly, the only big apartments available in Paris cost an arm and a leg to rent. Forget about buying, unless you were super rich.

It didn't matter though, Hélène loved her place. It was a two-bed, one bath with a separate toilet. The rooms weren't big, but they were just right for her. The second bedroom was her diving room. It was like a mini shop in there. Her wet suits hung from rails on the walls. Her flippers had their own hooks, as did her vest. The shelves that adorned every wall were stacked with all her gadgets and books. It was diving heaven.

The kitchen was miniscule, but the living room/dining room made up for it. It was a pretty decent size. The space easily held a full size family table, sofa, TV unit, and sideboard. The apartment faced a large courtyard. It was a pleasant view, especially in the summer when Hélène could leave the windows open. She'd lost count of the amount of times she'd sat on her sofa looking out over the courtyard with a nice glass of red.

Hélène sank into the couch, waiting for Sam to get comfortable at the other end. "Where should I start?" She had no idea what Anna had told Sam. It warmed her a little to think of Kim talking about her — as long as it was all good. That thought sent a little bolt of anxiety to her stomach.

"Well, the beginning is a pretty good place," Sam smirked, causing Hélène to roll her eyes.

"Okay, so you know she got stranded at the hotel?" Sam nodded. "I offered her the spare room in my suite. No big deal. Anyway, we started talking and drinking and laughing. Kim is so much fun."

"Oh, I know," Sam laughed.

"Everything was just so easy with her. She listened to my problems, and I listened to hers. I couldn't believe that it was the first time we'd really spent any time together."

"Me, too. Although looking back, you guys only really spoke through me or Anna." Hélène nodded in agreement.

"The first week was so much fun that I offered her to come along on my diving trip. God Sam, we had a blast. Kim is great in the water. She's also ridiculously smart. She's funny and adventurous."

"So, when did it turn into something more?"

"On the boat. We'd been flirting since the beginning, but I wouldn't have done anything about it. Kim's going through some stuff and I wasn't about to add to her troubles. But then…"

"Then?…"

"She kissed me."

"What did you do? Did you kiss her back?"

"I did, but then it was over and she went to bed. The next day she adorably tried to talk to me, but she was nervous. She knocked her orange juice everywhere and then hid in her room. I went to speak to her and… well… let's just say things developed."

"Developed." Sam chuckled. "That's how you're going to describe banging each other?"

"Banging, really you think that's better?" Hélène laughed.

"Better than 'developed' for Christ's sake."

222

"Anyway… we 'banged' for the rest of the holiday."

"Wow."

"You can say that again."

"So what now? Did you talk about what would happen when you got home?"

"We said we'd give it a go. I know she has stuff to sort out and it won't be easy…" Hélène trailed off as she remembered Kim on the phone with Greg. Her heart thumped a little harder.

"Hey what's that face? You just went all pale." Hélène shifted in her seat. Should she voice her concerns? Would it make a difference? "Hey, c'mon, tell me what's wrong."

"There's just a lot for Kim to work through, and I'm not certain that she's in the place to start something with me. I really like her and I think I'm already further down the road as far as feelings are concerned than she is."

"I know about the thing with Greg. Well, I know they broke up and that his behaviour was way out of line. Anna was fuming after Kim told her."

"Yeah, understandably, so was I. The thing is, they're best friends, as in they have grown up together. Kim is going to want to be there for him. It's just who she is, which is admirable. My worry is that once Greg has sorted himself out, Kim will want to be with him again. They have so much history, Sam, I can't compete."

Sam sat silently for a minute. Hélène could see she was processing. "Have you voiced your worries to Kim?"

Nope. She had not, and she wasn't going to. That would put pressure on Kim, which was unfair. "No, and I'm not going to yet. Like I said, she's coping with a lot. She doesn't need me adding on."

"Talking about how you feel isn't 'adding on'. You can't keep what you're feeling hidden. You saw the mess I made when I did that. I almost lost Anna. Don't make the same mistake."

Hélène could understand where Sam was coming from. The massive difference between what had happened with Sam and Anna was that they were desperately in love but were afraid. That wasn't the case with her and Kim. Was it? No, no, Hélène wasn't afraid — or in love — she was just cautious. The last thing she needed was to invest her heart, only to be let down again. Yes, it wasn't fear, just regular old caution.

Chapter 19

Kim had been sitting on the sofa for an hour, simply staring at the room in front of her. Nothing had changed and yet everything had. The apartment felt cold and lonely without Greg there.

The warmth and light that had encompassed Kim since Saint Tropez had vanished as she'd stepped through the door to her apartment. She'd been riding a high for weeks, only to come crashing down from the reality that lay in front of her. Greg was gone and Kim was alone for the first time since she was a teenager.

The apartment was is in disarray. Greg had left dirty dishes everywhere, cartons of half eaten Chinese food and several dirty glasses on the coffee table. The blinds and curtains had been drawn, making everything feel dark and dingy. The warm home that Kim had left three weeks ago now felt cold and unwelcoming.

Buzzing from her pocket finally shifted her out of her almost catatonic state. How could things have gone so wrong?

Anna
Nearly at your place. See you soon.

Kim didn't even have the energy to panic about Anna seeing her home in such a state. What would be the point? Anna knew things had gone sideways with Greg, she knew about Hélène, so no need to hide this.

A light tapping on the door, followed by the unmistakable sound of a key entering the lock, drew Kim to her feet. Anna had been given a key months ago and Kim was more than happy for her friend to come and go as she pleased.

"Hey you," Anna called sweetly. Kim stood rooted to the floor. Her voice had abandoned her and her throat felt thick with emotion. Anna rounded the corner and entered the living room.

Kim saw her misstep as she took in the state of the apartment. Anna's eyes grew big and a wash of emotion swept across her face. That was enough for Kim to break. The weight of everything became too much as she looked into Anna's eyes. Tears rolled down her face, her breath caught short. She braced herself as Anna marched over and took her in her arms.

"Shhhh," she cooed. Kim struggled to take a breath. She felt as if she was hyperventilating. "Slow breaths in, Kim." Kim willed herself to calm down. Finally, she drew in some deep breaths. "Let's get out of here. Come with me."

They stepped into Kim's favourite café a few minutes later. The noise was as welcome as a hot bath on a winter's night. Kim had only been in her apartment for an hour, but the silence had been deafening.

"Drink this." Kim looked at the tea Anna placed in front of her. When did she get that? In fact, how long had they been in the café? Anna sat silently watching her, waiting for her to say something. So far, she'd only sobbed.

"Thank you." Well, that was a start.

"Stupid question, but are you alright?"

"No, not really. Walking into my home, finding it like that, was devastating. Just another reminder that the man I have spent most of my life with has changed, and I don't know why. I spoke to him just before we returned home. He wants to talk to me and explain. I've just got back off of the best holiday of my life with the most beautiful woman I have ever seen and I'm trying to work out what that all means. The time away was supposed to help me figure everything out, but I'm more confused than ever." Kim inhaled sharply. She'd reeled everything off in one long and frantic rant.

"That's a lot." Anna reached over and took her hand that was resting on the table. "How can I help?"

"I've no idea, doll. It's just too much to wade through."

"Okay, no, we can do this. Let's break it down. One thing at a time. Starting with the Greg situation."

"I spoke to him briefly before leaving *Connie*."

"*Connie*?"

"The boat is called *Connie*, anyway he asked if I could travel to my parents so we could talk. He sounded better than the last time we spoke. It seems he wants to stay away from Paris for a while."

"That's a good first step. Speak to him."

"I'll book something for the long weekend."

"Okay, so that's planned. Next is the whole Hélène situation."

"We've decided to date, give the relationship a try."

"Okay, so what's complicated about that, then?

227

"Nothing, but when you mix it with the Greg situation, everything changes. Being on a boat in the middle of the Mediterranean was wonderful, but we were in a cocoon. There were no real life pressures to deal with."

"Are you having second thoughts about a relationship with her?"

"No!" Kim almost shouted her response. The last thing she wanted was to stop seeing Hélène, but the fact of the matter was everything just got a lot more complicated. She wasn't sure if Hélène was going to want to deal with it all. "I like her, Anna, like, I really like her. But what if dealing with all my shit proves to be too much? I mean, we've been dating for a short amount of time? Jesus, Anna, we haven't actually been out on a proper date."

"Alright, so go out on a date then. Yes, at some point, your worlds are going to collide. Greg and Hélène will have to coexist, but you have time. It's what, two weeks until the long weekend, so why not take that time to be with Hélène? Feel out the situation. Date her, talk to her. Hopefully, by the time you have to visit Greg, you will be in a clearer headspace."

Kim nodded as she contemplated what Anna was saying. Maybe if she just broke it down, dealt with one thing at a time, everything would work out. Was she being naïve? Possibly, but what was the alternative?

"Thanks, doll. God, it's great to see you. Sorry you've had to swoop in and deal with this."

"Stop. You did more than your fair share of listening and guiding when I needed it. I'm here for you, okay?"

"Okay. Now tell me all about Texas."

Kim's problems were far from fixed, but she felt the tiniest bit better after talking to Anna.

* * *

After a pleasant hour spent chatting with Anna, Kim found herself on the outside of her apartment looking at her front door. The thought of staying there filled her with dread. All she wanted was to go back to those lazy days spent in bed with Hélène as they cruised along the Mediterranean. Could she call Hélène? Maybe ask to see her?

Kim
Hey, what are you up to right now?

Hélène
*Sam just left, so now I am doing laundry. Living like
a rock star.*

Kim smiled, a warm comforting feeling surrounded her heart as she thought of Hélène doing her laundry. Thinking of Hélène doing anything, no matter how mundane, made her feel a thousand times better.

Kim
Would you like some company? I have mad folding skills.
Hélène
*How could I possibly turn down 'mad folding skills'?
I'd love to see you. Dinner?*

Kim: *Great. See you soon xx.*

It took Kim just over an hour to tidy up her apartment. Even though she wasn't planning to stay, she couldn't leave it in such a state. After a quick shower and a change of clothes, she was already feeling more like herself again.

A slight quiver of nerves rumbled through her stomach. Would they fit so seamlessly outside of their holiday bubble?

The taxi pulled up to Hélène's apartment building half an hour later. Kim wrapped her worries into a nice little box and stored it at the very back of her mind. All she wanted was to relax and feel Hélène's warmth.

Kim crossed the courtyard, which was brimming with flowers. Someone obviously took good care of the landscape. Hélène had told Kim which apartment was hers, so as she crossed to the door she looked up to see Hélène standing by her double windows sporting a smile that made everything feel okay in the world. Kim sucked in a good lungful of air. The mere sight of Hélène sent her into a whirlwind of excitement, happiness, nerves and longing.

The door buzzed open without Kim having to press anything. Hélène was just as keen to see Kim by the looks of things. The stairs leading to the first floor were spiral, each step squeaked under foot. The inside was a little dated, the place could do with a touch of paint.

As she rounded that last bend of the stairs, she caught sight of Hélène in her doorway leaning on the doorframe. She was dressed in cutoff joggers and a worn out T-shirt. It was the first time Kim had seen her looking so ordinary. Before their holiday, Kim had met Hélène in person a handful of times, and each time she was clad in designer skirt suits. In Saint Tropez and Corsica, she was either in a wetsuit or a bikini.

Seeing Hélène like this, completely comfortable, was breathtaking. Kim wanted to push her inside, slam the door closed, and take her up against it immediately. She didn't do that—she had some restraint. Kind of. Instead of fulfilling her fantasy, she stepped into Hélène's embrace, hugged her tightly and then kissed her deeply.

Once they had kissed themselves breathless, Hélène pulled back, guiding Kim inside. The apartment was on the small side, but it fit Hélène perfectly. Why that was Kim didn't know, she just felt it.

Kim dropped her bag by the door. She'd put an extra pair of knickers in there, just in case. Hélène wandered off into another room, allowing Kim time to peruse her space. The walls were littered with pictures of Hélène and her friends. Diving trips, nights out and several of Hélène with John and a woman Kim presumed must have been Claire.

Slowly, she made her way through to where Hélène had disappeared. Kim giggled as she looked at Hélène perched on the sofa with a pile of washing that was almost as tall as her. "Jeez, you weren't kidding, doll."

"I never joke about washing. I hope you brought those folding skills you were bragging about."

"Like you and washing, I never joke about folding. Stand back, H, you are about to witness a master at work." With a smirk, Kim ushered Hélène out of the way and set about folding.

"You know I was joking right, I did not expect you to come here and do my laundry." Hélène looked taken aback that Kim was actually sitting folding her clothes.

"The faster this is done, the faster I get to relax with you, so it's in my interest to chip in. Why don't you open some wine? You'll only slow me down." Kim shot Hélène a grin and a little wink, causing Hélène to chuckle as she left the living room in search of wine.

Clinking and thumping came from the kitchen. Kim happily sat folding away. She really was a pro. The sound of music drifted through the apartment. Hélène reappeared with

231

two glasses of wine. The surprise on her face when she saw the neat pile of washing folded on the table made Kim chuckle.

"That would have taken me an hour." She placed the wine on the coffee table, her eyes still trained on the clothes. Kim smiled internally. It felt good to impress her.

"Well, it's done now, so we can relax. Sit with me, please."

Hélène dropped into the seat, her body pressed close to Kim's. Clearly, their chemistry transferred to dry land. "Are you alright?" Hélène asked so softly that Kim almost missed it. Should she tell Hélène that she was, in fact, not okay? "Don't hide from me, Kim, let me in." Well, that decided that then.

"Greg trashed the apartment. It was… it was a shock to walk into." Kim's shoulders sagged.

"Hey," Hélène cooed, tipping Kim's chin up to meet her eyes. "It's okay to feel what you're feeling. I know it's complicated and you have a lot to sort out with him, but you have to let yourself feel whatever's running through you. Yes, he's your best friend, but he hurt you and it's okay to feel angry. He trashed your house, which I can only imagine felt jarring. A home is your safety, your comfort, at least mine is."

With just a few words, Hélène had pinpointed exactly what was running through Kim's mind. She was completely conflicted. Greg was so important to her she felt bad about having less than friendly thoughts about him. But why shouldn't she? He'd messed up, and Kim couldn't help but feel angry.

"Listen, why don't I order some food? Let's just relax tonight. It's been a really long day and I don't know about you, but I'm beat."

Music to Kim's ears. "That sounds wonderful."

Hélène smiled, leaned down, and gently kissed her. "Wait there, drink your wine." An order that Kim would happily obey.

Hélène skipped out of the room. The music became a little louder. Soft jazz soothed Kim's ears. Before long, she slipped off her heels, laid back on the sofa and watched as the sky faded through Hélène's window.

The squeak of floorboards drew her attention back to the room. Hélène stood by the door, beckoning Kim to follow her. Maybe the food had arrived, and she'd not heard the door.

Holding Hélène's hand, she allowed herself to be guided through to Hélène's bedroom and then through to the bathroom. The sweet smell of coconut permeated the air. The soft flicker of tea lights that had been strategically placed around the room gave off a warm and cosy light. Hélène stood aside as she pulled Kim further into the room. The bath tub had been filled. Kim looked at Hélène. Had this woman actually run her a bubble bath?

"I thought that maybe a soak would help you relax. Here, look." Hélène gestured to the glass of wine that sat on a small table at the head of the bath. "You could just have a bath and relax with some wine. I have books too if you'd like."

"You ran me a bath?" Kim still couldn't compute what she was seeing.

"Oh, yes, is that… was that a bad idea?"

A bad idea? This was the single most romantic thing that Kim had ever had done for her. "This is perfect." Her response came out as a whisper. She moved into Hélène's space, taking her face gently in her palms. "Thank you."

The kiss was supposed to be a "Thank you for this wonderful bath" kiss, but it quickly turned into "I'm going to fuck you in this bath" kiss. Kim wasted no time stripping Hélène of her T-shirt. It didn't seem that Hélène minded too much, not by the way she was cupping Kim's arse. Piece by piece, their clothing hit the floor.

"Get in," Hélène breathed. Kim had forgotten about the bath entirely. Her mind was one hundred percent on getting her head between Hélène's perfect thighs. "Kim?" Hélène laughed.

"Sorry, you distracted me."

"I distracted you, huh?"

Kim lowered herself into the water. It was deliciously hot, and the smell made her head swim wonderfully. The muscles in her back seemed to melt as she lay her head back. One thing was missing, though. Hélène. "Aren't you getting in?"

"I will in a minute, but first I want you to relax." Kim was about to protest until she saw Hélène snake her hand into the water, caressing her inner leg.

"Why, Ms DuBois, are you trying to seduce me?"

"Is it working?"

"You know damn well it is. I hope you plan on touching me soon, doll, because I'm not sure I can wait."

"Oh, and what exactly will you do if I make you wait?"

Kim loved this flirty back-and-forth. Hélène could hook and reel her in with just a few words. However, Kim was also pretty good at playing the game, too. She loved being able to take the power and watch Hélène become a puddle of want and lust.

With a wicked grin, Kim slid her hand between her own legs, cupping herself. Hélène's eyes grew to the size of saucers. Her breathing hitched and a little growl escaped her throat. "If you make me wait, I'll take things into my own hands."

Kim wondered if her sexy plan had backfired when Hélène withdrew her hand from the bathwater. Undeterred, Kim slid her fingers between her folds.

Unsurprisingly, she was beyond aroused. Her fingers glided up and down effortlessly. What surprised her was Hélène scooting away until her back hit the opposite wall. Kim watched eagerly as Hélène spread her legs and brought her fingers to her clit.

Was this really fucking happening?

"How does it feel?" Kim didn't recognise her own voice.

"Keep touching yourself." Hélène's eyes bored into her.

Kim picked up the pace of her fingers all the time, watching Hélène's skilled hands draw small light circles around her own sex. Both women were breathless as they continued to watch each other get off.

"I'm gonna come, H."

"Come now," Hélène demanded. That authoritative voice was enough to send Kim over. Her body slid down the tub as her eyes slammed shut. Her orgasm radiated in pulses from her stimulated clit. A loud cry echoed around the bathroom. Hélène followed shortly after. She was almost lying on the bathroom floor by the time her body had come down from her climax.

"Will you get in the bath now?" Kim pulled herself back into a sitting position, her face warm and glowing. Her legs felt heavy and her body felt sated. Still, she wanted Hélène. She wanted to feel her body.

On wobbly legs, Hélène heaved herself off the floor and slid into the bath behind Kim, her arms pulling them close together. What had started as a frenzied sexcapade finished in an intimate embrace. They stayed wrapped in each other's arms until the water became cold. "Let's get dressed and eat." Hélène mumbled in her ear, nipping at her lobe.

They left the warmth of the bathroom and went into Hélène's bedroom. Hélène produced a pair of sweatpants and a T-shirt for Kim, which were ridiculously long on Kim's short frame, but she didn't care because they smelled of Hélène.

They sat together in the living room, snuggled on the couch until their food arrived. With the lights dimmed and the music softly playing in the background, they spent the evening in beautiful silence. Now and then, they would kiss and hold each other tighter. Hélène had refilled their wine and turned on her little gas fire to add to the ambiance. This was what Kim needed. Somehow Hélène had plucked the perfect scenario out of Kim's mind and made it a reality.

"Shall we go to bed?" Hélène kissed Kim's temple as she spoke. They hadn't discussed if Kim was going to stay over.

"Okay." Slowly, they extracted their limbs. Kim waited for Hélène to stand before taking her hand and following her to the bedroom. As if it were the most normal thing in the world, they stood by the sink, Hélène handing Kim a spare toothbrush, Kim adding toothpaste to both brushes.

Anyone would think they'd been doing this for years. It had been the same on *Connie*. By the end of the trip, they'd stayed together every night, forming a routine. That routine had obviously carried over to the real world as well.

They slid beneath the covers, Kim backing herself into Hélène's body. Their breaths evened out and became heavier as they fell asleep.

* * *

A gentle brush against her cheek roused Kim. Her body was so warm and comfy she fought to keep her eyes closed, but it was no use. Her face split into a smile as Hélène continued to caress her face.

"Morning."

"Well, finally." Hélène mock huffed, pushing herself into Kim a little harder. Kim laughed at Hélène's sulky whine.

"Can I do something for you?"

"Oh, there's a loaded question."

236

"You're doing something for me. Keep rolling your hips like that and I'm going to have a fabulous start to the day." Kim felt Hélène's body convulse with silent laughter. Her hips rolled a little deeper. Kim reached back and grabbed Hélène's arse possessively. Her leg lifted, allowing Hélène to insert her own. Just as the night before in the living room, they remained silent. Their bodies were doing all the talking.

Hélène gripped Kim's hips, rolling hard as the friction between them built. Kim knew Hélène would be sporting a soaked leg as they continued to grind. Their release came suddenly. Hélène's hand had found its way to Kim's nipple. The feeling of her pinching and rolling almost sent her straight into a second orgasm.

"Mmm, now that's a good morning." Kim rolled over to face Hélène once their breathing had settled.

"Sorry to have woken you."

Kim couldn't help but laugh. Hélène's face did not agree with her statement at all. "No complaints from me, sugar." They kissed delicately.

"I hate to say it, but I have to get ready for work." Hélène looked genuinely gutted that she was going to have to leave the comfort of her bed. She looked downright stricken when Kim rolled on her back, the sheet dropping, leaving her breasts exposed. "Maybe I could take an extra day," she mumbled as her face dropped to take a nipple in her mouth. Kim laughed at Hélène's rapidly dissolving self-restraint. Kim wasn't going to make it into the office today.

Chapter 20

Swivelling in an office chair was rather relaxing. It was a little meditative. The back and forth motion lulled Hélène into a quiet state of calm. And, boy, did she need a state of calm. The week had turned into an emotional clusterfuck.

The delightful — and very satisfying — night she'd spent with Kim seemed like a lifetime ago, when in fact it had been six days and seven hours. But who's counting? Hélène. Hélène was counting because she would give anything to rewind the clock so that she was still nestled between Kim's magnificent breasts instead of in her office, pondering the past week of shittiness.

First point of disquiet was Kim's announcement that she was going to the UK a week earlier than expected because Greg seemed down. Kim and Greg had got back into a routine of messaging each other again and again over the week. Kim had become more and more restless, not knowing the full story of Greg's sudden downward spiral.

So she'd booked a last-minute flight to London. No problem, right? Well, only if you discount the fact that Kim had failed to realise — or maybe she did and found it not important enough to consider — that she'd made pretty specific plans with Hélène and hadn't involved her in the decision to leave the country, at all.

Hélène had bitten her tongue to keep her frustration at bay. Maybe it was for the best? The sooner Kim was there, the sooner she could sort it all out and come back. That line of thinking had become Hélène's mantra since Kim left. It was a pretty useless mantra in all fairness though, because Hélène couldn't stop herself from overthinking.

The thought of Kim being close to Greg sent bile shooting up her throat. Would he hurt her? Would he worm his way back? Would Kim realise she still loved him? Those questions sent terror shooting around her body like a bloody pinball machine.

Feeling in a constant state of stress was exhausting. Jesus, they'd only been together a few short weeks and already Hélène felt overwhelmed. Talking to Kim, or talking to anyone, would probably be the healthiest way to deal with her internal meltdown, but she just couldn't do it. Putting that on anyone else was unfair.

Once she'd received Kim's text that she'd arrived at the airport safely, Hélène's mental health took a nosedive into a rabbit hole of insecurity and anxiety. If Kim was eventually going to disappear, maybe Hélène should just cut her losses now?

Even though Kim had constantly tried to reassure her, it did little to assuage her nerves. However, the thought of willingly walking away from someone as perfect as Kim seemed utterly ridiculous. What the hell should she do?

Second point of disconcertment. JJ announcing he had found a woman to impregnate. Putting all the "Kim confusion" aside, Hélène had to face the fact that her brother was going ahead with having a baby, which scared the life out of her.

Was he ready? Could he really cut back his work and look after a child? Was the baby going to be predisposed to the DuBois shitty character traits? Okay, so those weren't reasons for her to be spinning out. It's not like she was having a baby, but she worried nonetheless.

Third — and possibly the most disturbing — point of perturbation was Veronique calling her up two days ago, two sheets to the wind. Crying down the phone, calling herself a failure, begging Hélène to pick up the phone — which she did not do. No chance in hell she was going to try to talk down a drunk Veronique DuBois.

Hélène had never seen — or heard — her mother be so self deprecating. Honestly, she didn't think her mother cared that much to feel so bad. After thirty-plus years of parental neglect, how was she supposed to reconcile everything that her mum had said? Could she believe Veronique wanted to do better? Was she really proud of Hélène? Who the fuck knew?

Hélène needed to double her therapy sessions after listening to Veronique describe *in detail* the reason she'd slept with Hélène's father, therefore producing Hélène nine months later and therefore the reason she'd married him. Nobody needed to know that Phillipe was a good lay, NOBODY!

Fourth point — admittedly less contentious, more exciting — was Holly calling to say she had an amazing opportunity for Hélène. Turns out Holly had done some serious thinking after their holiday. Apparently, she'd been unhappy for a while and she wanted to settle down doing something she loved. A friend of hers was selling his diving centre in the south

240

of Corsica. Holly had jumped at the chance to buy it off of him, hoping Hélène would join her as a partner.

Over the years, they'd spoken dozens of times about opening their own business. Diving was more than a hobby, it was their passion. As soon as Holly had laid out the plan, Hélène wanted to do it. She'd been working in an office for too long. As much as she enjoyed the people she worked with, the job was slowly killing her joy.

John and Kim were the only things that gave her pause. John had done so much for her, she didn't want to let him down and now with his plan for a baby, how could she ask him to search for a replacement for her and move even farther away?

Then there was Kim. That presented a whole new set of issues she didn't want to think about right now. Thankfully, Holly had given Hélène plenty of time to give her an answer. Either way, Holly was set to follow her dream.

All of that had happened within three days. It was a lot.

Her stomach protested at the constant movement. Halting her swing, she glanced at her watch. Kim would be nearly in the UK now. They'd promised to call and text, but already Hélène's skin felt itchy with anxiety. Great, was she going to feel like this until Kim came back? *If she comes back.*

Hélène jumped as her phone rang out. Kim's name scrolled across her screen. "Hey, did you make it okay?" She put every effort into making her voice sound relaxed.

"Uh, I hate budget airlines. It's like they think the general population has no need for legs. And that's coming from someone who is small. I practically had my knees wedged into my boobs the entire flight."

"They're very comfortable boobs, though."

"Ms DuBois, really. Here I am trying to get on my high horse about air travel and all you can do is compliment my rack."

"So sorry, please continue with your rant. I'll just think about your boobs in my head."

Kim's delicious laughter filtered down the line. Hélène smiled wildly, knowing she'd caused it. "I suppose it makes me feel better knowing my girlfriend is objectifying me from afar."

"I think that's the first time a woman has enjoyed me objectifying her."

"Well, this woman will never say no to a good ego boost, so objectify away, sugar." It was Hélène's turn to laugh. Just a few words from Kim and all Hélène's insecurities and worries melted away. For now, at least.

"Is someone meeting you at the airport?" *Please not Greg, Please not Greg.*

"Yeah, my dad, probably Mum too."

"Where are you now?"

"I have literally just stepped off the plane. I wanted to hear your voice."

"That makes me happy to hear. Will you call me tonight before you go to sleep?" Hopefully, Hélène didn't sound too needy. Oh well.

"You better believe your tight arse I'm gonna call. I need to see that beautiful face of yours before I can sleep. Hey, maybe we could…"

"Could?"

"Give each other something to dream about?"

"Kimberley, are you suggesting phone sex?"

"Please don't call me Kimberley. It's like my mother just entered the room and believe me, she's the last person I want to be thinking about right now. Not when the prospect of our late night call might turn sexy."

Hélène had never had phone sex before. The idea was titillating, but would she be able to do it? What the hell did you say to someone to get them off over the phone?

Oh Jesus, now she was overthinking it. It's not like she didn't know how to satisfy a woman. She'd never had a problem in that department, but doing it over the phone felt intimidating.

"You're panicking, aren't you?" Kim made the statement with no judgement.

"No, no, it's just… um… well, I haven't done that before. I know it's shocking, right?"

"I haven't either."

Kim's confession stumped Hélène. "Really?"

"Really. Look, I don't want to talk about our experiences with other people, but it's safe to say, my experience isn't vast."

"Okay, well, let's try it then. We can muddle through together."

"It's a date. A very weird date that will take place in my childhood bedroom with my parents down the hall."

"You'll just have to bite a pillow." Hélène laughed at the visual. Kim was not a quiet person in bed. Not at all.

"Wow, that's some confidence right there, Ms DuBois."

"Unless you want me to explain right now how I'm going to get you to the point of screaming, I suggest we end this conversation." Amazingly, Hélène's confidence had skyrocketed the moment Kim had started their playful banter. This phone sex thing was going to be a cinch. Kim's heavy breathing proved her point.

"Yes, I think you're right. Jesus, I'm turned on and now have to go hug my parents."

"You started it," Hélène chuckled.

"Yeah, and you better finish it this evening. I'll call you later."

"Okay, be safe… I… speak soon." Hélène almost threw the phone across the room. She'd nearly said those three words, you know, the ones that would have ruined everything because

243

they were no way near the point in their relationship where those words were acceptable. Was she actually losing her mind?

Merde.

* * *

Budget reports were put on this earth to slowly suck the souls out of anyone who gazed upon them. *I think I would actually prefer watching paint dry.* Hours and hours of Hélène's life had flitted away whilst she stared at her screen. The other option to pass the time until her evening rendezvous with Kim was to look at scheduling. Oh, or payroll. *Fuck my life.*

Hélène's brain was saved from melting by a ping on her work phone. It was an email from Otis Perez, her mother's assistant.

> *Dear Hélène,*
> *Veronique requests your presence tonight at 8pm. Usual restaurant.*
> *Cordialement*
> *Otis Perez*

Hélène slowly let her head *thunk* on the desk. Life was really testing her right now. The last thing in the world Hélène wanted to do was to sit through an excruciating dinner with her mother.

Maybe she could call JJ and ask him to fake an emergency. Even though Veronique wasn't his mother, she was always there for him when he needed her. If only she would show Hélène the same loyalty.

There was no way out of it. If she refused, she'd risk her mother's wrath or worse, a visit. She quickly fired off a reply, accepting her invitation. It was going to be a long night.

The first thing Hélène noticed when she entered the very ostentatious restaurant that her mother loved so much was that Veronique was not sitting at her usual table in the middle of the room, where she was bound to get all the attention she craved. Because you know, without being the centre of the universe, what was the point in life, right?

Instead, Hélène saw her mother waving from the back of the dining hall. *Well, this is new.*

"Mother." Hélène's standard greeting was met with a look of... something. Pain, maybe?

"Hélène, dear." Veronique stood and kissed her daughter on each cheek.

"Did your old table offend you?" Hélène wasn't trying to be an arse, but it was difficult to rein her tone in.

"I thought we could use a little privacy."

"Ah, I see. You don't want everyone to watch as you scold me. Bad for the brand." Wow, Hélène was going into full bitch mode.

"I understand why you would think that, but it's not true, I assure you. I have no desire to scold you or fight with you."

Hélène sat silently, eyeing her mother's face, looking for some evidence she was lying. The one thing Hélène knew was that Veronique could change her mood in a flash. She needed to keep her shield up, no matter how much she wanted to believe the honesty that radiated off her mother. "So, what do you need?"

"To talk and to apologise. I shouldn't have called you the other night. It was—"

"Horrifying. That's the word you are looking for."

"Yes, I'm a little mortified, if I'm being honest. Otis enjoyed regaling me with the conversation."

"Well, at least someone found it entertaining."

"Hélène. What I said shouldn't have been said when I was drunk. However, that doesn't mean everything I said was false. Forget everything I said about your father though."

"I would have to bleach my brain for that to happen, but I'm making a valiant effort to believe it just never happened."

For the first time in… forever, Veronique laughed out loud. A full bark of amusement shattered the thick air between them. Hélène couldn't help but smirk.

"Yes, I think that's a smart approach."

"Okay, I'm listening, maman."

Using "maman" caused Veronique's eyes to well up. "It's been years since you have called me that."

"It's been years since I felt I could."

Veronique nodded. "Yes, I can see why." She cleared her throat. "I've had a run of poor health recently." Hélène sat up straight. "I had to have a minor procedure to have a lump removed."

"When?"

"Last month."

"Why are you only telling me now?"

"Honestly, I didn't think to tell you." Hearing those words hurt more than Hélène could say. She'd always known her mother was uninterested in her, but to hear that she wasn't even a thought in her mother's mind was heartbreaking. "I understand your anger and hurt."

"Who said I was either of those?" Hélène said defiantly. Like hell she was going to wilt now.

"*Mon coeur*, it's all over your face. I hurt you with my words. I'm sorry, truly I am. After the procedure, I started to see things differently. My actions, the way I live my life." Veronique shifted in her chair, her gaze drifted to the table. "The conclusion I came to was chilling. I am my mother. Cold, distant, unloving to the ones that should have all my love."

Of all the things Hélène was expecting, this heartfelt confession was not one of them. Was she being punked?

"You won't remember your grandmother very well, and that's by design." Veronique had lifted her gaze back to Hélène. "She was a horrid woman with a heart of stone. Nothing I did was good enough in her eyes."

Well, doesn't that sound fucking familiar?

"She never wanted children. I was a mistake. She reminded me constantly that I'd ruined her life. I left when I was old enough and had enough money. It took years of hard work and dedication, but I succeeded. I built an empire worthy of her respect. Foolishly, I thought she would love me If I could just prove myself to her.

"Of course I was wrong. Even after she died, I could still hear her vicious voice in my head. I vowed to be different. I vowed to be nothing like her, but to my utter shame, I have turned out to be her replica." She sniffed as tears threatened to fall. "I can't give you a reason, Hélène. I can only say how very sorry I am. You *were* and *are* wanted. I loved you from the moment I knew you were growing inside me. I'm not sure where it went so wrong."

Hélène was struggling to breathe. She'd waited for this moment for decades and now it was here she had no words. "I…"

"Please let me finish. I think I clung to my work so desperately because I was still trying to prove her wrong. In doing so, I cast you aside, just as she did to me. Getting a healthy dose of my mortality shook something loose. I pictured my funeral. I pictured all of my 'friends' standing by my grave, mourning.

247

"But the one person I couldn't see was you. It terrified me to believe that my only daughter would shun my funeral because of how I treated her. I never went to my mother's. I couldn't put all the pain and hurt behind me. She didn't deserve my presence. I would be devastated if I had the same effect on you." Veronique reached over and took Hélène's hand. "As part of my treatment, I was offered counselling, which I accepted. The night I called you about The Sapphire incident was the wake-up call I needed. I hadn't even called you to reprimand you. I called to see if you wanted to meet for dinner so I could tell you about my health issues. I got the message about the hotel incident just before I called. It's inexcusable, but the old me took what I'd learned and berated you as usual." Veronique shook her head in shame. "I can do better, Hélène, I can. I am not ashamed to have you as my daughter. Nothing means more to me than you."

Brain injury would explain Hélène's current circumstances. Yeah, that made sense. She must have tripped somewhere, hit her head because this couldn't be real. She was hallucinating.

"Please say something."

"I…" *Ah, nice use of your vocabulary, H.* She could hear Kim's teasing tone as she sat there staring at her mother's tear-stained face, trying to unpack everything Veronique had just verbally vomited on her. "I honestly have no words, maman."

"It's a lot, I know. It's taken a therapist to help me get to this point, so I understand you need time. I have to fly to Milan tomorrow, but maybe when I return we can talk more?"

Hélène nodded. Time, that's what she needed.

"Okay, I'm going to go. I know we haven't eaten, but I doubt either of us wants to sit through a meal right now."

More nodding.

"I love you, Hélène." Veronique rose gracefully from the table, swiped away her tears and kissed Hélène on the temple. Her exit was quick and quiet. The waiter stopped at the table, placing a double brandy in front of her. Without pause, Hélène whipped up the glass and swallowed the contents in one gulp.

Not wanting to sit by herself like a deer in headlights, she pulled out a few notes to leave a tip and exited the restaurant. The night air was icy and biting, but it felt good. The nip of the wind helped refocus her mind.

Taking out her phone, she hit the call button. It rang... and rang... and rang. No answer. Where the hell was Kim? Tears fell down her face. She redialed. No answer. Wiping her face, she tried JJ. No answer. In a fit of confusion and frustration, she cried out a string of not so PG words. Where the fuck was everyone?

Her feet pounded the pavement as she walked. Her lungs burned, but she liked it. Her apartment was too far to walk the whole way, but right now, she needed to move. Her frustration grew as she tried Kim's mobile again and again. Five minutes passed until her phone pinged with a message notification.

Kim
Sorry doll, still with Greg, I'll call tomorrow xx

The message stopped her in her tracks. So it was beginning already. She was being put aside again. Her fingers pressed the call button.

"Sam, what are you doing right now?"

Sam must have heard Hélène's distress. "Nothing that can't wait. What's wrong?"

"I need to drink heavily. Can you meet me?"

"Yep, send me the address. I'm on my way." Thank God for Sam. Luckily, she was only around the corner from a bar she and Sam frequented when they'd first met. She shot off a message to Sam and headed off.

The place was heaving. It looked like most of the lesbians in Paris had congregated in this one bar. Pushing her way through, she snagged a free stool. Hopefully Sam would arrive soon, because Hélène had no intention of waiting. She ordered a double brandy which she necked. The bartender shot her an understanding look before pouring her another drink. Her brain was feeling fuzzy. A warm hand on her shoulder jolted her from her alcohol induced stupor.

"What's going on?" Sam asked as she squeezed in next to Hélène, signalling for the bartender to pour them two more drinks.

"Do you ever think the universe hates you? Or like you're cursed?" Yep, she was on her way to tipsy town.

Sam laughed. "No, not really. Is that what you think?"

"Yep, I think I must have really pissed someone off in a previous life, because karma is being a real bitch lately."

"Alright, fancy telling me what's caused this?" Sam made a swirling motion with her hand to convey "this" meant Hélène's state of pessimism.

"Kim is going to get back with her ex and leave me, just like everyone else. My brother is having a baby on his own with a random surrogate. Holly wants me to pack up and move to Corsica, and my mother has just given me enough emotional upheaval to keep my therapist in business for decades."

Sam stared at her wide-eyed. "Well fuck, we're going to need more drinks."

Chapter 21

Kim cradled the Martini glass in her hand. Her gaze was transfixed by the roaring fire in her parents' living room. What Greg had told her shook her to her bones. She'd been right coming to the UK early. How had she missed it? How had it gone on for so long without her noticing?

As soon as she'd arrived at her parents' house yesterday, she knew something was seriously wrong. Greg was thinner, his pallor was a sickly white. Beads of sweat traced his hairline. Immediately, she'd dropped her bags and taken him in her arms.

"What's going on? No more waiting. Please talk to me." They stood in her parents' hallway hugging, neither one wanting to let go.

"Let's sit down in the living room. I'll stick the kettle on." Peter said. Kim's dad was always a comfort in stressful situations. Kim, Greg, and Joy made their way to the couch.

"Greg?" Kim was losing patience.

"Okay, okay, it's just harder than I thought it would be." He cleared his throat. Joy placed a reassuring hand on his arm. "I'm in withdrawal."

Withdrawal? Like drug withdrawal?

"I can't pinpoint the exact time it got out of hand because it seemed to happen so fast."

"What did? Greg, what do you mean you're in withdrawal?"

"Drugs, Kim, I've been taking drugs for the best part of eighteen months."

Kim looked frantically from Greg to her mum. "What, how?…"

"It started as just a weekend thing when I had to go out with the guys from work. When I got put on Hervé's team, I quickly understood that they did things a little differently. Banking is all high pressure and money. I knew that, but these guys took it to a new level."

"Hervé, as in your bloody boss?"

Greg nodded his head. "Yes. I didn't want to be the bloke who couldn't keep up. They were giving me the opportunity to climb the ranks quickly. All I had to do was play nice. Honestly, it felt good to be a part of the 'in' crowd."

"By poisoning yourself?"

"Kim, let him finish," Joy whispered.

"I know it was daft, but I didn't see the harm, really it was just a bit of weed to begin with. A way for us to de-stress and bond. Then we took out some high-profile clients, the kind that like to party. The drugs got heavier. Cocaine, pills—"

"Jesus Christ," Kim almost yelled. This was unimaginable.

Greg waited for Peter to place the tray of teacups on the coffee table before continuing. "Before I knew it, the drugs were being brought into work. Hervé said it was a way to keep us motivated, to crank out the work faster. Believe it or not, I refused the first few times, but then Hervé started to distance himself from me. I was being pushed out. Kim, I'd worked so hard to get where I was. Hervé was the only one who could get me to the next level, so I started partaking in their daily habit."

"Why didn't you come to me?"

"And say what? Oh, by the way, love, I'm high as a kite most of the time now, but don't worry, I'm going to get a promotion out of it."

"You wanted a promotion that bad?"

"Yes Kim, I did! For once in my life, I wanted something I earned. Something that wasn't given to me by you or your parents."

"Greg, what on earth are you talking about?" Greg's statement was mystifying.

"Do you know how it feels to have to mooch off your girlfriend and her family? Since my parents died, you've had to do everything for me. Nothing was just mine."

"That's not true at all."

"Really? My first car, our first flat, clothes, pocket money. I could go on, but I think you get the point. Hervé was offering me the chance to earn a lot of money and secure myself a prominent position in the bank. We would have been set, Kim. I could finally start paying you all back."

"There is nothing to pay back. We're your family, that's how it works, kiddo," Peter said gently.

"I appreciate that, Peter, but that's not how I feel in here." Greg tapped his finger on his temple. "The drugs got heavier and more frequent. I couldn't control myself. I couldn't get through the day without a hit." A sob tore through Kim's chest. "I didn't realise how it was affecting my behaviour. I'm so sorry, Kim, you know I would never hurt you."

253

"But you did. You hurt me. Us."

"Yes, I did, and that was my wake up call. What happened in Saint Tropez was unforgivable. I was high and out of control. I'm glad Hélène was there." Greg dropped his head and sobbed, his body shuddered as he cried.

Kim was heartbroken for him, for them. Slowing his breathing, Greg pulled himself together. "I'm clean now, but I hope you understand why I needed to leave Paris."

"You did the right thing. Are you getting help? Have you seen someone?"

"I've started going to meetings. Your dad has been kind enough to go with me."

Kim hugged her dad. "Thank you."

"It's okay, kid. Greg knows my position on how he behaved towards you. We've spoken at length. I, like your mother, just want him to sort himself out."

"I suggested he take a sabbatical from the bank, looking to transfer back to his old office as soon as possible," Joy said. Kim's insides squeezed uncomfortably. Her life was in Paris now. She loved living there, but Greg was her best friend and he needed her now more than ever.

"Let's talk some more about that later." Kim didn't want to talk about it at all, but she had no choice.

They spent the rest of the afternoon and well into the evening catching up. Kim had questions, and Greg answered them honestly. They hadn't touched on the subject of their relationship yet. Kim definitely didn't want to bring Hélène into it.

She'd felt bad when she saw Hélène had been trying to call her. They were supposed to be having a sexy phone call, but instead Kim cancelled because she was still talking things through with Greg. She felt awful, but he needed her.

254

Today had probably been one of the longest days of Kim's life. There was so much emotion, the air was saturated with its unease. The Martini was helping — well, the third one, mostly. Greg had retired to the spare room a couple of hours earlier. Peter had left Kim and her mum alone for a while. Joy was always the one that Kim turned to in times of crisis.

"How are you, doll?" Joy asked, sipping her own Martini.

"I don't know, Mum. This was not what I was expecting. I wish you'd told me earlier."

"Love, it wasn't my place, or your father's. Anyway, it would have made no difference. When Greg came here, he needed space and time after what he did to you. If you'd have known, you would have come home and it would have made things worse."

"I still should have known. God, Mum, I feel awful. I was having a gay old time in the bloody Mediterranean whilst my best friend, my boyfriend, was having a crisis."

"Boyfriend? Don't you mean ex-boyfriend? I understand you wanting to support him, truly I do. That's why we stepped in, but, Kim, you needed a break just as much as Greg. If he'd have told you what was going on when he visited you in Saint Tropez, would it have made a difference? Would you still be with him?"

"I don't know." Would she have left with him and tried to sort out their relationship? She couldn't answer that. Maybe, but would it have changed anything for her in the long run?

Yes, Greg's behaviour had been the catalyst that started them down this path, but the truth of it was that Kim had been feeling lost for sometime. Her own life wasn't what she'd expected it to be, and that wasn't all down to Greg taking drugs, that was down to her and her own decisions.

"I think you do know, love. Can I be blunt with you?" When was Joy Richmond not blunt? Kim nodded, swallowing the last of her drink before pouring another. "You guys are the best of friends, and I always loved that. You know each other inside and out, which is wonderful for a parent to see. When you became lovers, I was less than chuffed." Kim did a double-take at her mother. Had she heard that correctly? "The reason I was less than happy was because when you're together, *you*, my darling, always seem to end up holding yourself back to make sure that Greg gets what he needs and wants. Which, as a friend, is great. You're his support. But as his partner, not so much."

"What do you mean?"

"If you guys had just remained friends, you would have met someone else. Correct?"

"Well, possibly."

"That other person would've been, I hope, the person who put you first, gave you what you needed and wanted. Allowing you the energy to help Greg without it becoming all-consuming. Kim, honey, you finished your degree and then dumped your entire career out of the window because Greg wanted to go to Paris. I'm sure you have a wonderful life there, but it's not what you dreamed of doing."

"Mum, you have to compromise in a relationship. I couldn't have it all my way. Greg waited for me to finish my Master's. It was my turn to let him do the thing he wanted most."

"Kim, you make it sound as if he was waiting around the house for you like an obedient puppy whilst you were in school. Greg lived his life. He did well in his job, he wasn't missing out on anything and, frankly, it pisses me off that he's made you believe anything to the contrary."

"He didn't. That's how I perceived it."

"Well, you got it wrong. Kim, you were so excited at the thought of getting your PhD when you started university.

You're so bloody intelligent it's scary, and you just let it all go. It frustrates the hell out of me."

As much as she usually appreciated her mum's candour, right in this second, she wasn't ready to hear it. "Okay, I get the point." Snapping at Joy was never a good idea. It's not how they operated as a mother-daughter unit, but Kim couldn't help it. Her frustration and emotional limits had been shattered. "I'm going to bed. Thanks for the drink. We'll talk more tomorrow." She left no time for her mum to respond.

Getting up, she quickly gave her mum a kiss on the cheek and scooted out of the room. She desperately wanted to call Hélène, but it was late. She'd do it tomorrow.

* * *

What a shitty night's sleep. Hours of tossing and turning. Today was going to be long and tiring. She looked at the time. 8 a.m. Hélène would be up and getting ready for work. Without thinking, she sent a message, hoping Hélène would respond quickly. Kim needed to connect with her. She needed to feel Hélène's presence, even if it was through a text message.

Kim
Morning, how was your evening, sugar?

Bouncing dots… nothing. Kim huffed out a breath of frustration. She'd hurt Hélène last night by cancelling their call. Kim wasn't stupid. She knew it would probably set off some alarm bells in Hélène's mind, but at that moment in time, Kim had had to make a choice between possibly upsetting her girlfriend and abandoning her best friend in his time of need. She just hoped Hélène would understand if she was allowed to explain what happened. The bouncing dots were back.

257

> *Hélène*
> Still in bed, not feeling too good. Will message later.

Short and clipped, that's how the message read.

> *Kim*
> Oh no, what's wrong?

> *Hélène*
> Too much to drink. Speak soon.

Why had she had too much to drink? Did Kim know Hélène was supposed to go out? No, they were supposed to have called, so that made little sense. Had something bad happened that caused her to drink herself silly?

"Kim, love, breakfast is ready." Her dad's low timbre vibrated through the door.

"Okay," she called back. Her phone felt too heavy in her hands. Was that the weight of her disappointing Hélène?

Joy, Peter, and Greg were all sitting round the table when she entered the kitchen. Greg looked better than the day before. Peter pushed a plate over to the open seat, where Kim plonked herself down. Oh, how she'd missed her dad's bacon butties.

"Dad, you're the best." Her dad chuckled as she sank her teeth into the breakfast delight. Ketchup squirted out the side and down her chin. Instinctively, Greg leaned over and wiped it off. The room froze. Awkward much?

"Sorry," he mumbled, taking his hand away.

"It's okay," Kim replied. It didn't feel okay. Greg's touch, which had once comforted her, felt unfamiliar and wrong.

258

"What's your plan today, love?" Her dad broke the tension. Thank god for him.

"Not sure."

"Tash and Steph are visiting. Why don't you call them?" Joy looked pointedly at her daughter. Kim knew why. Since moving to Paris, Kim had let her friendship with her two other best friends wane. Joy obviously wanted her to connect with them again.

"Yeah, that's a plan. Greg, you want to come with me? It's been ages since we were all together." Greg hadn't even opened his mouth before Joy interrupted.

"Greg's shopping with me today, love. Aren't you?" Jesus, were those actual daggers shooting out her mum's eyes. Greg wasn't stupid enough to argue, so he just smiled and agreed.

"Alright then," Kim mumbled.

* * *

Steph and Tash were delighted that Kim had reached out and, to be fair, Kim felt just as good. Kim, Greg, Tash, and Steph had all grown up together. Kim and Greg were the closest as far as best friends went, but that didn't stop them from having a great little friendship group.

They met at Beans and Buns Café — no one in their right mind would call their establishment that nowadays; the innuendo was ridiculous. But times were different back then.

The little coffee shop had been around forever. They served killer iced buns and scones. Kim checked her phone one last time before entering the café. Still nothing from Hélène. Kim sighed. What a fucking mess.

"There she is. Look at you all Parisian and shit." Kim burst out laughing. Steph was the loudest of the group and the one who cursed like a sailor.

"Hey, Steph." Kim walked into her friend's outstretched arms, hugging her tightly before doing the same with Tash. Kim settled in the chair opposite her friends. She took a moment just to look at them. Had it really been almost six years since they saw each other last?

Steph was a beanpole. She hovered around 6'2", which, compared to Kim, was ridiculous. Steph could literally lean her elbow on Kim's head. Her hair had changed since they'd last met. Kim remembered her sporting a cute pixie cut, but now it fell to her shoulders in chocolaty waves. As usual, she was in her workout gear, which was normal, considering she was a personal trainer.

Tash looked almost the same as before. She still rocked a pantsuit. Tash worked in banking, like Greg. They'd actually started at the same place all those years back. After climbing the ranks, she was now paid a ridiculous salary as an executive. Tash had straight blonde hair like Kim, but it was a lot more golden than hers. Tash wore it in a tight ponytail as usual. They both looked fantastic and happy.

"God, you two look great. I've missed you so much." She leant over and held both their hands. Her face lit up with a bright smile.

"Missed you too, lady," Steph replied. Kim looked over at Tash, who seemed a little less enthusiastic about their reunion.

"Everything alright, Tash?" As a group, they'd never shied away from airing grievances, and Kim could tell that Tash had something on her mind.

"It is great to see you, but I'm just wondering why now? You dropped off the face of the earth when you moved to Paris, so I'm a little surprised, is all." Oof, straight to the heart with that one.

"You're right. I'm sorry, really. I don't know, I could come up with a bunch of excuses, but I suppose I was just so focused on where I was, I didn't stop to look back." It was as honest as she could be.

"We've been friends forever, Kim. Moving shouldn't have been an issue. Hell, I moved a year after you, but Steph still texted me every day. We still meet up a few times a year."

What could she say? Did she know the reason she'd bagged off her friends? A memory swam through her mind. The three of them were sat eating just before Kim was due to move. Kim remembered the feeling of that lunch, and it wasn't pleasant.

Tash and Steph had vocalised their concern about Kim giving up on her education to follow Greg. If memory served, their discussion had gotten a little heated towards the end. That's the real reason Kim had run away and not looked back. She was angry that they challenged her decision. The worst part was that she felt angry because a part of her agreed with what they had said.

Whenever she spoke about her move to Paris with Greg, Kim always played it off as if it had been the easiest decision in the world and that she hadn't been too bothered about leaving her studies behind. In reality, it had been one of the hardest things she'd ever done, but in the end, guilt had won out.

Kim had felt guilty for her education monopolising hers and Greg's lives. When Greg had been a little short with her towards the end of her Masters, Kim had reasoned that he was right to want more for himself and that she should stop being selfish. Why should Greg stick around for another four years whilst Kim studied for her doctorate?

A mix of emotions coursed through her body. Shame that she'd pushed away her closest friends. Frustration that her life was not where she wanted it to be and sadness that she, along with Greg, were going through such a hard time.

"Tash, I'm sorry. I think that the last conversation we had hit a sore spot. I wasn't ready to hear what you guys had to say, and I distanced myself because of it."

"Kim, we were just looking out for you," Steph said.

"We didn't think you'd drop us for it, though. I mean bloody hell, Kim, we used to talk about all the hard stuff and nobody chucked the friendship away," Tash shot.

"I know, I know. I think I was just in a really shitty place. I felt guilty for keeping Greg waiting whilst I was in school."

"Guilty? What the hell for? He was doing his own thing, he had a great job, good money, and friends around him," Steph said incredulously.

"Funny, Mum said the same thing last night."

"Well, you can always count on Joy to say it straight." Tash chuckled. It was the first sign that her friend was thawing towards her.

"Have you heard what happened?" Kim wasn't sure if they knew about her and Greg. How would they unless Greg was still in contact?

"With who? Your mum, is she okay?" Tash asked quickly, her face marred with concern. Kim's heart warmed.

"No, between me and Greg."

"How would we?" Steph arched her eyebrow. Yeah, fair enough, Kim had been a shit friend. Message received.

Kim spent the next hour filling them in on everything. She caught them up with her life in Paris. She spoke of Anna and Sam. The change in Greg, the feeling of unfulfilment in her life. And last but not least, Hélène.

"Fucking hell, Kim, that's a lot," Steph laughed.

"Tell me about it," Kim sighed.

"So what's happening then? Do you think Greg will actually move back? Will you?" Tash asked her with pinched eyebrows.

"I think he will. He has a lot of work to do on himself and Paris is not the place for him to do it. He needs to remove himself from that environment. As for me, no idea. Paris is where my life is now and I love it, but Paris was supposed to be for me and Greg. He's going to need help and I'm his best friend. I feel like I'm abandoning him if I decide to stay in France."

"And Hélène?" Steph asked.

"God, I don't know. We have only just started, but I like her so much. For the first time in a long time I feel really good, hopeful almost. She pushes me and challenges me to think bigger. But there is so much history between me and Greg. How can I just throw that away? I don't want to be his girlfriend again. I know that much, but can I just leave him entirely?"

"This is what my problem was all those years ago, Kim." Tash almost barked in frustration, taking Kim by surprise. Tash's eyes were a little fierce. "I know you guys were the closest of us all. But Kim, what I don't understand is where this need to put him above you comes from. No offence, sugar, but he didn't do that for you. He was a sweet guy, but he never sacrificed anything to make you happy. So, where does your guilt come from?"

"I don't know, I just think he needs looking after and if I don't do that, who will?"

"He should be looking after himself Kim, he's a grown ass man. He's not the poor kid that lost his parents and couldn't fend for himself. You and your parents went above and beyond when that happened, but I think you took it a little too far in the end. You need to let him get on with it. The only person you should concentrate on is you. Be his friend, but for the love of all things sacred, do not give up your life for him," Steph stated. Tash nodded in agreement.

Jesus Christ, I need another holiday.

Chapter 22

Pain shot through Hélène's head and neck. Why the hell was she upside down? Cautiously, she pried one of her eyes open. Yes, she was definitely the wrong way up. Her head had slipped off the end of the couch and was dangling.

The rest of her body had been contorted in a way that would impress a master yogi. Hélène's muscles were *not* impressed. They were sore and stiff. Add to that the massive and hideous headache, she wasn't having the best start to the day.

As gently as she could, she lifted herself into an upright position. Wrong move. Her stomach revolted violently to the motion. Reaching for the paper bin that stood by the TV unit, she unloaded her stomach.

Oh, dear god. The smell of alcohol made her retch again, but nothing came up. Memories of the previous night darted before her eyes. Tequila, so much Tequila. Oh god, had they done karaoke somewhere?

Staggering to the bathroom, she tried to search her very spotty memories to piece together the rest of her evening. Lights, music, and dancing. Had she cried? Did Sam get home alright?

The soft moaning from the bedroom pulled her attention. "Sweet fucking Jesus," Sam groaned from the middle of Hélène's bed. By the looks of things, she'd simply collapsed in situ because she still had her clothes on and she hadn't even attempted to get under the covers. "I'm dying." Another long moan escaped the mess that was Sam.

"I threw up in my paper bin," Hélène stated, climbing on the bed. "Do you remember anything?" She sure didn't, not really. Good God, hopefully she'd not embarrassed herself.

"Tequila, there was lots of tequila. We danced and sang. You cried several times."

This time it was Hélène that let out a loud groan. Her head hurt, her body hurt, and her heart hurt.

"Coffee. We need lots and lots of coffee." Sam rolled over. She resembled something of a beached whale, the way she lolled about. Hélène listened as Sam set about banging around her little kitchen.

Several minutes later, Sam appeared with two mugs set on a large pizza box. "Apparently, drunk us are very conscientious. Look at this." Hélène sat up from where she had been slouched. Sam handed her a scrap of paper.

Eat pizr in mrnin. Pizr gud, drunk bad. Hed will feel ok after fud.

Not one to argue with her drunk self, she set about eating the pizza they had obviously picked up at the end of the night. Hélène's phone pinged from the living room. Able to walk

266

without wanting to vomit, Hélène retrieved her phone. It was a message from Kim asking how her night had been.

She was not in the right frame of mind to handle Kim right now. After a very short to and fro, Hélène set her phone on silent and went back to bed. Sam sat looking at her expectantly. "You ready to talk now? You drank enough tequila to down a horse and, by the look on your face, it did little to help with your problems."

"No, just added a hideous hangover to an already shitty situation."

"Yeah, I gathered from your outbursts last night. Wanna get into it?"

"Was I that bad?"

"Well, it wasn't good. The poor girl who was trying to get in your knickers all night ended up with you ugly crying on her shoulder for half an hour."

"Please tell me you're joking."

"Wish I was. I had to buy her a drink as an apology. Hélène, you were really upset. This thing with Kim has hit a serious nerve, am I right?"

Hélène had been pissed for sure, but was she really *that* upset? Yesterday had been an emotional rollercoaster, but it hadn't just been Kim ditching her for Greg. Holly, JJ, and her mother had played a huge part in Hélène's night of drowning her sorrows.

"Okay, let's start with the easiest one. JJ. I know you're worried about him, but he knows what he's doing and I'm sure he'll talk to you if he has any concerns. I reckon you just have to trust him and be the best aunt to that little kiddy when it comes along."

"I can do that."

"Alright, second. Holly's offer. It's huge, it's life changing, but it's something you've wanted for a long ass time,

267

Hélène. Forget about JJ and Kim. This is about you. Diving is your passion. I don't fully understand the thrill, but you do, and that's what matters."

"If you let me take you, you'd find out how amazing it is."

"Let's not hash this out again. I enjoy breathing on land. Anyway, back to it. Holly's offer. If it's serious and something that tickles your fancy, then I'm all for it. Call her. Get specifics and then make an informed decision."

Hélène rested her chin on her legs that were pulled into her chest. Yes, she'd call Holly and ask for her business plan. Once she'd seen that, she'd take it from there. "Okay, I'll call her."

"Great. Now your mum. This one is a biggy. I mean, you've got some major issues with that lady, so it's gonna take time and patience to work through everything she had to say."

"You're telling me. It still feels like a dream. I know that sounds cliché, but seriously, it does. I didn't know about my grandmother. No idea about their relationship or lack of. Veronique has never shown that side of herself to me, so our conversation yesterday was shocking."

"Completely fucking understandable. I mean, I only met the woman once, and that was enough. She's terrifying. But she's your mum. I couldn't imagine a life without mine. I hate that you never got to experience that kind of bond, so maybe that's something to take into consideration. A fresh start, the chance for a proper mum/daughter relationship."

"It's all I ever wanted, but I'm not sure I can trust it, you know?

"Yeah, totally. What would you need to get to that point with her?"

Hélène puffed out a long breath. She'd never dared believe that one day she would have the kind of relationship with Veronique that everyone else had with their mother. She'd seen how Sandy was with Sam and she'd felt that yearning deep within. All she wanted was to be able to laugh and joke with her mum. See pride in her eyes instead of disappointment.

"She told me she's been to therapy since her health scare. Maybe going together would be a good start. There are things I need to say. Things that are going to be hard for her to hear."

"I think that's an excellent idea. Maybe you should arrange a dinner or something? Float the idea past her and see where it leads."

"Yeah, okay, I can do that."

"See, it's not so bad. We've already sorted three of the four problems, well okay, not sorted, but straightened them out enough for you to deal with them without hard alcohol."

"And for that, Sam, I'm eternally grateful. You're a wonderful friend. Remind me to give Anna a bottle or five of red for letting me steal you last night."

"Ha, I think she was happy to get rid of me. Who knew I'd turn into a Bridezilla? At this rate, I'll be lucky to get her down the aisle."

"Pfft, that woman will race you down the aisle. Nothing will stop her marrying you, not even your overzealous approach to organising it."

"From your lips to God's ears."

"It's nice to see. I'll be so lucky to have a fraction of what you two have."

"Wow, is that the world's smallest violin I see? I think that little display of self-pity leads us nicely to the fourth and final problem. The reason you were snotting all over me last night."

"I do not snot."

Sam let out a loud guffaw. "Are you taking the piss? Hélène, you were a right bloody mess, a snotty tearful mess. And to be honest, I didn't really get what was going on. You just kept weeping, telling me you were 'cursed for eternity to walk this painful life alone'. It was dramatic."

Hélène could feel her face heating. "*Merde*, Sam, I'm so sorry."

"No apologising, just tell me what's going on."

So that's what she did. She told Sam about all the women that had left her for various reasons. She told her about her growing feelings for Kim and the fear of what that meant, especially because of how complicated it was between Kim and Greg. She told her about how Kim had cancelled their phone call to be with Greg and how that had played into every insecurity she had.

"I'm no stranger to letting past hurt affect a current relationship. Shit, Hélène, I almost walked away from the best thing in my life because of fear. You need to figure out if it's something that you can get past."

"How can I live with the constant worry that she's going to leave? Hell, we've been together a few weeks and already her situation with Greg has become a problem. I get she wants to be there for him, I do really. The thing is, though, is that I need a partner who is going to be there for me. Put me first, just like I would them.

"I called her last night, several times actually, because I needed her. The best she could do was a message telling me she needed a raincheck on the call. What was I supposed to do? Pour everything out in a message and hope she decides I'm more important than her ex? I'm tired, Sam, tired of always coming second." A tear fell down her cheek. Her body felt heavier than when she'd woken up upside down.

The weight of those words hung around her neck like an anchor. Sam shifted, so she was flush against Hélène's side, her arm wrapped around her shoulders. "I don't know what to do for the best. Kim is magnificent. I like her a lot, but I can't stand around and wait while she decides if I'm her person."

"You have to tell her how you're feeling. It's not fair to her to keep all this locked up and then decide for you both without her having all the information."

"What? Like she did when she ran off to the UK without talking to me about it? I think the timing is wrong. We both have too much going on to make this work."

"It sounds like you've already made your mind up."

Was Sam correct? Had she decided? "I don't know. I need to think." Hélène appreciated everything Sam had said and done to support her, but she needed some space alone. Time to process and decide what she wanted to do next.

"I'll head out, but Hélène… please, before you rush to a decision, think about talking to her. Openly and without fear."

"I will."

After a hug and a doggy bag of cold pizza, Sam left Hélène alone on her bed. Her hangover was still raging, but it was nothing compared to the queasiness that rolled around her stomach every time she thought of walking away from Kim. Even if it was for the best.

* * *

Lists were Hélène's friends. She loved a good "Pros and Cons" list. Was there a better way to figure out a conundrum than making a list? If the pile of paper surrounding her on her bed was anything to go by, then no.

There was a list for each of her problems. JJ, her mum, Holly, and Kim. Once she was satisfied that she'd got all of her thoughts down on paper, she was ready to mobilise. The first thing she would deal with was Holly. If the offer to partner up

271

was as good as it sounded, Hélène was going to take the plunge — pun intended.

Yes, it would be a huge upheaval, but one that would be worth it in the long run. Hell, you only have a certain amount of years on the planet, and by god she wanted to make the most of them.

Doing something she loved and was passionate about for the next fifty years sounded like heaven. She banged out an email, requesting Holly send her a detailed business plan. The speed of Holly's reply, along with all the excited curse words in the email, made her laugh out loud.

Drawing in a breath, she let herself bask in the excitement of her new adventure. Her heart felt as if little fireworks were going off. Smiling, she moved on to her second list. Her mum.

It was a no brainer. She wanted to seize the opportunity to get to know her mother. If there was the slimmest chance that Veronique could give Hélène what she needed, then that was good enough. Her second email of the day went to Otis asking him to set up a lunch. Hélène was going to discuss the idea of seeing a therapist together.

Wow, she was flying through her woes. Now time for JJ and his baby quest. The phone rang several times before he picked up.

"Hey, kid." JJ always sounded chipper.

"Hey JJ, have you got five to chat?"

"Yep, shoot, what's up?"

"Nothing's up. I just wanted you to know that I've been worrying about your plans. The baby plans."

"Oh?"

"I just want to make sure you're sure. Is this woman really the one?"

"You don't have to worry, Hélène, really. I'm not jumping into this blind. I've seen numerous doctors and psychologists. I've met Jane a lot and we've talked a lot. I feel it in my heart. She's the right woman, and I know Claire would be happy. I'm ready to be a dad. I want more than my businesses."

"Okay, I just needed to hear it from you, I suppose. There is something else, too, but I need to hash some things out first before I discuss it with you."

"Ah, Holly finally asked you to partner, eh?"

"She told you?"

"Yeah, she asked my opinion when we were on *Connie*. I told her to go for it. Hélène, it's what you want, it's what you've always wanted, and it's time to put yourself first. I'm behind you on this one hundred percent."

"Thanks, JJ, you don't know how much I needed to hear that. Okay look, I need to go but thanks for indulging my silly anxieties."

"Nothing silly in worrying about the people you love. Call anytime. Love you, kid."

"Love you, too."

Alright then, this was going brilliantly. Now all she had to do was stomp on the heart of the woman she was probably falling head over heels in love with, therefore breaking her own heart in the process. Great!

It had been roughly six hours and thirty-three minutes since Hélène had messaged Kim. In that time, she'd concluded that, as much as she wanted to pursue something with her, the timing just wasn't right for either of them. Hélène didn't need a conversation with Kim to know it either. The whole reason Hélène had whisked herself away to the south of France was to catch a break, specifically from women.

Instead of doing that, she'd stormed ahead and fallen for yet another unavailable woman. Because, in reality, that's what Kim was. Unavailable. Until she'd really sorted things out with her ex, Kim couldn't offer Hélène what she needed and frankly deserved.

They hadn't got too far into a relationship that it could fuck up a potential friendship. That's what Hélène hoped, anyway. Maybe in a few months they could look at dating again, if that's what they both wanted. Yes, solid plan. Better for everyone. Definitely. Right?

If she needed another sign that what she planned to do was the right thing, the message from Kim that had just popped up on her phone was it. Kim was extending her stay in England. Talking over the phone wasn't ideal, but she was damned if she was going to wait around until Kim came back. Gritting her teeth, she rolled her neck. This was not the type of phone call she was expecting to have with Kim.

Kim picked up almost immediately. "I know, I'm sorry, doll, I should have called. Are you feeling better? I'm sorry I need to stay here longer. It's just that Greg has asked if I would."

"It's fine. You do what you need to do, but we need to talk. It's not how I wanted this to go, but, well, I don't have much of a choice." Hélène's words felt like acid as they left her mouth. Her tone was hard because that's the only way she could do this.

"What are you talking about?" Hélène could hear the panic in Kim's voice.

"A lot has happened since you left. I wanted to talk yesterday, but you were otherwise occupied. Anyway, that doesn't matter now. I think I need to take a step back — "

"A step back from what?"

"From us. We've had a wonderful time, Kim, but I really don't think either of us can commit to something more. You need to take your time with Greg and I have things that need my attention, too."

"Where is this coming from? I know I shouldn't have cancelled our call, but this is extreme, don't you think?"

"It's not just about the call."

"Then what is it?"

Hélène's stomach dropped when she heard Kim sniff. Oh fuck, was she crying? "Holly has offered me a fantastic opportunity, which means I will be leaving Paris. I have some stuff with my mother too, but you don't need to worry about that. Look, let's not make this harder than it needs to be. We were only together a few weeks." Ice cold, that's how she sounded, and she hated every second.

"It really meant so little to you? Really, Hélène?"

"Maybe we could revisit this in a few months or not, depending on where you are with Greg."

"I will be friends with Greg, and that's it. You know — "

"I don't know, and that's a problem. I'm sorry, Kim, but I can't trust that you won't leave. It's my issue, I know, but it's enough that I don't want to continue with us." Boom, bomb dropped. The line went silent. Hélène's heart rate was hammering through her chest.

"I don't know what to say." Kim was defeated.

"Nothing. Let's take some time. Hopefully, we can salvage a friendship at least. Good luck, Kim." She put the phone down without waiting for Kim to reply.

That was the worst thing she'd ever had to do. The conversation began on a loop in her head. Hélène heard her harsh tone. She'd done a fantastic job channeling Veronique. It was a shameful way to have behaved, but it had been necessary.

Hélène dropped the phone to the bed. Her hands shook uncontrollably. The tears that she'd forced away came flooding back. The pain would fade eventually. It had to.

Twenty minutes of sobbing left her fatigued. The day had started out painfully and was ending the same way. Hoisting herself off the bed, she took herself to the bathroom. Maybe a scalding shower would help burn the memory of hurting Kim away? Unlikely, but she was going to try.

Her skin was bright red when she eventually turned off the water. It had made no difference at all. Nothing was going to make a difference, only time. It wasn't the first time she'd had to recover from heartache but it was the first time she'd caused it.

Slipping under the covers of her bed, she willed her brain to shut down. Her phone pinged. *Please don't be Kim. Please don't be Kim.* Her resolve to end it with Kim was hanging by a thread. She wasn't sure she could stay the course if Kim asked her to reconsider. She peeked at the screen.

Sam
I hope you know what you're doing.

Kim had probably called Anna.

Me too.

Chapter 23

Shocked, that's the best way to describe how Kim felt as she stood in her childhood bedroom clutching the telephone she had just used to talk to Hélène. What had just happened?

Okay so maybe telling Hélène over a text message that she was staying in the UK for a little longer was probably not the best way to have communicated, especially after cancelling their call through text as well.

Dammit. Kim had fucked up, but enough for Hélène to take their relationship out at the knees so brutally? She'd never heard Hélène sound so cold or distant. It had been like she was talking to someone else entirely. Should she call her back? No, with the way Hélène spoke to her, calling right now wouldn't help. Giving her some time was probably for the best.

Kim thought back to what Hélène had said. Something big had happened with her mother and Holly had presented her with an opportunity that would take Hélène out of Paris. Kim's racing thoughts were interrupted by Greg, who knocked once and then entered her room.

"Tea?"

"Uh, thanks." Kim was still reeling from her phone call.

"Everything okay?"

Kim hadn't divulged her relationship with Hélène to her ex. Somehow it didn't seem appropriate, but what was she supposed to say? She didn't want to lie.

"Oh, that was Hélène. We had a minor disagreement." Her shoulders slumped. If only it had been minor. That she could have handled.

"You seem really shaken. Did she upset you?"

"I'm not sure you're the best person to talk to about it."

"Oh, why's that?"

Jesus, he was going to make her spell it out, wasn't he? "We started seeing each other romantically." Could this be any more bloody awkward? She'd happily go for monthly smear tests than have this conversation right now.

Greg's face visibly dropped. "You slept with her?"

Oh, so it could get worse, okay good to know. "Do you really want to talk about this?

"I think I have a right to know!" he snapped.

Oh no, hell no, he did not get to take that tone. "You really want to start down that road? After everything, you think I'm in the wrong?"

"Jesus, Kim, you've just skipped right ahead. Never mind me. Yes, I hurt you and yes, I fucked up, but we were supposed to be together forever. You didn't even wait a week."

"Hang on a sec. I tried for months and months to get you to open up, to talk, to work on the relationship. You made your choices, and I made mine. Honestly, I think I'd checked out of 'us' a while ago. Probably when I spent my birthday alone, or when I had to spend the day trying to get all my money back on the holiday you bailed on.

"You were going through something, but so was I. I didn't just magically move on, Greg, I agonised for months and then I met someone who offered me everything I needed. She didn't push me, she didn't seduce me, she just listened, and we got close. It had nothing to do with you. It was about me."

"So you had no intention of coming back to me? It doesn't matter what I do, you're really done with us."

"Am I missing something? You told me it was a good thing that we weren't together."

"Yeah, but I didn't mean forever. I have some work to do, but I'll get better and then we can get back to how we were."

"I don't want to get back to how we were, Greg! I was bloody miserable. I've had time to think about what I want. As much as I love living in Paris, I want more."

"More?"

"I want to go back to school. I should have gone for my doctorate when I was in university."

"So you regret choosing me. Is that what you're saying?"

"Why did it have to be a choice in the first place?"

"Well, how else could it have gone? Did you want me to go to Paris whilst you stayed here?"

"Why not? Would that have been the end of the world?"

He was getting irritated, his face was flushed. "Why can't you just be happy with our life? Fuck, Kim. I just wanted to look after you."

"I didn't ask for you to look after me! You made that decision for us both. God, where did we go so wrong? It's pretty clear we want very different things."

Greg dropped his head to his chest, blowing out a sad sigh. "We never really had those conversations, did we?" He wasn't being accusatory, just honest.

279

Their friendship had morphed into a relationship seamlessly when they were teens. They hadn't spent their time getting to know each other as separate people.

"No, we didn't and I think that was a big mistake on both our parts. I love you, Greg, you know that. I'm your best friend, always, but I think I have to take some time now to figure out where I go from here."

"Why did Hélène get cross with you?"

"Because I did something I shouldn't have. When you asked me earlier to stay longer, I didn't take her into consideration. I did what I always do, where you're concerned. I put everything to one side regardless of how that would make me, or in this case, Hélène, feel." The reality of what she'd done crashed down like a wave. Why had she done that?

"I'm sorry—" Greg began.

"No, it's my fault. I don't know why I keep repeating the same pattern."

* * *

Shopping was invented for these types of shitty situations. Kim had zero answers over the past few days. Hélène had disappeared off the face of the earth. She'd given Hélène space, three days in fact, but even then she obviously didn't want to talk at all. Messages were left unanswered, phone calls went to voicemail.

After the conversation with Greg, Kim called Anna. She needed to speak to someone who knew Hélène. Maybe she or Sam could shed some light on the situation because, no matter what Kim's mistakes had been, she didn't deserve to be dumped so brutally.

They had a connection. Okay, so they'd been together a few weeks, but what did that matter? There were people in the world who met the love of their lives and knew it after one look.

Anna had hinted that there were some significant things going on in Hélène's life, but she didn't feel comfortable spilling the details. All she said was that Sam had come home severely hungover and a little worried about her friend.

Everything was one big mess. In three weeks, Kim, and Hélène were supposed to be a part of Anna and Sam's wedding. Major parts. Kim was going to be standing with Anna whilst Hélène performed the ceremony. They had to talk, but what could she do if Hélène refused to engage?

Her credit card was taking a good beating. Three new dresses and two pairs of heels later and her heart still felt as bruised as it had done three days previously. Joy had tried to talk to her on several occasions, but Kim couldn't open up anymore. She could feel herself folding inwards.

For months, she'd felt raw with emotion over her failing relationship with Greg. She was supposed to be healing. That's why she'd gone away, to get some peace, but it'd backfired spectacularly, hadn't it?

Breaking up with Greg, finding Hélène, losing Hélène, losing herself. Hell, her mother, and friends had told her in no uncertain terms that she'd made a huge mistake with her life when she'd followed Greg to France. That was a lot, right?

Surely anyone would be struggling. She felt untethered. Paris, for so long, had been her safe port. Anna, Sam, Greg had been her comfort, but all that had changed in such a short space of time.

Well, she had to think of some way to cope because she couldn't afford to keep spending money on retail therapy.

"Ms Richmond?" A low, gravelly voice called from across the store. Kim turned. Standing by the winter coats was her old professor.

"Professor Plum." Yes, that was her real name. "What a pleasure to see you."

"Likewise Ms Richmond. How are you?"

Ha, good question. "Very well, thanks." Lies. "Just getting a bit of retail therapy in before I go home."

"I would have thought the shopping in Paris would be far superior."

"Well, yes, but it's also more expensive."

"Indeed. So tell me what you've been up to."

Kim wasn't ashamed of her job or her life, but as she stood in front of her old professor, she was suddenly less happy to be sharing her life after university.

"Oh, I'm a PA to a very good friend who owns a publishing company."

"Excellent. Are you enjoying it?" There was no trace of judgement in Professor Plum's voice or face.

"Very much so." Her voice trailed off. Could she talk to Professor Plum about her future? Maybe someone impartial would be a good idea. "Actually, professor, I've been thinking recently about returning to my education."

"Oh, well, that would be fabulous, Kim." The use of her first name made her feel better. The excitement in her professor's face warmed her.

"The thing is, I'm not sure I want to return to the UK. Any chance you could help me look into some programmes in France, that's if you have time?"

"Absolutely. How long are you here for?"

"As long as I need to be."

"Come along to my office in a couple of days. That gives me a bit of time to look into it."

"Wonderful, thank you, professor, really."

"Pleasure's all mine, Kim. It was a shame when you left us, but I understand that sometimes life takes us on different paths than we'd planned. I'm just thrilled you're wanting to resume your education. You are one smart cookie, Kim."

Okay, that was a step in the right direction. For the first time in months, Kim felt in control.

* * *

"Patricia called me today." No good morning, just straight to the point. Joy had her professor's voice on again. Kim shouldn't have been too surprised to learn that her former professor had reached out to her mother. And yes, once again, Professor Patricia Plum was her actual name.

"I'm sure that was a lovely conversation." *You want to know something, Mum, you can just ask.*

"It was enlightening. I'm just wondering why I'm finding out from Pat that you are thinking about going back to university."

"I saw her the other day, and it crossed my mind that she would be a good person to talk to casually. I haven't decided if it's what I want to do."

"But you could've talked things through with me, doll, you usually do."

"Honestly, Mum, I didn't come here intending to change my life. I just wanted to support Greg, but after talking to you, Steph and Tash, I had to admit that some of what you said stuck. I just wanted to decide on my own, no outside influences."

"Alright, love. No pressure. I am pleased you're thinking about you for a change, though. That's the last thing I'll say."

"Okay, and I promise that if I make any actual decisions, I'll come to you."

In truth, the more Kim thought about returning to university, the more excited she became. At the end of the day she was a scientist, and she missed being around her people and the work.

Speaking of her people, Kim needed to get a move on. Professor Plum had extended her an invitation to a dinner party. It was the opportunity Kim needed to reconnect with her academic roots. Professor Plum had assured her there would be plenty of people for her to mingle with that could point her in the right direction.

Smoothing down her pencil skirt, Kim took a deep breath. It had been years since she'd spent time in this kind of social situation. The prospect was a little terrifying, if she was being honest.

The party would be packed with academics that spent their time either teaching or researching. Kim had spent her time organising Anna's diary. No time for doubts now, though. If she was serious about returning to university, she had to put her concerns to one side and jump in.

Professor Plum's house was beautiful. The building was a traditional three storey Victorian property and would definitely come with a hefty price tag.

Kim straightened her shoulders and knocked on the grand oak door. The wait ramped up her heart rate. A few seconds passed before the door creaked open. Professor Plum greeted her with a beaming smile.

Instead of her usual brown skirt suit, the professor wore a gorgeous black cocktail dress. Her hair, that was normally in a tame bun, was loose around her shoulders. Had her professor always been hot?

"Kim, welcome."

"Professor…"

284

"Now, none of that, it's Patricia, please I insist. You're not my student anymore."

Kim smiled shyly. Why the hell was she acting like a timid teenager? "Patricia, thank you so much for the invite."

"Oh, the pleasure is mine. I have a few people I want to introduce you to. Nearly everyone is in the living room. Please go through and grab a drink."

Kim stepped through the door and into the hall. The interior was as beautiful as the outside. Kim wasn't sure what she was expecting to find, but a modern, sleek house wasn't it. Patricia must have caught the surprise that flashed across her face as she took in her surroundings.

"The interior is all my wife. I have the interior design skills of a caveman, I'm afraid."

"It's beautiful." No lies there.

"Well, Callie will be over the moon. Come on, just through here."

Kim followed Patricia into the room immediately to the right of the entrance hallway. A dozen people were standing around with various drinks in their hands.

Kim recognised a couple of people who, in return, recognised her. The group spent several minutes catching up, and Kim was delighted that none of them made her feel bad about her choice to leave after graduating. In fact, they'd been very excited to hear about her life in Paris.

"Kim, let me introduce you to my wife, Callie."

Holy moly. Callie was a fox. She had long ash blonde hair and piercing blue eyes. Kim's heart hurt. She was looking at Hélène twenty years down the line. She'd done a valiant job at putting Hélène to the back of her mind, but it was proving impossible as she stared into the eyes of Callie Plum.

Swallowing hard, she extended her hand. "It's a genuine pleasure, Callie."

"You, too. Pat hasn't stopped going on about you for the past few days. She's always been impartial with her students, but there is no doubt you are one of her favourites. Apparently, you're one of the most gifted students she ever had the pleasure to teach."

Well gosh.

"That's too kind. Patricia was my favourite professor, though. She always made the lectures fun."

"Careful, she'll get an enormous head." The three women laughed.

"Have you been reacquainted with everyone?" Pat asked, scanning the room.

"I think so, although there are plenty of people I don't know."

"Yes, and there is one you must meet. Aurelie is a visiting professor from Nice. It's serendipitous you both being here. Aurelie is the head of the science department. Have a chat with her. She can answer any questions you may have and she will point you in the direction that will suit you best."

"Wow, yes, definitely."

"Fabulous, but first, let's have some fun. We have all night to talk shop."

Kim chuckled. She couldn't recall ever seeing her professor so relaxed. The wine was divine, a delicious red from Chinon. Kim would bet money that Pat and Callie spent a lot of their holidays in the French wine country.

An hour must have passed by the time Kim found herself in front of Aurelie. As with most French women — in Kim's humble opinion — Aurelie was gorgeous. She had long, straight auburn hair. Her figure was to die for and the long blue dress she wore was just the icing on top of a very delicious looking cake. Okay, so she was probably fifteen to twenty years Kim's senior, but that didn't stop her from looking.

"Ah, the famous Kim Richmond." Oh boy, that accent was yummy. Not as yummy as Hélène's. More heart pain. She had to do a better job at putting Hélène aside, for now at least.

"Aurelie, thank you for taking some time to talk to me."

"No problem. Pat has told me you're looking at getting back into academia."

"I have been giving it some serious thought. I'm currently based in Paris and would prefer to stay in France if possible."

"Well, I'm sure you know my position is in Nice. We have an excellent science programme. You have a MSc in Biology. Is that correct?"

"Yes, that's right. At the time of choosing my degree, I hesitated between Biology and Marine Biology. I feel that Marine Biology would be the path that I would choose now. Do you think it's a possibility?"

"There's no question of it being a possibility. From what Pat has told me, you are more than capable. You will, however, come back to your studies as a mature student. That *can* be difficult sometimes."

"I think the added years will only help." Sure, it could be hard fitting in if she was the only "mature" student, but she'd only been away from education for a few years. It wasn't as if she was returning in her forties.

"How about we set up a meeting when you're back in France? You could visit the campus. See what you think."

"Brilliant, thank you. I'll get your contact details from Patricia before I leave."

"Great, now let's drink." Aurelie laughed heartily.

It was nearly midnight before Kim got back to her parents. Thank god she was a master in heels because she was more than a little tipsy. A lesser skilled person would have face planted the floor by now.

287

If she only had the same skill in her love life. She was like Bambi, stumbling about, trying to navigate her way through her feelings. Her alcohol-soaked brain gave her the great idea to call Hélène. Of course, it was the perfect time to sort out their troubled situation.

Hélène had been screening her calls for days, but as luck would have it, she picked up. "Kim." Cool and aloof, just like before.

"Kim," she mimicked, trying to sound as cold as Hélène. Silence.

"Hélène, you suck right now, doll. However, we have to get through our friends' wedding in a couple of weeks, so you can't just ignore me forever."

"Are you drunk?" Hélène's tone softened.

"Yes, and your voice is sexy. Your stupid face is too, but that doesn't matter now. Are you going to stop being an ass so we can get through Anna's nuptials?" Hélène chuckled down the line. "And what exactly are you laughing at?" Kim didn't find any of it funny.

"Sorry, I'm not laughing. I just forgot how entertaining you are when you're drunk."

"Yes, well, you don't get to be entertained anymore."

"Yes, you're right. I promise I won't be anything but friendly when we see each other next."

"Oh, wonderful, friendly, just what I wanted. You're such a douche canoe, it's unbelievable. Just remember that it was you that walked away because I'm certain you are going to come to regret that. I'm a catch. I was your catch, but you threw me away. Remember that when you're being so bloody friendly."

Not waiting for a reply, Kim disconnected the call. She'd probably regret that call tomorrow, but not now. Hélène had been an arse, and it felt good for Kim to express that to her face — well over the phone.

Hélène might not see her value, but finally she was seeing her own worth.

Chapter 24

Was there anything better in the world than listening to nature? Two buzzards circled above the expanse of green that surrounded the little cottage Hélène was staying in. Well, she was sleeping in the converted barn on a blow up bed, but still it was pretty idyllic.

Birds chirped from the hedgerows and small lizards scuttled around the floors. If she had to pick a favourite place to go bar the sea, the countryside would win out every time.

Anna's parents' cottage was beautiful. It was clear to see they had invested a lot of time and money into it, and it was no surprise that Anna and Sam had chosen it to host their wedding. The gardens alone could rival something you would see at the Chelsea flower show.

Hélène continued her walk around the property. Time was counting down to Kim's arrival. It had been weeks since they'd last seen each other and the last time they'd spoken was when Kim had drunk dialled her. Kim's words echoed through her mind. Hélène was sure that she was going to regret walking away, hell she already did, but on the flip-side, it had made Hélène sit up and really take stock of her life.

For far too long, Hélène had been waiting on other people to make her happy. Sure, every time she'd had someone leave her, it had hurt, but in reality, she shouldn't have relied on them to give her what she needed.

Every one of those women had left her because they had to put themselves first. And they were right. Hélène had always struggled to put herself above anyone else, but now she had to try.

Her career wasn't something she wanted, but she'd stayed for JJ and her mum. But no more. Hélène had read Holly's proposal and snapped her offer up because it really was her dream come true.

The relationship between herself and Veronique had always been one-sided, but that had also changed. Hélène had summoned the courage to ask her mum to attend therapy together, which, to her utter shock, Veronique had agreed to.

They'd had three sessions so far and although it had been difficult and emotional, they'd made some breakthroughs. Veronique was learning to open up. It had been strained a few times, with Veronique slipping back into fashion mogul obsessed with optics rather than a mum, but Hélène could talk to her about it now and together they were building something.

JJ was already waiting to hear if his surrogate was pregnant. Hélène had had to let that one go. She couldn't spend her time fretting over something that was out of her control. She had to trust that JJ knew what he was doing and was ready for it.

So, leaving Kim may feel like hell, but it had needed to happen. Hélène had taken the time she should have taken weeks ago to put herself first. Still, the thought of seeing Kim both excited her and broke her at the same time. Kim Richmond wasn't the kind of woman you simply got over and moved on from.

Surprisingly, Kim hadn't arrived at the cottage early. Hélène wondered if that had been intentional, so she didn't have to see her. But as Anna's maid of honour, she was sure cutting it fine. The wedding was due to start in three hours. She couldn't think about that, though. It wasn't her business. All Hélène should focus on was her own part. Conducting the ceremony.

For the past two days, she'd been studying her lines. She could do the thing in her sleep by now. Out of the corner of her eye, she spotted Sam pacing near the barn door. Dressed in an ivory suit, Sam looked every bit the stylish bride. The cut of the suit was perfect. It hugged all of Sam's curves. Her sandy hair was down by her shoulders. The sun reflecting off the golden strands wonderfully.

"Everything okay, Sam?" Hélène wandered over. Sam was looking a little manic.

"Umm, yep, totally fine." Wow, she was a terrible liar.

"Want to try that again, but with the truth this time?"

Stopping her pacing, Sam faced Hélène with an almost comical expression of panic on her face. "She's going to turn up, isn't she?"

"Kim? Of course she will."

"What? I'm talking about Anna."

Yes, Hélène, not everyone is bloody obsessed with Kim. Obviously, Sam was referring to her bride-to-be. "Sam, mon amie, do you really have any doubts? For one, you're staging this whole shindig at her parents' place. Two, you saw her last night.

Myself and Charlie had to drag the pair of you away from one another. I really don't think you have anything to worry about."

Her pep talk seemed to help a little. "But she could realise it's not what she wants, she could see how out of my league she is, she could regret settling down with the first woman she met." Sam was back to full out panicking again.

"Whoa, *calme toi*. You are being silly and you know it. There is nothing that will stop you from becoming each other's wives. She loves you more than anything and that's all you need to focus on, okay?"

"Okay." Sam nodded vigorously.

"Where is Charlie?" Charlie Baxter was Sam's best friend and business partner. She kept their office running in the UK. Charlie was one of the nicest people Hélène had ever met. She was also stupidly good looking.

Charlie was tall, slender, and had the greenest eyes Hélène had ever seen. Don't even get her started on Charlie's hair, which was pitch black, pin straight and so soft it should be illegal. Hélène knew because on one of their nights out Charlie had passed out next to Hélène in her bed. No funny business had occurred, but Hélène had woken up to Charlie's hip length hair sprawled all over the place.

"She's picking Kim up from the station. Her flight was delayed and then the train had to stop for something, so it's been frantic."

Well, that answered the question of Kim's absence then. Already Hélène could feel her heart beating a little louder. Sam sensed the change in Hélène's stature at the mention of Kim's name.

"Hey, you two going to be okay?"

Jesus, Hélène, didn't want Sam worrying that her love life was going to interfere with her wedding day. "Absolutely, we've spoken. Everything is fine." A little white lie never hurt anyone, right? She hadn't even really told a fib. They had spoken. The situation may be far from resolved, but for today they would be okay with one another.

The sound of gravel crunching under car tyres stole their attention. Charlie's bright green VW bug came to a screeching stop. "We're here, nobody panic," Charlie announced, bouncing out of the driver's seat.

Hélène watched the passenger door open and Kim step out. Their eyes met briefly before Kim turned back to the car. Bending down, she unfastened the seat, allowing access to the rear. That's when Hélène realised there was another person in the car. A person who Hélène recognised. Greg. He was here with Kim.

So there it was, further proof that Hélène ending things between them had been the right choice because Kim had gone back to her ex, just like Hélène predicted. Spending time in Kim's company just got a helluva lot more uncomfortable.

"Sam, get your arse inside. You don't want Anna seeing you, and I need to get ready so we can have a drink." Charlie looked from Hélène to Kim. The tension was palpable. ". Hells bells, you can come with us. I need you to help keep this one from losing her shit." She hooked her thumb toward Sam, who had resumed her pacing.

Hélène could've kissed Charlie for giving her an out. Happy to oblige, she scooped Sam's elbow, ushering her inside. "Well, that was fucking awkward." Charlie didn't mince words. "You two gonna be able to keep it civil?"

"Of course, we're adults!" Hélène sounded more confident than she felt. Seeing Greg standing by Kim's side made her rage. Smug son of a bitch. Needing to get her head back in the present, she set about pouring three mimosas. Sam gulped it down in one. Charlie laughed at her and then followed suit, leaving Hélène feeling a tad daft sipping at her glass. Oh, sod it. She upended the glass and downed the lot. *Ah, that's better.*

It took Charlie ten minutes to change, and she looked fabulous. Her suit was the same shape as Sam's but in a navy blue. Instead of wearing a blazer or shirt, she only wore the vest, leaving her tattooed arms on full display. Charlie really was a sight to behold. Well, that was until she spied Kim across the garden. In a knee-length navy blue strapless dress with killer heels. Hélène's breath was taken clean away. Her beautiful platinum blonde hair was in a styled high bun with one of her signature scarfs wrapped around it.

Seeing her exposed shoulders and back transported Hélène back to the bed they'd shared and all the delicious things they'd done to each other. Hélène recalled vividly the bite mark she'd left on Kim's left shoulder after a marathon morning of sex. Her body tingled and her clit stood to attention. Her vision was shattered when Greg sidled up to Kim, placing his hand on her lower back. A low growl erupted from her throat. Another mimosa was in order.

The time finally came for everyone to take their places. Hélène stood at the end of the makeshift aisle waiting for the brides to make their way to her. The music started, and Kim and Charlie walked arm in arm towards her. It took every ounce of her energy not to stare at Kim.

Together Anna and Sam walked hand in hand down the aisle. Their faces radiated love and happiness. Hélène's time practising had been worth it. She performed the ceremony sans problems. Admittedly, she'd struggled not to look at Kim as she spoke of trust, love, and soulmates. Her words may have mirrored her feelings toward the sublime blonde, but it made no difference, not now anyway. Too much time had passed, leaving Kim to return to Greg.

The reception was held under a large marquee tent in the south garden. Anna had wanted a sitdown dinner but nothing overly fancy. They'd chosen to have a local butcher roast a pig on a spit. Hélène found it highly amusing watching the few English guests stare in wonder at the hog.

Glancing at her watch, Hélène began to mentally countdown the hours until she could make her escape. The day had been wonderful, and she was so happy to have been a part of her friends' union, but now the only thing she was a part of was the avoidance game that she and Kim were playing.

Several times she'd seen Kim walking in her direction, causing her to veer off in another and vice versa. They should probably talk, but Hélène couldn't do it whilst Greg hung around like a bad smell.

Inevitably, though, she found herself alone with Kim. They'd been sitting at the same table—not next to each other, thankfully—for the meal. There had been enough people around them so that they didn't need to talk, but that soon changed when the little dance floor opened up.

Nearly everyone on their table buggered off when ABBA's "Dancing Queen" blared from the speakers. Everyone, except Hélène and Kim. For an instant, they held eye contact. Who was going to break it first? Hélène, that's who. She couldn't look into those eyes without wanting to break down. *It was for the best. You walked away because it was for the best.*

Kim cleared her throat. "So how have you been?" Ah, the polite chit chat.

"Good, thank you." Hélène glanced at Kim as she spoke, but quickly averted her eyes. Alcohol, she needed more alcohol. Thank Christ, Anna, and Sam hadn't skimped on the booze. Taking the bottle of red that sat just in front of her, Hélène poured a very generous glass and gulped half of it down in one.

"Sam mentioned you're moving next week."

Hélène nodded. *Cheers Sam, remind me never to tell you anything again.* "Yes, south Corsica."

There was a flicker of something in Kim's eyes at the mention of Corsica. Was she remembering all the fun and adventures they'd shared? "Wow, so you really are going into business with Holly?"

"Sam has certainly been keeping you well informed." It came out a little snarkier than she meant. Eventually, she would have called Kim and told her about her plans. She really had meant it when she asked if she and Kim could be friends again, but they both needed time.

"Well, Sam wouldn't have to keep me apprised if you hadn't vanished from the face of the fucking planet, would she?"

God, Kim was hot when she got all fiery. *Stop it, you masochist.* "I was just giving us both space."

"Weird. I don't recall asking for space. Ah, then again, it turns out you're just someone else who thought they knew what I wanted and decided without consulting me."

What the fuck did that mean? Was she seriously comparing her to Greg? "That's rich considering you're here with the very person who treated you that way." Yeah, two can play this game, love.

"I don't know what you think is going on, but me and Greg are —"

"Kim, let's dance, sweets." Greg slipped into Kim's space, planting his hand on her shoulder. Hélène could see him gently squeezing it affectionately. Acid was threatening to burn a hole in her stomach as she watched his little display of possessiveness play out.

That was more than enough for one day. Hélène was very much over this scenario. She would not sit and watch Kim fall into that asshole's arms. "Greg." Short, but at least she acknowledged his existence. "Good catching up, Kim. You look beautiful, by the way. I'll see you around."

Okay, she should've left the "beautiful" comment out, but it was true. Kim was radiant, and she deserved to be told. Rising swiftly from the chair, Hélène made a beeline for the brides. Time to say goodbye and get the hell out of there.

"You two are adorable, and I'm beyond happy for you both." She slid her arms around Anna and Sam as they danced.

"Thank you for doing the ceremony. You were perfect. We couldn't think of anything better than having one of our best friends marry us." Anna beamed.

"Yes, seriously, Hélène, thank you from the bottom of our hearts." Well, damn, she'd kept a lid on her emotions for most of the day, but her tears sprung out like a leaky tap at their heartfelt thanks.

"*Merde*, you two. Have a wonderful honeymoon. I have to leave now, though. My flight is soon and I can't afford to miss it." That was a bare face lie. Her flight to Corsica wasn't scheduled until the next day, but she hadn't told anyone that just in case she needed to make a hasty getaway.

"No, no, no, no. You can't go yet. We haven't even done a conga line." Sam huffed.

Hélène laughed. "Oh no, how will I ever survive missing that delight?"

"Hey, it's tradition," Sam mock sulked.

"I promise that when you guys come down for the grand opening, I'll throw a party that has the best conga line ever. How's that?"

"You're too good to her," Anna smirked.

"Fine, but I wish you were still staying." Sam hugged Hélène tightly.

"I know I'm sorry, but we'll have plenty of time to party soon."

298

"Alright, be safe and message us when you arrive, okay?"

"Will do. I love you two."

"We love you." Anna and Sam wrapped her up in one last hug before letting her go. Turning towards the tent entrance, she caught a quick glimpse of Kim, still sitting at the table. Hélène was positive Kim was looking right at her, but she didn't dare look to find out for sure. She needed to leave now. So, with her aching heart and tail between her legs, Hélène slunk out and headed for her rental car.

* * *

The heat packed a punch even for October. Europe was suffering through a heatwave even though summer was long gone. Hello, global warming. To be honest though, Hélène needed the warmth of the sun because after escaping Sam and Anna's wedding, the only thing she'd felt was the icy embrace of sadness.

Seeing Kim at the wedding had sent her mind into overdrive. All those reasonably well thought out excuses that she'd used to justify walking away from Kim now seemed utterly ridiculous. Her brain was screaming at her that she'd made a colossal mistake. *Tough shit, you're too late now.*

The soft top car she'd rented was supposed to make her road trip to Santa Giulia fun, but she was struggling to summon any enthusiasm whatsoever. Her new life was waiting for her. The life she'd wanted for so long, but without Kim, everything seemed so lacking.

What was the point of living her dream if the woman of her dreams was with someone else? That was her stream of thought as she traversed Corsica. She didn't stop for coffee or food. She just plowed through, letting her mind take her deeper and deeper into a pit of despair. By the time she reached *Go Deep Diving Centre,* she was completely despondent.

The *Go Deep Diving Centre* was a relatively new building. It was perfectly located by the water in Santa Giulia. The previous owner had set it up as a dive centre, so everything they needed was already installed. The front of the building was made up of floor-to-ceiling windows which were tinted, so they reflected the water. They couldn't have got any luckier, especially with the price they'd paid. It seemed Holly's friend wanted a quick sale, something about a costly divorce.

"Jesus, was it that bad?" Holly opened the door to her rental once she'd come to a stop in front of their building. Apparently, that's when you were supposed to shut off the engine and get out. Hélène had sat there with the car idling until Holly had come over with a severe look of worry on her face.

Hélène tilted her head up to Holly, her brain finally engaging. "The wedding itself was great, just the guest list I struggled with."

"So you saw her then?"

"Yes, I did."

"And?"

"She was breathtakingly beautiful." Hélène let out a deep sigh.

"Did you talk at all?"

"In a fashion. We couldn't really get into it."

"I get you didn't want to cause a scene, but you guys need to hash this out."

"Well, it wasn't just the fact I didn't want to screw up Sam and Anna's wedding day. It was also because she came with Greg."

"Oh, shit."

"Yes, well, at least I know I got it right. She was always going to go back to him."

Holly ran her hand up the back of her neck. "Sorry, mate, this sucks."

"Yep, it really does. Can we talk about something else now?"

"Yeah, let's go in and have a drink. After all, we should be celebrating. All the paperwork came through when you were away. This place is officially ours."

Hélène snapped her head up to Holly. They hadn't had a reason to worry that anything with the sale would go wrong, but you never knew, right?

It was a massive relief to know that her dream would not be taken away. She had *Go Deep*, and that's all she needed. Eventually, her heart would heal. Maybe there would come a time that she could be in the same room as Kim and Greg and not feel violently sick. That was a way off yet, but hopefully one day.

"Okay, let's go drink." Hélène cheered.

"Already ahead of you, chuck. There's a bottle of Champagne waiting."

"*Parfait.*"

And it *was* perfect, mostly.

Chapter 25

Pissed didn't even come remotely close to how Kim was feeling. Who the hell did Greg think he was? Yeah, sure, their transition from partners to friends was bound to be rocky, but they were supposed to be on the same page.

Kim had made it abundantly clear that their romantic relationship was over. So why, for the love of all things sacred, had he acted like a dog marking his territory when Hélène had tried to talk to her? He may as well have cocked his leg on her. And now as she sat glaring at him, he had the audacity to look innocent, like butter wouldn't fucking melt.

Kim had been waiting weeks for the opportunity to talk to Hélène. The only way she'd been able to keep on top of what Hélène was doing was to pester Anna and Sam. After the disaster that was her drunk phone call to Hélène, she'd gone straight to Anna — well the day after, when she was sober — and begged her to get Sam to tell her what the hell had happened in Hélène's life the night she'd tried to call Kim.

From what Sam had said, Hélène had already been on the fence about their relationship. Her fear of being left had trumped her feelings towards Kim and by Kim running off to support Greg, she'd played right into Hélène's anxieties.

Adding the fact that Hélène's mother had opened up a torrent of emotion between them, it was no wonder Hélène had gone off the deep end and cut Kim off. She had been protecting herself in the best way she knew how.

Instead of calling Hélène back, Kim had taken some time to think. Hélène was a beautiful and complex woman. Her issues with commitment and intimacy were all valid. Kim couldn't imagine how she would feel having no emotional support from her parents and then dealing with people who never stuck around.

The wedding was supposed to be the perfect place to start a line of communication between them. Well, so much for that bloody idea. "Why do you look like a bulldog chewing a wasp?" Greg barked. Had he really asked her that? Was he that clueless?

"Why did you feel the need to act like a Neanderthal when Hélène was near me?"

"I did no such thing!" The red patches on his neck disagreed with that statement. Even his own body thought he was a jackass.

"Oh yes, you bloody did. Greg, you knew I wanted to talk to Hélène. Christ, you encouraged me. I thought we were making headway in becoming friends again, but clearly I was mistaken after that little performance."

At least he now had the decency to look contrite. "Alright, look, I'm sorry. Seeing you with someone else was harder than I thought it would be, okay?"

"I wasn't with someone else. I was just trying to have a conversation."

"Fine, fine, I buggered up."

"No, not fine. That was the one chance I had to talk to her. She's gone now. I saw her leave." She rubbed her hands roughly over her face. She'd made a mistake bringing him with her. Honestly, the only reason she had was because he had travelled back to Paris to collect his belongings and arrange shipping to England.

Kim had had a flurry of panic when she thought about leaving him on his own at the apartment. Having Greg so close to the place and people that had led him astray was too much to think about, hence the invite to the wedding. She'd made it perfectly clear they were there as friends only.

Over the last few weeks, they'd talked until they were blue in the face. Kim was determined to salvage her friendship with him and she was positive they were in a good place, but obviously not.

"I'm going to talk to Anna. Stay here." He didn't even attempt to move.

As she made her way through the marquee, she did her level best to plaster on a smile. After all, it was a wedding. "Hello you two lovely people." Sam and Anna turned in unison.

"Oh, Kim, thank you for making today so wonderful," Anna cooed.

"I didn't do anything, doll, I just stood up there with you." Kim giggled at the love-struck puppy eyes Anna was shooting at Sam.

"And that was more than enough. You made our day," Sam said.

"Well, I wouldn't be anywhere else." They fell silent. Kim caught the look Anna shot Sam. Did they know why she'd come over? Was she that transparent? Sam answered that question.

"She left for the airport." Kim's heart sank. "The opening of the dive centre is coming up, so she had to get down there pronto."

"Yeah, of course." What else could she say?

"You know it's not the end of the world, right?" Sam added, squeezing her shoulder. "You could just jump on a plane and go there."

"After our very brief discussion, I don't think I'd be welcome."

"I think you'd be surprised. She's running. I don't think she'd be reacting this way if you didn't mean that much to her. I think she needs someone to show up, prove that they're gonna stick around."

Kim looked at her friends again. She could show up, couldn't she? She could prove to Hélène that she was all in, because she was. They may have only been together for a short amount of time, but Kim knew her own mind and heart, Hélène, was the person who complemented her.

Kim had never needed someone to *complete* her. She needed a partner that helped balance her out, challenge her when needed, and support her through life. Hélène made Kim's life better, just by being close. There was a lot they would have to sort through, but she was confident they could, if Hélène would just give them a chance.

"What are you going to do?" Anna asked, pulling Kim out of her reverie.

"I'll plan to fly down there in a few weeks."

"Good choice. Whilst you're heading south, maybe it's time to take up the offer to tour the university you were telling me about?"

Kim had relayed Aurelie's offer to tour the University of Nice to Anna. She was still stuck on the decision. The more she thought about it, the more she knew it was the right call.

305

Returning to science was all she thought about nowadays — well, apart from the ash blonde woman she had fallen for.

It was tricky, though. Upending your life to pursue something that gave no guarantee of a good income or job was daunting. Paris had been a good move; even if she'd come to regret it recently. Her job with Anna was fun and uncomplicated, she had friends and a pleasant apartment. Chucking all that away seemed foolish. Even so, her heart wanted what it wanted. She just had to pull the trigger, which was proving harder than she thought it would be.

"We'll see. I haven't decided yet."

"Hmm, I thought that would be the case. So, I'm going to make it a little easier for you." Anna was giving Kim all her attention now, which made her feel a little uneasy. Gone was the love-struck bride. Anna had transformed herself into "boss mode" in the blink of an eye. "Kim, I love you and I couldn't have asked for a better assistant, but the time has come to let you go. You're fired."

Had she heard that right? "I'm sorry what?"

"You're fired, effective immediately. You will get a generous severance package and a glowing reference if you should ever need it." Kim's eyes darted from Anna to Sam, who, for some ridiculous fucking reason, was smiling like she'd won the lottery. How was this the time to be smiling?

"Firing me? You… you can't fire me."

"Actually, I can." Anna was beaming. And then it was as if a switch had been flicked. Instead of the unbridled panic that had swirled in her chest moments ago, she felt lighter. Not having to worry about her job and loyalty to Anna had just made her decision infinitely easier.

"Kim, you deserve to do the thing that brings you happiness. We've had so much fun working together, but your passion is in science. I don't want you holding yourself back because of me, or anyone else. I think it's been a long time since you put your wants before anyone else's."

Tears pricked at the edge of her eyes. "Thank you. God, I love you." Kim wrapped her arms around Anna's waist. Even in her heels, she was much shorter than her friend. "I'm a little terrified," she laughed.

"Don't be. You're going to do great things. I can feel it. You're one in a million, Kim."

"I'll second that." Sam chimed.

* * *

Today marked the second week since Anna had unceremoniously fired Kim. It also marked her last day ever at *Tower Publishing*. Over the course of the last fourteen days, Kim had tipped from one end of the emotional scale to the other. She'd been upset that Anna had fired her, then she'd felt elated, then back to annoyed. Oh, not forgetting the fear and anxiety of the unknown that plagued her nightly.

As she sat at her desk for the last time, all she could feel was gratitude. She was grateful to Anna for taking a chance on her. There weren't many people in the world that would've chosen Kim for the role as their personal assistant knowing she had no experience. Anna had though, she'd hired Kim based on a gut feeling which turned out to be spot on, because — without tooting her own horn — Kim had made this job her bitch. She was a damn good PA.

The hardest part of the week had been helping Anna choose her replacement, although Anna had assured her there was no way she could be replaced. That was sweet. After a grueling three days of back-to-back interviews, they finally found Anna's new PA.

Becca Simmons was, in a lot of ways, just like Kim. She'd just arrived from the UK after graduating university. Unlike Kim though Becca had a BA in business. Her sense of humour and positive disposition, however, was just like Kim.

It was important that Anna had that kind of influence in her life. Anna was a control freak sometimes and didn't know when to switch off. She also took things way too seriously in Kim's book, but she had relaxed more since meeting Sam. Anna's job was high pressure, so finding her the right PA was essential. Becca would need to be everything that Kim had been in order for it to work.

"So, you'll start next Monday, is that okay?" A sadness gripped Kim's heart as she thought about not being in the office from next week.

"That's perfect. I can't wait to get started." Becca beamed. Knowing that Anna was in safe hands made Kim's decision to leave even easier.

Everything was in motion now. The lease to her apartment still had another month left on it, giving her enough time to find somewhere in Nice. It felt a little like she was counting her chickens before they'd hatched because she still hadn't taken the tour Aurelie offered, but it was scheduled for the middle of next week.

Yes, she could get there and hate it, but something in her gut said that wouldn't be the case. Hours scouring the university's website had assuaged her of any concerns. The course she would study looked fabulous, something she could really sink her teeth into. It would also pave the way for her to complete her doctorate.

All that was still a week away. Right now, she had to concentrate on sifting through her belongings and packing them in boxes. In the unlikely event that Nice wasn't the place for her,

Kim had decided to move out of the apartment she shared with Greg, regardless.

Greg had accompanied her back to Paris after the wedding. He'd spent several days packing up his things and having them shipped to the UK. His recovery was going well. He was taking it all day by day and it was clear that their breakup had had a positive effect on him, well on both of them, actually.

Whatever hang-ups Greg had regarding Kim and her parents helping him, it was clear that he wouldn't be able to get past them if they remained a couple. That didn't stop him from acting like a jealous arse sometimes, but it was a process. Kim got that. Both their lives had changed so drastically over a very short stretch of time and they both needed to work through it in their own way.

The clock on her desk read 5 p.m. She'd officially finished her last day. A sad sigh tumbled from her mouth.

"You ready?" Anna called. Her office door had been propped open. Kim watched as her boss — no ex-boss — gathered up her bag and slipped on her coat.

"Yup, I suppose so." Anna had convinced Kim to go to a bar for a quick farewell drink. It was the last thing she wanted to do, really, but how could she say no?

"*On y va*," Anna chirped.

The bar was one of their locals. It was only a five-minute walk from the office, which is why they frequented it so much. Kim, being a bit of a social butterfly, had befriended all the staff and bouncers. It would be nice to see them before she left, she supposed.

Anna pushed through the bar door, obscuring Kim's view. Kim didn't need to see anything to know there was something odd going on. The place was silent until Anna stepped out of the way and then there was an eruption of noise.

309

Kim reflexively took a step back as a wall of sound hit her. Stood in front of her were the entire office staff, the bar staff, her parents, and Steph and Tash.

"Holy hell," she blurted. Anna threw her hands around Kim's neck, giving her a big kiss on the cheek.

"I can't believe you thought we would let you go without a party."

For the next twenty minutes, she was swept up in hugs and kisses from her friends. It was all a little overwhelming, but she was floored by the outpouring of love and support.

"What are you guys doing here?" Kim directed to her family and two friends.

"We wouldn't miss a good knees up, love," her dad smiled and winked.

"Free trip to Paris," Steph laughed.

"French blokes," Tash chimed, causing everyone to laugh.

"I'm so proud of you," her mum cooed, pinching Kim's cheeks.

"You guys," Kim giggled.

Wine and Champagne flowed throughout the evening. It was when the second round of YMCA was being screamed out that Kim decided she needed water and her bed. She thanked everyone several times over for coming. She really was stunned by their support.

Admittedly, the one person who should have been there wasn't. No matter what had happened between them, Hélène had helped her realise she wanted more out of her life.

Unfortunately, it wasn't to be. Sam had quietly informed her she wasn't sure if Kim was okay with Hélène knowing about her plans to leave Paris. Maybe it was good that Hélène was in the dark. Kim wanted the chance to talk to her and put forward a plan to get them back on track. As vintage dresses were her witness, she would not let Hélène go so easily.

* * *

Her nerves had been playing silly buggers for the past three days leading up to the university visit. The morning after her party was when it had really hit her. She was leaving, starting a new adventure all by herself. Well, maybe not entirely alone if everything went to plan.

The University Côte D'Azur was beyond what Kim had expected. Aurelie had personally taken the time to show Kim around the campus. It was difficult to really concentrate when they were surrounded by such wonderful sights.

Living by the Côte D'Azur wouldn't exactly be a hardship. She could definitely see herself parading around Nice, basking in the sun with a cocktail. After she'd studied her arse off, of course.

The Mediterranean landscape was so far from what she was used to. She'd experienced it a little in Saint Tropez, but that was a holiday. Everything looked magical on holiday.

The houses around Nice were painted in a variety of colours with terracotta roof tiles. One could forget they were in France at all. The area could easily be mistaken for Spain or Italy.

After taking her on a tour of the university, Aurelie suggested they find somewhere in the heart of Nice for food. They meandered around the brightly coloured, small streets. The buildings that towered above were covered in a variety of plants and vines. Little tables and chairs littered the pavements from the cafés, and restaurants nestled in the small streets. They settled into a hole in the wall to eat.

"So, what do you think?" Aurelie was perusing the menu as she spoke.

"I'm very impressed."

"Enough to join us?"

"Yes, definitely." She'd made her mind up the moment they'd started the tour.

"Excellent. Do you still want to begin part-time?"

"If possible. I have a lot of things to sort out, which will require me to travel. However, I would like to take on a full-time role in the next semester."

"I can't see a reason for it to be a problem. I'll talk to admissions and get the ball rolling. Now you will be a few weeks behind, but I have every confidence that you will catch up quickly."

"I'm not too worried. I haven't been away from academia that long and I pride myself on having a strong work ethic." Aurelie gave her a quick tip of the head in agreement.

The one thing Kim was good at was adapting. After seeing how diverse the group of students in her class were, she held no worry about her age or the fact she'd been away from education.

With the tour wrapped up, it was time for Kim to set her sights on the next part of her plan. Hélène. They'd definitely had a rocky road ahead of them, but Kim firmly believed they could navigate it. It wasn't every day that two people connected the way they had. If she had to be the one to make some changes to show Hélène she was all in, then she would.

Studying part-time would help. Once the apartment in Paris was sorted and she was settled in Nice, she could look at travelling to Corsica. Aurelie had set her up with work that could be completed online, meaning she could study anywhere.

Maybe if she and Hélène had a few weeks together, she could build up the trust that Hélène needed to take them seriously.

312

First thing first, though, she had to see Hélène and talk to her. Hopefully, she would listen. The problem was that Hélène's protective walls were so high, Kim feared it was going to prove impossible for her to scale them.

Her flight was scheduled for later that night. It would have been a wise choice to stay over in Nice for the night and *then* head down to Corsica, but at the time of booking, the only thing running through her mind was getting to Hélène as soon as possible.

The plane would arrive at midnight, which was not ideal. She'd have to put up with an airport hotel for the night. If everything went to plan, she'd pick up her rental car at 8 a.m. and begin the drive to Santa Giulia.

It had crossed her mind to contact Holly, give her a heads up, but the thought of Holly warning Hélène and Hélène bolting put pay to that idea. Hell, turning up sans warning could be a big mistake. Hélène could take one look at her and tell her to bugger off. Everything was up in the air and it was awful.

The next few hours were going to be long and tiring, but what other choice did she have? For the first time in years, Kim felt good about putting her needs first, and Hélène was one of those needs. Her heart told her that Hélène felt the same and that they could be something wonderful together.

Chapter 26

The soft rocking of the boat kept Hélène from emerging from her bed. Buying a small sailing boat instead of a townhouse had been the perfect choice. She was close to work. Literally, she could see the centre from her little porthole in her sleeping quarters. There was no rent as the jetty belonged to the diving centre, and she got to wake up to the sound of the sea and the gentle sway of the waves.

The smell of coffee was a pleasant, albeit surprising, delight to have wafting in from her little galley. Hélène rolled her eyes. Holly had obviously made herself at home again.

Two weeks ago, when Hélène first took ownership of the vessel, she'd named *Blonde Bombshell*, Holly had spent all her time onboard with Hélène. It had been like having an extended holiday, but now all Hélène wanted was some privacy and space.

Holly had her own apartment, a nice one in fact, but that didn't matter, apparently. No, Holly had made a vow to someone somewhere that she would not leave Hélène alone for more than an hour a day, it seemed.

Okay, so Hélène had been in a bit of a funk recently. And yes, maybe Holly had caught her day drinking, but that didn't mean she needed a babysitter. She was a fully formed adult woman, with her own business, for Christ's sake.

With her irritation spiked, she rolled out of bed and stomped through to the galley. "Hols, why are you here again?" A little curt, but she wasn't in the mood for niceties.

"I brought you breakfast," Holly shot back.

"I have food, I have coffee, I don't need you smothering me." No more nice guy. Holly needed to get it through to her head that Hélène was just fine.

"Ah, if you're referring to the stale bread in the cupboard or the empty packet of filter coffee in the fridge, then yes, you have food. How silly of me to want to help my best friend when she is clearly struggling."

"I am not struggling. *Merde*, Holly, I'm fine."

"You're fine, really. That's what you're going with. How about you say that again when you're not wearing a cheese-stained tank top and sweats that have another stain on them? Have you just started throwing things at your face, hoping they land in your mouth now?"

Hélène looked down at her stained clothes. Alright, so maybe she wasn't totally fine. Even so, she could deal with her emotional turmoil alone. "I just got out of bed. I'm still in my nightwear," she mumbled.

"That's even more fucking disturbing, Hélène. You were wearing those clothes yesterday afternoon, which means you haven't even bothered to wash and change." Hélène didn't have a good comeback because it was true.

315

Since Sam and Anna's wedding, she'd found herself in a pit of misery, which pissed her off. Starting *Go Deep* was supposed to be the thing that got her out of her funk. She'd had every intention of cracking on with work the moment she'd arrived back from the wedding, only that hadn't happened at all.

Once Holly had popped the Champagne and they'd begun celebrating, all of Hélène's emotions had come spilling out. Blame the alcohol, she did. But then the next day was the same. Tears and grief. Losing Kim to Greg had torn her to shreds. Knowing it was her own fault was crippling.

"Look, I know you're worried, but really, I'm as fine as I can be. I just need some time and space." Surely Holly would take the hint and leave now.

"And normally, chuck, I would be happy to give you that time and space, but we have a business to run. So far, I'm doing all the bloody work, love. I'm run off my feet, and it's becoming too much. Thankfully Leo just called and told me he can work with us for a while because I need the help, Hélène. You're brokenhearted but you won't talk about it, and that love is the only way you can start healing. Hiding away on your boat is not the answer."

Ugh, she felt even worse now. Wallowing in her own self-pity had been all-consuming. She hadn't stopped once to consider Holly and the business, which was atrocious. Why Holly would want to run a business with her was anyone's guess?

Even so, the thought of entering the world again felt wrong. The sun was shining and there were still enough tourists to do a few dives before the end of the season. But all Hélène wanted to do was stay in the dark, away from their stupid smiling faces.

"I'm worried about you, really worried." Holly's voice conveyed the sincerity in her words.

316

"God, I'm sorry Hol, I'm a terrible business partner."

"No, you're not. You are the only person who I want to be in business with, but you have to deal with your shit. Right now you're hurting and that's all you can deal with, but I need you to actually deal with it so you can be my partner again, chuck."

"How? I don't even know where to start." A sob ripped through her throat. How could she accept she would never hold Kim in her arms again?

"Come and sit down, have a bit of coffee and calm down, love. Let's talk, and I mean properly talk about it. All you have told me is that you broke it off before she could and that she's back with Greg."

"Everyone I get involved with leaves and that's what it looked like Kim was doing."

"But did she actually give you a genuine reason to believe she was running back to her life with the ex?"

"She ran off at the first moment he called."

"She went to help her best friend, Hélène. If me and you had had a relationship that broke up and I called you in need, would you tell me to sod off?"

"That's not the same thing." Hélène's frustration with the conversation was getting the better of her. Why didn't Holly understand?

"It absolutely is. And, in all honesty, if you hadn't got so many hangups about being left, you would see it too. Don't get me wrong, I understand why you feel the way you do. Dating is a shitty arena, getting to know people and then them leaving is tough, but you're letting those experiences shape your future. Hate me all you like for saying this, but you really screwed up, walking away from her."

"What's wrong with protecting myself, huh?"

317

"Nothing at all but you over-corrected. There was nothing you needed protecting from. Kim was in that relationship. That was clear as day. Okay so everything happened quickly, and the timing wasn't ideal, but she told you she was in, right?"

"*Merde*," Hélène growled. "It doesn't matter now, does it? She's gone, I blew it, end of."

"Well, that's the stupidest thing you've said recently. Call the woman, explain, open up to her, and let her decide what she wants."

Hélène shook her head. No way. She couldn't listen to Kim tell her she was happy with Greg. What was done was done. Now she just had to learn to live with it. "I'm going to shower. I'll be in the centre in half an hour, ready to work. I appreciate you, Holly, you're my best friend, and I'm sorry I let you down recently. That's going to stop now."

"So, you're not going to call her then?" Holly looked exasperated.

"I'll see you later. Thanks for the coffee." Leaving Holly in the galley, Hélène made her escape. There, she'd done the talking, she'd opened up and Holly hadn't understood. Or had she? Jesus, she was so conflicted.

* * *

It was a slog to get herself off the boat and into work mode, but right now, as her body plunged into the warm water of the Mediterranean, she could kick herself for hiding away for so long.

Diving always brought her peace. Why hadn't she done this sooner? The sounds of her breathing crackled through the water, her heart rate slowed and the sadness that had engulfed her for weeks eased.

318

Thankfully, the client she was diving with was a seasoned diver. He didn't need her to guide him or look after him, but that was her job. He just wanted a diving centre that did all the heavy lifting, which was what they offered.

Today's dive was round the islands located roughly five miles from the centre. It wasn't a technical dive, just a calm meander. It was the first time in weeks that Hélène felt herself. The pain was still there, but it had dulled. The sea had done its job.

Happy that the client was satisfied, Hélène began unloading the zodiac. Her body was aching. Even a short time away from hauling diving gear had rendered her body fatigued beyond recognition. She should hit the weights more often.

Holly had already signed off for the day, which was great. Maybe Hélène could actually get some peace and quiet. After a quick shower in the staff quarters, she headed down the jetty. About ten metres from her boat, she stopped dead.

Sitting on the stern of her boat at her little wooden table, with arms crossed and a rather intimidating glare, was Kim. Hélène should have been terrified. Kim painted quite the picture of a woman scorned, and rightfully so. But Hélène wasn't terrified. She was elated and her heart beat for the woman glaring at her with piercing blue eyes and ridiculously high heels.

* * *

Travelling to Santa Giulia had not gone well. The plane had sat on the runway for two hours after it had landed, and no one had any clue why. Stumbling into the airport hotel at nearly three in the morning was not fun, especially when the reception desk took another thirty minutes to check her in.

319

They'd struggled to find her reservation, which nearly tipped her over the edge. Flashbacks to The Sapphire didn't help. Kim *would not* spend the night in the hotel lobby. So after a heated chat with Francine, the receptionist, she was finally given a key to a bog standard room.

Her sleep had been interrupted three times by other guests stumbling past her door, banging it with their luggage. The alarm that sounded at 7 a.m. nearly gave her a coronary. The shower got to a lukewarm temperature and the breakfast she was offered consisted of burnt toast and orange juice. Add on to the fact that her rental car was late being returned, which set her back a whopping three hours, Kim was not feeling hopeful towards her task of winning Hélène back. Was the sodding cosmos against her or something?

Mercifully, the road from Ajaccio to Santa Giulia had been a breeze. In that, there was no traffic. The mountain roads had been a little panic inducing at times. The landscape was gorgeous; the sky was a light blue with no clouds in sight. The temperature for the time of year was above average, and Kim was happy to roll down her windows as she cruised along. The sea air caressed her senses and left her feeling a hell of a lot calmer.

Close to three hours later, Kim pulled her rental car into the drive of the Airbnb she had rented for the week. A week may have been a little presumptive. Hélène could tell her to sling her hook after five minutes. She was prepared to stick it out, though.

If Hélène told her to leave, she would, but only as far as her accommodation, and then she would try again. That was the plan anyway, but after the past twenty-four hours she wasn't all that confident it would go the way she expected.

The small villa was perfect. It was nestled in a sweet little neighbourhood about five minutes from the town centre. When booking Kim hadn't spent a lot of time picking through the listings, she just needed something affordable, and close to the diving centre.

Her choice had been pretty stellar, though. It was a two-bed villa with its own pool out back. The garden and surrounding space was enclosed by palm, pine, and Italian Cypress trees. The house was secluded, but not to the point where it felt isolated. Kim could foresee a little skinny dipping in her future. The bedroom she decided to call her own was on the back of the property, overlooking the luscious landscape and pool. It also had its own balcony that she would definitely have her morning coffee on.

A quick glance at her watch told her it was past lunch. She hadn't eaten since her woefully lacking breakfast this morning. To her delight, she found a small basket of local products and a bottle of wine on the counter in the kitchen. She would give these hosts a five-star rating.

Olives, charcuterie, and cheese adorned her plate as she sat outside by the pool. She'd left the wine for later. Either she'd celebrate with it or she'd drown her sorrows.

With a full stomach, Kim gathered her things and headed back to the car. There was no point in waiting around. She had to get this over and done with now.

The drive to *Go Deep Diving Centre* took all of five minutes. There was enough space out front for several cars, however, they were all occupied. *The centre must be doing well.* The cosmos seemed to have had an attitude change since yesterday, because just as she was about to pull away to find parking elsewhere, a man exited the centre and freed up a space.

Kim took a deep breath. She turned off the car and sat there for a moment. Summoning all the confidence she could, she hauled herself out of the car and went inside.

The foyer was large and open. A counter ran along the back of the room. Posters and price lists hung from the wall behind it. The floor-to-ceiling windows let the sunshine in, lighting up the blue walls. It was like being in an aquarium and Kim liked it.

So far, there had been no sign of Hélène or Holly. Maybe they were out on the water? If that was the case, though, surely they would have locked up? A noise from the back grabbed Kim's attention. Someone was hauling gear by the sounds of it. Kim could feel her pulse spike, and blood pulse in her ears. Was it Hélène?

"Kim?" A broad Australian accent shot through the silence. In her excitement, Kim hadn't seen Holly walk through the door leading to the back rooms.

"Hi, Holly."

"Crikey, what are you doing here?" Holly was standing stock still with her arms full of wetsuits.

"I'm here to sell Girl Scout cookies. What the bloody hell do you think I'm doing here?" she laughed. Holly's face softened and a smile spread from cheek to cheek.

"You do not know how glad I am to see you, chuck."

"Right back at ya, doll. Is she here?"

"No, she's out with a client." Holly checked her watch. "She should be back in an hour, though. Tops."

"How are you?" They might as well catch up whilst they waited for Hélène to return.

"You don't really want to know about me, do you? You want to know about Hélène."

"Actually, I would like to know about you." She cast her gaze around the room. "This place looks awesome. You've done a fab job."

Holly beamed with pride. "Ah thanks, love. I'm pleased as punch. It wasn't the best time to open, with the season coming to a close so soon, but honestly, we just wanted to get some dives in and if people want to pay to come along, then that's bonza."

Kim laughed. Holly's exuberance and Australian slang were very endearing. They may have started out with issues, but now Kim considered Holly a friend. "When do you close for dives?" Kim wanted to get a couple in, if possible.

"Probably next week. The weather's due to turn. We've been super lucky that the summer has held on way longer than usual."

"Well, hopefully if all goes well today, I can dive with you before you shut."

Holly eyed her. "And what are you hoping will happen today?"

"I'm hoping Hélène will at least give me the time of day to talk to her. Properly talk. She bolted so bloody fast neither of us had the chance to say what needed to be said."

"What do you need to say?"

"I think Hélène should be the first to hear it, don't you?"

Holly studied her longer. Kim never shrunk away from anyone. She stood as tall as she could with her shoulders back as Holly looked her over. What was she thinking?

After several charged seconds, Holly let out a deep sigh. "She needs you."

"Does she? Because that's not the impression I get."

"C'mon, you know why she did what she did. You haven't come all this way just to shout at her."

"Yes, I think I know why, but I need to hear it from her."

"What about Greg?" That question took her by surprise.

"What about him?"

"Well, last I heard, you'd shacked up with him again." Kim's blood boiled. First, because Greg had acted the way he had at the wedding, causing Hélène to make assumptions, and secondly at Hélène for making those assumptions.

"You were misinformed."

Holly nodded. They remained silent for a few seconds. Holly looked contemplative again. "Head down to the beach. Walk about fifty metres to the right and you'll see where you need to wait. I think you'll also understand why I said she needs you." Oh good, a riddle, just what she needed. "I've got to get on, chuck, these wetsuits won't clean themselves. I'll see ya later." Holly gave her a sincere smile before retreating to the back again. Alright, she'd follow Holly's cryptic clue and head to the beach.

The stretch of beach was huge. Kim followed the white sand as instructed. Fifty metres later, Kim stood looking at a boat that could only belong to Hélène. She now understood why Holly had sent her there. Hélène had named a boat after her.

The *Blonde Bombshell* was a gorgeous vessel. Spacious, but not over the top. It showed signs of use but was still in excellent shape. She shone brightly under the Mediterranean sun. The wood trim was polished and smooth. It was perfect for Hélène.

Kim's ire peaked again. Hélène was not over them, not by a long shot. Nobody named a boat after a woman they weren't interested in. All this bloody buggering about. Why hadn't Hélène just communicated, opened up? They could be sitting sipping Champagne on the back of *Blonde Bombshell* right now in their underwear. Instead, they'd spent weeks apart hurting.

Climbing aboard, Kim headed for the little table that sat at the stern. It was tempting to go inside and have a nosey, but that didn't feel right. She sat at the table and crossed her legs, staring in the direction of the diving centre.

The longer she waited, the more irritated at the whole situation she became. By the time she saw Hélène descend the wooden walkway she was livid and she was positive her face construed her emotional state too.

Hélène had come to a standstill about ten metres away. Her face was a picture of shock and something else, happiness?

324

"K… Kim?"

"Hélène." Kim knew that being anything but kind towards Hélène wasn't the best start, but she couldn't help it. Well, not until she saw Hélène flinch at the coldness attached to her name.

Damn it, she just wanted to wrap Hélène up in her arms and tell her everything was going to be okay. She couldn't do that, though. They had to talk. She needed to hear that Hélène wanted to be with her.

"What… What are you doing here?"

"What do you think I'm doing here?" Hélène opened and closed her mouth several times before clamping it shut. Kim saw her take a deep breath before closing the distance between them. Hélène threw her bag on deck and climbed aboard.

Finally, after a few seconds of hesitation, she sat in the chair opposite Kim. "I'm here because you never gave me a chance to talk. You bolted and left me in your wake with nothing but confusion and heartache." Hélène dropped her gaze from Kim to the table in front of her.

"I'm sorry." Hélène shuffled in her seat before looking back at Kim. "I am sorry, Kim, I really believed it was the right thing to do, but I shouldn't have cut and run like that."

"And now?"

"Now?"

"Do you still think it was the right thing to do?" Hélène shrugged, which irked Kim to no end. "Don't shrug, that's not enough. Tell me if it was the right thing to do."

"At the time, yes." Well, that stung. "But now… I don't know."

"I'll tell you what I know." Kim had had enough of this prating about. It was time to get to the nitty gritty. "We had a whirlwind romance that turned out to be so much more than either of us was expecting. Both of us were in a tough place to start something, but we did, and it was glorious. You —" Kim pointed at Hélène, "—kept one foot out the door from the beginning. All that bollock about being cursed. You walked away at the first sign of trouble. I'll hold my hands up and say that the way I ran off to help Greg was insensitive. My only explanation is that I was acting on instinct. Watching someone lose their parents is traumatising. Greg was in so much pain, I spent my time helping and looking after him.

"I concede I took it beyond what it should have been and put myself to one side in favour of his wants and needs. That has ended now. We are not, I repeat, *not* together in a romantic capacity, but he will always be my friend, something you're going to have to get used to.

"The time we've been apart has given me the opportunity to make some changes. Positive changes, but it's also given me the room to assess us. You shouldn't have walked away and you most certainly should not have decided what was best for me. I'm the only one who gets to do that." Kim sent a penetrating glare at Hélène, reinforcing what she had just said. "You don't get to tell me I can't love you. I choose who my heart belongs to, not you."

"You love me?"

"Yes, unequivocally. It's quick, but I know my mind and I know my heart. Which, Ms DuBois, you have broken. Saying all that, I'm still here today on the boat you clearly named after me to ask you to reconsider. I want us to be together, Hélène. I can help you with your insecurities if you let me. We can do this and we can be happy."

Hélène regarded her for a minute, making Kim squirm. She let out a squeal of surprise when Hélène swiftly pulled her from the chair and into her arms, crushing their mouths together.

326

"I'm sorry, I'm sorry, I'm sorry," Hélène mumbled against Kim's lips. "I love you too, good lord, Kim. I fell for you right from the start. I've been miserable and stubborn and selfish, but I need you. I need you with me."

"Then you have me. It's not always going to be easy, but you can't run, understand?"

"Never again. I'll only move towards you, never away."

"Good, now take me below deck and show me how much you've missed me."

Epilogue

"You didn't have to do this, H."

"Yes, I did. I have a lot of ground to make up." Hélène nuzzled Kim's neck from behind.

It was three years to the day since Kim had turned up in Santa Giulia. Three perfect and sometimes painful years.

"No, you don't. We're way past that. It was unavoidable missing my graduation. Plus, you got to see it through the live stream, so technically, you were there." Kim cooed as she turned in Hélène's embrace.

Standing on her tiptoes, she kissed Hélène's jaw. A shiver ran down Hélène's body. Kim drew out her primal needs every time she touched her. She had to chastise herself regularly because if she let herself, she'd drag Kim to bed every time they were in touching distance, regardless of the situation.

"Remind me to thank Greg for setting the live stream up." Who would have thought Hélène would be in a position where she was happy to thank Greg and actually class him as a close friend now?

It had taken several months for Hélène to open herself up to Greg. It was still difficult to reconcile the man she saw when he was acting irrationally and the man who was sober.

Kim had made it perfectly clear that Greg would be a part of her life, and Hélène certainly didn't want her feelings to create a problem in their relationship. She followed Kim's lead and over a couple of years; they began meeting up more often.

Once Hélène got to know him, she quickly cast aside the man who had lost control. That wasn't Greg. He'd been in a dark place, but he'd worked hard and was now three years sober. He was kind, funny, and completely supportive of Hélène and Kim.

"Look at it as my way of congratulating you," she continued. "I'm so proud of you, my love." They kissed again. "Plus, you're going back to Nice in a few weeks to start your doctorate, so this little getaway gives us time together before we spend weeks apart." Hélène had taken charge of *Connie* for a couple of weeks. She'd whisked Kim away for some quality time alone.

From the moment Kim arrived in Santa Giulia, she'd mucked in with the diving centre. She'd become their unofficial receptionist. Kim was wonderful with the customers and when they closed for the season, she chipped in with any manual labour that needed doing.

All that work meant that Hélène and Kim hadn't got the alone time they thought they would, which was hard considering Kim could only visit every few weeks because of her uni schedule.

Running *Go Deep* was a partnership. Hélène couldn't just take weeks off at a time to spend with Kim, so they ended up hanging out with Holly and Leo more times than not. That wasn't conducive to quality romance time.

Holly and Kim had formed a close bond quickly. Their quick back-and-forth banter was hilarious. They had a wonderful group of friends, which made Hélène stupidly happy. She loved that the group were *their* friends, not just Kim's and not just Hélène's.

The harder parts of their years together, aside from the time spent in different places, were the emotional ones. Hélène had spent so long shoving her feelings to one side, it took a lot of time and patience for Kim to coax them out. Kim pushed Hélène to open up. She pushed to make sure that Hélène expressed herself, even if that meant upsetting Kim. They rode out the choppy waters together and every day led to Hélène feeling more secure in their relationship.

In the beginning, the hardest part for Hélène had been when Kim explained she would be leaving for university. The thought of Kim living elsewhere had sent slivers of panic into every one of her limbs. Her anxieties had raised their ugly heads on more than one occasion.

At one point, Hélène had almost told Holly she was leaving the centre to follow Kim to Nice. Kim had overheard Hélène talking to herself in the mirror, trying to pump herself up to break the news to Holly. Thank god Kim had overheard because it led to Hélène confessing how utterly terrified she was of Kim leaving.

Hélène's brain had convinced her that Kim would meet someone else or the work would become too much and she'd leave her in pursuit of her career. Kim had treated Hélène with love and patience. She'd acknowledged Hélène's fears and helped her talk them through. It had taken some time, but eventually Hélène realised they didn't need to follow each other, or live in each other's pockets to be happy.

They could do the things that made them happy separately and still be together. The distance between them geographically didn't diminish their love for each other or their commitment.

Kim was doing something she was passionate about, and that made Hélène ecstatic. Hélène had her dream job, too. The centre had become a success in the first season. The past two years had been booked solid, and they were now scouting other locations to set up new centres.

"I had your bags put in your room," Hélène commented. Kim raised her eyebrows questioningly.

"My room? Don't you mean our room?"

"No, I meant your room. I thought we could get set up like the last time we were here. You know, play it coy for a while until you use your womanly charms to seduce me." They hadn't made it back to *Connie* since their first time together.

"Until I... the nerve of you, Ms DuBois." If Kim wasn't such a remarkable scientist, she should have tried acting. The fake outrage was almost too good to be fake until she quirked her mouth up at the side. "You're going to pay for that."

"Oh, good." Hélène drew Kim in for another mind melting kiss. *Connie* was operating on a skeleton crew, which was good because Hélène and Kim were getting more than friendly on the observation deck. "I'm taking you to bed." Hélène growled. Her libido was through the roof.

"Oh, are you really?" Kim asked defiantly. Hélène threw her a wicked smile before launching Kim over her shoulder, causing her to squeal in surprise. The squeal turned into laughter as Hélène jogged with Kim to their suite.

The door had only just clicked shut when Hélène held Kim up against it. Kim's legs naturally wrapped around Hélène's waist. "God, you're sexy," Hélène moaned. Kim was rolling her hips, trying to build some friction.

They were still in their travelling clothes which, thankfully for Hélène, meant Kim wearing an easy access dress.

Hélène cupped and squeezed Kim's back side, massaging it as her hips continued to roll.

"Bed," Kim gasped. Hélène moved them to the bed. They'd arrived later in the day and the sun was setting. The sky was a mass of golden hues. The light poured in through the windows. Hélène looked down into Kim's eyes as she gently placed her on the bed. Kim was a vision of exquisite beauty. The golden rays made her glow, and Hélène couldn't stop the tears from falling.

"Hey, hey, hey, what's wrong?" Kim cupped Hélène's face with her palm.

Hélène gently shook her head from side to side. Sometimes she would look at Kim and her breath would be stolen from her lungs. Knowing that she'd almost lost this perfect woman was sometimes too much, even after all this time. "I just love you so much."

"Oh, Hélène, I love you too, sugar." Kim smiled sweetly, then drew Hélène's head down for a kiss. "Make love to me, H."

More than happy to oblige, Hélène gently slipped the dress up and over Kim's body. She had to bite her lip to stop a moan from escaping. That's the reaction Kim's lace clad form elicited.

She let her fingers roam over Kim's sculpted abdomen. She noted the increased speed with which Kim was breathing. Her fingers brushed delicately over her tight nipples, then down to the edge of Kim's lace thong. Every brush of skin sent magical pulses through Hélène's fingers and up to her chest. It would be so easy to lose herself in Kim's creamy, soft skin.

"Hélène." Kim's body squirmed underneath her. She hooked her fingers underneath the waist of the lacey garment and gently pulled them away, dropping them to the floor. Kim's sex was mouthwatering.

Extracting herself, Hélène stood and undressed. She didn't rush. She enjoyed Kim watching her. She loved to see the love and lust in her eyes as Hélène revealed a little more of her body. Kim sat up and discarded her bra. They were both naked and wanting. Lowering herself back down to Kim, she took one of her breasts into her mouth, causing Kim to shift and moan.

Their lovemaking was so different to fucking. They enjoyed taking each other, sometime ferociously, often up against walls or other furniture. They played with toys and experimented with positions. They would whisper dirty things in each other's ears, but not when they made love. That was silent. They let their bodies do the talking. Their movements were slow, deliberate and all-consuming.

Instinctively, Kim parted her sex as Hélène settled between her legs. Hélène slid her pussy against her lover's. Together, they moved. Their hips rocked as they settled into a rhythm. All the time, their eyes remained glued to each other. There was nothing quite so extraordinary as looking into her soulmate's eyes as she gave Kim all of herself in that moment.

Kim's chest was red, small beads of sweat had formed. Their breathing was equally ragged as they continued to move. "Oh, baby," Kim gasped. Hélène pressed herself harder into Kim. Her own orgasm began to swirl and build in her core.

"Come with me," Hélène moaned. Her climax was fast approaching. Their cries of ecstasy broke the surrounding silence. It took several minutes for their breathing to normalise. Hélène remained between Kim's legs. She'd stay there forever if she could.

"I'm going to miss you." Knowing that Kim was leaving soon was hard to cope with, but she knew it was important for her to do it. Kim had waited and worked far too hard to do anything else.

"About that," Kim began. Hélène looked at her with furrowed eyebrows. Kim grinned wildly. "There's something I need to talk to you about."

Not what Hélène was expecting. "Okay, is everything alright?"

"Oh yes. I've been given the opportunity to take part in a research study. I'll be required to travel around the world for about a year."

Hélène was stunned into silence. Her feelings were a mess of contradictions. Proud, Happy, sad, fearful — you name it, she was feeling it. Weeks apart from Kim were torture. How the hell was she going to cope with an entire year? "Wow... I... Kim, congratulations." She sounded sincere, right?

"Thanks, doll." Kim was beaming. Hélène was a little upset. She seemed so happy to be going. Her face obviously gave her away. "No need to look so glum, sugar. You're coming with me."

Okay, now Hélène was stunned. "What?"

"So, I've been plotting," she cast a devilish smile at Hélène. "You were going to be travelling to look for new locations and I thought you could do that with me. I've squared it with Holly and with the research team I'll be joining. We can sail ourselves around the world whilst we work. Together." Hélène's mouth gaped open. "What do you think?"

"What do I think? I... I think we have a lot of planning to do before we leave. You need to fill me in on all the details and then you need to agree that on one of our stop offs, preferably a tropical beach-y one, you agree to become Mrs Kimberley DuBois."

It was Kim's turn to gape now. No, she hadn't got down on one knee and asked, but she'd meant it all the same. Hélène knew Kim was the only woman she wanted to experience life

334

with. They would make new memories, experience new adventures, and they'd do it together forever.

"Only if we can have piña coladas during the service."

"I suppose that can be arranged." Hélène chuckled. Trust Kim to joke right now.

"Well, in that case, yeah, a beach wedding would be good."

"Good? Well, what would make it unforgettable?"

Kim leaned up and captured Hélène's bottom lip between her teeth. "Every moment in time is unforgettable with you, my love." They deepened the kiss. "Now sugar, get strapped, we have a proposal to celebrate." Kim grinned, slapping her arse.

Hélène laughed out loud. Their lives were going to be magnificent.

Afterword

Thank you so much for reading my book. I hope you liked reading it as much as enjoyed writing it! Please spare a few seconds to add a review on Amazon and/or Goodreads. Even just a star review without a comment helps Indie authors so much!

Goodreads
Amazon

Sign up to receive my monthly newsletter. Just visit my website and enter your email address.

www.alysonroot.com/sign-up

Acknowledgement

As usual, I would like to thank my wife for her unwavering support. I would also like to thank all the people that have reached out and given their insight and support. A special thank you to Monna, Ingrid and Fran.

About Author

Alyson was born and raised in the heart of England. She moved to Paris in 2015 when she met her wife. Together they moved to the west of France where they now live with their two dogs and pet bird. Alyson spends her time running a small campsite and holiday home. During her off time, she loves to read lesbian romance books, write and Scuba Dive.

Praise For Author

A Dance Towards Forever

"This is my first Alyson Root book and F/F book. I actually really enjoyed it. The story was funny and sweet and at a few moments had me wanting to strangle Kim, Helen and Greg. I liked that she used common problems in relationships like education, careers, family, friendships and addiction. It really makes the story more relatable. I am definitely looking forward to reading Sam and Anna's story and more books."

Goodreads review

Books in Series

The French Connection Series Book 1

A Dance Towards Forever

There are three things that Sam Chambers knows to be fact. One, her heart is broken, two, her career is sinking, and three, she hasn't a clue how to turn any of it around.

When her new boss John Spencer shakes things up at the photography company she works for, the last thing she expects is to be sent to Paris on a career changing project. Unbeknown to Sam, the brief glimpse of a dark-haired beauty at St Pancras is about to tip her world upside down.

Anna Holland has the life she worked hard for. She's successful, she lives in the city of love and she is in a steady relationship with a nice guy. The problem? Her nights are filled with the vision of a red-haired woman. Nothing makes sense when the woman of her dreams shows up in Paris and her office.

Together, they start a journey of exquisite discovery. Is there something more to their chance meeting? The unfathomable connection between them would suggest so.

Available to buy on Amazon.

Printed in Great Britain
by Amazon